ANIKA TAKES THE LONG WAY HOME UP SOUL MOUNTAIN

Eliza Andrews

Cover credit:
Thanks to the wonderful photographers at Unsplash.com for providing their hard work and amazing photos for free, without the need of licensing or attribution. Your work is appreciated.

Other books by Eliza Andrews:

To Have Loved & Lost: A new adult lesbian romance

Paradise: A (short) lesbian romance

Both titles available from Amazon.com.

GET A FREE SHORT STORY:
AuthorElizaAndrews.com/readersclub

Learn more about Eliza:
AuthorElizaAndrews.com

To anyone who's ever been through a mid-life crisis.
You'll be fine.

Table of Contents

You can't outrun your past. If you try, it will chase after you in a silver DeLorean.

The last thing Anika Singh wants is to go home to Ohio, but when her mother is diagnosed with cancer, what choice does she really have? She'll go home if she has to, but she won't stay long. Because all Marcine, Ohio, has for Anika is bad memories — memories of being an outcast, even within her own family, and memories of a perfect love that was soured by betrayal.

Jenny's betrayal. Anika's high school sweetheart-turned-ex-wife. Anika hopes she won't run into Jenny... Or maybe she hopes she *will* run into her. It's hard to say.

Then there's Amy, a dark-haired beauty Anika meets on the flight to Cleveland, who happens to be in Marcine for a friend's wedding. Nothing serious can happen with Amy; she's only going to be in town for a week. Which means that falling for her would be stupid, especially given the fact that Jenny might be available again.

But Anika is famous for doing stupid things.

A story flavored with curry and cornbread, family drama, and a whole lot of f-bombs, *Anika takes the long way home up soul mountain* will have you laughing, crying, and grimacing as Anika gets chased around by a silver DeLorean and attempts to answer the age-old question:

Can you ever really go home again?

This lesbian romance is rated R for
- A lot of really bad language
- Sexual content
- Adult situations

"People like us, who believe in physics, know that the distinction between past, present, and future is only a stubbornly persistent illusion."

— Albert Einstein, Letter to Besso's Family (March 1955)

"The middle of life has these cul-de-sac days. In your twenties you think, Surely I am going somewhere, and later — as in now — you think, Nope."

— Leslie Daniels, *Cleaning Nabokov's House*

Chapter 1: I fucking hate airports.

Monday

Mom has cancer.

The thought irritates me, nags at my brain the same way a mosquito that gets trapped in your room at night and circles and buzzes and dives and bites and basically won't leave you the fuck alone.

Mom has cancer mom has cancer mom has cancer mom has cancer mom has —

Shut. Up.

It's bone cancer, by the way. Osteosarcoma. In her left hip bone. I looked it up a couple of weeks ago, right after my dad called me, voice trembling, to deliver the news. I'm not saying I believe every single word on the Internet, because, hey, it's the fucking Internet, the same miracle that gave us fake news and videos of people getting their dogs high and September 11th conspiracy theories, but the medical sites seem reliable enough. Which sucks, actually, because they all agree that osteosarcoma, at Stage IIB, which is what Mom has, isn't good. It's not a death sentence, not yet, but it's definitely *not* fucking good, either.

I know it's a strange thing to wonder, but you know what I keep thinking? Why her hips? Why those things?

My momma's always been thick and strong, and she squeezed four babies out of those hips. They're the things she propped us on when we were little, holding us in place with one hand while she flipped bacon with the other, the things that double as door-openers and drawer-closers and the thing she'd pop to the side and put a hand on when someone got in trouble with her.

The only thing bigger than my mother's hips is her mouth, and as I slouch down grouchily in the blue plastic airport seat with my bad, British attempt at coffee, I have this image of her mouth getting even bigger to compensate for the chunk of hip they're going to chop off in her surgery next week. I imagine her mouth expanding, stretching on her face, full lips all warping out of fucking control, getting so big her chin and neck practically disappear, and then she says something, and her voice has gotten louder, stronger than ever, and what she says to me is,

"Anika! Get over here! Right fucking now!"

Well, okay, so she wouldn't say "fucking." She always complains that I say it too much. Which is probably true. But *Anika-get-over-here-right-now,* that's her favorite thing to say. I thought "Get Over Here Right Now" was my middle name when I was a kid. And getting cancer, it's like the ultimate way to say it, right? It's like her way of sending me a NastyGram all the way from Ohio to tell me, *Girl, get over here. Come home. Right this instant.*

I sigh, take a sip of my coffee.

Ohio.

The place is a fucking rubber band. No matter how far I manage to pull away, it always snaps me back into place eventually.

I take another sip of coffee.

Fucking *Costa.* The British don't understand anything about coffee. I could get better coffee for half a Euro out of a vending machine in Switzerland than I can in all of fucking England. But I drink it anyway. It's caffeine, and I need the caffeine, because I don't even have to guess about what kind of day it's going to be. It's going to be a long, shitty fucking day. The rain drizzling down on the Manchester Airport tarmac says it, the monitor above me flashing DELAYED says it, the coffee says it.

And the cancer says it. Well, not the bone cancer so much as the words "chemotherapy" and "followed by surgery" and "possibly metastasized" that come with it.

I'm sitting there, thinking all this, in what is basically the airport waiting room — a bunch of uncomfortable blue vinyl seats facing a bank of departure monitors like we're all at the fucking DMV waiting for our numbers to be called — when a girl walks by, meets my eye, gives me a small smile.

I try to smile back, but I'm sure it comes across more like a grimace. I recognize the girl from my flight over here from Basel; she sat a few rows ahead of me on the plane. She'd smiled when I walked past her boarding the plane, too, like she knew me. But I didn't smile back that time; I was busy maneuvering my gym bag ahead of me,

13

stooping to avoid whacking my head, trying not to let my big, awkward fucking body embarrass me more than it already naturally does. When she'd smiled at me on the plane, honestly my first thought was, "Is she *laughing* at me?" But then I'd realized no, just because a pretty woman smiles at you doesn't mean she's laughing at you.

Now I watch her go as she weaves through the crowd towards the escalator. She looks like she's about my age, maybe — late thirties? Early forties? — but it's hard to tell because she's got this fancy business suit on, the kind that's designed to make older women look younger and younger women look older, and plus she's short and her hair's cut to where it's short in the back, a little longer in the front. My first thought when I see the haircut is *"Jane Lane,"* who, if you have no idea who the fuck that is, was a character on this late-90s MTV cartoon called *Daria.* (My sister Dutch discovered *Daria* reruns on late-night cable and we used to watch it in high school sometimes. Google it.)

Anyway, that's what I think when I see the woman from the Basel-Manchester flight again — Jane Lane from *Daria.* Jane Lane, but Tinkerbell-sized and smiley and probably a hell of a lot less surly.

I lose Jane Lane in the crowd when she disappears up the escalator and into the food court above. There's some kind of bar on the upper level, and the faint scent of a meat-and-potatoes-and-tomatoes English breakfast wafts down to me. On the tables closest to the escalator, I see half-empty pints of beer.

Brits.   It's not even ten in the fucking morning, and they're already on their second pint.

This guy wanders over to me — young, doofy, wearing an '80s-style, orangish vest over a button-down shirt, hands shoved into the pockets of his tight-rolled jeans.

His name is Marty McFly, and by the way, he's a figment of my fucking imagination.

Remember him? *Back to the Future?* Actor Michael J. Fox as *Guitar Hero* Marty, the high school loser who gets dragged along by his elderly mad scientist bestie through space and time in a silver DeLorean with batwing car doors?   Marty saving his parents through time traveling back to 1955?   Biff the bully?   Dorky George McFly? Pretty girl Lorraine?   Please tell me you know who I'm talking about. Not knowing Daria... that I can understand. But surely anyone under the age of seventy-five who didn't grow up on a fucking television-free hippie commune knows *Back to the Future.* If you don't, you need to stop what you're doing and go watch all the *Back to the Future* movies with a quickness. Right now.

I'll wait.

Anyway, back in the Manchester airport, (imaginary) Marty McFly sits down next to me, slumps into his seat, hands still in his pockets. I glance over at him, look him up and down, remember how short the shrimp actually is. Sitting next to me like this, we could almost pass him off as my ten-year-old son.

If he was real, that is. And if I were as white as he is, or he was as Blasian as I am.

He nods in the direction of the escalator. "Smell remind you of anything?"

"I don't want to talk about my childhood, McFly," I say (but I don't say it out-loud because he's only in my imagination and I'm weird but not fucking delusional).

He inhales deeply. Keeps talking like I never said anything. "Smells almost like home, doesn't it? Like Mom's kitchen?"

"I told you. I don't want to talk about it."

I don't tell him *why* I don't want to talk about it, but he already knows why. I don't want to start crying like a big fat baby right here in the airport waiting room.

He points up at the monitor in front of us. "Flight's still delayed."

"I can see that."

He jerks a thumb towards the escalator. "May as well get some 'brekkie.' And you know... the English usually do ale better than coffee."

"It's not even noon. You're suggesting I drink before my flight?"

"It'll make the day go faster."

I groan. *"Nothing* will make this day go any fucking faster."

He makes a face like he's offended. "Who's the expert in time travel?"

I eye him. "And if I go upstairs for breakfast... You're going to take me back in time again, aren't you? Whether I like it or not?"

Marty McFly stands up, gives me a shit-eating grin. "Maybe. What's wrong with a few childhood memories? What's wrong with going back to your mother's kitchen for a few minutes?" He extends a hand.

I sigh, but then I grasp the hand he offers anyway, almost tugging him into me as I haul myself to my feet. I shake my half empty coffee cup, drop it in the trashcan — excuse me, *rubbish bin* — next to the escalator.

"Lead on, McFly."

Chapter 2: Back to the Future.

Back to the fucking future (or past — I never understood that stupid title. I mean, why would you say "back to the future" when most of the time they were going into the past?):

Set the flux capacitor back-in-time clock on the DeLorean for seventh grade, and the location to the kitchen table inside the brick ranch at the corner of Maple and Greene Streets in Marcine, Ohio.

Ready? Here we go.

Momma slides still-crackling bacon and fried potatoes onto my plate out of the cast iron skillet she holds with a scorched oven mitt dotted with little pink flowers. I push my bacon and potatoes to the side, reach for the bowl of scrambled eggs.

"More eggs?" she says skeptically when I pile them onto my plate. Her tongue clucks against the roof of her mouth. "Lord, child. How you stay so skinny, eating like that?"

I shrug my shoulders, because how the hell would I know? All I know is that I'm hungry, all the time hungry, and even though I already had one big pile of eggs and one helping of bacon, I know I'll be trying to sneak snacks by the time Social Studies hits if I don't put a little more food in my stomach.

"She eats like a pig," quips my sister Dutch. Her name's not actually "Dutch," it's "Dechen," but I had trouble saying that when I was little, so she's been Dutch since I was two.

I make a face at my sister that my mother can't see, opening my mouth wide so she has a good view of my mouthful of half-chewed scrambled eggs and bacon.

"Disgusting pig," Dutch amends.

"Dutch," Mom snaps, and she doesn't need to say anything else, just gives Dutch that *look* that's warning enough, the look that says *You say something else like that, you goan get popped.*

Dutch waits til our mother looks away, mouths "pig" at me one last time as if I needed a final reminder of her opinion of me. I answer with a mighty eye roll like a good younger sister and turn back to my plate.

Truthfully, I can't stand to look at Dutch. At fourteen, two years older than me, she's everything I'd like to be but am not. She's pretty, for starters, and she does it without even trying. Her hair isn't as kinky and frizzy as mine, and it cascades over her shoulders in thick, artful waves, perfectly framing her round, tawny face and high cheekbones.

She tells me my hair could be like hers if I'd only try a little harder, or let her mess with it, but I know the truth: In the DNA Power Ball Lottery, Dutch won long and lanky and elegant; I won Godzilla.

Even if she wasn't the oldest of us four kids, Dutch would be in charge anyway. She's got that unique power to command that only the pretty girls have, an over-confidence that's both snide and irresistible simultaneously, that repels at the same time you just can't fucking help but admire it.

"PJ! Gerry!" Momma calls, booming my younger brothers' names through the kitchen loudly enough to make my ears ring. "Y'all get in here and eat!"

Y'all get in here and eat. They are the words that bind my rainbow family together. In dal bhat and cornbread, we were the same; in all other ways, different.

Dutch shoots me another look, and this time it's the conspiratorial kind that siblings share over the antics of their parents, and I answer with a carefully muffled chuckle. Mom's ten minutes-to-eight yell for our brothers to *Y'all get in here and eat* is as predictable and consistent as the eggs and bacon and fried potatoes themselves.

My two younger brothers meander into the kitchen like child zombies, bleary-eyed and bickering with each other in indecipherable whines and groans. PJ — Pathik Junior — is a round, brown butterball, and even though he's only ten, you can tell he's already destined to be short like my father but thick like my mother. Of all of us, his features are the blackest — flat nose, round eyes, black hair stuck to his scalp in thick curls, and yet despite this, he is the one who most desperately wants to be Nepalese. He's got the double triangles of the Nepalese flag on his bedroom wall, a cheap little Buddha statue surrounded by sticks of incense stuck into bowls of rice sitting on his dresser. It's like he thinks he's going to accessorize his way out of his blackness and into his Nepalese heritage.

PJ hates that he shares his room with Gerry, our youngest brother, who cares nothing for Buddha or incense or curry. But with only three bedrooms and an unfinished basement, PJ and Gerry are stuck together, just like Dutch and me.

Gerry's as different from PJ as I am from Dutch. That's going to get more obvious as we all grow up, but at this particular moment in time, Gerry — whose full name, unfortunately for him, is "Geronimo," for my mother's grandfather — is a skinny, adorable kindergartener. The apple of my mother's eye.

Dutch is fourteen.

I'm twelve.

PJ's ten.

Noticing a pattern? Two years stair-stepping between each kid?

Yeah, so Gerry's six. We're pretty sure he's the accident kid. But I would've been more than happy to be an accident if I got treated the way Gerry does. He's as small and cute as I am tall and awkward, as bony as PJ is round, and as insanely cute as Dutch is domineering.

He's the only one who earns a loud, smacking kiss from our mother every time he enters the kitchen, the only one who gets a second helping of bacon without having to ask for it. It means the rest of us are fascinated by him and ridiculously jealous of him at the same time.

#

And now we've come back to the present day — the Manchester airport, two pints and a full English breakfast later.

My phone dings with an incoming text. It's just a number with an Ohio area code, no name associated with it, so whoever it is must not be in my address book.

I'm picking you up
it reads.

Who's this?
I type back.

Gerry. What time you get in

Gerry? I raise an eyebrow at the pronouncement. I'm surprised to be hearing from him. Hell, surprised he owns a cell phone, period. If he's picking me up from Cleveland, I guess that means he's back home again. I hope that's a good thing. But forgive me if I'm just a little suspicious of his motives.

I write him back anyway, telling him my flight details without any other comments or questions that might hint at my surprise. I haven't seen my youngest brother in a couple of years. I don't think I've even talked to him in at least a year.

I get a fist-pound emoji for a response. Then nothing.

I linger near the gate, gym bag carry-on hanging behind me at an almost vertical angle, like I've got a fucking sword strapped to my back.

A line starts to form; I wander into it. Something knocks against my gym bag, and I turn my head automatically.

Well, look who it is.

Tinkerbell-sized Jane Lane. The girl who smiled at me on the Basel to Manchester flight. She's getting into line behind me, which means she must be headed to Toronto, too.

"Sorry, I wasn't watching where I was going," she says with an apologetic smile.

American accent? Or Canadian? It's certainly not Swiss, at any rate.

"No worries," I say with a shrug. They call zone three for boarding, and I turn my attention back to the front of the line.

Chapter 3: Snakes on a plane.

I hear that the actor Samuel L. Jackson (you know, the black dude with the Jheri curl from *Pulp Fiction*?) agreed to star in the movie *Snakes on a Plane* only if:

(1) The movie continued to be titled *Snakes on a Plane,* and

(2) He got to have a line of dialog saying, *"I have had it with these motherfucking snakes on this motherfucking plane!"*

No shit, true story. Google it or whatever.

I can't say I've ever seen the movie; it was a little before my time and my dad was overprotective with anything rated R, but I think the whole concept is perfect, right? I mean, what could be worse? You're thirty-thousand feet above the Earth's surface, trapped in a confined area, surrounded by aggressive, lethally poisonous creatures. What a fucking nightmare.

Do I need to point out here that it sounds pretty much exactly like my upcoming trip to Ohio? I have to keep remembering that I'm doing it because it's important, because it's *Mom* and it's *cancer* and I might not be a great daughter, but even a crappy daughter knows to go home when her mom gets cancer.

Anyway, by the time I finally make it to Toronto, go

through customs, go through TSA pre-check for the good ol' US of A, and make it to my gate for the final flight to Cleveland, I'm whipped. I eat a sandwich, watch muted CBC, wait for my plane to board.

When it does board, it ends up being one of those itsy-bitsy puddle-jumper planes, the kind where you don't even get the dignity of walking down an enclosed ramp but have to walk out onto the tarmac and up a flight of stairs. It's starting to drizzle by the time I'm climbing up the stairs, and I have to admit that I kind of glare at the propellers like they've offended me when I see them, because, God, the only thing I hate worse than fucking airports is leaving an airport in a fucking propeller plane.

They've given us a *"the plane's super full so if you have a large carry on you'd better check it at the door"* speech, so I give up my gym bag without even grumbling that much, leave it on a damp cart with a guy wearing a bright-orange safety vest and a gap-toothed grin.

I follow the crowd and start looking for 8B, an aisle seat, and do you want to guess who's sitting in 8A, the window? I'll give you some options:

(A) Samuel L. Jackson

(B) Jane Lane (not the cartoon version, but the one who ran into my gym bag in the Manchester airport)

(C) Peanut the poisonous cobra

(D) All of the above

If you said D, all of the above, you're wrong. The correct answer is B, Jane Lane, and when I stop in front of my seat, she looks away from the window she's gazing through and glances up at me.

She kind of does a double-take. "Oh," she says, and for the fourth time in this long-ass day, she smiles at me.

I do my best to return her smile (and the one she just graced on me was actually like a *real* smile, and I don't know how she manages it, given that I know how far she's traveled), but like I said, I'm whipped, and so I'm sure my return smile makes me look like a gorilla baring its teeth.

I settle into my seat, which is difficult when you're scraping six-foot-four. My knees press against a tray table for the third time in this endless day, and just as I start to stretch one foot out into the aisle to give myself some relief, a heavyset guy holding a briefcase in front of him picks charges down the aisle towards his seat. I barely pull my foot back in time to avoid disaster.

"I bet you're ready to be finished with flying," Jane Lane comments after watching me nearly trip the fat guy and tuck my knee back against the tray table. She looks downright cozy in her seat, being Tinkerbell-sized and all. Like a kid curled up in daddy's armchair.

I shrug like it's no big deal, like my knees and back and neck aren't all screaming at this point. "Yeah," I say. "I bet you are, too. Weren't you on my Basel-Manchester flight?"

She nods. "And Manchester to Toronto. I thought we

were never going to board that plane!"

I chuckle — and it's not quite so gorilla-like this time. It's actually nice to have someone to chat with, given that I haven't really spoken to anyone all day, unless you count exchanging texts with Dutch, Dad, and Gerry.

Speaking of which.

I pull out my phone, send Gerry a quick text:

About to leave for Cleveland.

See u in an hour or so

and put my phone back in my pocket.

"Is this your last flight for the day?" asks Jane.

I nod. "Thank God, yes. You?"

"Yes." There's a pause, the kind that always comes when two strangers strike up a conversation on a plane but don't really have much to talk about. "Are you from Ohio?"

"Yeah, south of Cleveland. But I haven't lived there in a long time. Since high school." (I leave out the fact that I moved back to Ohio for a few short-lived months nine years ago, because it's not relevant and because I don't want to have to explain.)

She cuts her eyes away, nods, seems to think about this. It looks like she hesitates for a second, but finally, she says, "Must be something big going on at home, for you to leave Switzerland in the middle of the basketball season."

Now *I'm* the one doing a double-take. She already

knew I was a basketball player?

"No shit — oh, sorry, I mean... *you* follow women's basketball? Nobody follows basketball in Switzerland. Hell, *I* don't follow basketball in Switzerland."

Her smile turns shy. "Well, not quite nobody. *I* follow women's basketball. When I first moved out there, I was channel surfing one night and came across a game. It reminded me of home — and I was *so* homesick. So I started watching and... I guess you could say I've become a die-hard fan over the last few years. Which, actually — "

A staticky voice crackles to life overhead, cutting her off. They start talking about the safety demonstration, please pay attention to the stewardess, blah blah blah, put your devices into airplane mode.

I pull my phone out to switch it off and see that Gerry's texted me back.

Stuck at the restaurant, can't
leave
reads his reply.

Probably going to be an hour
late. At least.

I want to chuck my phone down the aisle in frustration.

"Should I get a rental car?" I'd asked Dutch when we were putting all this together.

"No, no, no, of course not," she'd assured me. *"We'll*

all be home, and Mom's not driving her car right now anyway, so I'm sure you'll — Nathan! Put that down! — I'm sure you'll have no trouble getting around."

"Because I don't want to be stuck in Marcine for an indefinite length of time without a — "

"Will you stop it? It'll be fine."

Oh, it'll be *fine.* Sure. Mom just has *cancer,* the bad kind, but no *big fucking deal.* And the fact that Dad's flipping out? He'll be *fine.* And that that PJ's probably coping by reverting into workaholic mode? Also just *fine,* Dutch. Fine like the fact that you're managing Mom and Dad, *and* let's not forget that our junkie baby brother Gerry is home for some reason, don't know what *that's* about but I'm sure it's *fine.*

And you know what else is *fine?* The fact that Gerry's going to leave me stranded at the Cleveland airport for at least an extra hour.

Why didn't I trust my gut and book a rental car? Maybe I can still get one when we arrive.

I've had it with these motherfucking siblings in this motherfucking family!

The announcement overhead finishes up; the plane lurches backward.

Jane Lane takes in my face, which is apparently pretty all screwed up in frustration, because she gives a concerned brow-furrow and asks, "Are you okay?"

ANDREWS / ANIKA TAKES THE LONG WAY

Chapter 4: In case of emergency, keep the person next to you busy.

I straighten up, adjust my face back into Polite Stranger Mode, pull the edge of my foot further away from the aisle as the stewardess bustles past. "Yeah, fine. What were you saying before the announcement?   Die-hard women's basketball fan...?"

The furrowed brow melts a bit. "Well, yes, actually. I even..." she blushes, leans forward, fishes through a purse at her feet practically as big as she is.   She pulls out a hardback book, flashes the cover in my direction.   "I got this just before I left yesterday. Ordered it specifically so I could read it on this trip. Have you seen it yet?"

Had I seen it yet. What a question. She's holding up a book titled *Only One Shot,* and there on the cover, looking very Head Coach-y, is the girl I've called my best friend since we met at the age of eighteen as freshmen basketball players at Rosemont University — Alexis Woods.   Had I seen the book? Hell, I'm *in* that book. I *lived* that fucking book.

But I don't say that. I only nod. Polite Stranger Mode and all.

"She mentions you in here a few times, you know,"

Jane says. She looks down for a moment before looking back up, laughs nervously. "I hope it doesn't weird you out that I recognized you right away when we were getting on the plane back in Basel."

Instead of answering, I kind of lift an eyebrow. I guess I know why she's been shooting smiles my way all day.

The plane's engines rev, and we jolt forward. False alarm, though; pilot's just moving us down the runway, and we stop again a moment later. But next to me, poor Jane Lane is pressed back against her seat, gripping the book in her lap, mouth tighter than it really should be.

"Don't like flying?" I ask.

She loosens up on the book a little. "It's not that I don't like flying. I actually don't mind it so much on the big transatlantic jets. Except for the takeoff. I hate all takeoffs. And these little propeller planes…" She lets out a long-suffering sigh. "On top of that, it looks like it's going to storm outside."

I follow her gaze out the window. Rain beads on plastic, and the wet tarmac reflects back kaleidoscope of orange, red, and blue lights. But it's barely drizzling — "storm" is pretty much a gigantic fucking overstatement of the situation.

So I decide to do Jane Lane a solid, distract her from her nerves.

"I've read the whole thing," I say, nodding at *Only One Shot* sitting in her lap. "It's not bad. Alex made me read the early draft when she got it back from the guy who did all the actual writing. She can't write worth a fuh... flip herself. Plus she wanted me to okay the parts that I'm in."

My plan to distract her works. Jane Lane half-turns in her seat, dark eyes twinkling with curiosity, rainstorm forgotten. She pushes some brown hair behind one ear, revealing an earful of silver studs and loops, just like the original Jane Lane had.

"So is it true?" she asks. "All the stuff about her coming to games drunk her junior year?"

I snort. "No, it's not true."

She looks disappointed. Deflates.

I grin. "The truth is it was *way* worse than what she admits to in the book."

This gets her attention. She sits up straight again, the twinkle's back. It makes me want to laugh — which is nice because I haven't felt much like laughing since the moment Dad called to tell me *Momma has cancer.*

I open my mouth to say something more — basically to throw Alex under the bus (Alex wouldn't mind, and what she doesn't know won't hurt her) — but the plane revs again, accelerates down the runway, and poor Jane Lane, she's not even holding onto the book anymore, she's clinging to both armrests, dark eyes staring straight ahead, unblinking, and it looks like she's either going to barf or scream at any second.

And... liftoff. Out the window, Toronto falls away, a million streetlights and taillights and empty office buildings shrinking against the black, expansive maw of the Earth.

We bank left, and the horizon line tilts into a disorienting angle, revealing sepia-colored cloud bottoms tinted with the last rays of the sinking sun.

It's pretty, really. I've always liked taking off at night.

Not that my seat mate sees any of this nighttime beauty. She's still got her eyes glued to the seat in front of her, still balances Alex's book in her lap while she hangs onto the armrests.

It's sort of hard to watch, and I want to pat her on the shoulder, give her arm a squeeze, remind her to breathe, or something, but it seems like a weird thing to do given that she's a stranger, so I just lean my head back and wait, stretching out my jaw a few times as I try to pop my ears.

When the plane starts to level off five or six minutes later, Jane turns to me and says, "Takeoffs are the scariest part."

I shrug. "I dunno. I've always kind of liked them."

The plane shudders and dips — hard enough that I feel my body moving down while all my innards seem to move up. We're climbing again a moment later.

"It's a good thing you're here to keep me occupied," Jane Lane says through clenched teeth. "Otherwise I'd be a total wreck. Or — *more* of a total wreck." She lets go of an armrest long enough to tap the book that she somehow managed to keep on her lap this whole time. "Not to sound creepy, but it doesn't surprise me that you'd like takeoffs. Based on what I know about you — from the book, I mean — it seems to fit."

A laugh finally escapes my throat. "I'm not as bad as Alex makes me out to be, you know."

The plane shivers, bounces again. Something in the overhead compartment above us rolls, pops hard against a plastic surface. Another bump and drop come a moment later, followed by the high-pitched *ding-ding* telling us all to keep our seat belts on. As if we needed the reminder.

I don't mind turbulence, but this flight's starting to feel like the stewardess should've been holding one of those *You must be at least this high to enjoy this ride* signs when we boarded. And I know I qualify, but I don't know about Jane Lane.

"Jesus," she murmurs under her breath. The way the word comes out, I can't say for sure if it's intended as a curse or a prayer.

I turn my head in her direction, determined to get back to distracting her. "So you know *my* name, obviously. What's yours?"

She looks at me like she's completely forgotten I was there, a blank expression on her face. It's like I've asked her for the solution to a complicated physics equation instead of her name. Then she comes back to life again. "Amy," she says. "Amy Ellis."

I stick out my hand to shake. She lets go of the armrest long enough to take it, and her hand is so small by comparison, it feels like a child's in my ginormous paw.

"Nice to meet you, Amy Ellis. And what were you doing in Switzerland that makes you so homesick?"

"I work for a software company," she says, seeming to unwind a tiny bit as she warms to the idea of conversation. "And they sent me to Basel for what was supposed to be a six-month assignment to sort out our European office, but that was a couple years ago, so…" She shrugs. "At this point, I don't know how long I'm going to be there. Fortunately, I get the European-style six weeks of vacation every year, instead of the American-style two, so I get to go home for a few weeks every year. But anyway — what about you? I'm surprised to see you headed state-side, given that it's the middle of the season."

"Yeah. My team's not exactly happy with me, but… Family stuff," I conclude gruffly. There's a silence that threatens to get awkward, so I fill it with, "So are you from Ohio?"

"No. Went to college there, but I was an army brat, so I don't really claim any roots anywhere. But I've got an old friend from college who's getting married this weekend. So I'm stopping off in Ohio to see her and be there for the wedding this week, then I'll do a bit of traveling after that — see some friends and family in different parts of the country — and then it's back to Basel."

I open my mouth to ask *Where are you traveling to,* but the intercom crackles to life and our captain comes on.

"Folks, this is Captain Paul Snider from up here in the cockpit, and I'm joined tonight by First Mate Georgia Halston. We're just about at our cruising altitude of twenty-two thousand feet… Don't know if you've noticed, but we've had to fly through a few storm cells this evening and we're dealing with a pretty strong headwind. Wish I could say that's the last bit of turbulence we'll have this evening, but it's looking like it might be a bit of a rocky ride to Cleveland tonight... That's the bad news. Good news is, it's a short flight; we'll have you there on time or even a little ahead of schedule. So sit back, relax, and enjoy the flight."

Amy blanches at the captain's news.

"Guess you were right about the storm," I say lamely. I wrack my brain for something else to say but come up empty, and so, a little reluctantly, I say, "Well... I guess I should let you get back to Alex's book."

She manages an almost-smile as the plane rolls like a ship out at sea. "Not a chance. Sitting next to Anika Singh in person? That's *so* much better than anything I could read about. Besides, if I tried to read right now, I'd probably lose my dinner."

I smile, a little embarrassed. When we won back-to-back national championships in college, I got used to being in the lime light, occasionally getting recognized in public. (And I do mean "occasionally;" this is *women's* basketball, people.) That recognition faded when I was in the WNBA; it ratcheted back up when Alex and I both played for team U.S.A. in the Olympics and took the gold medal, but since moving to Switzerland, I've gotten used to invisibility again.

Well — as invisible as you can be in Switzerland when

you're a fucking six-foot, three-and-a-half-inch Godzilla Amazonian who's half-black, half-Nepalese, and a hundred percent loud-mouthed American. The stares I get don't have *anything* to do with playing basketball, trust me. I wish they did.

So Amy recognizing me… it's unexpected, to say the least. Unexpected, but not necessarily… bad.

The plane suddenly drops again, enough to earn a chorus of "Oh!"'s from people around us. Amy looks absolutely terrified, and this time I can't help myself — I do pat her on the shoulder.

"I'm sure it'll be fine," I tell her. "At least there's no motherfucking snakes on this motherfucking plane."

She gives me an odd look.

"Sorry — Samuel L. Jackson? *Snakes on a Plane?*" When her face doesn't light up in an *Ah, yes, of course* recognition, I silently kick myself and forge ahead with, "And it's like the captain said — it's a short flight. Right?"

"Right," she says, but there's no conviction in it. After a few seconds, she turns her head my way. "Hey — Anika?"

"Yeah?"

"Will you tell me a story? — to distract me, I mean."

"A story? What, like 'Once upon a time, in a galaxy far fucking away…?'"

She lets out a nervous laugh again. I kind of like the way it sounds.

"No, not that kind of story. A story about *you.*

Something that's not in Coach Woods's book."

I think for a few seconds, trying to remember what Alex did and didn't say about me in the book. "Does her book say how we pranked Coach Tynan sophomore year, superglued a basketball to his ass?"

She nods. "Yeah. That's in there."

"What about the prank when I told Alex she — "

"No," she says again, emphatic and commanding this time. "About *you. Your* life. Not about pranks."

I get back to thinking, trying to come up with a story that doesn't reveal to Amy how much I hate playing basketball in Switzerland, or how much I miss Alex, or how much I'm starting to feel like my four years at Rosemont might've been the high point of my life and my career. God, I never wanted to be one of *those* people, pining for their high school / college glory years that were already well past, but maybe that's exactly what I'm becoming.

And in particular, I'm trying to think of a story to tell Amy that won't remind me of Jenny. Being reminded of my ex-wife — especially when I'm about to go back to our hometown, where *everything* reminds me of her — is the last thing I want right now.

"How about your family?" Amy suggests when I don't come up with anything on my own after a minute.

"What about them?"

"Well, what are they like?"

"I don't know. They're just… a normal family."

Her eyebrows lift and she gives me a skeptical look.

"There's no such thing as a 'normal' family. Do you have any brothers and sisters?"

"Yeah. One older sister, two younger brothers."

Amy lights up, turbulence suddenly forgotten. "Seriously? Same as me! Well — I mean, my older sister is actually my step-sister, but... wow. So we're both the second of four, two girls, two boys? Crazy. Are you close to them?"

I shake my head. I refrain from saying, *Close to them? Why the hell do you think I live in Europe?* and instead I say diplomatically, "Not really. This trip home will be the first time I've seen them in a couple years. And my baby brother, Gerry... it'll be the first time I've seen him in a couple years. He's kind of the black sheep. Or the Blasian sheep, I guess."

"Blasian...?"

"Yeah — black and Asian. *Blasian.* That's what we call ourselves."

She nods. "That's right, I remember that now — it's in the book. Coach Woods says your dad was an immigrant from Nepal — "

"Yep. It's true."

" — and he married an African American New Yorker. But yet you grew up in Ohio? Now *that* sounds like a story I'd like to hear."

I nod, smiling, thinking of all the times I've heard one of my parents recount the story of how they first met, fell in love, and moved to Ohio. They tell it differently, of course.

I can almost hear Momma shouting *"That's not how it happened, Pathik!"* in the background just thinking about it.

"It *is* a good story, actually," I say, and I launch into it.

Chapter 5: This is how my parents met.

My mother's from New York City. East Harlem, to be exact. Grew up there in the 70s and 80s, surrounded by Puerto Ricans and Dominicans and Cubans, along with black folk and a smattering of Italians, long before anyone had ever seriously considered putting the words "gentrification" and "Harlem" in the same sentence. East Harlem hadn't exactly been a "good" neighborhood for a long time — actually, lots of it had been pretty crappy for a while — but at least where my mom lived, it wasn't... well, it wasn't absolutely-fucking-awful.

She lived on a block where people sat outside on stoops on nice evenings, gabbing and laughing and bitching about whatever nonsense was going on in the neighborhood at the moment, playing cards, rolling dice, listening to music, spitting sunflower seed husks onto the sidewalk and telling each other things like, "Where little Jimmy at? I heard he broke up with Maria last week," and, "Your Momma still sick? You tell her she been in my prayers," and, "Nah, what I heard was that *he* was messing around on *her,* and she came home one day and chased him right out the 'partment with a *broom!"* and then everybody would cackle and pass a pitcher of lemonade or a beer can or a pack of Kools or whatever they were sharing that day.

ANDREWS / ANIKA TAKES THE LONG WAY

And then the crack epidemic hit in the mid-80s, and everything went from "mediocre-bad" to "really fucking shitty." It isn't noticeable at first; it starts with little Jimmy not coming home one night, then turning up on the street a few weeks later, disheveled and stinking of stale urine, clothes a mess and lips chapped, face ashy, pockets clinking with empty vials and a glass pipe, begging for money.

Then other things happen. People who'd always had steady jobs all the sudden can't keep them. Kids get this haunted, wide-eyed look on their face when momma disappears for a few days at a time. Young dudes wearing oversized parkas stand on street corners with 40-ounces in brown paper bags in one hand, baseball bats in the other hand to keep customers in line, and they're loud and they're feral and they're posting ten year-olds on the corners as lookouts.

New York got bad. East Harlem got worse. It became the kind of place where you had to pretend not to see some of the things you were seeing unless you wanted you or your family to be the next drive-by victims.

People stopped hanging out on stoops.

Well, some people still hung out there. But they weren't the kind of people you really wanted to spend time with.

#

1984 and my mother was twenty-two years old, working a stable job at the Port Authority, the kind of lady who sits behind plexiglass for eight hours at a time, selling bus tickets to locals and giving out directions to tourists.

That's where she was when my father found her. Six years older and six inches shorter than my mother, Dad followed his sister and his brother-in-law from Kathmandu to New York City, wooed by tales of easy riches and abundant jobs and a stable government. It was still ten years before the Maoists in Nepal tried to overthrow the government and ended up embroiling the country in a fucked-up civil war that lasted a decade, but even before the war, Nepal was isolated and corrupt and lacked opportunity. And for an ambitious young guy like my dad, who, entranced by the rock 'n roll and the wandering white hippies who'd just started filtering into his country, the United States seemed like a fairy-tale land, a place where anything could happen. A place where a man could make a mark on the world. So a year after his brother-in-law whisked his sister away to Queens, Dad followed.

Black woman from East Harlem. Tall and thick and tough, not willing to take nothing from nobody.

Shrimpy Nepalese guy fresh off the boat. Skinny and smiley and sheepish about his broken English, speaking and moving in halting stutter-steps, like he's afraid that at any moment, somebody's going to tell him he's doing it wrong.

When people meet my parents, they're like, "Wha —? How the fuck did they —?" And then they do things like shrug and look skyward, as if to say, "Heaven only knows how your parents got together. Clearly some people really *are* destined for each other."

But me, I don't bring destiny into it. I *get* my parents. Anybody with a few brain cells who thinks about it for longer than a fucking minute can get them.

To get the weird mismatch that is my parents, you just have to think about Kathmandu and East Harlem. Because, really? Those two places, at that particular moment in history, they weren't that different in the end. Take a poor city, get its own government to neglect it, bring in outsiders to exploit it, leave the locals feeling angry and hopeless — that kind of environment, it'll produce a certain kind of person. And Mom at twenty-two and Dad at twenty-eight, they were *both* that certain kind of person — each in their own way. They were these strong, stubborn, passionate young people who went back and forth between being pissed off at the world and being determined to turn it on its head.

To hear my dad tell it, the story of their love was an epic tale, a fucking Frank Sinatra song come to life, a remake of *West Side Story* minus anything resembling tragedy or Italians.

This is how it happens for him:

He sees her behind her plexiglass window, and boom, something clicks into place inside him. Like he's been working on a fucking jigsaw puzzle his whole life and finally found the missing piece that's been caught beneath the rug this whole time.

He's in love from moment one.

He makes his way to the front of the line, asks about bus tickets. She answers him. He's not ready for the conversation to be over, so he asks her more questions. She starts to answer again, but he interrupts, saying what he needs to say slowly and as clearly as he can, trying to keep his accent out of the way:

"You're beautiful. Please, let me buy you dinner."

He asks this because he loved American movies long before he loved America, and from the movies, he knows a little about American dating, and he knows this is what you say when you ask a beautiful woman out on a date. You invite her for a drink, or for dinner, and since this is America and not Nepal, if you're polite and you're funny, she'll let you take her hand, let you help her take off her jacket, let you walk her to her door at the end of the night and maybe even give her a kiss.

This, I imagine, is what he's thinking as he asks my mother out the first time.

Ask Mom, she'll tell a totally different story. There's no love at first sight in her version. In fact, mainly what she remembers is this short little Asian guy annoying the hell out of all the customers in line behind him as he takes up her time with a bunch of stupid-ass questions she can barely understand thanks to the thick plexiglass and his thicker accent. And when he asks her to dinner, her whole face scrunches like she's sucking a lemon and she says:

"*Hell,* no. Get outta my line. Next!" And she dismisses him with an annoyed wave of her hand.

But he comes back the next day with a bundle of daisies he bought for three dollars on the street. He's working as a bus boy at a restaurant that belongs to his brother-in-law's brother. He's earning enough to get by, but it varies from week to week, sometimes not even hitting minimum wage. And everything's under the table, off the books. Three dollars is a small fortune, but he spends it on this beautiful woman he's going to take to dinner.

And she's surprised but still annoyed to see him back, won't accept the flowers, shoos him away while her coworker grins behind her hand. He leaves the daisies on the counter.

Comes back the next day with tulips.

The day after that it's a single rose.

Then another bunch of daisies.

On the fifth day — I know, it sounds like fucking Genesis, right? — on the fifth day, there's a plastic vase taped to the countertop with a handwritten sign above it that says "FLOWERS" in black marker and has an arrow pointing down at the vase. He puts his mums in the vase, waits to see if Sheronda (he's learned her name, at least) will turn around, but she's fake-busy with fake paperwork, back to the plexiglass, and the only person who will look at Pathik (that's Dad) is Sheronda's coworker, who's grinning behind her hand.

Day six is daisies again, day seven lilies, day eight peonies.

Day nine he doesn't show up. Sheronda's kind of disappointed, and disappointed that she's kind of disappointed.

Day ten she asks him where was he on day nine, and he hangs his head and tries to explain about the other bus boy being sick, and how he himself wasn't feeling great, and he worked even longer that day, and he's sorry — he'll bring extra flowers for day eleven to make up for that. And what Sheronda thinks about his story is, "He's got a job."

Day eleven he brings extra flowers like he promised.

Day twelve she smiles at him, and he tells her she is a living goddess.

Day thirteen the plastic flower vase and the handwritten sign that says FLOWERS is gone, leaving only half-scraped-off Scotch tape behind on the plexiglass, and Sheronda tells him about how her supervisor came by, and was upset about the vase, and Pathik *really* has to stop doing this. Really. He has to stop coming by every day like this, bringing her flowers and trying to talk to her.

On day fifteen, she asks him, "If I let you take me to dinner, will you *promise* to stop?" At first, he doesn't understand the question; she has to rephrase it a couple more times before he nods in understanding. He beams at her; he swears she'll never have to see him again after they go out. It's the happiest day of his life. He will be back at the end of her shift.

Sheronda says, "Okay, fine. Five-thirty."

He walks away on bouncy steps, on top of the fucking world. Sheronda only sits down on her side of the counter with a sigh. But when Sheronda's coworker keeps grinning at her behind her hand, Sheronda swivels and snaps at the woman, "What?"

"Nothing," says the other woman. "That Chinaman, he really like you."

Normally, Sheronda would never go out with a man immediately after work. She would go home, she would take a bath, fix her hair, put on something nice, add some jewelry. But she has every intention of blowing Pathik off as quickly as possible, feigning a headache or a stomachache halfway through dinner and insisting she can find her own way home. She plans to be home by seven-thirty tonight. Eight at the latest. And then no more harassment from Pathik.

(Who, she knows, is from *Nepal,* not China. People can be so ignorant.)

He's back at exactly five-thirty, clean-shaven and smelling of a shower, and when he walks her away from the Port Authority, he runs ahead to open doors for her; when they make it to the sidewalk, he walks on her outside, between her and the street; and when a crackhead comes too close, begging for change, he positions himself between the crackhead and Sheronda, puffing out his narrow chest and ordering the man away in English that doesn't stutter.

They wind through Manhattan for several blocks this way, getting closer to Hell's Kitchen, which makes Sheronda nervous, and she asks "Where are we going?" to which Pathik, who has been beaming the whole time, gives a confusing answer that has something to do with an Indian restaurant, his sister, his brother-in-law, his brother-in-law's brother, cumin, and a fire escape. Sheronda nods along skeptically, catching only every two to three words of the story, wondering when they pass a subway stop if she should bail *right now* and head back uptown.

But — and you can call it fate if you want, but I just call it fucking curiosity — she follows the wiry little man until he stops on the sidewalk and points excitedly and says, "Bhaswar's. This Bhaswar's restaurant." She follows his jabbing finger and suppresses the puckered lemon-face look just in time, because the place is an utter dive. Greasy spoon, Indian style, probably with cockroaches clinging to the underneath sides of the tables while patrons' elbows rest on the sticky tops.

She opens her mouth, feigned headache speech already prepared, but Pathik waves his arm down the sidewalk. "Other side, fire escape," he says, like this is some sort of explanation.

She follows a few steps behind as he rounds the corner into an alley, eyes alert, ears scanning for danger as she grips her handbag tightly against her chest and prepares herself to fight. She's pretty sure she can take shrimpy little Pathik — he only comes up to her chin — as long as he didn't bring any friends to this party.

But when she steps into the alleyway, Pathik has stopped a few feet ahead of her, that idiotic, gap-toothed smile still plastered on his face, and he points up and behind him. Sheronda follows his finger for the second time, eyes climbing the brickwork, snaking up black iron fire escapes and around laundry lines, and finally, she sees it. A round table with a pristine white tablecloth that flutters in the wind five stories up, a glass vase on top filled with bright red roses, two chairs on either side.

Pathik pulls down on the whining, screeching bottom stairs of the fire escape, his smile faltering a bit. "I sorry so far up," he apologizes to Sheronda. Then he points down at her feet. She's still in her work shoes — ugly black sneaker-like things with thick rubber soles. "I glad safe shoes," he says.

Sheronda hesitates for a moment. Moment of truth. Go through with it like she said she would, or turn back around.

("It was my smile that won your mother over that night," my father says to me a couple decades later, his English perfect and most of the accent gone. "She couldn't resist my good looks and my charm."

She slaps his arm, clucking her tongue at him. "That's what you think. Truth was, I'd been at work all day and I was just hungry."

He arches a black eyebrow at her, and crow's feet

crinkle around the folds of his dark eyes. "Whatever you say, my darling."

And I roll my eyes because I was fifteen when I heard that story, and by default, their love story was impossibly maudlin, impossibly fucking dorky.)

Whatever the reason, Sheronda walks up the fire escape. Pathik follows a few steps behind her.

And she surprises herself by having a good time. When Pathik can make himself understood, he's funny. He regales her with stories about growing up in Kathmandu, making up for his limited English with wild hand gestures, miming, and sound effects. He tells her about the time he and his friends released the grumpy old elephant from the man who used it to give rides to American tourists; he shows her pictures of his aging mother and his dead father, his five siblings, his tribe of nieces, nephews, cousins, aunties, uncles, and on and on. And Sheronda laughs at the right moments and gasps in surprise at the other moments and leans over the faded, dog-eared photographs, and the rows of smiling faces remind her of East Harlem before it was *that* bad, and when he walks her back to the subway stop just before nine o'clock, she says to him, "You bringing me flowers tomorrow?"

His brow clouds, probably thinking his English is failing him. "Flowers? I promise, no more flowers."

She repeats her question, slower. "I know I said that. But I'm asking: Are. You. Bringing. Me. Flowers.

Tomorrow?"

Finally, he gets it. His face splits into a trademark broad smile, and he says, "Yes. Flowers tomorrow."

Chapter 6: Since I don't like the YMCA, maybe we should do brunch...?

My story keeps Amy occupied for the rest of the trip. It's not that long of a story, but then again, it's not that long of a trip. She sighs with relief when we finally touch-down, and I try not to laugh or bust her chops about it because, frankly, it *was* a really awful fucking flight.

She shakes my hand one last time when we finish taxiing to our gate. "Anika Singh, you're even more charming in person than you are in Coach Woods's book. Thank you for keeping me from focusing on what was going on up there."

I grin. "Thank you for..." I start, but I don't really know how to finish my statement. Saying *"Thank you from distracting me from the fact that my mom has cancer, from the fact that I'm about to have to deal with my neurotic siblings for an indefinite period of time, and from the general horror show that is returning to Ohio"* doesn't seem particularly... well, you know. I try again. "Thank you for being an interesting seat mate."

When the aisle opens up, I help her get her bag down from the overhead bin and wave goodbye. I wave to her again while I wait for my gym bag at the edge of the exit ramp with the handful of other passengers who had to check their carry-ons at the last minute.

I take my phone out of airplane mode while I wait. Nothing new from Gerry, so I text him.

Just landed.

No reply. I decide to try Dutch.

Gerry says he's stuck at the restaurant.

Any chance you can pick me up?

And why is he at the restaurant?

Sorry, can't, Dutch answers.

**I'm with Nathan at karate, the babysitter's home
with Sherry, and Matt's working late.**

At least I'll get to see my nephew and niece this trip. I guess there's that. Except... Seeing Nathan and Sherry means I'll probably have to see my brother-in-law, too.

I grimace.

The light-hearted mood from chatting with Amy is already evaporating.

What about PJ? I ask Dutch.

Not here yet.

Still in Philadelphia.

I figured as much. PJ owns a string of high-end restaurants in Philly. Getting him to come home for anything, even a parent's major surgery... I suppose I shouldn't be surprised.

Marty McFly appears at my elbow. "Makes sense," he says, apparently referring to PJ. "He's always responded to stress by working harder. At least you two have that in common."

"I'm not a workaholic. Not like he is."

McFly scoffs. "No? You don't spend every minute you can in a weight room, on a track, or on a basketball court?"

"That's different. Physical movement relieves stress," I say. "It's a scientific fucking fact."

"Stress and basketball. Reminds me of high school." He gazes up, looking pensive. "Reminds me of the time — "

"Oh, no you don't," I say quickly. "No more trips to the past today."

"It'll be short," he says. "I swear."

#

Ready for another road trip in the time-traveling

DeLorean? No? Well, too fucking bad.

Back to the future: Twenty-one years ago, junior year in high school. Marcine, Ohio.

I'm stressed out, so I'm out on the court, despite the fact that it's only thirty-four fucking degrees outside. I shoot from the key, miss, chase the ball as it clangs off the rim and threatens to bounce away into the slushy mixture of melting snow and mud. I snatch it just before it can land, but then lose my balance when an unexpected "Hey" comes from behind me. My right foot lands hard in the mud, splashes some of it up into my face.

I wipe off the speckles of mud from my cheeks, take a breath, and turn around to face the owner of the "Hey."

It's what I thought. It's her.

"Hey," I say, nervously spinning the ball between my hands.

Jenny tilts her head up toward me, and the blonde hair that cascades out from under the stocking cap whispers against her parka. It's a conspiratorial kind of noise, like her hair has a secret to tell.

"What are you doing out here?" she asks. "It's so cold." And as if to prove it, she wraps her arms around her midsection, hugging herself against the chill air.

"Practicing."

"Aren't you guys on break from basketball?"

"Yeah."

"So shouldn't you be... I don't know, resting or

something?" She pauses. "Or at least playing inside. I hear the YMCA is free with a student ID."

Now is probably not a good time to mention to her that I practice out here in part because I know she walks by it every day on her way to school. And even though school's on winter break, this neighborhood court is still the best place to be if I want to "accidentally" bump into her.

But she doesn't need to know that I know that. Not after what happened last night.

"I like practicing out here," I say. "It's quiet. The fucking Y is fucking *loud,* filled with little fucking kids running around all over the place. They're like fucking cockroaches or something — stomp on one, five more appear to take its place."

"Anika," she says. I love the sound of my name in her mouth, the way she says it like I'm about to get scolded for something. Still, a smile plays at the corners of her lips. "Do you *really* have to use the f-word multiple times in every single sentence?"

"Do you *really* have to say 'f-word' instead of fuck?" I shoot back. "What are you, ten? Just say it. Fuck. Fuck, fuck, *fuck.*"

Jenny shakes her head. "I have a broader vocabulary than just curse words," she informs me in an uppity tone, but the smile's still there.

I palm the basketball I'm holding. Drop it to the pavement. Catch it when it bounces back up. She tracks the ball with her eyes.

"Listen," she says, and all the uppity is gone from her voice, replaced with something more hesitant. "Do you want to go get brunch? I thought maybe... I thought maybe we could talk about what happened last night."

"What's there to talk about? You already told me. You had too much to drink; you got carried away; you didn't mean to kiss me." I shrug, all casual nonchalance as if it makes no difference to me. "I get it — people do crazy things on New Year's Eve. No harm, no foul. End of story."

The arms around her midsection tighten; her gaze drops to the pavement at my feet.

"That's what I wanted to talk about. Maybe — maybe it wasn't so crazy after all." She lifts her eyes to meet mine. "What would you say if I told you that I don't think kissing you had anything to do with how much I had to drink last night?" She pauses, waits for me to answer, but I'm so thunderstruck that I couldn't speak even if I wanted to. So she drops another bomb on me: "What if I told you that I haven't been able to stop thinking about it since?"

I dribble the ball a few times so that I have an excuse not to look at her. Looking directly at Jenny? It's like staring straight into the fucking sun. You can only do it for a few seconds at a time.

Still feigning nonchalance, I ask, "Are we talking *hypothetically* what if you said that? Or are you actually *saying* that?"

"Do you really have to make this difficult?" She

pauses. Maybe waiting for me to answer a question again. But it's obviously rhetorical. *"Yes.* I'm actually saying that."

"Then what I'd say is, 'Where are we going for brunch?'"

Chapter 7: SAT questions and first kisses.

I sit across from Jenny, twitchy. Her hands are still, neatly laced on top of the table; my own fingers fiddle with the white wrapper of my straw.

"We should eat black-eyed peas and collard greens," I tell her, breaking the silence.

"Why?" she asks, genuinely confused.

I shrug, still not looking directly at her because it's still like staring straight at the sun. "It's what you're supposed to do on New Year's Day. For prosperity and good luck. It's a southern thing."

"Southern? Your dad's Asian, and… didn't you tell me your mom's from New York?"

"Yeah, but my mom's Grandpa Geronimo, he was from Alabama. Moved to Harlem during the Great Depression. And he was the one who taught my mom to cook. So I guess it comes from him."

There's a long silence emanating from Jenny's side of the table, and finally she says, "Are you talking about black-eyed peas because you don't want to talk about what happened last night?"

"I never said I don't want to talk about it," I say, defensive. "I'm here, aren't I? If you want to talk about it so bad, talk. I'll listen."

She takes a deep breath, opens her mouth to speak… and is immediately interrupted by the waitress.

Fucking hell.

"You girls ready to order?" asks the fifty / sixty-something lady with dyed red curls. She looks tired and bored and like she'd rather be just about anywhere other than here, waiting on a couple of high school kids who don't have the good sense to still be in bed like everyone else their age.

I get how the waitress must feel. Ever since my parents opened their crazy Nepalese soul food fusion restaurant last year, I get roped into waiting tables almost every weekend, plus a lot of weekdays after school — basically anytime I'm not at basketball practice or a basketball game. Waiting tables is a shitty job that leaves you with sore feet, too many one dollar bills, and clothes that never quite stop smelling like kitchen grease and garlic.

We order some food and a couple of sodas, and once the waitress walks off, I go back to fiddling with my straw wrapper. Waiting for Jenny to speak.

In the ensuing awkward silence, my mind flips back to the SAT prep class my dad's been making me take. I've told him about the college scouts coming to watch me play ball, even though I'm still just a junior, but he doesn't seem to get it. I've tried to explain that these schools aren't after me for my brain, and they don't give a crap about what kind of score I get on the SAT as long as I pass all my classes. But Dad won't listen, yammers on about not taking my education for granted, and so I'm staying up late at night after ball practice, after waiting tables, and after homework with my fucking SAT verbal workbook putting together analogies like

Anika is to Jenny as

(A) A mountain gorilla is to Dutch

(B) Frankenstein is to a Disney princess

(C) The future crazy, crotchety old cat lady is to the future Miss Ohio

(D) All of the fucking above

"Anika..." Jenny starts, lamely saying my name because maybe, after what seems like three fucking hours of waiting, she can't think of anything else to say. And although her clasped hands don't move from their spot on the tabletop, I can see the knuckles going white. When she speaks again, her voice is so low that it's practically a whisper. "I shouldn't have manipulated you into kissing me last night. It was wrong to use you like that, and I - I'm sorry. I'll understand if you never want to speak to me again after this."

My brain freezes up like an old computer with too many tabs open, because I'm not capable of processing what just came out of her mouth. I rip the straw wrapper up into itsy-bitsy bits.

She manipulated *me* into kissing *her*.

She... used me?

Not possible. It was the other way around.

I shake my head slowly, finally look up and meet her eyes. "I don't get it. How did *you* manipulate *me?* The way I remember it, I'm the one who got you under the mistletoe last night right as the clock hit twelve."

I'd had a few drinks the night before, true, but with a frame as big as mine, it actually takes a lot for me to get good and drunk, and between that and the fact that I don't have that many opportunities for teenage debauchery anyway, I rarely get drunk.

Jenny, on the other hand, drank almost as much as I did, but she more-or-less comes up to my kneecaps — *when* she's wearing heels (which she was last night). Arguing that *she* was the one to initiate the kiss didn't make any sense. She was too drunk to do any manipulating.

I was the one who'd put my palms on the wall on either side of her head when the kids started yelling, "TEN! NINE! EIGHT!..."

I was the one who'd leaned forward and down when they got to "TWO!," the one whose eyes had skittered down to Jenny's smirking smile, lips half-parted already, at "ONE!"

I was the one who had kissed *her* at "Happy New Year!". *She* was the one who'd mumbled, "I'm sorry; I can't do this," and ducked out from underneath my outstretched arms ten seconds later, just as a drunken knot of jocks by the TV started singing their own off-key version of "Auld Lang Syne."

But now, Jenny shakes her head, mouth twisting into an irritated grimace.

"No, Anika. You don't get it. I set you up last night. Think about it — who invited you to the party in the first place?"

You did, I think silently, remembering the unexpected text message chiming on my phone on the last day of school before winter vacation.

"And who kept bringing you drinks all night?" she asks.

You did.

"And who kept complaining about her stupid ex-boyfriend and lamenting the fact that she wasn't going to have anyone to kiss at midnight?"

You did.

I stab one of the white bits of wrapper straw with my index finger, the realization slowly dawning on me that Jenny's telling the truth — she *did* set me up. She *wanted* me to kiss her last night. She was *hoping* I would. She'd engineered the whole night, guiding it to *that* moment, the moment where she leaned her back against the wall, hands pinned behind her butt, gazing up at me with big brown eyes and an open-mouthed smirk.

I look at her — the sun — and look away again. "Why? Why did you want me to kiss you?"

"Because I... I knew you were into me. I could see it in the way you watch me, in the way you can't quite ever..." One of her small, porcelain-white hands reaches across the sticky surface of the diner table and gently covers two of my fiddling fingers. "Look at me."

I follow her command, my hand falling still as I look up from the shredded wrapper, eyes meeting hers. And then I realize *"look at me"* wasn't a command at all but the completion of her sentence.

She knew I had a crush on her because I can't ever quite look at her.

She must not realize that she's the fucking sun.

The little white hand withdraws, and then both hands disappear beneath the table. Jenny glances around the diner furtively, and the waitress returns with three plates of food — two for me, one for Jenny.

I take my fork immediately, but Jenny's silverware stays untouched next to her hot plate of eggs and hash browns.

"I thought I could kiss you as a joke," she says, resuming her half-whispered explanation. "It would be a story I could shock my friends with, something that might make Brett jealous."

(Brett is her most recent ex-boyfriend, by the way. And Anika is to Brett as the ugly step-sister is to Prince Charming.)

Should've known.

Fuck, Anika, you should've known.

I look down at my plate because tears sting my eyes and I don't want Jenny to see them. I attack the short stack of pancakes with a knife, not bothering with syrup or butter, just shoving the biggest forkful I possibly can into my mouth before I say, "Great fucking joke, Jen. Fucking most hilarious thing I've heard all year."

All year, we've been sitting next to each other in trigonometry. All year, we've been checking each others' homework. Working together on group projects. Studying together on weekends, before quizzes and big exams. And all year, *I'd* been the jokester, always telling stories to make her laugh, making fun of her to get her to relax when she came into class stressed about Brett or her friends or who-said-what at band practice. *I* was supposed to be the jokester, but I guess

"Joke's on me," I say, finishing my thought out-loud as I swallow a mouthful of dry pancakes. What Jenny doesn't know — and what I'll never tell her — is that last night's kiss was my very first one. My very first fucking kiss, and I'd already been played, already been the butt of someone else's joke.

It fucking figured.

"I'm so, so sorry, Anika. God, I'm *so* sorry."

A small white hand reappears above the table, hovering uncertainly for a moment before it reaches across the divide again, fingertips brushing against my forearm.

"But what I'm trying to tell you," she says, "is that I made a mistake. Because what happened with us last night... it wasn't a joke to me." The fingertips stay on my arm. The touch is light, barely there, but it burns like acid against my bare skin. I should move out of reach, but I don't. I can't. "It wasn't a joke at all. From the moment

you touched me… Something happened. Something I
didn't know I already knew until you kissed me." She
sighs. "That didn't make any sense, did it?"

I shake my head.

"What I'm trying to say is, Anika… do you believe in
love at first kiss?"

Slowly, I put my fork down. And slowly, I look into
those wide, innocent brown eyes again. This time, I don't
look away.

"Yes," I say, my voice barely audible.

Chapter 8: Home smells like curry, collard greens, and fried chicken.

Back to the present

I travel light.

Maybe that's hard to understand, since I'm flying in from fucking Europe and don't know how long I'm going to be here, but an airline lost my checked bag once when I was country-hopping for basketball, and ever since then, I only take a carry-on with me. So I don't have any reason to go to baggage claim, but I end up walking past it anyway on my way to ground transportation.

The baggage carousel from our tiny propeller plane flight is rumbling rhythmically, metal slats letting out a high-pitched squeak every few seconds as they scroll by, but no bags ride the conveyor belt.

Amy's standing there with a handful of others, oversized purse on her shoulder, hands folded in front of her, and as I walk by, she catches my eye, waves me over.

I check my phone, but there's no reply from Gerry, which means the restaurant's probably still in the weeds, so I saunter in Amy's direction, gym bag bouncing against my waist.

"You didn't check anything?" she asks when I arrive.

"I fundamentally do not fucking believe in checked baggage," I say, then add, "Sorry, I should watch my language."

She shrugs. "I work in a software company. I'm the one female in an office full of men. Believe me, an occasional f-bomb is the least of my worries."

I grin. "So where do you go next, once you get your bag?"

"I pick up my rental car. Then it's off to Bumblefuck, Nowhere, for this wedding."

"And where exactly is Bumblefuck? Sounds suburban. Is it close to Columbus?"

Amy pulls out a phone, thumbs it awake, flips through a few screens. "No, it's… Marcine. Have you ever heard of Marcine, Ohio?"

"You're fucking kidding me. Marcine? The wedding you're going to is in *Marcine?*"

"Yeah," she says, eyebrows furrowing a little. "Why? What's wrong with Marcine?"

"Nothing — everything, actually. It's my hometown. It's where I'm going. Marcine's between here and — "

"Akron?"

"Exactly."

Her eyes light up. "We should ride together!" Then her face falls just as quickly. "Unless — sorry, I'm sure you have someone picking you up, or other plans, or — "

"You said you're renting a car?" I ask.

"Yeah, as soon as my — "

"I'm in."

"Really?"

"Really. Lemme just text my brother, tell him I don't need him to come get me."

#

I don't give Amy directions to my family's home; I give her directions to Soul Mountain. After all, this is why I'm here, isn't it? To fill in with whatever needs doing at the restaurant while Mom recovers from chemo and surgery, and Dad nurses her back to health. I try to explain this to Amy as we drive without giving away too much family drama.

"The 'Soul' is for soul food," I tell her. "You know — collard greens and coleslaw and cornbread and fried chicken. The 'Mountain' is for traditional Himalayan cuisine. Nepalese food is similar to Indian food, but... different. Usually not quite as intense. More lentil soup, fewer hot peppers."

Amy contemplates this, adjusts the glasses on her face as she looks over her shoulder before changing lanes. She switched into glasses before we left the Cleveland airport, complaining that her eyes were burning after sixteen hours wearing contact lenses. The glasses make her look kinda professorial. Which I mean in a good way. In a hot-for-teacher way.

"So... soul food... and Himalayan food... fusion?"

"I swear it's not as strange as it sounds. My mom and dad, they're both amazing cooks. They make it work."

"They must make it work, if they've owned a soul-Himalayan fusion restaurant in small-town Ohio for — how long did you say, again?"

"Twenty-five years. Give or take. After my dad got laid off from the auto parts plant for the third time, my folks realized that running restaurants was the only other marketable skill they both had. So they borrowed some money from my dad's brother-in-law, and... *voila.*"

So — let me just skip ahead here and explain that I did *not* go on and on and on about my family's restaurant the entire car trip to Marcine. I made sure to get Amy talking, too. And here's what I learned:

Begin Summary

As a kid growing up with a military dad and a stay-at-home mom, Amy had grown up in

- Germany
- France
- South Korea
- Alaska
- North Carolina
- New York state

Of these, her two favorite places were South Korea and Alaska.   South Korea because it was so wired; Alaska because it was so not-wired.   She got an undergraduate degree in business management from Ohio State, then returned for business school a couple years later because she was a "practical idealist" — her words, not mine. After growing up in the shadow of pretty much the biggest bureaucracy the government had to offer, she decided that governments and militaries and politics and policies were not going to fix the world's problems.   Socially and environmentally responsible businesses, on the other hand, now *they* might just be able to tackle big issues *and* turn a profit at the same time.

("I have an Elon Musk approach," she says, and I nod knowingly rather than admit I don't know who the fuck Elon Musk is.)

That's how Amy ended up in "b-school," as she calls it, with the intention to either work for a business that had social responsibility as its primary objective, or to start one herself.   But by the time she actually graduated, the economy was down, pickings were slim, and the software company made her an offer she couldn't refuse.

("Golden handcuffs," she explains with a shrug.)

The rest was history.

End Summary

"And that was almost — God, I think it's been eight

years already," she concludes, eyes on the road. "It's strange, isn't it? How time works as we get older? When I was a kid, 'eight years' meant two or three different pushpins on the map. Two or three different houses, two or three different schools, two or three different sets of new friends. And now? Now, it's like eight years can pass" — she snaps her fingers — "like that. And you look back and you think, 'Where'd that time go? Where *was* I for those eight years?'"

"Eight years ago, I'd just turned thirty," I muse.

She nods. "I was thirty-one."

"And thirty felt so fucking old, right?"

"So fucking old," Amy agrees. "Ancient. Over the hill. Or at the very least, it felt like we'd finally arrived at an irrefutable adulthood."

I nod. "But now... thirty year-olds are already starting to look like babies."

"And you look at forty year-olds, forty-five year-olds, and you think, 'Eh, they're still young,'" she says, grinning. "You see forty-three, forty-four on someone's dating profile online and you're like, 'Oh! My generation!' When did that happen? That 'our generation' is in their forties?... Um, not that I spend all that much time looking at people's online dating profiles." She glances sideways at me. "Speaking of forty. How long will you keep playing basketball for?"

I sigh, because this is the question of the hour. Forty might look young to a software executive; to a professional athlete, forty is beyond ancient. Forty is career-ending.

"This might be my last season," I admit. "If not this year, then…" I trail off with a shrug. "My thumb hasn't been the same since I hurt it a few years back."

"I remember when you were out for almost half a season after the surgery," she says.

I nod. "And I've gotten to the point where ice baths after every game are a necessity."

"So what will you do next? After basketball?"

After basketball.

After. Basketball.

I was afraid she was going to ask that. It's what I ask myself almost every day now. And I don't have an answer for myself, let alone for her.

"Coach?" I suggest, shrugging my shoulders. "Maybe. I don't know. Alex can probably help me get a job somewhere if it comes to that."

"You don't sound that enthusiastic about it."

"I suppose coaching's better than… I don't know, sitting behind a desk all day, staring at fucking computer screens." I realize what I've just said a moment later. "Sorry," I say quickly, my cheeks burning. "I'm sure staring at computer screens…"

Amy only chuckles. "I would *love* it if I actually got to sit behind a desk and stare at screens all day. Sitting behind a desk would probably be more productive than traveling all over Europe, schmoozing with fat old men at conferences and dinner parties."

"This is our exit," I say, pointing at the green and white highway sign, glad to find a topic-changer.

I've been away from the U.S. for so long that the green and white sign seems more foreign than familiar. But despite my long absence, I don't have to check my phone for directions. I could find my way back to Soul Mountain blindfolded. I'm like a fucking homing pigeon. A mile later, well before the crowded parking lot comes into view, I can smell our family restaurant. These mingled smells of rice and lentils, black-eyed peas and curried vegetables, chicken masu and golden-brown hush puppies, formed the backdrop of my childhood and my adolescence.

It smells like home.

And it makes me goddamned twitchy.

Chapter 9: These weeds aren't the kind you smoke.

I pull my bag from the backseat and give Amy one last goodbye wave. She waves back and drives off, and it's weird, but I kinda think I'm going to miss her.

I thread through the cars and push into Soul Mountain's outer foyer, greeted by the same series of framed, black-and-white family photos of Kathmandu, Harlem, and Ohio that have been hanging in the entryway for the past twenty-five years. They rattle precariously on the wall when the open door sucks in a cold draft of early spring air.

By the way I have to say "Excuse me" when I reach through the crowd for the second glass door and "Oh, sorry" when I bump the heavyset man on the other side with my gym bag, I know Soul Mountain is deep in the weeds.

(Time-out for restaurant lingo explanation: If you haven't ever worked in a restaurant before, let me explain: "In the weeds" means you are backed-up and probably totally FUBAR (and if you don't know what "FUBAR" means, sorry. You're going to have to just look that one up). By the time you're in the weeds, the kitchen staff is yelling at the waitstaff, the waitstaff is yelling back, the customers are grumbling, and the hostess is standing at the podium with a plastic smile that wouldn't convince a gullible puppy, telling people things like, "Sorry for the long wait. We're clearing off your table just now — it'll be ready any second.")

I glance around, looking for Gerry or my dad, but I don't see either one of them, which is ominous. The teenage hostess behind the podium has eyes that are wide with panic, but she tries to smile anyway and asks me, "How many in your party?"

I shake my head. "Where's Mr. Singh?"

Her face falls, like I'm about to deliver some really shitty news. "Which one?"

"Either."

"Mr. Singh's in the kitchen," she says. "His son is helping a guest right now."

"Right. Okay." I nod my thanks and squeeze between her podium and a family of towheaded Ohioans, "pardon-me-ing" as I try to keep my gym bag from knocking over a chubby first-grader. The kid's got so much extra padding on him that if I do knock him over, he'll probably just bounce right back up.

I know. It's wrong to say, but it's true. I've obviously been living in Europe for too long if the girth of your average American resident is starting to surprise me.

"Ma'am?" the hostess calls to my back as I make a beeline for the kitchen. "Ma'am, do you need me to get Mr. Singh for you?"

I ignore her and keep walking, pushing through the white, saloon-style doors into the kitchen.

It's as bad as I assumed it would be when I walk in, with my dad lifting a basket of chicken from the deep fryer with one hand, forehead beading with sweat, while he shuts off a beeping timer and opens an oven door with his other hand.

Meanwhile, there's a guy trying to clear the backlog of dishes in the back and clearly losing the battle; a Hispanic guy I don't recognize plating *dal bhat tarkari*, garnishing it with artfully cut carrots and cucumbers, dropping a sprig of parsley on top of his perfect mound of rice; and another guy I don't recognize on the hot prep side next to my dad, stirring a giant rice cooker for all he's worth.

Becker, a second cousin of my mom's who's so huge that he makes me look petite, booms out "Order up!" just as a skinny young waitress scurries into the kitchen and slaps a new ticket on the rack.

She glances at me for a single impatient second, not curious about who I am or why I'm standing in the middle of the kitchen so much as wondering why I'm suddenly in her way. "Where's the side of mashed potatoes for table seventeen?" she barks, not directing her question at anyone in particular. "I told you about it at least ten minutes ago."

Becker smiles, white teeth gums a sharp contrast to his purple-black skin. His bass voice rumbles out of his chest like a truck engine starting. "Don't stress, lovely. I've got your mashed potatoes right here." A ham-thick fist reaches over the head of the Hispanic guy, pulls out a small bowl from the stack, plops an ice cream scoop of mashed potatoes inside and adds a ladle of gravy before handing it to the girl.

"I need a fucking saucer," she snips.

Before Becker can reach over the little Mexican's head again, I do it myself, fishing off a plate from the top of the pile and shoving it at the girl. She nods curtly and disappears out of the kitchen without so much as a *"thank you,"* the bowl of mashed potatoes clinking on top of the saucer.

"Well, hello, young pup," Becker says to me when she leaves, the same easy grin still on his face. He's so mellow it's like he's got the other kind of weed working for him. "Did'n expect to see *you* here."

My dad glances over his shoulder at Becker's words. "Anika," he says, voice full of relief. Relief because I'm at the restaurant to help, relief because I'm safely home, relief because I'm his daughter and he loves me — I don't know. There's no time to ask.

My dad is the only person I know who pronounces my name the way it's actually supposed to sound. My name coming from his mouth is both familiar and disconcerting at the same time. Familiar because it speaks of family, disconcerting because it means I'm indisputably home.

After uttering my name like it's a prayer, he turns away from me and back to his basket of fried chicken, shaking the hot oil into the fryer before reaching for a set of tongs.

I pull the gym bag off my shoulder and point to the office door on the left. "Be right back," I say.

Two minutes later, I've got on a hair net, an apron, and I'm sticking my hands under the tap at the hand wash sink. Two minutes after that, I've got a place on the line next to the Hispanic guy, taking over the artful slicing of carrots and cucumbers to free him up to do other things.

#

I don't sit down again until almost eleven PM, when the fluorescent lights in the dining room flip on, the sweeping up starts, and the last customer leaves. I slouch into an empty chair in the dining room, sipping a glass of ice water and pulling the hairnet off my sweaty head.

The annoyed waitress from earlier is finishing up her side work, rolling clean silverware into clean napkins for tomorrow. The hostess is cleaning up, chatting with a bus boy as they clear the last few tables, and behind me, I can hear Becker laughing about something in the kitchen.

My brother Gerry plops into the chair across from me. He's built like me — tall and broad (though not quite as tall as me) and naturally athletic. He's grown a thin, trim mustache and goatee since the last time I saw him; the mustache is pencil-thin and winds around the edges of his lips in a style that's way too Fu Manchu Asian stereotype for my taste. But then again, everything about Gerry has always been "way too [fill in the blank with absolutely fucking anything]" for my taste.

He grins at me, reaches across the table and slaps my

shoulder playfully. "Hey, sis. You're here. Your flight okay?"

"Yeah, it was fine. Got held up in Toronto for a while, but otherwise uneventful." I stifle a yawn and rub at my dry, heavy eyes.

"Glad you found a way home from the airport. I guess you understand why I couldn't leave to come get you right away."

"Yeah. But it all worked out," I say with a nod. I pause, then decide to address the elephant in the room head-on. "So you're here. In Marcine."

He sighs, glances down at the table. "I moved back home about six months ago. Been living with Mom and Dad."

That's surprising. The last I'd heard, Dad had basically excommunicated Gerry from the family and told him never to come home again.

"Nobody told me you were back home."

Gerry chuckles. "No offense, Ani, but if I'm the black sheep in the family, you're the dark grey one. And nobody tells you anything because you act like you don't give a flying fuck. Not like you exactly make much effort to keep in touch."

I take another swallow of my ice water and shrug.

It was true. I couldn't remember the last time I'd been the one to initiate a conversation with my parents or siblings. Other than occasionally liking their posts on social media, we didn't interact much.

"So what's changed? *No offense,* Gerry, but I thought you weren't welcome around here anymore."

He runs a hand through the dark, close-cropped curls on his head. "I got clean. Once and for all."

"Once and for all?" I repeat skeptically. It was a line we'd heard before over the years.

"Once and for all," he says again, nodding. "I can tell you later if you want to hear, but basically, I had a scary fucking experience in Oakland about a year ago, and that was it. I decided I was done. Went to rehab, took it seriously this time. Reached out to Mom and Dad and Dutch when I got out. And so..." He splays his hands palms-up in front of him. "Here I am. Clean as a whistle for a little over a year. Moved back almost seven months ago, and I've been working here in exchange for living rent-free at home. And I'm applying to school."

I lift an impressed eyebrow. Maybe there was hope for my baby brother after all.

Maybe.

"Good for you," I say, and when the yawn comes this time, I don't suppress it.

Gerry laughs. "You must be fucking exhausted. Want me to run you home? I'm sure they can finish closing up without us."

I push up from the table, swaying on my feet. "You get the car keys. I'll get my bag."

#

Fifteen minutes later, I'm flicking on the light switch in the basement bedroom that became mine when I finally got my own room around the middle of high school. My parents converted it into a guest room at some point in between my high school years and now, so the basketball and hip hop posters that used to decorate the walls are long gone, but there's still a pile of dusty old plastic trophies and plaques on top of the bookcase in the corner. Maybe I'll throw them away while I'm here. High school's been over for more than twenty years, and it seems stupid to keep them.

I walk around the double bed, drop my bag between it and the book case. A framed snapshot catches my eye from amongst the dusty trophies, and I lean down to pick it up, wiping the layer of dust off the glass with my thumb.

It's a selfie of Jenny and me from high school, our faces pressed close together as we laugh / scream on an Ohio State Fair roller coaster ride. The pic's blurry and crooked; our hair flies out wildly behind us and the orange body of the roller coaster is visible rising above our heads in the background. Jenny's got one hand wrapped tightly around a stuffed animal I won for her, and although the other hand isn't in the frame, I know it's in my lap, squeezing three of my fingers so tightly that it hurts.

I put the photo back on the shelf, face-down. Then I kick off my shoes, collapse spread-eagle onto the bed. I don't even bother getting up to turn off the light. The last thing I do before I fall into a deep sleep is promise myself to bring a garbage bag down here as soon as I get a chance, to get rid of everything that no longer belongs. Trophies, plaques.

Pictures.

I'm fast asleep twenty seconds later.

Chapter 10: Why I'll always have a soft spot for park benches.

Back to the future: Summer before my senior year in high school.

Jenny's hand finds its way to mine, wrapping around three fingers as we wait in line for the roller coaster ride. My heart embarks on its own short roller coaster at her touch, because usually, she doesn't like holding hands in public. And by "usually," I mean it's never happened before. But I don't let my surprise show; I just give her a gentle squeeze back.

"I'm nervous already," she says, looking up at me. "What if they don't maintain it the right way and there's some kind of freak accident? That happens, you know. You hear about people dying on roller coasters every couple of years."

I shake my head. "Stop. You're being paranoid."

"I don't know that it's all that paranoid. It's not like this is some place sophisticated, like Disney World. It's the Ohio State Fair. And wasn't there an accident at the Indiana State Fair just last year?"

"If there was, I don't remember hearing anything about

it," I lie.

"That's because the only news you pay attention to is sports," she says disdainfully. "It wouldn't even surprise me if you don't know who the current president is."

I tap my chin thoughtfully. "It's Al Gore, right?"

She bumps her shoulder into me. "Oh, stop it."

I grin and then — daringly — I let go of her hand and wrap my arm around her shoulders, pulling her into a quick, sideways hug before I let her go. I know better than to try to keep an arm wrapped around her; the hand-holding was already at the edge of her PDA comfort zone. "It'll be fine. If we start falling or something, I'll just position myself under you to make sure that you land on me instead of the ground."

Her eyes flash briefly with affection. "What about you?"

I shrug again. "I'm tough. Not breakable like *some* people."

It's a reference to the nasty fall she took a week ago at band practice — like the football team, band practice starts before the school year itself does. Jenny tripped over her own two feet walking off the practice field and into the parking lot, landing on her wrist and badly bruising it. The bruises are only beginning to heal now, but her pride is still wounded.

She makes a face at me. "That's not nice. I didn't break anything."

"I know," I say. "And I'm glad you didn't." I smile,

because without her realizing I did it on purpose, I just successfully redirected her attention away from her roller coaster paranoia.

A few minutes later, with Jenny screaming with delight next to me, I pull out my phone and snap a selfie.

#

I've got the Ford Explorer tonight for our trip to the state fair, the one that I share with Dutch and PJ. Dutch usually has possession of it, because even though she already graduated, she's still living at home and driving back and forth to community college, so she actually has the most legitimate need for a car. The other reason she usually has possession of the old Explorer is because she's Dutch. But tonight, I've argued and bribed and pushed for use of the car, and so, like some sort of overgrown, Blasian fucking Cinderella, it's mine until my midnight curfew.

Which is why Jenny and I drive around aimlessly around Columbus after we leave the state fair instead of heading straight home. It's almost a two-hour drive back to Marcine, but it's not even nine yet, and I can tell she doesn't feel like going home any more than I do.

We end up at the Highbanks Metro Park thirty minutes later, wandering through an empty playground because the park officially closed an hour ago. Now that we're all alone, Jenny holds onto my hand without hesitation, rubbing absent-minded circles over my knuckles while she leads me to a bench and chatters about some guy in band who's been flirting with her recently.

"...And it's like, I told him, 'I'm with someone already,' and then he was like, 'Who?' And I said, 'Anika Singh. The basketball player,' and he made this face and was like, 'You're dating a girl?' And I was like, 'Yeah,' and then he said — I can't believe this, Ani — he said, 'Well, when you decide you're ready to date someone *for real,* call me.' As if being with you doesn't count!"

I roll my eyes and pull Jenny onto my lap before brushing a strand of blonde hair away from her heart-shaped face. "Want me to beat him up for you? 'Cause I'm pretty sure I could take Jeremy Wheeler. In the dark. With one fucking hand tied behind my back."

Her brow furrows and she sticks out a bottom lip. "Don't be so violent, Ani. He can't help being ignorant."

"I was only kidding, Jen."

Her lips twitch into a smile. "Halfway. If I'd said 'yes, I want you to beat him up,' I bet you would've."

I press a kiss onto her forehead, taking in her smell of laundry detergent and flower-scented lotion. "Only because I'd do anything you wanted me to do," I say.

She nestles down against my chest, using the hand that's not pinned between us to trace a whisper of a line down my neck. "How did I get so lucky to meet my soulmate when I was just seventeen?" she murmurs. "Most people spend their whole lives looking for their soulmate, travel the whole globe looking for them, and all I had to do was register for trigonometry."

I keep my face carefully blank, but my heart is thudding hard against my ribs. This is the first time she's ever said anything like "soulmate," and what the fuck are you supposed to say when someone springs that kind of shit on you without any warning? We'd already said "I love you" to each other a couple months ago, but somehow, "soulmate" feels like taking it to a whole new level.

I kiss her gently again, first on the corner of her tiny, dainty, perfect mouth, then brushing my lips against hers, letting our tongues find their way to each other.

When she pulls away, I clear my throat and say, "I think you're my soulmate, too, Jen."

She meets my eyes, and hers are extra-big, nervous about something. But she doesn't say a word; she reaches behind her, takes one of my hands from where it sits behind her back, and pulls it around to the front, placing it on her breast.

My heart starts hammering even faster, jumping around inside my chest like a fucking puppy trying to escape a cage.

Slowly, still watching me with extra-big eyes, Jenny slides my hand down the front of her body. With only a thin, tight t-shirt between my hand and her skin, I feel every contour, every tense muscle rippling beneath the surface. She doesn't stop until my hand comes to the place where the form-fitting t-shirt tucks into cut-off jean shorts.

I can feel her stomach rising and falling to the rhythm

of shallow breaths beneath my palm. I swallow audibly, heat cascading in waves through my body.

She tugs my fingers forward until they rest on the top button of her jean shorts and presses them against the warm surface of the smooth metal. "You said you'd do anything I wanted you to do?" she asks in a breathless whisper.

"Yes," I manage, just as breathless.

"Then I want you to touch me," she says.

Another wave of heat floods through, flushing up my neck and face, coiling down into a tight knot deep inside my lady parts.

But you have to fucking hand it to my eighteen-year-old self because what I say in response, with a restraint I didn't know I was capable of, is, "Jenny, are you sure?"

Because you have to understand: On this infamous night of the Ohio State Fair, we'd been together for about eight months. And in eight months, there was a lot of kissing, there was a lot of groping, and sometimes there were some clandestine meetings between boobs and nipples and tongues, but there was never any south-of-the-border action. Instead, there were a lot of late, post-date nights that involved me locking the door to my basement bedroom and flopping down onto my bed, shoving a pillow against my face while I let my fantasies and my own goddamned hand take me further than Jenny wanted ever go.

But now, sitting on a park bench on the outskirts of Columbus, holding my hand to the top of her shorts, Jenny nods and closes her eyes.

"I'm sure."

A tangle of nerves and inexperience, I glance down at where my hand sits at the top edge of her shorts. Acting on instinct and what little I've dared to look up on the Internet, I push my hand down along the outside of the zipper flap and into the hot space between her legs, then squeeze experimentally.

Jenny sucks in a breath, eyes still closed.

She grabs my hand by the wrist again, and at first, I think I've already done something wrong and she's changed her mind, but instead of moving my hand away, she pushes my fingertips beneath the waistband of her shorts. And when my enormous paw doesn't seem to fit in the tight space, she reaches down and pops open the button and slides down the zipper.

"Touch me, Ani. Please," she says again, pressing her small hand against the back of my big one.

"Well, since you asked nicely," I say, joking like a dumbass in an attempt to cover up my nerves, but the words sound half-strangled coming out of my tight throat.

I lean her back, one arm still behind her, holding her weight, while my other hand angles down against the flat plane of her stomach and slips beneath the line of her unzipped shorts, then her underwear. I stop breathing when the tips of my fingers encounter the thick mat of wiry hair, gasp in a sharp breath when my middle finger touches the top of her slit, then encounters the wetness pouring out from her.

Jenny lets out a soft moan, her back arching against my arm. "More," she says in a pant, wrapping her hand against my wrist and pushing it further beneath the fabric of her underwear. My eyes flutter and close of their own accord as my fingers slide between Jenny's slick folds. Still not knowing exactly what the fuck I'm supposed to be doing, I guess and do what I've only ever done to myself before in the quiet privacy of my bedroom: I start rubbing.

Just gently, tentatively at first, constantly checking her face to see if I'm doing anything she doesn't like, savoring the wet, hot textures of her skin against my fingers. Gradually, letting her rocking hips and quiet moans guide me, I add speed and pressure. I lower Jenny down against the bench and shift until I'm basically above her, one knee digging into the bench beside her, my other leg slung over the side, foot trying not to slide through the mulch beneath. It's not particularly comfortable, but the fuck if I'm going to complain.

Jenny's hips buck and she slides her hand over mine. *"Oh.* More. *Harder,"* she breathes, pushing on the back of my hand.

And I, the girl who would forever do anything she wanted, obey. Her hand still on top of mine, I press up into her soft flesh, every bit as aroused and wet as she is, and try not to groan in pleased surprise when she pushes on my middle finger, sending it deep inside her. She tilts her head back against the bench, mouth falling open, and the sight of it obliterates the last traces of my nervousness because I realize in that instant that I was born to please this woman.

Soulmates, I repeat silently to myself.

Still just guessing, still not really knowing what I'm doing, I send my index finger up the same rabbit hole where my middle finger disappeared to, finding a new rhythm as I thrust inside her. She lets go of my wrist and claws her nails down my forearm, and it's so sexy that my insides go hot and numb and gelatin, all at the same time. I want to form words, I want to say "I love you," but I seem to have lost my capacity to speak.

She comes a couple minutes later, in a rocking series of spasms and hushed moans. When she finally stills, I bring my hand back out, wiping Jenny off of me onto the rough wooden slats of the bench.

I stay perched above her, searching her closed eyes and frozen face for signs of life.

"Jenny?" I ask when she still doesn't open her eyes a few seconds later. Worry starts to overtake arousal as I wonder if this was all just too much at once, despite what she asked for. I run a damp finger down her cheek. "Are you alright?"

Finally, heavy eyelids break open and she blinks up at me a few times. She lets out a long, contented sigh.

"I'm more than alright. I'm... If I'd known I could feel that way, I would've made you do that a long time ago."

I grin, more pleased with myself than I have been in a while. Then I shrug. "Beginner's luck," I suggest.

She uses my arm to lever herself up. She zips up,

buttons her shorts.

"We should probably get out of here and head home, right?"

The stupid grin on my face falters, spell broken. "Yeah. We probably should."

Chapter 11: A tutorial on how NOT to come out.

That night before our senior year in high school at the Ohio State Fair that started out so magical ended up totally FUBAR.

We stop for milkshakes at a highway diner not long after we leave the park, giggling and swapping bites of our shakes and playing footsies under the table until we lose track of time, the way sappy teenagers in love do. I drop her off at her house close to one in the morning, an hour past her curfew. We think we're being sneaky and quiet and there are no lights on in the house, but unbeknownst to us, Jenny's mother's waiting for her in the living room, peering at us through curtains we think are closed.

Which is how we get caught a minute later, making out inside a soft yellow cone of porch light.

Jenny's hands are halfway up my shirt, and she's literally sending fucking moans down my throat when the front door flings open. And all the sudden, there's Mrs. Pearson in the doorway, standing there in a blue nighty, eyebrows nearly meeting her hairline, mouth hanging open as wild eyes dart from Jenny, to me, to Jenny again.

"Jennifer Anne *Pearson!*" she bellows as a startled Jenny breaks away from me. "Inside! Now!" And she yanks her daughter roughly away from me by the arm and slams the door in my face.

I freeze, panicked. Total fucking deer in headlights. I want to help Jenny, but I know bursting in isn't the right thing to do, and I don't have any other ideas, so I just stand there stupidly on the front porch for a while, listening to the shouting match that's unfolding inside. After a couple minute, I realize there's nothing I can do, so I tuck my tail between my legs and go home, hoping but not really expecting that my own parents will have long since gone to bed.

They haven't, of course; they don't usually even get home from closing the restaurant until close to midnight, which means they're sitting shoulder-to-shoulder, watching television on the couch when I try to tiptoe past them through the kitchen and down the stairs.

Like my mother would ever be fooled by that.

"You're late," she says just as the door to the basement squeaks open.

"Sorry," I say. "Bad traffic on the way home."

She turns around to face me, clicks the tongue against the roof of her mouth with unadulterated disdain. "I *know* you're not late *and* lying about it to me, too," she says.

I drop my eyes, rubbing my thumb over the same fingertips that had reached inside my girlfriend a few hours earlier. I know it's only my paranoid imagination, and shit, it's not like I didn't wash my hands when we stopped for milkshakes, but I feel like my mom can fucking smell Jenny on my fingers all the way from where she sits.

"Sorry, Momma. We just left Columbus too late. Lost track of time."

"Wrong answer." She gets up from her place on the couch, walks towards me with arms crossed against her chest. My father follows her, and his face is stony.

That's when I know I'm really in trouble.

"Mrs. Pearson called a few minutes ago."

Aww, shit.

Then my mother, who I've known for eighteen fucking years and yet I've only seen her cry *once,* when her own mother died, starts to get tears in her eyes. "She told us what you and the Pearson girl were doing."

"Momma, I — "

"How could you, Ani?" she asks me through tears. My father's lips press tightly together, and he puts a comforting arm around my mother's shoulders. "We raised you to be Christian," she says. *"Christian!* Your *relations* with that girl are not acceptable to us."

"But Momma, she's my *girlfriend!* She's been my girlfriend for — "

"Do *not* say that again under my roof again, young lady."

"I love her," I say quietly.

"You do *not* love her. That is disgusting, and unnatural, and you will — "

"But she's my soulmate! She's my girlfriend and I'm in love with her and she — "

"Anika Regina Singh!" she shouts, and she's crying in

earnest now. "I did *not* bring you up to raise your voice to your mother!"

I try lowering my voice, and it's trembling with tears of my own. "I'm sorry, it's just that I want you to understand — "

"You are not to *see* her," she says, talking over me. "You are not to *call* her. You are not to *text* her. You are not to *talk* to her in school. Mrs. Pearson, your father, and I already discussed this and — "

"You can't stop me from seeing her!"

"I can and I will!" Her hand snakes out, and at first, I think she's going to slap me. I flinch instinctively, but she simply opens her hand before me. "Give me the keys to the car."

"But I — "

"Give me the keys!"

I drop the keys to the Explorer in her open palm.

"You are grounded until school starts. And once school starts, you'll go straight to Soul Mountain every day after school and stay there until Dutch, your father, or I can take you home."

"This isn't fair," I say, and I'm crying as hard as she is.

"You're acting against God. All I'm trying to do — " Her voice catches in her throat as she stifles a sob. "All I'm trying to do is protect your soul."

#

For two weeks, I follow my mother's orders. I move through life as a ghost. I don't see Jenny, don't call her, don't text her. My mom's checking my phone log every day, and I'm sure Jenny's mom is doing the same, so there's nothing for me to do but play basketball incessantly at the court near her neighborhood and hope for her to come by. She doesn't.

School starts, and I find that Jenny has transferred to another trigonometry class. That first day after school at Soul Mountain, I take continuous breaks to go into the bathroom and cry.

Dutch is working that day, too, and she volunteers to drive me home when our parents let us go home early after the dinner rush.

I'm not in the mood to talk on the way home, and I try to make it as obvious as fucking possible, but Dutch has never been one to take a hint.

"So," she says, "you finally opened your closet door. Hallelujah."

I glance over at her, confused, and look back down at my lap.

"I've known you were gay since you were about twelve," she continues. "Came into our room to find you reading one of my magazines, and the way you tried to hide what you were looking at..." She chuckles, shaking her head at the memory.

"I don't want to talk about it, Dutch."

"At first I thought, 'Is she actually interested in makeup

now and she's just afraid to tell me?' But that didn't seem right, so I — "

"I *said* I don't want to talk about it."

"Will you shut up and let me finish? I'm on your side here and I'm trying to tell a story."

Her pronouncement — that she's on my side — shocks me into silence. Because when in our entire lives has Dutch ever claimed to be on my side?

"Anywho, I saw the actress who was on the cover that much — that girl in all those weird-ass science fiction movies you liked so much — and it just sorta clicked." She glances over at me, then back to the road. "Why you were reading the magazine. Why you looked so embarrassed when I came in. Why you tried to hide it." She shrugs. "So yeah, I've known for a long time. Maybe you'll stop being so afraid to be who you are now."

I look at my sister in sheer wonder. Did I actually just get encouragement from *Dutch?*

She reaches into the center console, fishes around until she pulls out her phone. Tosses it to me. "Here. We'll swap phones. You use mine to call your little girlfriend, I'll use yours. We can swap back afternoons at Soul Mountain."

"You… you're giving me your phone? So I can call Jenny?" I say, still dumbfounded.

"The words you're looking for here are 'Thank you, Dutch.'"

"Thank you, but… why are you being so nice to me?

What do you want?"

She laughs out loud. "Is it so hard to believe I'd want to see you happy, Ani? Really?"

"A little, yeah."

She holds out her palm, and it reminds me of Mom demanding the car keys. "Then give me my phone back, if you're going to be a little shit about it."

I put a phone in her hand, but it's mine, not hers. Then I grin. "You can have this one."

Chapter 12: You know what? Screw "Amazing Grace." I'll just stay lost.

Tuesday

I trudge upstairs and into the kitchen, hungry and still half-asleep. I'm pretty sure that staying in my old room put me into some kind of wacky time loop, and I'm pretty sure I dreamed about high school — and Jenny — the night before.

My mother's sitting at the kitchen table, gazing down with a glassy stare at the front page of the newspaper.

I give her a hug from behind and kiss her on the cheek. "Hey, Momma."

"Hey, baby," she sighs without looking up. "Glad you got home safe last night."

The pre-surgery chemotherapy has left her worn and thin, like an old rug. Her skin is almost grey; a do-rag covers her head to hide the hair loss. It's *not* the way I'm used to seeing my mother. I frown.

"You alright?" I ask.

"Yes, baby, I'm fine." She stops. Looks up at me. Then she shakes her head. "No, I'm not alright. Not really."

I get an empty plate down from the cabinet and load it with bacon and eggs from pans that are still warm on top of the stove. I sit down next to her. She glances from the eggs to me and shakes her head, smiling.

"Still the hungriest of all my children," she says.

"Still the biggest of all your children," I retort.

"True."

I pour a glass of orange juice and take a sip before I say, "So what's wrong? You feeling bad from the chemo? Or are you nervous about the surgery?"

She looks up, studies me a moment before answering. "No. I'm sure the surgery'll be fine." She rubs her hip absentmindedly, the one with the tumor hidden inside it.

"You sure? It's okay to be nervous."

"No, I'm… " She heaves another sigh, eyes moving past me and staring at nothing in particular. "'Course I'm nervous 'bout the surgery. Why you gotta ask a silly question like that in the first place?"

I smile at the sharp edges in her words because *that* sounds more like my momma. As long as she can snap at me like that, there's still hope.

"Heard you jumped in, helped your baba and your brother last night at the restaurant," she says, changing the subject.

I decide to go with it, not press the issue of her surgery, because when has my family ever been particularly good at talking about our feelings? We either don't talk about them at all, or we yell. And I'm too tired to yell. So I shrug, tear off a chunk of bacon with my teeth.

"That's what I'm here for, right? Help out with things til you're all recovered?"

She nods and goes back to rubbing her hip. "Didn't figure you'd start last night, though. Not after flying all day."

"They were in the weeds. It was the right thing to do. But anyway, what's going on today?" I ask. "You want me to go with you to that chemo treatment?"

"Actually… I was hoping that your baba could go with me. And you and Gerry could watch the restaurant?"

My eyes narrow, not over being asked to babysit Soul Mountain, but at the million-and-one questions I still have about my brother. I decide to brave the topic.

"So about that. About Gerry, I mean. He said he's been clean for over a year and he's living here and working at the restaurant? Are you really sure you should let him do that?"

"Your brother has turned a corner." She says it in her non-negotiable fact voice. "He's different now. I believe the Good Lord gave him a bona fide revelation. And *you* need to give him a chance to prove that to you." She jabs a finger at me when she makes this last statement, which makes me feel a little like, fuck, between me and the heroin addict, how did *I* suddenly become the bad guy?

But then Gerry's words from the night before come back to me. If he's the black sheep, then I'm dark grey. Except maybe he's not the black sheep at all anymore.

("For this my son was dead, and is alive again; he was lost, and is found. And they began to be merry." — The parable of the prodigal son, fucking gospel of Luke, 15:24. Look it up. And yes I know the word "gospel" is supposed to be capitalized, but I don't fucking feel like it, okay?)

Maybe Gerry's the prodigal son. The "Amazing Grace" once was lost, now he's found ex-junkie. Always the favorite, underneath it all.

But me? Yeah. Still the fucking dyke.

I hold up my hands defensively. "Okay, alright. Don't bite my fucking head off."

"Watch your mouth, Anika."

"Sorry. I was only asking. 'Cause last I heard, he was officially not an official member of the family anymore. That's all. I just wondered what had changed."

"You want to know what's changed?" she asks. "Everything's changed."

Not quite everything, I think bitterly. I rip into the bacon again like a savage.

#

It's Gerry and Becker and the Hispanic guy (who's name is Emir, I learn) and me who open up Soul Mountain at eleven that morning. We're more of a dinner place, and almost all of our lunch business is take-out from people who swing by on their lunch hour, so it's blissfully quiet and restful, and I mainly spend my time running people's credit cards in between playing games on my phone.

Jodie and Ben come in right on time at noon for their weekly game of Scrabble. Jodie's a hairdresser who owns a salon down the street; Ben owns the failing record shop on the corner. They used to date, years and years ago, but they're still friends and get together once per week at Soul Mountain so that Jodie can beat Ben senseless in Scrabble. I haven't seen them since the last time I was in Ohio, which was almost five years ago, and now Ben's pony tail is streaked with silver and white and Jodie's hair color looks like it definitely came out of a box.

Jodie gives a high-pitched squeal of delight when she sees me behind the podium, shoving the Scrabble box at Ben and then prancing up to me with outstretched arms, wrapping me in a tight hug before I really have time to object.

"Oh my God! *Anika!* Nobody told me you were coming home!" she exclaims against my shoulder. She pushes me back, still gripping my forearms. "Let me get a good look at you. Your hair's still a disaster, but I like the shorter cut." She pulls on the curly ends so that they come down just past my chin. "It frames your face nicely."

"Thanks... I think."

Her eyes scan up and down. "And you look like you haven't aged a *day*. Like you're going to walk in here in your high school uniform."

I give her a half-smile, but I'm thinking to myself, *You*

have no idea how much I've aged, lady.

Instead of saying that, I say, "You guys look good, too."

She finally lets go of me, but she's still inspecting me like like she's a fucking *CSI* lady-detective.

"So what are you doing home? I thought you were playing basketball in Switzerland. That's what your dad told me."

"I still am," I say, although I wonder if it's still true. Technically, I broke my contract by coming home. I don't know how much the town of Marcine knows about my mother's cancer, so I tell her, "My mom's taking a break. So I came home to help out for a while."

I see Ben nod knowingly behind Jodie, so I'm thinking that maybe they know she's sick, but then Jodie's brow furrows in confusion.

"You guys still get the same thing?" I ask, redirecting before she can ask more. I point to Ben. "Dal bhat tarkari for you, collards and chicken masu for Jodie?"

Jodie beams up at me, already forgetting my mom's mysterious absence. "I can't believe you still remember, after all this time. *Yes.* You know, you always were my favorite Singh."

I ignore the last comment, because I've got a headache and because I already had to play fucking sibling rivalry games in the kitchen this morning with Mom.

"You guys sit down. I'll bring out your iced tea and mango lassi," I tell them.

"Oh — no more mango lassi for me," Jodie says

apologetically. "My old lady stomach can't handle the dairy anymore. I'll just take tea."

I nod and escape into the kitchen while Ben leads Jodie to their table in the corner.

I'm carrying out a pitcher of iced tea for them a few seconds later when I catch a glimpse of some girl with neck-length dark hair and an expensive-looking pea coat jacket standing at the podium, her back to me.

"Be with you in a second," I call. I feel her tracking me with her gaze as I walk into the sunny spot in the corner and pour drinks for Jodie and Ben. Jodie starts babbling as soon as I arrive, asking me *Have you visited so-and-so yet? Did you hear about what happened with so-and-so? Business at Ben's record shop is really picking up, you should go by some night when they have live music,* and on and on. I'm glad for the girl waiting at the podium because it gives me an excuse to jerk my chin in her direction and say,

"Sorry, Jo, I gotta go help this customer"

and Jodie can only give me a disappointed but understanding nod.

I high-step it back to the podium and say, "Can I help — " before freezing mid-sentence.

Because guess who it is?

"Hi," yesterday's Tinkerbell-sized Jane Lane seat mate says to me. "I heard this place had the best Nepalese and soul food fusion in town. Thought I'd check it out."

Chapter 13: Racist generals and cryptic fortune cookies.

I tilt my head, grin at Amy. "It's not bad," I say. "I hear there's a better place in Cleveland, but, you know, for a small town, Soul Mountain's pretty good." I grab a menu. "So... you really want some lunch?"

"Well, I hear eating when you're at a restaurant is the thing to do, and I didn't have breakfast, so... yeah. I do want some lunch."

I wave my arm at the dining room, which is empty except for Jodie and Ben. "Where do you want to sit?"

"Anywhere in the sun," she answers, and I grin again because Basel was grey, cold, and rainy when we left a few days ago, and so far, Ohio has been warm and sunny. At least it has that going for it.

"Lead the way," I tell her.

She sits down at a table across from Jodie and Ben and asks me for menu suggestions. I give them to her, and fifteen minutes later, after running a few more credit cards and taking a few more take-out orders over the phone, I'm bringing her a bowl of thupka with sides of collards, cornbread, and my mother's pimento mac 'n cheese.

Jodie gives me a curious look when I sit down across

from Amy and rest my elbows on the table.

"So how's Marcine so far?" I ask.

She butters her cornbread. "I've only been here for about sixteen hours, and this is the first time I've actually made it out of my hotel room, but... so far, so good?"

I chuckle. "When's your friend's wedding, again?"

"This weekend."

I think for a second. Today's Tuesday. "And what are you doing between now and then?"

"Helping out, mostly. She's got a dress fitting tonight after work, I'm helping the wedding planner down at the church where they're holding it tomorrow, then there's a bachelorette party Friday night, the rehearsal dinner Saturday... blah, blah, blah."

"Too bad," I say. "If you weren't going to be so busy, I thought I'd show you around the bustling metropolis of Marcine. Show you all the most exciting places. Like the statue of George Custer in the park across from the courthouse."

She frowns. "George who...?"

"Custer. You know, famous dead general? Responsible for the deaths of thousands of Native Americans? Battle of Little Bighorn? Custer's Last Stand?"

"Oh, right," she says. "*That* Custer."

I raise an eyebrow. "Is there another?"

She laughs. "Quit busting my chops. I only just woke up a couple of hours ago, and my body hasn't figured out what time zone I'm in yet." She takes a bite of her cornbread and closes her eyes. "Oh — this is *good.*"

"Toldya. You won't find cornbread like that anywhere else in the state."

"I believe you," she says. She swallows, washes it down with a mouthful of water. "So — about Custer."

I chuckle. "About *Custer?* You just started a new topic of conversation with 'about Custer'?"

Her pale cheeks redden immediately, and I like the effect. "Didn't I tell you to stop busting my chops? But it's not about Custer *per se.* More about going to see his statue. And all the other 'big sights' of Marcine. If you're not too busy, I was wondering if you — "

The phone rings at the podium and I lift up a finger. "Hold that thought. I gotta get the phone."

I take another call-in order, asking the guy to repeat himself five fucking times because the connection is so bad, and I feel Amy watching me the whole time. It's distracting, so I turn my back and lean against the wall, putting my palm over the ear that's not against the phone so that I can finally hear him.

I go back to the kitchen to give the order to Becker and am not *at all* surprised to find Gerry sitting on his ass in the office, smoking a cigarette. I think about leaving it, because I *still* have a headache and I *still* think it's too fucking early for sibling rivalry games, but I'm also stinging from the conversation with Momma this morning, so I fling the door open and step inside.

"You're fucking *smoking* in the kitchen."

He looks up from the stack of paperwork he's got in front of him. "I'm in the office. And the door was closed," he grumbles, but he stabs the cigarette out in the coffee saucer sitting in front of him anyway.

"You know we don't smoke in here." I wave my arm around the hazy office. *"God,* Gerry," I say, and then I quote the ominous fortune cookie I've been carrying in my wallet for the past ten years. "Take the time to *think* before you act."

"Think before I... Jesus *Christ,* Anika, since when did you become such a law-abiding tight-ass?"

"Since I didn't want our customers' food to taste like licking a fucking ashtray!"

"Sorry — I smoke when I'm stressed out, okay?"

I cross my arms against my chest. "And what the fuck do *you* have to be stressed out about? You live with Mom and Dad for *free.* You have the same fucking job you've had since you were sixteen. When you were sober enough to show up for work, that is." I gesture at the desk. "But apparently you don't have to work even when you *are* sober since you're sitting back here on your — "

"Come on, it's been slow. I came back here to work on payroll. Thought I'd surprise Dad by getting it done today so he doesn't have to worry about it this week."

"Whatever," I huff, even though it's a legit excuse and I'm a little jealous that I didn't think of it myself.

"Except — look." He pushes a paper across the desk at me. "I don't know if there's enough money in the bank to *make* payroll this week."

"Wait — what?"

I snatch the paper up, which turns out to be a bank statement. He's right — the balance is much lower than it should be. He points at the computer screen.

"And look at this."

I bend over his shoulder, read the figures in the accounting software he's pulled up.

I'll be damned. He's right. We're barely going to be able to make payroll — *if* we make payroll. And after payroll, there's not going to be enough cash in the bank for the week's groceries. Dad can always charge them, but the cashflow situation...

I drop the bank statement back on the desk, shaking my head. "I'm sure Dad's got it figured out. There's probably another account we don't know about or something."

Gerry shakes his head. "I don't think so, Anika."

His pronouncement echoes in the small office.

"I've got a customer waiting on me," I tell him after a few seconds of tense silence, during which time we sit there and stare at each other like confused mutes. I walk out of the office, out of the kitchen, and drop back into the seat across from Amy, where she nibbles at her mac 'n cheese.

"It's good, right?" I say, hoping I don't smell like cigarette smoke. "Baked mac 'n cheese with pimento and paprika. My mom's secret recipe."

She sets her fork down. "Every bite I take, I swear I'm

probably gaining another five pounds."

"I don't think that math really works."

I start my next sentence at the same moment she says "I was — "

We both laugh. "You go ahead," I say.

"Before you went to answer the phone, I was going to ask if you — I'm not busy tomorrow night, and I don't have anything else to do when I'm not with my friend except sit in my hotel room and watch Pay Per View, so I thought... maybe you'd like to do something? Grab a coffee? Look at statues of dead generals?"

My heart speeds up, does a little happy dance in my chest like I'm eighteen again and holding Jenny's hand in public for the first time. "Amy *Ellis*. Did you just ask me out?"

More red cheeks and it's adorable. She lifts both eyebrows. "Only if you're going to say yes. If you're going to say no, then I was just asking because I was bored and I don't know anybody else in town and my friend's going to be too busy to hang out tomorrow night."

Before I can answer her, the phone rings again.

"Hang on, okay? I need to answer that." I get up, push the chair back in.

She groans and shakes her head. "You're killing me."

"Just — hold on a sec," I say over my shoulder, laughing.

But Amy doesn't have anything to be worried about. *Of course* I'm going to go have coffee with her tomorrow night.   My only disappointment is that she asked me out before I got a chance to ask her out.

I feel fucking lighter than I have in *weeks* when I strut to the podium.

Still got it.

Chapter 14: I only came to talk (yeah, right).

Wednesday

We're in the weeds again Tuesday night, and I come home exhausted and sore and smelling like lentils. It's practically enough to trigger PTSD-style high school flashbacks. Dad doesn't come to the restaurant at all after Mom's morning doctor's appointment, so Gerry and I are the ones who manage the restaurant and close up at the end of the night.

Wednesday morning rolls around and I'm back at Soul Mountain by ten o'clock, rolling silverware and double-checking the toilet paper supply in the bathrooms before our eleven AM open, and I'm already completely fucking over this and counting down the hours til my coffee date with Amy.

Dutch comes by right after eleven with my toddling baby niece in tow, and we chat and it's awkward and Gerry hides in the office and everyone, including Dutch, seems glad when she leaves again.

Jodie and Ben show up at noon, even though their weekly Scrabble date was the day before, and Ben surprises the whole damn restaurant by ordering fried chicken instead of dal bhat tarkari and I think, *That'll be the most*

*exciting thing that happens the whole goddamned shift —
Jodie and Ben showed up on a Wednesday, and Ben
ordered chicken.*

Couldn't have been more wrong.

Because at two-thirty, right as the lunch business starts
to peter out and we begin thinking about getting ready for
the dinner rush, in walks a woman with long, braided
blonde hair, and yoga pants. She's got an infant snug inside
a sling against her chest and a pre-schooler with his
mother's big brown eyes holding onto her first two fingers.

She pauses for a second in the foyer, and I watch her
with clenched fists and a stomach that burns like I just
gulped down a bowl of Momma's five-alarm chili too fast.
I wonder if she's looking at the black and white photos of
my family, or just stalling because she's trying to decide if
she really wants to pull open the second door and waltz into
the main body of the restaurant.

Just as I'm sure she's about to turn back around and
escape into the parking lot, she opens the second door and
walks in. Uses her free hand to brush stray hair out of her
face when the cold draft catches it and pushes it forward.

Instead of looking directly at her, because it's like
staring straight into the fucking sun, I look down at the kid
hanging off her hand. He's got his mother's eyes, true, but
it's already obvious he's going to end up a spitting image of
his father.

My fingers uncurl long enough to find a dry eraser cap
sitting on top of the seating chart. I start fiddling with it.

Jenny hesitates, walks up to the podium.

"Hi," she says.

I grab a menu, nod down at her son. I unclench my jaw. "You need a high chair for him?"

She shakes her head. "I didn't come to eat, Ani."

"Don't call me that."

"I just wanted to talk."

"I don't."

She releases a long, slow sigh. "I got my hair trimmed yesterday afternoon, and Jodie told me you were in town. I thought I'd come by. Say hello." She glances down at her son and smiles softly. "Introduce you to my wild things."

I glance over involuntarily to the table in the corner. Is that why they came on a Wednesday? Jodie wanted to see the show play out in person?

Fucking *Jodie*. Woman can't keep her mouth shut for longer than two minutes at a time. Never pauses to consider that what she says to someone in her salon chair might lead to unwanted consequences for other people.

"I'm busy, Jenny."

She looks pointedly around the empty restaurant, arches an eyebrow. "Really? Doesn't look like it." She hesitates before speaking again. "C'mon, Anika. Can't we act like adults here? It's been more than five years since we talked. I just wanted to see you. Hear how you've been."

I cross my arms against my chest, ignore the way I can feel my pulse slamming against my ribcage. I lean back against the wall. "You're right — it's been years since we

118

talked. I don't see why we should start now."

She takes a step closer, lowers her voice even though she just pointed out that we are alone in the dining room. "You never gave me an explanation. I thought we'd been doing really good at being just friends. Then you blocked my number. Deleted me off social media. Why?"

"I don't want to talk about this."

"But why? Why the sudden change? Friends for years… and then nothing? With no warning?"

I squeeze the marker cap in my hand, feel its open end bite into my palm. "Being friends turned out to be too hard. You cheated on me."

Her perfect brow wrinkles. I used to think it was cute when she got mad. Now… Oh, hell. I don't know how it makes me feel now.

"I cheated on you?" she says, voice ticking up an octave or two. "Don't you think that's the pot calling the kettle black?" Then her eyelids drop closed; she draws in a long breath, lets it out slowly. It's Jenny's reining-her-temper-in look. I used to think that was cute, too. "If it was so hard to be friends with me, why were we friends for so long before you stopped talking to me?"

I shrug. I know the real answer, but there's no fucking way I'm telling her. Especially not now. Not after five years of carefully maintained radio silence.

"Maybe I got tired of being expected to comment on every fucking picture of your kindergartener you posted or texted or emailed." I point at the baby against her chest, then at the kid hanging off her arm. "Where's the other one? You thought it'd be easier for me if I didn't have to look at the one who broke us up?"

Hurt spreads across her face. But she's always been a better person than I am, so instead of responding to me using her child as a weapon against her, she reins in what's left of her temper and changes the hurt into a smile. "Andy's in school. He's nine already — fourth grade this year."

"Great. *Nine,*" I spit out. Nine years since I came home to find a positive pregnancy test in the bathroom trash.

"Anika. Don't be like this. Andrew isn't who broke us up, and you know it. *Mason* isn't even who broke us up. *We* broke us up."

I snort. "Oh, so it's 'we' now, huh? I guess that's an improvement over it being all my fault."

Jenny bends down, hands her phone to the boy who comes up just past her waist, says something softly in his ear. He dances off, jumps onto the waiting area bench with that eager energy only little boys have, swings his feet below him. Watching him, I feel something *pop* deep inside my heart, like some sort of inner fan belt split apart and I'm about to overheat.

She steps closer to the podium, cupping the back of the infant's head protectively.

"Please let's not fight. I just... I honestly just came by because I was hoping you would finally be ready to talk to me again. Can't we at least *try* having a civil conversation? One that's not about the past?"

She's looking up at me with those wide, innocent brown eyes, and for a split second, it's like no time has passed at all. I'm back in high school, at a New Year's party, leaning over her the moment before our first kiss. I'm back in college, trying not to wake up Ophelia with our whispered Skype session. I'm back in Phoenix, coming home from basketball games to a woman who stands on tiptoes to reach tiny hands around my neck and pull me down into a kiss.

And because I'm a complete fucking pushover who apparently hates myself, and because I still feel guilty, and because of sheer force of habit — after all, for thirteen years I always did whatever this woman asked of me — I hand her a menu and I say, "Go find a table. I'll get you a high chair."

"I told you I'm not here to eat."

"It's a restaurant, Jenny. People don't come here to stand around in the lobby."

She glances over her shoulder, to the adorable little boy playing with her phone behind her. "If we sit down and order some food, will you join us? Will you talk with me?"

I tip my head back, stare at the ceiling for a second before letting out a breath and looking down at her. "If it stays quiet, maybe I can sit with you for a minute."

She beams a smile at me that's all heart, a laser beam of concentrated sunlight that nearly blinds me, and even though there are the beginnings of crow's feet crinkling around the corners of her eyes, even though three babies have added a bit of padding to her petite frame, she's still the perfect vision she always has been.

Jenny. My Jenny.

Chapter 15: Things you don't reminisce about over lunch.

Preamble

We end up having a civil lunch like she wanted. Jenny talks about her kids and avoids the topic of her husband Mason; I talk about being back in Ohio and avoid my mom's cancer diagnosis. Once I stop resisting, we fall into comfortable conversation and banter with less effort and in less time than I expected, and she even makes me laugh a few times.

The whole ninety minutes she's there goes like that, friendly and jokey things that snake around all the things we don't talk about, but the past still there, bubbling beneath the surface like a fucking dormant volcano, and I can feel it and I know *she* can feel it and it's shitty because as soon as Jenny leaves, kids in tow and one last glance over her shoulder to give me a friendly wave, the volcano erupts. Everything that goes unsaid rushes to the surface, and it's all I can fucking think about for the rest of the afternoon, a whole list of unanswerable what-if questions, impossible thoughts that will land you in a fucking mental hospital if you're not careful.

Which, case-in-point: Marty McFly shows back up in the middle of all my reminiscing, shoves me into the DeLorean, even though I tell him I don't want to go. But he's insistent and it doesn't help that the restaurant's slow as fuck and I don't have anything else to do except lean on the podium and think about the past.

Back to the future: Ten years ago. I'm twenty-eight.

I drop my gym bag by the front door and walk over to the couch, where Jenny's watching TV and sipping a glass of white wine. An empty Chinese food container sits on the coffee table in front of her, chopsticks jammed into a mound of white rice still in its box, a cracked open fortune cookie next to it.

I lean over the couch, kiss her cheek. "Hi, babe."

"You smell nice," she says distractedly, not looking at me.

I climb over the back of the couch with my shoes still on, even though she hates it when I do that, and land next to her heavily. "I know you like it better when I shower before I come home."

She sips her wine, still won't look at me when she says, "As if you ever come home."

I frown. "What's that supposed to mean? We had a game tonight. The team went out for drinks afterward; I came home. I thought you'd be happy to see me."

She puts her glass down, covers her face with both her

hands and shakes her head. "I am, I'm sorry. I shouldn't have said that. I've had a long day."

I reach an arm around her, about to pull her into my lap, but she pushes my arm off.

"Don't," she says.

"Don't what?"

"Don't try to make me feel better."

I huff out an acidic laugh. "Oh, right, because it doesn't make *any* fucking sense to try to make you feel better after you just said you've had a hard day."

"I didn't say I had a hard day. I said I've had a long day."

I want to say, *Is there fucking a difference?,* but I manage not to. I reach for the fortune peeking out of the cookie, because I need something to fiddle with if we're going to do this right now. *Take the time to think before you act,* the fortune reads cryptically.

I rub the little slip of paper between my thumb and my forefinger, and for once I try to think before I speak. After a moment, I ask her softly, "What's happening with us, Jen?"

She stares straight ahead at the television screen.

I crumple the fortune in my fist. "Talk to me. Please?"

She runs a hand over her head, finger-combing long blonde hair to one side, and folds her legs up beside her. Still doesn't look at me.

"You're never home," she says at last.

"It's basketball season. Travel is part of the job. You

know that. But we had a home game tonight, and... I'm here now, aren't I?"

She lets out a long breath. "I made it through college because I kept telling myself — because *you* kept telling me — that it would be different once we graduated. We wouldn't have to keep doing the long distance thing. We'd be together at last. We'd be in the same state, the same city, under the same roof, sharing the same bed." She glances at me long enough to meet my eyes, then looks away again. "We'd build a life together."

Now I'm confused. "We *do* sleep in the same bed. And we *are* building a life together."

"No, we're not," she says sharply. *"You're* building a life. *I'm* working as a secretary and coming home to an empty house *every* night."

"Baby, come on. That's not fair. You know things are busy during — "

"Do *not* fucking tell me again that things are busy during basketball season, Anika!" she shouts, hands curling into fists. And I know she's really mad now, because Jenny never, ever cusses. "You're *never* here. No matter what time of year it is. We've been living here for six years, and how much of that time we've actually spent together?"

I don't answer.

"Do you know how many friends I have here, besides Cindy from work?"

I don't answer again.

"All I do is sit here, on this couch, and wait for you to

come home every night. *When* you come home." Her voice drops, cracks. "I'm lonely, Ani. I miss my family. I miss Ohio." She gives a humorless laugh. "Hell, I even miss winter." She turns to face me, holds my gaze. "And I miss *you.*"

"But I'm right here," I choke out, fighting back tears. "I've been right here the whole time. *You've* been the one pulling away — for years now. And it's like it doesn't matter how many times I reach out for you. The more I reach, the more you pull away."

"I pull away because it's like you've forgotten how to listen to me. To *see* me. Every time I try to tell you that I don't like Phoenix, that I wish you were home more, that I wish we had more friends here, all I get is excuses. 'Baby, I'm trying to build my place on this team.' 'Baby, I'm so tired when I get home, I don't want to go out.' 'Baby, what do we need a bunch of drinking buddies for when we've got each other?' Baby-this, baby that." She shakes her head, eyes welling with tears. "I can't keep putting *my* life on hold for *your* life, Ani. I've been doing it since high school, and I'm tired of it. I don't even know who I am anymore; it's like the only thing people know me as is Anika Singh's wife. And that's not enough for me. Not anymore."

"I never asked you to — "

"I know. I know you never asked me to be your little housewife. Not directly, at least. But that's what our relationship has *always* been. For the whole ten years we've been together, it's *always* been about *me* following *you. Me* waiting for *you.* And I can't do it anymore."

"Baby…" I reach out for her again, but she shrinks away from my touch. I'm not sure which hurts more — the fact that she won't let me touch her, or the fact that she's been feeling like this for way too long and I've been utterly oblivious.

I sit back on the couch, giving up trying to hold her, to comfort her. I straighten out the fortune that I crumpled in my hand, smoothing it against my palm.

Take the time to think before you act.

And it hurts to ask the question I know has to be asked, because I don't know what the answer is going to be. "So what do you want to do?"

Chapter 16: People I wish I'd never met. Things I wish I'd never done.

Back to the future: One year after that tense fucking conversation in Phoenix. I'm twenty-nine.

I'm traveling the last week in September, playing a game in a big, dirty city that looks like all the other big, dirty cities I play in, and for once I'm actually sharing Jenny's nostalgia for small-town Ohio. Or for Rosemont. If any place ever felt like home, it was there.

The team goes out for drinks after our win, and I get invited, but I turn them down. Instead, I head back to the hotel and talk with Jenny for an hour before I take my shower.

Things are better than they were a year ago — at least, that's what she tells me. To me, it feels about the same. It feels like we were always magnets before, drawn together despite all odds, stuck together with an inevitability that felt as predictable and permanent as the laws of physics and JFK conspiracy theories. But now, it was like our magnets had reversed their polarity, and we kept pushing away from each other no matter how hard we tried to come back together.

Our hour-long conversation is familiar and strained at the same time. We fill it with safe mundanities, reviewing things like weather, errands, plane flights, basketball plays. (We don't know it then, but the conversation we have ends up being a lot like the one we'll have in Soul Mountain, ten years later, when she comes to see if I'll finally talk to her again.) She tells me about her new classes — because she's going back to school now, working on a degree in Early Childhood Education so that she can become a kindergarten teacher — and I tell her about the weight-lifting regimen Coach has put me on.

"So when can I look forward to some six-pack abs?" she asks, and it's supposed to be teasing and flirty, but it falls flat somehow, like our whole conversation, and so I just say,

"I don't know," and there's a long pause heavy with unsaid words, and finally I decide I've had more than enough of this. "I need to hit the shower. I'm stinking up the hotel room."

She lets me go. I shower. I call Alex when I get out, but she doesn't pick up, and I imagine she and Graham out somewhere, having a late dinner or catching a movie, and for some reason, the thought stings.

So I decide maybe I'll hit the bar after all, see if my teammates are still there.

#

"What do you have on tap?" I ask the barkeep, a cute young thing with way too much eyeshadow and a long brown ponytail streaked with blonde highlights.

She rattles off my choices, and I pick one and put a stool beneath me, because even though I don't see my teammates anywhere — maybe I got the bar wrong or they decided to go somewhere else in the end — I'm here now and I'll stay long enough to at least have a fucking beer. Or two. Maybe three. Drinking by myself in a bar might be depressing, but it's less depressing than watching TV in a hotel room by myself.

I sit there nursing my beer, my back leaned against the bar rail so I can people watch.

Which is how I spot the top of a blonde head, a long face ending in a square jaw, winding its way through the crowd and towards the bar. Towards *me*.

"Mother*fucker,*" I mutter under my breath.

She walks straight up to me but doesn't look at me; hails the barkeep with that attitude of superiority she's always fucking had, orders herself a beer. It's only after she knocks the cap off the bottle and refuses the glass offered to her that she leans sideways against the bar and looks me up and down.

"Where's everybody else?" Rhianna-Fucking-Jerkins asks me, sweeping a hand around the sparsely populated bar as if I didn't fucking realize the rest of my team isn't here.

I shrug, stare straight ahead.

She laughs. "What, are we pretending we're in high school now? You're going to pout and act like you don't know me?"

I look at her. "Why would I be the one pouting? I beat you tonight. Again."

"You beat me? I out-scored you, just like I always do. Shut you out of the paint, just like I always do. Almost succeeded in fouling you out. Like I always do." She straightens a little, like she wants to remind me that she's still got two inches on me. She gives me a cocky smile.

Rhianna is to Anika as Thor is to the Incredible Hulk: One's a blonde goddess and the other's green with envy.

I roll my eyes. "And you *did* foul out. Like you always do. You've got no grace, you rely solely on brute strength and size, and my team *won*. Like my team *always* does when my team plays yours."

Rhianna frowns and shakes her head. Sore loser. She takes another sip of her beer. "Not my fault we have a shit-for-brains point guard. She turns the ball over like it's going out of style."

I can't help myself. I give Rhianna a really smug fucking smile. "Your point really did screw you guys over pretty good tonight. I'll bet it makes you nuts."

She arches an eyebrow, studies me as the beer goes back to her lips, and after a long pull, the bottle comes away with lipstick smeared along its neck.

Huh. So Rhianna Jerkins wears lipstick when she's not in uniform. Not that I'm staring at her lips. Not that I think the color looks good on her. Without a jersey on, in boots instead of high tops, she looks kind of feminine. Like a Valkyrie instead of Thor.

"I've been stuck with bad guards ever since UConn," she admits, changing the topic away from the night's game. "What about you? Ever wish you still played with Woods?"

I break eye contact, watch a group of women laughing around a pool table. "Meh. We were good together on the court. But I like being in Phoenix."

I'm lying through my teeth, of course. And somehow Rhianna seems to know it because she lets out a low chuckle and nods at my empty glass.

"Loser buys," she says. "Let me get you another."

#

My fidgety fucking fingers are shaking so hard that the door card slips out my hand and tumbles to the ground before I can fit it into the slot.

"Fucking *Christ,*" Rhianna says behind me, hot, alcohol-saturated breath too close to my ear. "Get it open already." Her hand slides up the back of my shirt, and her palm is as hot as her breath, but it makes me shiver anyway.

I manage the door after two more tries, and the woman behind me doesn't waste any time — she's shoving me forward, ripping at my shirt simultaneously, pushing me against the bed until I stumble and land hard on the mattress back-first.

She's straddling my waist in the next moment, hands working at the zipper of my jeans, and I sit up, grab her by the shoulders, wrestle her down to the bed, fumble at the buttons of her shirt with my fidgety fucking fingers.

"No you don't," she laughs, and she rolls me over, pinning my wrists to the bed on either side of my head and dropping her weight onto my torso. "When are you going to learn that I'm bigger than you and stronger than you?"

Her mouth dips down into the space where my throat meets my collarbone, and I'm expecting a kiss. Instead I get a bite. A hard bite. And it fucking hurts. I try to buck her off, but she's right — she's stronger. And heavier. And she laughs against my neck and I don't get far before I give in and just let her pin me.

"I hate you," I say, and she bites my earlobe, and it hurts even more than the bite to my collarbone, and I tilt my head back and suck in a sharp breath.

Rhianna kisses me with such sudden intensity that our teeth clack together, which draws a giggle from her that bubbles into my mouth. She pushes herself up with hands that are still holding down my wrists and looks me in the eye.

"You might hate me," she says, "but you *love* this. Don't you?"

And I can't think of how to answer, maybe because I'm drunk, maybe because shame and guilt burn in my chest as I think of Jenny, maybe because I've never been with anyone else except my beautiful, Tinkerbell-sized wife, and in our eleven years of being together, Jenny's never been able to pin me on my back, even if she wanted to. And I'm pretty sure she's never wanted to.

I arch my head and shoulders up — not trying to throw Rhianna off anymore, just trying to get to her mouth so I can shut her up. I take her bottom lip between my teeth and pull, making her yelp, forcing her to follow me back down to the pillow. The kiss that follows is long and wet and sloppy, smearing thin strings of saliva against my cheeks and my chin.

I hate it and I love it and I need to stop *right now* and there's no way I'm stopping this and I can't believe it took me until I was twenty-nine to be with someone besides Jenny.

Rhianna ends the kiss long enough to sit up, pull my bra off, then drops her sharp fucking monster teeth to one taut nipple.

It hurts. In the best possible way.

"God, I *really* fucking hate you," I gasp out.

Her mouth works its way down my torso, alternating between biting and sucking and kissing in a way that I know is going to leave a trail of purple bruises behind, bruises that will still be there when I get back to Phoenix, but I can't bring myself to care. She lets go of my wrists at last, and I use the opportunity to put both hands on top of her platinum blonde head, push her down towards my hips. She laughs, but her hands start working at my jeans again, tugging them down over sweaty underwear.

A surprisingly gentle, slow series of kisses follows the line where my underwear meets my abdomen. Rhianna looks up. "I'm about to fuck you so hard, Singh, you're going to wish you never met me."

I close my eyes, rock my hips up to help when she starts pulling off my underwear.

"I already wish I'd never met y — oh, *fuck.*"

A hot tongue slides against me, and I go breathless and silent.

But before my brain even has a chance to fully process the tongue sliding against my wet fucking clit, there's a long finger pushing hard inside me. Then another finger. Then a third. Somehow, she manages to squeeze even her pinky finger up there, and now I've got Rhianna-Fucking-Jerkins whole fucking hand working its way inside me. It hurts, and I think about telling her to stop, but it doesn't hurt enough that I want her to stop. And I can't help it — I find myself wondering why Jenny's never tried this, given that her hands are so much smaller. Rhianna's face becomes Jenny's. Jenny's morphs back into Rhianna's.

Lips and tongue and hand all work together, and I'm thinking about taking back what I said earlier. Maybe Rhianna has some grace, after all. A little, anyway.

Her hand pumps in and out of me — pleasure on the knife edge of pain.

"Jesus-motherfucking-*Christ,*" I groan. "I still — *God* — I still... oh, fuh... I still hate you."

"Stop talking, Singh."

It takes me longer to climax than usual, maybe because of my guilt, maybe because it almost hurts, maybe because of the booze. At any rate, I don't waste any time once she's finished me. As soon as I catch my breath, I roll her off of me, pin her to the twisted, sweaty sheets below us. I straddle her bare chest, my knees biting into her forearms.

"Payback's a bitch, you know," I say.

Her smile is sultry. "It had better be."

I've always been gentle with Jenny. She's smaller than me in every way, in every place and every crevice of her porcelain body. I've never been rough with her in bed, because I'm afraid I might break her. And I have the feeling she wouldn't like it, anyway.

But with Rhianna...

I flip her onto her stomach, use my knees to push her legs apart, use my hands to knead at her ass. She lets out a small moan of pleasure when I reach inside her and wiggles her legs wider. It encourages me at the same time that it irritates me, so I push harder. Her hips jerk up, slap against my bare abdomen, and that does it — something inside me goes wild. I've never done anything like this with Jenny before, and I love it. I push my fingers so far inside Rhianna that she practically swallows my knuckles, and she only groans louder. I move faster, deeper, and pretty soon I'm panting along with her, bracing myself on a forearm as my tits alternate between sliding and sticking to her sweaty back. Unlike with me, it only takes Rhianna a couple minutes to tip over the edge, and when she does, she clenches her thighs together so hard that she practically breaks my fucking hand.

I collapse on top of her when her legs finally relax, pull my aching, pruned-up fingers out and wipe them on the sheets beside her.

"Still hate me?" she asks, words muffled by the pillow beneath her face.

"More than ever."

#

When Rhianna leaves a couple hours later, I take another shower and put on fresh clothes, kicking the dirty, sex-and-bar-smelling ones into the corner. I fish my phone out of the pocket of my discarded jeans before sitting on the foot of the bed, open the screen to my list of favorites. My thumb hovers over Jenny's name. It's one in the morning where she is; there's a chance she might still be up.

Tears swell in my eyes like water balloons; a fat one breaks, rolling down my cheek and splashing onto the phone. It blurs Jenny's name. I sniff hard, wipe the tears from my cheeks with the heel of a hand.

I press my thumb against the screen, knee bouncing up and down as three rings pass in painful slowness.

"Anika?" Alex says, voice gravelly with sleep.

Words don't come out right away, just a pained cry.

"Anika? Are you there?"

"I fucked up, Lex. Jesus *fucking* Christ, I just fucked up really fucking bad."

Chapter 17: Amy's surprisingly extensive knowledge of the Greek alphabet.

Wednesday night

Seven hours after my lunch with Jenny, seven hours after my trip into the past with Marty McFly, I'm saying "Sorry I'm late" as I slide into the chair across from Amy. I knew I'd end up being a few minutes late, but I wasn't going to show up without running home to shower first. Even if I didn't smell like curry to her, I would've to me. And that's not the way to start a first date.

Amy puts her phone down, graces me with a smile. She dressed up a little, I note — a button-down top with a light purple cardigan over it, silver hoop earrings hanging from the bottom of ears lined with silver studs. Light lipstick, a little bit of eyeshadow. Jane Lane dark hair pinned away from her face on one side.

I'm just about to compliment her when she points at the counter. "What do you want?" she asks. "I'll go put in our orders."

I shake my head. "No, no, let me get — "

"Not a chance. I asked *you* out, remember? That

means *I'm* the one treating here."

I can't argue with the logic, so I give her my drink order, fiddle with the petals of the fake flowers while I wait for her to come back.

She returns a couple minutes later, sets a latte in front of me, sits back on the bench side of the table.

"I didn't peg you as a latte drinker," she comments.

I raise an eyebrow. "No?"

"No." She squints at me like I'm a distant street sign she's trying to make come into focus. "No… you look more like a Gatorade and Vitamin Water kind of girl."

I make a face. "Hate that shit." I sip the latte. "Well — okay, I'll drink Gatorade in a game. But only because it's necessary."

She chuckles; a few seconds pass. I worry we're going to descend into irretrievable awkwardness before we even really get started, so I search my brain for a question, just to get the conversation going again. But we both start to speak at the same time again, just like at Soul Mountain the afternoon before. I wave for her to go ahead.

"So what's it like being back in Ohio?" she asks.

I think of everything that's been going on — of Mom, Dad, Jenny, and Gerry, of discovering the restaurant might not be financially solvent. I take the thin wooden stirring stick that's still in my coffee and swirl it around a few times as I try to think of a polite way to word it.

"It's been… interesting." I figure I should say more, so I add, "I came home because my mom's sick. Since she comanages the restaurant with my dad, and since my other siblings are all busy with their own things, I said I'd come home and help out til she got better. But I don't know how long that will be, so…" I trail off with a shrug.

"None of your siblings are helping out?" she says, sounding skeptical.

"Well, I mean there's Gerry. If he counts. But PJ and Dutch are too busy."

"But you're busy, too, right? What about basketball?"

"It's like I said before, this might be my last season anyway. So it was a better time for me than for the rest of them. And I felt like I owed them — the last time I was living in Ohio, I kind of left in a hurry. My parents ended up cleaning up the mess I left behind."

She hesitates a second, then says, "I won't ask."

"Probably better if you don't," I agree, thinking of my epically dramatic breakup with Jenny that gave Jodie's hair salon gossip fodder for weeks. "Anyway," I say with a dismissive wave, "how's it going with your friend's wedding?"

Amy rolls her eyes. "This is the last time I will ever agree to be a bridesmaid. I've been here for three days and already it's like I'm back in the sorority again."

"You were in a sorority?" I ask, mildly surprised.

She nods. "Oh, girl. Not just *any* sorority. I was a Pi Phi."

"No the fuck you were not."

"Yes the fuck I was."

I shake my head hard to show her what I think of her obvious big fat lie. "No, there's like a fucking rule that all Pi Phis have to be blonde and rich and pretentious."

She raises both eyebrows like it's a challenge. "And you don't think I could be any of those things? Or did you just imply that I *am?*"

"Well, obviously you're not blonde — "

"You've never heard of dye?"

"And you told me your dad was military and you had a stay-at-home mom, so no offense, but I doubt you were rich growing up. Plus Pi Phis… they're like the *straightest* of the straight girls," I add.

Amy flips her hair dramatically, bats her eyes a few times, gives me a smile that makes me think of a cat sneaking up on an unsuspecting bird. "You'd be amazed how good I am at faking things."

I open my mouth, close it again. Open it. Finally say, "Okay, I'm not touching *that* with a ten-foot pole."

She lets out a light, musical laugh, and gives me a broad grin that sends her dark eyes twinkling.

I have to look at my latte for a second, because that smile? Yeah, it's like staring straight at the fucking sun.

When her laughter dies out, she takes a sip of her own drink and says, "I was good at faking, but not so good at not getting caught."

I cock my head to the side, intrigued. "Okay. I'll bite. Getting caught at what?"

"More like 'getting caught at who,'" she answers.

\#

Back to the future: Twenty years ago.   Amy's college coming out adventure.

Amy's just turned nineteen when she joins the Formal Recruitment process to rush Ohio State's sororities. She's got plenty of good fakes going for her back then — she's got long, fake blonde hair; she's bent the truth about what her father does for a living (says he's a department head at an "international organization," which is technically true, she just makes it sound like he's a business man instead of a Lieutenant Colonel); she plays up the fact that she's lived in Europe and entered college already fluent in German and semi-fluent in French.

What she's not faking is her interest in Pi Beta Phi. She knows, like plenty of young women like her know, that Pi Phi takes only the prettiest, most popular girls to be a part of their self-congratulatory club. And self-congratulatory or not, she wants in.

Because Amy's never been "in." She's always been outside *looking* in. As soon as she thinks she's made a solid new group of friends, it's time to move. She tries keeping in touch with them for a little while, but inevitably they stop taking her calls, stop answering emails, disappear off her Facebook feed. It's been like this her whole life.

Now that she's in college, she'll be in one place for

four. Straight. Years. An unprecedented luxury that her father's next post can't change. And Amy's going to make the most of those four years. She's going to make the Friendships That Last a Lifetime. And when she graduates, she's going to list one of the most exclusive sororities in the country on her resume. With those three little Greek letters tacked onto her name, she'll never be on the outside looking in again.

No matter where she goes after college, she'll be a Pi Phi. She'll have Sisters everywhere. Friends everywhere. No starting over ever again. And it's something no one can take away from her.

So she charms and fakes and lies her way through the recruitment process, endearing herself to one Pi Phi after another. But when she talks to her future sisters, she expresses her doubts about the sorority. She drops the names *Kappa Kappa Gamma* and *Tri-Delt* in her conversations with them, talking about how kindly the girls there have treated her, how interested she is in them, how interested they are in her.

Amy, it turns out, is a total fucking con artist.

By the time she gets her Pi Phi invitation on Bid Day, they're practically surprised that she chooses them. Like she graced *them* with her acceptance, rather than them gracing *her* with an invitation.

#

Annual mixer with Sigma Chi, spring semester of Amy's freshman year

Amy staggers into a bathroom, mostly drunk, and is about to hitch her dress up over her hips so she can pee when she spots a girl leaning against the sink, touching up her lipstick.

"Oh," Amy says. "Sorry — I didn't know there was anyone in here."

The girl's silvery dress hugs her lanky frame in all the right places, and it makes her seem even taller than she is (but Amy comes in just over five feet, so everyone seems tall to her). The tall girl looks Amy up and down, giving the kind of snooty inspection Amy endured over and over again during rush. Then she lets out a half-laugh, telling Amy the inspection's *obvious* conclusion was — Amy's been found wanting.

It's irritating. Amy's a *Pi Phi* now, goddammit. And who's *this* girl, and what the hell did Amy do to offend her?

Amy gives as good as she gets, crosses her arms against her chest and does her own inspection. The tall girl in the silver dress has long, wavy brown hair only a few shades darker than her tawny brown skin. Amy's first thought is that she looks Hawaiian. Maybe Polynesian. Or Indonesian. But she doesn't ask, doesn't let her eyes reveal how striking she finds the other girl. Instead, she says,

"What?" and gives the word as much haughty Pi Phi venom as she can.

146

The girl looks her up and down once more. "Nothing. *Clearly.*"

The icy stare-down continues for a few seconds more, but then something dawns on Amy. "Wait a second," she says. "I know you. You're Quinn Kama. You're a varsity soccer player."

Quinn Kama is momentarily caught off-guard. "Yeah? So? I'm here with my boyfriend. He's Sigma Chi," she says. It's all unnecessarily defensive, and she's justifying her presence at the mixer, Amy realizes. Compensating for the insecurity of feeling like she doesn't belong. It's something Amy gets.

"Do you remember me?" Amy asks. "I write for *The Lantern*. I interviewed you after the last home game. You scored twice."

Quinn's face softens a little; her stance relaxes. "Yeah... Actually, yeah, I do remember you. Your name's... It's, uh..."

"Amy."

"Amy. Right." Quinn relaxes further, lets out half of a smile. "I remember you watching from the stands. You seemed like you were really into the game."

"I am — or, I mean, I was. I love women's sports." Amy shrugs self-consciously, because her obsession with women's sports is something none of her Pi Phi sisters understand. Hell, it's something that Amy herself doesn't entirely understand. All she knows is that she loves watching female athletes. She loves the power, the strength, the skill — but also the grace. A grace that male athletes rarely match.

There's a long pause. "Look, Amy," Quinn says. "I'm sorry I was such a bitch. I just... Rod's always dragging me to these mixers for his fraternity. Most of the time, people treat me like I don't belong here, so I've just gotten into the habit of..." She drops her gaze to the floor.

"Of preemptive strikes," Amy supplies with a nod. Her father's a career military man, after all. She can appreciate Quinn's strategy. "Believe me. I get it. Sometimes I hate these things, too."

Quinn looks back up, meets Amy's eyes. Smiles fully this time. Perfectly white teeth provide a beautiful contrast against her tawny skin, and butterflies flutter into Amy's stomach for reasons she doesn't entirely understand yet.

"Umm," Amy says. She gestures in the direction of the toilet. "I kind of need to use the, uh..."

The spell is broken. Quinn clicks the cap back onto her lipstick and titters out an uncomfortable giggle. "Right — I was hogging the bathroom. Sorry. I'll just..." She turns sideways to step past Amy, her chest brushing against Amy's shoulder through the silvery dress as she does. "... I'll get out of your way," she says.

Quinn leaves, closing the door behind her.

Alone in the bathroom, Amy lets out a breath she didn't know she was holding.

#

Amy can't stop thinking about Quinn after that, and when she's offered a chance to cover the women's soccer game against Ohio the next week, she jumps at it, immediately seeking out Quinn in the locker room after the game.

Amy was a high school sports reporter at both of her high schools, and she signed up to write for *The Lantern* the very first week of school. And since most of the sports reporters were guys, and since most of them had very little interest in covering women's sports, Amy practically had interviewed, highlighted, or at least known of almost every female varsity athlete on campus.

It means she's no stranger to women's locker rooms.

But there's something different about being in the locker room after the Ohio versus Ohio State game this time. There's something about the smells of heat and sweat and grass stains and floral shampoo that make Amy feel out-of-balance. She walks through the locker room unsteadily, like a woman with vertigo, mumbling apologies as she bumps into more than one bare arm and bare back before she makes it to Quinn.

Quinn's hair is pulled up and back; sweat-darkened curls are plastered to her temples and the back of her neck. In a sports bra, soccer shorts, and cleats, she's somehow both more intimidating and more beautiful than she had been in her silver dress in the frat house bathroom.

Amy steels herself. "Hi — Quinn? It's Amy. From

the, well, from the bathroom at Sigma Chi — remember?"
She's rolling her eyes at herself even as she says it,
blushing even as she tries not to. "I'm doing the write-up
on the game for *The Lantern* again."

Quinn looks up at the sound of Amy's voice, flashes
that perfect, bright white smile again. The sensation of
vertigo gets so strong that Amy plops down on the bench
beside her interview subject.

"Amy," Quinn says. "See? I remembered this time.
Nice to see you again."

The interview goes smoothly — so smoothly that the
two are laughing and joking like old friends by its end. The
next time she spots Quinn on campus, they smile and nod at
each other as they walk past. The time after that, Amy
offers to buy Quinn lunch.

Chapter 18: I'll show you my General Custer if you show me yours.

Guys & Dolls party, Sigma Alpha Epsilon house, next-to-last week of Amy's freshman year

It's the last week before finals when Amy sees Quinn again, this time at a *Guys & Dolls*-themed party at a different frat house. Amy loves costume-themed parties; she arrives in a perfect 1920s flapper dress, complete with a fringe at the dress's bottom, a headband adorned with a peacock feather, and a black boa draped around her shoulders.

She bumps into Quinn at the edge of the makeshift dance floor, where she hangs on the arm of her beefy Sigma Chi boyfriend. He's wearing a fedora cocked at an angle and a bowtie, but Quinn's wearing the same silver dress as the last time Amy saw her at a mixer, the only change to her outfit a long necklace of fake pearls. Quinn twists the pearls around her index finger listlessly, gazing out at nothing in particular with a slight crease in her brow.

The boyfriend says something into Quinn's ear, pecks her on the cheek, and walks away. The crease in her brow gets deeper.

Uncomfortable again. Clearly.

Amy, who's already had one strong mixed drink and is feeling extra cheery and extra social, bounces over to her.

"Quinny!" she exclaims. "You're back from Indiana! Did you win?"

"Yeah," she says without enthusiasm. "We won. It was a good game."

"You don't look like you're having a very nice time," Amy observes.

"I'm not."

Amy jerks a thumb over her shoulder to the dance floor behind her. "Then dance with me."

"I don't dance."

"Pssh," says Amy. "I've seen you dance."

"I don't dance, Amy."

Amy pouts, sticking out her lower lip. "Not even for me? You're not going to leave me all alone on the dance floor, are you? What if I get you a drink? Will you dance after a drink?"

The crease in Quinn's brow softens; the corners of her mouth twitch into what doesn't quite amount to a smile.

Amy gets her onto the dance floor a drink and a half later.

They dance to a song. They dance a little closer on the second song. They grind together playfully on the third, much to the hooting delight of the nearby frat guys.

A drink and a half after that, they're stumbling up the stairs towards the bathroom, laughing about something they'll forget by the next day, if not the next hour.

Before they make it to the line for the bathroom, Quinn grabs Amy's wrist, pulls her into the shadows of an alcove.

"Thank you," she says.

Amy's laughter dies down. "For what?"

"For getting me to dance. For... rescuing me down there."

"Rescuing you?" Amy asks, confused. "From what?"

"From these awful parties."

Amy starts giggling again but trails off when she realizes Quinn isn't laughing with her. Quinn reaches out, pushes some of the hair that's escaped Amy's headband away from her face. Amy stills.

"You're a beautiful girl, you know that?" Quinn says.

Amy is too stunned to speak. And she's afraid that if she does speak, Quinn might stop touching her.

"You're not a natural blonde, are you?" Quinn asks. "What's your real color?"

"Brown," Amy answers, barely managing to breathe. "Just... plain brown."

Quinn smiles — perfect, bright white against tawny skin. "There's nothing plain about you, Amy. I'd like to see your natural color one day."

She leans forward, and her lips brush Amy's tentatively. Amy remains statue-still, afraid that the slightest movement might break the spell, savoring the sensation of such soft lips against her own. No boy she's ever kissed has been as soft or smooth or gentle as this.

But Amy's stillness has the opposite effect from what she'd hoped for. Quinn pulls back a moment later, shakes her head like she's angry at herself.

"I'm sorry," she says to Amy. "I guess I've had more to drink than I thought."

Amy grabs her wrist before she can pull away completely. "Don't be sorry."

Their eyes meet; a moment pulled as taut as a thread on the verge of breaking passes between them. When Quinn leans in to kiss her a second time, Amy's ready. She grabs at the silver dress with both hands, bunches the sheer fabric in her fists. She pulls Quinn forward so hard that the soccer player loses her balance, snakes out a steadying hand to brace them both before they crash into the wall behind Amy. They kiss like it's the last kiss they'll ever have, they kiss like it's what they've been waiting for their entire lives.

When they break apart this time, they're both panting for breath.

"I've never kissed a girl before," Amy whispers.

"I have."

Quinn pushes Amy back, pinning her against the alcove's curved back wall. It occurs to Amy that something was meant to be in that alcove other than them — a potted plant, maybe, or a bust of a famous fraternity member on a pedestal. Even as Quinn kisses her again, reaching under the fringed hem of her skirt, Amy finds herself wondering where the bust or statue or plant is.

She thinks, *Frat guys. Somebody probably broke the statue during a kegger a long time ago.* And as if the thought is the conclusion of a long-standing inquiry, she realizes her time with men — dating them, kissing them, accepting their flowers and laughing at their jokes — is over.

Quinn's hand slides up the outside of Amy's bare thigh. "I want you," she breathes into Amy's ear.

Amy reaches down, moves Quinn's hand from the outside of her thigh to the inside. Quinn's fingers dance upward, push the crotch of Amy's underwear to the side. Amy lets out a soft moan when Quinn's fingers press against her. Amy's thoroughly wet. She's probably been wet since the dance floor.

"You can have me," Amy whispers, and pulls Quinn into another kiss.

#

Back to the present

"Long story short," Amy says, swallowing the last of her coffee, "one of my roommates caught us in bed about six months later, right at the beginning of my sophomore year. I didn't stay a Pi Phi for very long after that."

"The fuck. They didn't kick you out for sleeping with a girl, did they?" I ask. "I mean, you could sue them or something, right?"

Amy shrugs. "They didn't kick me out for being gay, no. Not directly, anyway. Officially, they kicked me out for telling my sisters a collection of mistruths and half-truths. They found out about my relationship with Quinn about the same time my dad showed up on the doorstep in full fatigues. I moved out of the sorority house a month or two later. It was fine, though. By then I was way over being a sorority girl."

I fiddle with the wooden coffee stirrer, dragging it through the pools of frothed milk at the bottom of my empty cup. "Whatever happened to Quinn?"

"She broke my heart," Amy says simply. "I should've known better. She stayed with her boyfriend even after we'd started sleeping together. Took her *months* to finally break up with him. But I was in love and insecure and twenty." She shrugs. "We're all stupid back then, right? Not long after we were finally an official couple, she cheated on me with a girl in the sorority house next door to Pi Phi." Amy smiles, but there's a sadness in her face when she looks down into her coffee. "But anyway. It's ancient history. First gay relationships pretty much always crash and burn in the most tragic and dramatic way imaginable, right?"

I roll my coffee stirrer between thumb and forefinger, thinking of Jenny. Thinking of the halfway decent conversation we managed to have over lentils and cornbread earlier this afternoon.

"More or less," I agree at last.

"What about you?" Amy asks. "Tragic first girlfriend story...?"

A couple seconds pass, and based on the way Amy's face changes, I guess my silence says a lot more than I wanted it to.

Before she can follow up with another question, I point with my chin towards the plate glass window at the front of the coffee shop and the falling sun beyond it.

"Do you want to take a walk before it gets too dark?" I say. "I could show you that General Custer statue."

She scoffs. "Dead mass murderer on a bronze horse. That's so romantic, Anika."

My cheeks get hot, but my skin's coffee with a good dose of cream, and it's stuffy in the crowded shop, so I doubt she notices my blush.

"I know. But the park's nice," I say lamely. "Especially at sunset."

She gestures towards the door. "Lead on."

Chapter 19: Of mice and women, rednecks and government conspiracy theories.

We make the short walk to the park, and as promised, I show her the statue of General Custer. It's like she said — not much to see, just an old dead white guy who killed a bunch of brown guys and got turned into a statue later. He's fucking cocky and full of himself even in bronze death: cowboy hat tilted to the side, chest forward. Sword out and at his side, holding it like he'll run an Injun through any second.

Amy gazes up at the statue, and the dying sun plays on her head, bringing out red-brown highlights I hadn't guessed were there before. I step forward until I'm standing right behind her, and the urge to pet her head like she's a fucking puppy and I'm that big, dumb oaf from *Of Mice and Men* is strong. But I keep my hands on my hips.

She turns around, squints up at me. The sun's directly behind her now, splicing through General Custer, giving Amy's head a halo of golden light.

"Explain to me again why we're looking at the statue of General Custer?"

"Because it's literally the only fucking thing to look at

in Marcine."

The wind picks up, blows at my back. I got my hair cut to just a little longer than chin-length before I flew to Ohio, thinking it would be easier to deal with, but now the breeze pushes it forward and into my face. Irritated, I try to blow it away with little puffs of breath, and when that doesn't work, I try to tame the mane by shaking my head.

Amy reaches up, smiling, uses her two Tinkerbell-sized hands to push the thick, wavy stuff off my cheeks. But instead of letting go, she holds it there, behind my ears, stopping the wind from blowing it into my face again.

"It's not the *only* thing to see in Marcine," she says.

I give her a lopsided grin. "No?"

"No. I've found something else I rather like looking at."

My hands come off my hips, find Amy's waist, gently tug her forward. She keeps her eyes locked on mine, hands on either side of my face, waiting.

I lean down into the kiss we both feel coming.

It's not awkward or sloppy, the way some first kisses are, with two people discovering each others' rhythm for the first time. Kissing Amy feels natural. Easy. Like it's something I don't have to try at but can just *do,* fall into like shooting a basketball or trimming carrots into decorative garnishes. Like something I've done a million times before.

Or might do a million times again.

Maybe she feels the same way?

I can't say for sure, but when she pulls away, it's with a contented sigh that ends with closing her eyes for a brief moment before opening them again and bringing her hands away from my face.

I lace my fingers together in the small of her back; she leans against my hands, squeezes my arms.

"There's got to be something besides General Custer you can show me," she says after a few moments of comfortable silence. "This park, for example." She lets go of one of my arms long enough to sweep a hand around the expanse of rolling grass, budding dogwoods, park benches, basketball courts, covered bandstand. "I bet this is the kind of place you used to come to with your family when you were a kid, right? July Fourth picnics? Outdoor concerts in the summer? Barbecues?"

She waits for me to nod. Which I do.

"Then show me around. Tell me another story — like the one you told me on the plane."

I glance around the park, looking for something to trigger a memory. Everything does, of course — park benches I'd made out with Jenny on. Basketball courts I played on in the evenings after work after I left the WNBA in Phoenix and moved back to Ohio with Jenny to "focus on our relationship."

The apartment just the other side of the courts, where I found the positive pregnancy test in the bathroom six months after we moved back home.

So much for focusing on our fucking relationship. I

look away from the courts and search for something else.

Marty McFly appears at my elbow. He tugs on my sleeve. "Hey," he says. "What about that?"

I follow his pointing index finger, and finally my eyes land on a memory that doesn't have Jenny in it, at least, not directly: the covered band stand.

I laugh out loud.

"What?" Amy asks. She follows my gaze to the bandstand.

"What've I told you about my brother Gerry?"

"He's the one who... owns the restaurants in Philadelphia?"

"No, no, that's PJ. The good brother. This is Gerry. The screw-up."

"The one who's going back to school?" Amy says, and I hear the reprimand in her voice.

"Okay," I concede with a roll of my eyes. "The one who *used* to be a screw-up. Maybe." I rotate her towards the bandstand, start walking. She takes my hand, laces her fingers with mine, and again it feels like the most natural thing in the world. I give her hand a little squeeze and start in on the story about Fourth of July, summer after my sophomore year in college. Gerry was fourteen at the time, and I caught him high as a fucking kite hiding behind the bandstand, ranting about a government conspiracy theory that involved rats equipped with sonar equipment.

"...So my friend and I — " (and I say friend because I'm skimming over Jenny's involvement in the whole thing) "— took him back to my house before my parents got home, sobered him up enough to get him quiet."

I chuckle, shaking my head at the memory.

"The things we do in our teens, right?" Amy says.

I nod. "Though in Gerry's case, it's 'the things we do in our teens, twenties, and thirties.' If I had it to do all over again, knowing how Gerry's life turned out, I wouldn't have covered for him that night."

I take Amy's hand again; we meander through the park.

"And how did it turn out?" she asks cautiously. "If it's okay to ask."

"It's okay," I say with a shrug. "Gerry's story isn't anything half of Marcine doesn't know anyway. Probably even your friend getting married knows if she's from here." I take a breath. "Gerry... Well, everyone in my family dealt with being exotic freaks in different ways."

"Exotic freaks?" Amy asks, nose crinkling in a way that I have to say I find kind of adorable.

I wave my arm around, trying to include in its sweep the whole of quaint-fucking downtown Marcine. "In case you haven't noticed, this is a white bred, redneck little town. There's maybe three other black families in the whole Marcine zip code. No Asians to this day. And then there's us. Definitely not white but never quite black enough for the, like, ten other black kids. My brothers and sister and I, we were fucking *zoo* animals growing up. Spectacles." I shrug. "Dutch bent the attention to her advantage, of course, because that's what she does — made herself Queen Bee. And since I was… well, *big,* I poured my energy into being an athlete. I figured no one would mess with me if everyone knew I could beat the shit out of them. PJ thought he could win people over if he was smart and charming and worked harder than everyone else. But Gerry? Gerry just rebelled."

I let out a bark of a laugh. "And in a twisted kind of way, I respected him for it. The rest of us were all searching for approval even if we said we weren't; Gerry had a sort of 'fuck you' attitude from the time he was eleven or twelve, but it turned into a drug problem by the time he was fourteen, fifteen. He went into rehab for the first time when he was seventeen; started using again as soon as he got out. Dropped out of high school. Fought constantly with my parents. They tried to fix him, but you can only be fixed if you wanna be, y'know? So he just got worse and worse and finally ended up running off with a bunch of friends when he was eighteen. We tracked him down to California, but he was full-on junkie by that point — a fucking walking, breathing public service announcement, living under bridges and eating out of dumpsters and shit. My parents brought him home, he stole from them, split again, they brought him back, he did it again. In and out of rehab. On and off the streets. Finally, a couple years back, he gave my mother a black eye and my father put his foot down. Told him he wasn't a part of the family anymore, wasn't welcome at home. And that was the last I'd heard about Ger. Until I came home a few days ago."

I look down at Amy, who has a pensive look on her face. Like she's taking it all in.

"Sorry," I mumble. "Maybe all that was TMI."

She shakes her head. "Not at all. Thank you for trusting me enough to tell me."

We arrive at the edge of the park, across the street from the coffee shop we started from. Without discussing it, we end up next to her parked rental car a moment later.

She leans against the car door, reaches up to brush hair out of my face again. Lets her fingers brush down my cheek and jaw.

"Thanks for coming out with me tonight," she says.

I take both her hands. "Thanks for asking me out. Although I am a little jealous you beat me to it."

She smiles; I lean in for a goodnight kiss, but am startled out of it when I hear a male voice boom out from across the street, "Get a room, fucking queers!"

I jerk my head in the direction of the voice, anger smoldering, and spot a twenty-ish, heavy-set kid with a beard and a baseball cap. He and a couple of his sniggering buddies are coming out of Dillan's Bar & Grill down the street, not far from Ben's record shop.

As if we'd discussed it ahead of time, Amy and I both give the boys the one-fingered salute in perfect fucking synchronized timing. They return the friendly gesture. I open my mouth to yell something, probably like *Fuck you!* or *Kiss my big black ass!*, but before I can get a word out,

Amy wraps both her hands around my shirt collar and yanks down hard, pulling me down into a ferocious kiss. She has to stand on her tiptoes to reach me, and even then I'm too far away for her taste. I get what she's up to, so I help her out, hoisting her up, hands under her thighs, pressing her back against the car.

Our PDA annoys the shit out of the rednecks down the street. They holler and cuss and I hear an empty aluminum can hit the asphalt in the middle of the road and slosh and roll pathetically in our direction. Amy grins against my lips and starts to giggle through the kiss, but still won't let go of my collar.

I wait until I hear the pick-up truck in front of Dillan's roar to life and peel out, honking at us, all three rednecks still yelling from the cab, before I break the kiss. I set Amy gently back down on the ground, and she wipes her mouth with the back of her hand.

"Now *that* was a fun good-night kiss," she says, still giggling.

I smooth dark hair away from her face, tuck it behind one ear. "No. That was your official 'Welcome to Marcine.'"

The answering smile she gives me has mischief and sympathy in it at the same time. They kind of cancel each other out, and the resulting crooked curl of her lips mainly make Amy look like she's got a secret she's not ready to share yet.

"Well," she says at last, pulling the rental car's key

from her pocket. "I should go. Are you going to be at your family's restaurant tomorrow?"

"How can I stay away? I'd miss all the fun."

"So then… Is it alright if I drop by for lunch?"

I nod. "That'd be nice. I'll introduce you to the fried chicken."

She puts a hand on her stomach. "In case you didn't notice, we've already met."

I put my hands on her sides, run them down her waist and around the curve of her hips. I know what she's implying, but Amy's not fat. Curvy, maybe. But curvy like an old European oil painting — elegant and voluptuous. My hands end their journey on her butt, and I start to squeeze, but she pushes my arms away.

"Nuh-uh. You already got the good-night kiss to end all good-night kisses. Don't push your luck."

I laugh. "You're spunky."

"You don't know the half of it." She puts her palm on my chest, pushes me gently back so she can open the door and get in. "See you tomorrow?"

"If you don't, I'm tracking you down at your hotel."

"You don't know where I'm staying."

"I grew up in this town. And there's only three hotels. If I want to find out, I will."

She rolls her eyes, but she's grinning when she closes the door and starts the car.

I stand there with my hands in my pockets, watching until she drives out of sight. When I walk back to Mom's car, I've got a big, dumbass smile on my face.

Chapter 20: Nicknames (Part 1).

Thursday

Jenny's back for an early lunch the next day, the baby girl only this time since Andrew is at school (he's *nine* already, I remind myself) and the bouncy boy from yesterday, Jake, is at pre-school. Since I've never officially met Andrew, Jenny shows me pictures on her phone, scrolling through with her thumb as she gives a running commentary, skipping over the pictures that also feature her husband, Mason.

She puts her phone away when I get up to help a customer, and when I come back and sit down again, she asks, "Why did you come back to Ohio, Anika? And be honest with me."

"I *was* honest. It's like I told you — I'm helping out with the restaurant for a little while."

"You hate the restaurant. And it's the middle of the basketball season in Europe. I looked it up."

I raise an eyebrow at that but decide not to comment on it. Instead, I sigh and admit, "Mom's got cancer. Osteosarcoma. She's having surgery on Monday to remove the tumor from her hip. And there's a good chance everything will work out fine, but... Dad's a total wreck —

you know how he is with her."

I look away as soon as I finish the sentence about my dad because I probably shouldn't have said it. My father is more in love with his wife than any man I've ever known, and I used to tell Jenny that I treated her the way that I did because I'd learned from the best.

Jenny seems to catch the look on my face when I mention my father, because she leans back, suddenly very interested in her infant daughter, who is sleeping peacefully inside her sling.

I clear my throat. "So I offered to come and help. Broke my contract to do it, but…" I shrug. "It's family. I owe them. And… It was probably going to be my last season anyway."

She glances up, brow furrowing. "Your last season?"

I nod.

"What are you going to do? You already have a plan?"

Of course she would ask me that. Because she always has a plan, and I never have a plan, and she knows it.

"I'm not sure yet," I answer.

She picks up the fork, pushes the collards around on her plate. "That's… that's really big news. No more basketball. How are you feeling about that?"

Totally fucking lost, is what I want to say. But I don't. "All good things come to an end," is what I say instead, which is *another* fucking stupid thing to say to Jenny, of all people. I scramble for something else to say that will take the conversation in a different direction, hoping she doesn't hear the same double-meaning in my words that I do. "What about you? Last time we talked, you were still doing the stay-at-home-mom thing. Is it... how's that working out?"

"I really miss teaching," she admits with a sigh, then points at the baby fast asleep on her chest. "I'm hoping I can go back to work again, at least part-time, once this one gets old enough for pre-school."

"What's her name?" I ask.

She blinks in surprise. "I didn't tell you yesterday?"

"You probably did and I just don't remember."

"No. You would remember." She gazes up at the ceiling, takes a deep breath, and her eyes are watering all of the sudden.

Geez. All I'd asked was the kid's name.

"Her name is Annie." Jenny meets my eyes again, staring me down like she's waiting for a challenge.

"Okaaayyy," I say, not really getting why she's descended into weirdness. Since I remember how much she liked the musical, I say, "Like, uh, Little Orphan Annie, right?"

She's still staring hard at me. "No. Not like Little Orphan Annie. More like... Ani."

My eyes narrow. "Ani? Wait. Ani as in... are you saying...?"

"Yes. *Ani.* I named her for you."

"That's... that's... pretty fucked up, Jen."

She laughs, and the sound crackles in her throat like

splintering glass. "I know." She sniffs hard, wipes both eyes. "I always thought you and I would start a family one day. Annie's the closest I'll ever be able to come."

There's a long, breath-holding silence between us, broken only when the baby girl stirs and whimpers like she knows she's being talked about.

"Jesus, Jenny. Does Mason know? That you named your daughter — *his* daughter — after your ex-wife?"

She rocks the daughter who will grow up to look like her father but who has my name. "No. No one knows except for me. And now you."

Shit. I wipe a hand down my face. "Jen..."

"I'm sorry," she says hastily. "You're right, it's crazy. And I shouldn't have told you. Plus we agreed not to talk about the past. So let's get back to talking about the present. Like figuring out what you're going to when you stop playing basketball. Have you thought about coaching?"

My head's still spinning over her revelation, because for someone who's supposedly straight now, she just pulled some really classic fucking lesbian drama. But I grab onto Jenny's change of subject like I've fallen overboard and her question is a rope.

"Yes. I've thought about it. But... I don't know. Coaching is Alex's thing. Ophelia's. I'm not really sure that it's mine. If I had to coach players as obnoxious as I was in high school and college, I'd probably — "

"Turn into Bobby Knight and get yourself fired," she

says, smirking.

"Yeah," I agree, and I return her smirk, pleased that she remembers who Bobby Knight is. And there it is again — the simple ease of talking to someone who knows you better than anyone else. Maybe someone who knows you better than you even know yourself. "So I don't know. I..."

But instead of finishing the statement, I turn my palms face-up on the table, indicating in a single gesture how utterly lost I've become. I know it's a gesture Jenny will understand, because of the aforementioned fact that she still knows me better than anyone, even after nine years apart and five of those years not speaking.

She nods, and just like she understands my gesture, I recognize the change in her expression: Jenny's put on her serious let's-fix-it face.

"Well," she starts, "how do you feel about Switzerland? Would you want to stay there? Is there anything holding you there? Or..." Her eyes flick down to her plate, then back up. "Is there any*one* holding you there?"

My thoughts flash briefly to Amy, who will be headed back to Basel in a few more weeks, but a single date and two kisses hardly count as someone "holding" me in a foreign country.

"No," I say. "There's nothing holding me to Europe. No one, I mean."

"Oh." She seems relieved by the admission, and it makes me want to defend myself, to tell her I *have* dated in the nine years since our breakup, including a nearly two-year relationship with one of my teammates that only ended because she got a better offer to play ball in Australia.

But then I remember I don't need to defend myself to Jenny. I haven't needed to in a long time.

"Okay," Jenny says, getting herself back on track with fresh determination ringing in her voice. "So you don't need to stay in Europe. And you don't want to coach..." She thinks for a moment, taps her chin pensively, which is part of the let's-fix-it routine. "What about here? What about coming back to Ohio? Especially since your family's here. And with your Mom sick — "

I cut her off with a groan. "I'd rather be almost *anywhere* besides Ohio. You, of all people, know that. Fucking Antartica comes to mind."

She covers her daughter's tiny ears. "Try to control your mouth for at least a single lunch," she says. "Or at least in front of Ani."

I'm just about to make two pointed comments — one, that the words Ohio, fucking, and Antartica are all the same to an infant, and two, that I *really* don't think she should be calling Annie "Ani," but the door jingles behind me and I turn to greet the customer who just walked in.

And see that it's Amy.

She glances over at me from the podium, smiles, lifts her hand in an easy wave. I smile back, grinning like big, doofus, puppy-petting George from *Of Mice and Men* again, and glance at my watch. Twelve-thirty already.

Which means I've been chatting with Jenny for over an hour, and totally forgot that Amy said she'd be dropping by for lunch.

She walks in our direction as I rise from the table, stopping a few feet away from us. Looks from me to Jenny.

"Hey," I say, and after one plane ride, one car ride, and a coffee date, we're definitely not at a point of a hello kiss, but I reach for her automatically anyway, my hand landing on her forearm and giving it a squeeze before I think to second-guess myself.

"Hi," she returns, but it's a little cool. She glances at Jenny again. "Are you busy? I can come back later if you need me to."

I follow Amy's gaze and look over my shoulder. For a brief second, Jenny's eyes meet mine, and there's another one of those Jenny-looks that would slip by other people but which is obvious to me — it's a silent and slightly territorial, *Who's this chick?*

Don't need to defend myself to Jenny.

"No, no, I'm not busy," I tell Amy. "We were just... catching up. This is Jenny, by the way. Jenny, this is Amy."

I take a half step back so that I'm not blocking Amy's line of sight and watch as the two women size each other up. For a moment, something tense buzzes in the air between them, and I'm reminded of Amy's story from last night about her first meeting with Quinn in the bathroom of the frat party. But the tension only lasts a second before Amy leans forward and extends her hand across the table with a practiced, professional politeness.

Jenny meets her halfway, and they shake.

"Nice to meet you, Amy," Jenny says.

"And you." Amy straightens, looks up at me. "So how do you two know each other?"

Jenny looks like she's about to answer, and I know exactly what she'll say, so the words rush out of me quickly, beating my ex-wife to the punch. "We went to high school together."

I can tell Jenny's going to elaborate, even though I'm trying to tell her with my eyes and my psychic powers not to, but it's little Annie who saves the day by waking up from her long nap and starting to fuss.

Amy watches Jenny soothe the infant, I watch Amy watching her, and *holy shit,* I realize all at once that the women are photo negatives of each other. They look like they're exactly the same height, with exactly the same small frame, the same Tinkerbell-sized delicate hands. But whereas Jenny is blonde and rosy, long hair flowing down her back in a loose braid, Amy's skin is paler, creamy instead of pink, and her shorter hair is a dark, rich brunette.

Despite the differences between them, there's something about Amy and Jenny that *echo* each other, and it instantly makes me uncomfortable, like I've done something wrong and I'm gonna get caught any second.

I suspect Jenny feels it, too, because she looks up at me

and says, "I think Annie's hungry. And I'd probably better get going, anyway."

Annie. Ani.

I nod and start helping Jenny gather her things, while Amy settles into the same sun-bleached table near the window that she sat in the day before. A few minutes later, after I've cleared Jenny's table, I set a glass of water down in front of Amy.

"Have you already eaten?" she asks.

I look past her for a moment, through the plate glass window and into the parking lot, watching Jenny load the baby into the car seat in the back of her car.

I shrug, and instead of admitting that I kind of forgot she was coming and ate with Jenny, I say, "When you work at a restaurant, you end up eating on and off all day."

If she picks up on the fact that I dodged the question, she doesn't show any sign of it, because she just smiles and says, "I remember those days. I told you I waited tables all the way through college, right?"

Chapter 21: Nicknames (Part 2).

Amy eats, and we slip into easy conversation, talking about waitressing and college and how hard it is to resist the urge to tip while in Europe, and how Swiss cuisine doesn't have anything on my dad's chicken masu or my mom's cornbread.

And again it's a photo negative of my time with Jenny — all the same ease for none of the same reasons. Unlike with Jenny, Amy and I share no history. We don't know each other inside and out. But that also means there are no topics from a shared past that we cautiously inch around, no words that are better left unsaid, no double-meanings hidden like I.E.D.s inside volatile phrases or baby names. On the other hand, of course, I have to spend extra time explaining everything to Amy — when I tell her about what a wreck my father's been, it's not like she automatically understands that he's more in love with his wife than any man I've ever met, and when we get to talking about what I'm going to do after basketball, I have to actually *explain* why I'd prefer Antartica to Ohio.

"They both have harsh winters," I say, "but Ohio's got a lot more fucking racists in it."

When she finishes laughing, she says, "Maybe you're giving the penguins more credit than they deserve. They're pretty homogeneous, you know."

I grin. "They're pretty homo? Sounds okay."

"No. Homo*geneous.*"

"I don't even know what that means."

"I doubt that." She pats her mouth with the napkin. "But... you're not the only one who's thinking about leaving Switzerland."

"No?"

She shakes her head. "It's not just the wedding that brought me back to the States; part of the reason for my long vacation is that I'm trying to figure out what I want to do next. Where I want to *be* next, since I'm sick of traveling all over Europe for work. I got my fill of travel growing up. Some people fantasize about traveling; I've always fantasized about staying in one place for longer than a few years."

"So what are your options?" I ask.

"Well, that's what I'm trying to figure out. Which — I meant to tell you last night — it looks like I'm going to be staying in Marcine for a few more days after the wedding."

I smile. "That's something I won't argue with. What's keeping you here? Is it my charming wit or my dashing good looks? I know it's hard to choose between the two."

She rolls her eyes, bats at my hand playfully. "Sorry to burst your bubble, hot stuff, but neither one. A friend of mine from business school got a job teaching recently. She knows how burnt out I am with the corporate world, so she keeps trying to get me to interview for a position. Which she swears I'd be perfect for. So... I thought that as long as I'm town, I should take her up on it. The interview's scheduled for Tuesday."

I cock my head to the side, because the thought that Amy might actually stay in the United States begins opening a few quiet doors inside my head. The janitor who lives inside my brain had previously attached a big red fucking STOP sign on one of the doors, with a caption underneath that read: *Don't bother looking for anything more than a quick fling with Amy; she's going back to Switzerland in a few weeks and you aren't.*

Now the janitor walks by, whistling a pop song and casually pushing a wheeled yellow mop bucket in front of her, and when she gets to the door, she pauses long enough to take down the stop sign and its caption.

"Teaching what?" I ask Amy, careful to keep the question on the I'm-only-asking-to-make-conversation side. "And where would it be?"

"International business," she says. "And as for where, it would be here — well, not 'Marcine' here, but 'Ohio' here. In Columbus. At the Fisher College of Business at Ohio State."

The janitor in my brain pulls a well-isn't-that-interesting face. She unclips this enormous carabiner ring from her belt loop, and it jangles with dozens of keys. She flips past a key labeled *Shitty racist experiences from childhood,* then another one that says *Two years of utter emotional fucking bankruptcy after things with Jenny ended,* fiddles around some more until she finally arrives at one that says *Willingness to reconsider living in Ohio again.* The janitor walks down a corridor, still humming her pop song, comes to this thick metal door that looks like it belongs to a bank vault, twists the key into place. A rusty lock mechanism grinds inside the door, and the door groans mournfully, opening two or three inches.

Amy's brow furrows. "What?" she asks.

"What, what?"

"What is that look on your face?"

"Nothing. Hey — are you done with that?" I ask, pointing at her mostly empty plate. When she nods, I pick it up and rise from the table. "I'd better go see what my brother's up to. He's trying to get payroll done while it's still quiet."

"Okay," she says, but I detect some disappointment in her voice. She looks at her watch and stands up. "I should probably go — told my friend I'd meet her at the church. But... would you be up for doing something later? If you're not too busy here?"

My head bobs up and down with a nod that I realize too late is very dumb-oaf-ish. I make my head stop moving and try to look more like the intelligent, sophisticated adult that I am.

"Sure. I don't have any more statues to show you, though."

Amy's answering smirk is the kind that sets my stomach to knotting in on itself and my heart rate to galloping. "I'm sure we can think of something else to do."

I glance around the dining area to make sure we're still alone (we are) and step into her personal space, my hands finding their way to Amy's. I bend down, and my mouth fits perfectly against hers. It's not a long kiss, but it has *way* more heat in it than the two from last night, even more than the exaggerated one we performed for the benefit of the rednecks coming out Dillan's Bar & Grill. When I pull back, I must have a dumb-oaf look on my face again because Amy giggles and touches the tip of her index finger to the tip of my nose.

"See you tonight, Ani," she says, stepping around me into the aisle.

A piercing alarm blares inside my brain at the sound of my nickname, red and white lights strobe brightly enough to give me a fucking seizure, and somewhere, a door swings shut, closing with a loud BANG.

Fuck. Why'd she have to call me that? Nobody but my family and...

Annie. Ani.

...Jenny calls me that.

#

By four o'clock, no one's in the dining room, no one's calling in a late lunch order, and all of us — me, Gerry, Becker, and Emir — are prepping for dinner. Gerry emerges from the back with a stack of white envelopes in his hand. He sets them down and sits heavily in the chair across from me.

"I finished payroll," he announces.

"Okay," I say, waiting for what's coming next.

"It's worse than we thought."

I set down the rag and spray bottle on the table next to me. "How much worse?"

"Twenty-three dollars and fifty-seven fucking cents. That's how much is still in the account, once everyone's paychecks are cashed."

I frown. "How can that even be? We've been busy every night since I've been home."

He nods. "We've been busy every night since before you've been home. We've been busy every night since *I've* been home, and that's been more than seven months now."

"Then how can we…?"

"Dad's making an enormous payment every month that's only labeled 'loan' in his accounting software. Even though Soul Mountain's making money hand-over-fist, whatever this loan payment is, it's draining out the account as fast as it fills. Which means we're barely scraping by. He's charging all the groceries — I checked. All it's going to take is — "

"A couple bad weeks. A slow week when school lets out and everybody goes on fucking vacation — "

"Or a bad weekend or two, and we won't be able to make the loan payment."

I sit down, lean back in the chair. "Why do they even

have a loan out? A loan for *what?*"

"I don't know," Gerry answers, shaking his head. He takes off the Buckeyes baseball hat he's wearing, runs his hand through his curls. "We should talk to Mom and Dad."

"It's not our business."

"It *is* our business," he insists.

"It's not."

"It will be if the fucking restaurant closes, and Mom's getting fucking chemo, and they can't pay her fucking medical bills or afford their insurance, and then they lose the fucking house. Are *you* going to be the one who takes them in?"

"You're overreacting, Geronimo."

"Don't call me that."

"Then don't be an over-reactive pussy. They aren't going to lose the restaurant. Soul Mountain's an institution in this town. It's been around for twenty-five — "

"Twenty-three dollars and fifty-seven *fucking* cents!" he shouts, slamming his fist on the table.

I cross my arms against my chest. The dining room is silent except for the faint sound of the muzak playing in the background. Gerry scratches absentmindedly at the crook of his arm. I watch him do it, stomach curdling. It's a gesture I've seen plenty of times before, an ill omen that comes right before tales of needles and purple track marks and opiates.

"Gimme your arm," I say, holding out my hand.

He looks up, startled. His eyes dart from his arm back

to me. "What? No, that's not, I'm not — "

"Give me your fucking arm, Gerry!"

"Anika, I'm not — "

I don't wait for him to finish. I shoot up from my chair, lean across the table, pin his wrist with one hand while I use my other hand to push up the sleeve. He's protesting and yelling and his words don't even register. I'm faster than him, I'm bigger than him, I'm stronger than him, and goddammit, he's still my baby brother and I'm still his big sister and he shouldn't try to fight me.

I pull the sleeve up over his forearm, over his elbow, halfway up his bicep.

And the copper-brown skin below is smooth. Unmarred but for a couple small white scars from his using days.

"Everything alright out here?" comes a deep voice from the direction of the kitchen.

I turn to see Becker staring at us, concerned expression on his face.

"Yeah," I say. I steady the chair teetering behind me, lower myself back down. "Sorry. Just sibling squabbling. It's nothing."

Becker gives a crooked smile and disappears back into the kitchen.

My eyes find Gerry's. His chest is heaving up and down, and he's rubbing his arm like I hurt him.

"Sorry," I repeat. "I saw you scratching, and I…"

"I told you. I'm *not* using. I'm done for good."

"I've heard that before."

"I mean it this time, Ani." His eyes start to glisten. "I'm turning my life around."

"I know. It's just..." I trail off again, shrug. My palms turn face-up, my classic I-don't-know-what-to-say-here gesture.

"You don't know what it's like to be back here," he says. He looks up at the ceiling, seems to struggle with himself for a second, clears his throat. "Everyone's looking at me like you just did. All the time. *Waiting* for me to fuck up again. Waiting for me to prove them right, to prove that I'm the asshole loser they always thought I was. Even Mom and Dad. Well, you know what? *Screw them.* I'm not who they think I am and I never fucking have been."

A lump forms in my throat, and I'm twenty years old again, chasing my baby brother through the park so I can take him home, sober him up before our parents find out. I reach out to him, put my hand on top of his.

"You're really done for good?" I ask.

"Yes. I swear it."

And there's a little bit of the old Gerry hardening his voice when he says it, the rebel who gave the middle finger to the rest of Marcine before too many drugs dulled the rebellion out of his eyes, the kid I admired for not even trying to fit in while the rest of us fought so desperately for some tiny crumb of acknowledgment and acceptance.

"Then I believe you, Ger." I pick up the stack of envelopes, finger through them one by one. "But... we need to talk to Mom and Dad about this."

He adjusts his baseball cap. Nods.

"And then," I sigh, "we're figuring out how to save this fucking restaurant."

Our gazes connect, and it's almost like looking in the mirror. We share the same dark eyes with the same subtle folds around them, the same high Nepalese cheekbones, the same long, flat nose, the same tawny skin. And when his face breaks into his best cat-who-swallowed-the-canary bad boy grin, I match it with a grin of my own.

"Damn straight we will, sister," he says.

He holds out a fist. I bump it.

An hour later, just as the first few trickles of the dinner crowd starts coming in, Kiersten — the snooty young waitress I met my first night home — calls in sick. She doesn't sound sick, though. She sounds like she's got Thursday night plans she doesn't want to break. I tell her sarcastically *Thanks for the advanced notice,* and slam the phone down so hard against the receiver that for a second I'm sure I cracked the plastic casing.

I have a feeling it's going to be a long night.

Chapter 22: *That's* a fucking romantic second date.

Thursday night

This is what being deep in the weeds feels like:

You scoop ice into a plastic pitcher, stick it under the sink to fill, and while you wait, you search for a clean fork because the kid at table nine dropped his, but you realize there are no clean forks, and the teenager with the backwards baseball cap standing in front of the dishwasher is full-on sweating, and his hands are chapped to a bright red and he has a sink full of dishes, so you grab a fork and wash it by hand, dry it on your apron, turn the sink off because the pitcher's overflowing at this point, and you snatch the pitcher on your way back to the dining room, only to hear "Order up!" just as you shoulder the door open to exit the kitchen.

And in the comparatively cool dining area, there's muzak playing, quiet laughter coming from the young couple in the corner, louder laughter coming from table nine, where the mom and dad have had one too many beers and the kid's still waiting for his fork. And the hostess glances over at you; her eyes are wide and rolling like a

ANDREWS / ANIKA TAKES THE LONG WAY

panicked horse, chewing on her bottom lip as she looks between you and the lobby full of patrons waiting for a table, and as if you're playing a game of connect-the-human-dots, your eyes bounce from the hostess, to the knot of waiting patrons, to the bus boy hustling to clear the table by the window, to the young couple, back to table nine again. The kid at table nine's looking your way expectantly, trying to catch your eye, and you know he's waiting on the goddamned fork, so you plaster on a smile, carry the fork and the water pitcher their way, gaze darting from the wife to the husband to the kid with no fork to the screaming baby sister in the high chair while you refill their waters and apologize when, in your haste, a bit of ice water splashes out onto the table.

"I think we're going to order dessert," is what the wife says, and you're looking at the fat rolls that hide her elbows thinking, *Lady, the last fucking thing you need is dessert,* but you just smile even bigger and say,

"Sure, what do you want?"

and you listen and mentally count up how many more clean forks you're going to need to bring them, and then head back for the "Order up!" that's still waiting in the kitchen for the young couple in the corner.

It's this wolves' den of pure chaos, with me and Gerry trying desperately to turn tables, the hostess doubling as an extra bus boy, and even the unflappable Becker utterly silent as he tries to keep up on the hot side of the line, that Amy walks into about seven-thirty.

From the corner of my eye, I see her *excuse me, pardon me,* scoot around the families waiting in front of the podium, and weave her way over to my station in the corridor, where I'm swiping a credit card.

"Hey," she says.

"Hey, Amy. Listen, I know you were hoping to do something tonight, but I — "

"But you're deep in the weeds and there's no way you can get away."

"Yeah," I say, and I try to convey my disappointment with my voice and eyes as I look down at her.

"You guys have a clean apron back there?" she asks, nodding at the kitchen.

"A clean apron?"

"Yeah. I told you I've been a server before. I can help."

"Amy, you don't have to — "

"No, I don't have to. But…" She lifts her shoulders. "It's still better than sitting in the hotel by myself."

"You don't know the menu."

"So? I don't need to take orders. I'll just help out. Run food, fill drinks, bus tables."

"You're serious?"

She nods. "If this is the only way I can spend time with you tonight, I'll take it."

My face splits into a grin, and I'm wondering to myself how she always manages to elicit these dumb fucking smiles from me. "Okay. Clean aprons are hanging from the shelf in the office."

She nods once, struts into the kitchen like she owns the place.

#

It's two more hours of straight-up hustle before things slow down again and we all have a chance to catch our breath. By the time it's over, Katie, our high school hostess, looks totally fucking traumatized, like we told her that her puppy got hit by a car. But Gerry looks like he's having a blast; Becker's smiling; Emir and the dishwashing kid are joking around in Spanish.

And Amy...

She pops up on her toes and gives me a quick peck on the cheek in the shadows of the corridor next to the wait station.

...Amy's fucking amazing.

"Thanks for letting me stay," she says. "I haven't had this much fun in a long time."

I'm about to thank her for the fourteen millionth time and inform her that she has a pretty fucked-up idea of fun, but she spots an empty glass and darts off with a pitcher of ice water in one hand and a carafe of fresh coffee in the other. She walks with purpose towards the table, like refilling an empty glass is serious goddamn business. As if she's a career waitress and not a globe-trotting software executive.

As if she's serious about how much fun it all is, and she actually truly *enjoys* running around Soul Mountain and smelling of curry and cumin and collards and cornbread.

I chuckle and shake my head and turn back to the credit card machine.

#

It's just after ten when Katie finally turns on the overhead fluorescents, the universal restauranteur's signal to customers that *Okay, we're really happy you came and ate with us and all, but now get the hell out, alright?* and the last table of patrons looks up in surprise, blinks a few times, and then they're shuffling into jackets and grabbing purses and making their way to the exit.

I slump into an empty chair as Gerry finishes wiping the table down with a greying rag.

I feel a cool hand on my neck and I tilt my head up, not surprised to see Amy standing next to me.

"So I guess we got to do something tonight after all," I say. "Though this wasn't exactly what I'd had in mind for our second official date."

She lets go of my neck, glances at her watch before shrugging. "It's only ten," she says. "Night's still young."

I start to say something else, but Gerry strides back over, sticks out his hand to Amy. He claps her on the back as he shakes her hand.

"You're a fucking lifesaver," he says, sitting down

across from me. "I can't believe you jumped in like that."

Amy smiles, looking pleased with herself, which makes me smile, too.

"It was no big deal. I think I'm getting too old to do it every night, but it was kind of fun." She glances between Gerry and me. "So — you're Anika's brother, right? We didn't really get an official introduction."

"Yeah, I'm Gerry. Around here they call me the 'bad brother.' And you said your name's... Amy?"

She nods. "Amy Ellis. Guilty as charged."

He laughs, points from me to her. "So... you guys know each other from high school or something?"

I shake my head. "No. We, uh, we met on the plane from Toronto to Cleveland a few days ago, actually."

"Oh," Gerry says, and his eyebrows travel up his forehead a little as he studies Amy more closely.

I can tell he's putting two-and-two together and arriving at four, and normally I'd feel a little embarrassed, because it sort of makes it seem like I came all the way back to Ohio just to hook up with some chick I met on the plane three days earlier, but for whatever reason, I don't feel embarrassed about Amy. If anything, I've got to say I'm feeling kind of proud. Like *Hey, lookit me, I've got good goddamned taste, and I can still turn a few heads.*

Amy's face brightens with a new idea. "Do you guys want to grab a drink or something? Once we close up?"

Gerry shakes his head. "I don't really drink anymore." He adds quickly, "But you two should totally go. In fact —

ANDREWS / ANIKA TAKES THE LONG WAY

just go ahead and get out of here. We can handle closing without you."

"No, no. Closing can be a bitch," Amy says, shaking her head. "I didn't work all night just to skip out on you guys at the end."

Gerry looks at me. "Seriously, sis. Get out of here. I've got this."

"You're sure?" I say, but I'm caving already.

He nods reassuringly, punches my arm lightly. "Go."

I push up from the table, tug at the string of Amy's black apron. She pulls it off, hands it to me.

"Your jacket's in the office?" I ask.

"And my purse."

"I'll be right back."

Chapter 23: And now we're back to tragic first girlfriend stories.

We post up at a small table in the corner of Dillan's Bar & Grill a few minutes later, order drinks for each of us, plus a plate of nachos to share.

While we wait for the girl to come back with the drinks, I pluck up the corner of my shirt and sniff it. "Gah. I smell like a fucking restaurant."

"It could be worse. When I was an undergrad, I worked at a place that was maybe half a step above a burger joint. Always came home smelling like a deep frier. It's where I met my friend, Grace — the one who's getting married this weekend."

My brow dips as the name flashes me back to a green-eyed redhead, tossing her hair and swinging her hips as she sashayed down the halls of our high school, arm looped through Jenny's. "Grace... She's not from Marcine, is she?"

The waitress sets our drinks down in front of us, promises to be back with the nachos momentarily. I pull the maraschino cherry from the glass, pop it into my mouth.

"Yeah, she is," Amy says. "Why — do you think you might know her?"

"Her last name isn't 'Adler' by any chance, is it?"

Amy grins broadly. "You do know her! That's so funny. Small world, right?" She takes a sip of her drink, sputters, nearly chokes it out back into the glass.

I reach over, slap her on the back. "You alright?"

"I'm fine, that's just… stiffer than I expected it to be."

"Dillan's doesn't skimp." I chuckle. "You saying you can't handle it?"

She meets my eyes, lifts her glass up before taking a long few swallows, runs her tongue over her lips when she finishes.

I raise an eyebrow. "I guess that's a no."

"So how do you know Grace?"

I think back to a New Year's party twenty-one years ago, to a drunken Jenny and her even drunker red-headed friend.

"Like you said. She's from Marcine. And she's our age. Which means I've known her since more-or-less kindergarten." I fiddle with the cherry stem, rolling it between thumb and forefinger, and decide to be honest. "Actually, you know my friend Jenny? The one you met briefly at lunch?"

Something changes in Amy's face, and she nods.

"Well, Grace and Jenny were best friends in high school. They had a falling out the summer after we graduated, and they kind of fell out of touch for a while, but…"

\#

Back to the future: Marcine, Ohio. Nine years ago.

It's a sunny early evening, and I'm just arriving home from work, tossing my jacket on the back of the recliner with one hand as I swing the flimsy apartment door closed with the other. My gaze travels out the window, lands longingly on the basketball court in the park below. Both palms practically itch with the anticipation of holding a ball again, and I start unbuttoning my fancy blue work shirt, one of a half-dozen Jenny bought for me when we moved back to Ohio and her friend Mason helped me get my crappy job working for the crappy staffing company in crappy fucking Marcine.

"Jen?" I call as I work on the buttons. I suspect she's in the bedroom, papers spread around her on the bed as she works on progress reports for fifteen kindergarteners. I turn towards our room. "Are you back — "

But I stop because she's sitting right there, on the couch, next to Grace Adler. Jenny's eyes are puffy, her nose is red, and she's clutching a Kleenex.

"Um, sorry, I didn't realize you were…" I say.

One of Grace's arms is slung around Jenny's narrow shoulders, and she's looking at me like I've done something wrong.

I've never particularly liked Grace Adler. She's a catty gossip who I thought was out of Jenny's life for good after high school ended, but over the years, she's wiggled her way back into Jenny's life, and now Grace is here, sitting on *my* couch in *my* apartment comforting *my* wife, but still has the gall to look at me as if *I'm* the intruder.

"Am I interrupting something?" I ask, looking from Grace to Jenny.

"No, not at all," Jenny says hastily. She stands from the couch and crosses the room, greeting me with a light kiss and an embrace, both of which feel forced. "Grace and I just got to talking about the old days, and I started feeling... nostalgic, and we shared a few tears."

"Oh. Okay." I kiss the top of her head automatically, but I'm looking from Jenny to Grace, Grace to Jenny. Jenny's prone to nostalgia and she's prone to crying — so darn sensitive she even cries during television commercials she finds touching, so her explanation isn't entirely suspect. But... they *shared* a few tears? Then why are Grace's eyes completely dry?

Maybe I'll ask about it later. After Grace is gone.

After I've had a chance to shoot a few hoops.

Except we don't end up "talking" much that night. We scream and we cry instead. Because when I get back from the park, I head into the bathroom to take a shower.

And I find the pregnancy test in the trash can.

#

Back in the present

I drop the cherry stem, turn my palms face-up on the sticky table, and conclude lamely, "So, yeah. I've known Grace for a really long time."

Amy cocks her head to the side. "Jenny's best friend, huh?"

I nod.

"And I guess you were close to Jenny, so…"

It's a leading question. And I can tell by Amy's expression that she already suspects.

I sigh. "Jenny's my ex," I blurt. At this point, I feel like if I don't just fucking say it, then I'm being dishonest. And I like Amy too much to be dishonest with her.

She nods slowly. "That's kind of what I thought."

"Why? You meet a cute straight girl with a baby asleep on her chest for all of two minutes and you're just like, 'Oh yeah, clearly that's Anika's ex'?"

She chuckles, shrugs. "I could just tell. Something about the way you guys move around each other. It was… like two people who know each other really, really well. So I knew you were either very good friends, or you had been… more than friends."

I raise my glass. "I toast to your excellent powers of observation, Doctor Watson."

She clinks her glass against mine, and we both take a drink. Fortunately, the nachos choose that moment to arise, giving us something else to focus on for a minute. After a bit of flirting that includes me wiping guacamole from

ANDREWS / ANIKA TAKES THE LONG WAY

Amy's chin and Amy trying to toss black olive slices into my mouth, she asks the inevitable question.

"So when were you and Jenny together?"

I lick some sour cream from my index finger, buying time while I contemplate my answer. "Remember how you asked about my tragic first girlfriend story?"

Amy's eyebrows raise as she nods. "So she was your first girlfriend? High school sweetheart?"

"Something like that." I stick a tortilla chip in my mouth.

Amy waves the waitress over, orders us a second round of drinks. After the girl heads back, Amy turns to me belatedly and asks, "You're okay with another round, right?"

I nod. "Only so long as you stick to your promise of letting me treat tonight." I gesture at the plate of nachos we're sharing. "So far, though, you're a cheap date."

"Maybe I should've asked for the top shelf stuff," she says, bouncing her eyebrows up and down suggestively.

"I don't know," I tease. "Judging by how the first sip affected you…"

She pokes my arm. "You stop it. I can hold my liquor. What else do you think I do at all those schmoozing parties except drink?"

"Good question. What else *do* you do at those parties?"

This leads to some more poking, some more flirting, until finally our fresh drinks arrive and I eat my second maraschino cherry of the night.

But you-know-what is still bothering me, so I put on my big girl pants and say:

"Listen, Amy. Just to be honest about Jenny... She was a lot more than my high school sweetheart."

The mirth fades from Amy's face, and she leans back, twirling the ice in her drink with the little plastic toothpick impaling her cherry. "Okay. And what does that mean, exactly?"

"She was... we were married for a while."

"Married. How long's 'a while'?"

"Well... we got married right after we graduated college. So if you count the year and a half we were together in high school, plus college, and then after... We were together for a total of thirteen years. And married for about seven of those years."

Amy's silent for a long moment. "Wow. I guess your 'tragic first girlfriend story' beats mine, huh?"

"Sorry, I didn't plan on bringing it up. But I figured — well, I figured if you're hanging out with Grace Adler, and just knowing the way Marcine is, you might've found out anyway. And I'd just rather you hear it from me than someone else... I didn't want you to think I was hiding anything from you."

She nods, a thoughtful look on her face. "Thank you. I appreciate your honesty." She sips her drink. "Thirteen years, starting at the end of high school... and you're thirty-eight... so that means you broke up when you were thirty? Thirty-one? It's been over for seven or eight years?"

"Eight years. Almost nine, really. We'd just turned thirty when we split." And because I think I know what she's asking without directly asking it, I add, "Jenny's been in the rearview mirror for a long fucking time, Amy. In fact, we hadn't even talked in five years. Not until she showed up at the restaurant yesterday with her kids."

Annie. Ani. I decide to leave that part out.

"I hope you don't mind me saying that I'm glad to hear it," Amy says. "Because I've enjoyed hanging out with you these last couple of days, getting to know you. I like you. I like you a lot, actually. And it's been a long time since I met a girl I really liked."

I drop my hand to Amy's knee, give it a squeeze. "Same here."

She smiles, puts her hand over mine. "I like you enough that I'm kind of hoping we might be able to keep in touch after I leave Marcine."

I move the hand that's on her knee slowly up her thigh, tracing the inner seam of her jeans as I lean in a little closer. "You'd better keep in touch. I wouldn't want to have to track you down."

Amy's eyes flutter closed for a moment, and when she opens them again, there's something smoky in the look she's giving me. "You need to take your hand off my leg. Before I do something I regret."

My mouth is almost on her ear when I reply softly, "What would you regret?"

"I'd regret inviting you to follow me back to my B&B tonight."

"I don't think — "

But the waitress picks that moment to come over to check on us.

I straighten up, take my hand off Amy and scoot a few inches away, like a little kid caught goofing off by a teacher.

"You ladies okay?" she asks. "Need any refills?"

Amy glances at her watch, shakes her head. "No. If I had a third, I wouldn't trust myself to drive home."

"You can bring me the check when you get a second," I tell the waitress, who nods and scurries away.

Amy reaches over, takes the hand that had been traveling up her thigh a moment earlier, squeezes it once before letting go again.

"Sex on the second date is something I reserve for the girls I *don't* like that much," she says. "I hope you understand. It's a compliment that I'm not taking you home."

"I'll try to feel honored," I tease.

"But hey," Amy says, eyes lighting up. "Why don't you come with me to the bachelorette party tomorrow night? You could be my date."

"Are you supposed to bring a date to a bachelorette party?"

She shrugs. "Probably not. But a full night of straight girls shoving dollar bills into a stripper's thong? I'm probably going to need a distraction at some point."

"That's all I'm good for? A distraction?"

"Oh, I'm definitely hoping you're good for more than that," she shoots back, and the smoky look is back in her eyes.

It's enough to convince me that the only place I need to be tomorrow night is Grace Adler's bachelorette party, which is a surprising fucking revelation, trust me. "Then I guess I'll be there."

"Bring an overnight bag."

"An overnight bag?" I echo. "So sex on the second date isn't okay, but on the third date, surrounded by straight girls and male strippers, *that's* okay?"

She rolls her eyes. "Don't you wish. The party's out of town, at somebody's lake house cabin. I think everyone's going to make it into something of a slumber party."

"You are *such* a sorority girl."

"You can't tell me you didn't spend the night at a few sorority houses when you were in college."

I raise both palms in defense of my innocence. "You're forgetting — I just explained that I was with Jenny all the way through college. I was already spoken for. I had a very tame four years at Rosemont. Your hero Alex Woods is the one who used to wake up in sorority houses. Amongst other places."

"So you say."

"So I do say. I'm an extremely loyal fucking girlfriend."

Something passes across Amy's eyes, a look that's hard to interpret but that definitely signals an end to the flirty banter. Instead of answering, she just nods. I pay our tab a couple minutes later.

"Walk me to my car," Amy says.

And because I can feel an urge to obey whatever commands this brunette Tinkerbell gives me growing inside my chest, I follow her out of Dillan's and back to the parking lot of Soul Mountain. Her car and my Mom's, the one I've been driving since I've been back, are the only two vehicles left in the dark parking lot.

It takes nearly fifteen minutes and a whole series of increasingly sophisticated good-night kisses before we finally part for the night. My legs are actually trembling when I start the car, and I can't manage to wipe the grin off my face.

Why do I feel like I'm in high school again, like an idiotic fucking teenager falling in love for the first time?

But I shouldn't be thinking like that. I've known Amy since Monday, today's only Thursday, and she'll be leaving Marcine by next Tuesday.

Possibly permanently.

Chapter 24: Families. Jesus.

Friday morning

I sleep in the next morning, and in my sunless basement room, I would've been quite content to *keep* sleeping in, but voices drifting down from the kitchen above wake me around nine. At first, I just lie in bed, listening to the cadence of my mother's voice, noting how the softer rumble of my father interrupts it at predictable intervals, and the melody of their mixing voices forces my eyes closed again, not because they're lullabying me back to sleep, but because there's something painful about it. Something about their voices that makes me think of Jenny, and the daughter who isn't ours, the children who aren't ours, the whole fucking family we'll never have, and how we could've had kids who grew up listening to the intermingling sounds of our voices lullabying them back to sleep on lazy spring mornings.

I'd managed to stop thinking about Jenny, for the most part, over the last five years. That was why I'd stopped talking to her — not talking to her had made it easier not to think about her, and not thinking about her had made it easier not to miss her so fucking much, and not missing her was supposedly helping me to "move on."

Whatever the fuck *that* means.

And then I come back to Ohio, and Jenny waltzes into Soul Mountain with her adorable little kids, including a daughter she'd named for me, and five years of "moving on" evaporated in an instant and I was back to where I'd started.

She's like a fucking ghost limb, still hurting despite being amputated years ago. I press the heels of my hands into my eyes, push the thoughts away.

"Nine years," I mutter out loud. "It's been nine fucking years, Anika, so fucking stop it with your fucked-up lesbian drama shit."

There's another voice vibrating its way through the floorboards above, and I know it's not goddamned Marty McFly, so I'm guessing it must be Gerry.

An upset Gerry. The voice gets louder, higher. My mother breaks in, then my father.

I throw the covers back, pull a hoodie on over my sleep t-shirt, and climb the stairs.

I open the door to the kitchen to find Gerry angry and red-faced, my mother matching his temper inch for inch, my father looking hesitantly between them.

Whatever's happening stops the instant I walk into the kitchen, everyone falling into tense silence in the way people do when they've been arguing and someone not involved interrupts. Mom looks down, picking at the corner of the *Marcine Observer* laid out in front of her. Dad stands, walks over to the industrial-sized rice cooker that's lived on the corner of the kitchen counter for as long as I can remember. Gerry adjusts the Buckeyes cap on his head and folds his mouth down into an unhappy grimace.

I decide not to comment on the toxic atmosphere, make my way to the cold remnants of scrambled eggs still sitting on the stove.

"Is there any bacon left?" I ask, voice froggy with sleep.

"I ate the rest of it," Gerry confesses. "Sorry."

"There's more in the freezer if you want to cook it," my Dad says from his spot next to the rice cooker.

I sit down at the table next to Gerry, stealing a glance at Mom. At least her eyes aren't red-rimmed from crying this morning, so that's good. I'll take an angry Momma over depressed Momma any day of the week.

"So. Today's the big day, right?" I say, referring to the surgery.

Dad walks over behind my mother, places his dal on the table and his hands on her shoulders. She reaches up automatically, squeezes his fingers. It's a gesture I've seen repeated countless times over the decades, and it brings out another painful whisper of *Jenny* from somewhere deep within the recesses of my mind.

I look down, focus on my eggs.

Dad shakes his head as he massages Mom's shoulders. "The surgeon called yesterday. We've been rescheduled for Monday afternoon."

I glance around the table, taking in the faces. Gerry's

gazing off into the distance, still stewing on something. Likewise, Mom's also distracted, and Dad, as always, is distracted by Mom.

I decide to confront whatever's happening head-on. "Is that what you guys were fighting about? The surgery?"

Gerry brings his attention back to the table, looking at me, then our parents. "No. I brought up the payroll situation."

Oh, Jesus. I might actually need coffee for this.

"And we told your brother it's none of his business," Mom says, biting off each word.

"We *made* payroll," Dad says, and by the way he says it, I get the feeling it's not the first time he's said it this morning.

"We *made* payroll, yeah, but not with enough money left over to buy groceries next week," Gerry retorts.

"We're managing just fine!" Momma yells, one of her hands curling into a fist on top of the *Observer*. "We've managed Soul Mountain for twenty-five years, and we've out-lasted almost every other business in downtown Marcine. We don't need *you* telling us how to run it."

"Buying groceries on a credit card every week isn't sustainable," Gerry says. "And from the looks of your credit card bill, you've been doing it for a while."

My mother tilts her head back, looking up at my father's face above her. "Why does he have access to your accounts, Pathik?"

He ignores her question, addresses Gerry instead. "The

restaurant goes up and down. You know that. We won't always be in trouble the way we are now."

Gerry wipes a hand down his face, trying to contain his temper. (Dutch, Gerry, and I all take after my mother in the temper department. PJ is as mellow as his namesake.)

"How can you not be concerned about this?" Gerry presses. "Dinner's been busier than I've ever seen it, we're getting more customers than ever before — "

"Which is why we aren't concerned, babu," Dad says.

"Don't call me that, I'm not anybody's little boy anymore," Gerry snaps, rejecting the Nepalese term of endearment. "We're barely scraping by. We're one disaster away from shutting our doors."

Everyone reverts to tense silence.

"It will work out," Dad says after a few seconds. He sits down to eat his dal.

I argue with myself for a moment, oscillating back and forth between wanting to weigh in and wanting to stay out of it. But frankly, I've never been fucking capable of keeping my fucking mouth shut, so the internal argument doesn't last long.

"What's with the loan?" I ask my parents. "Gerry showed me the books. Seems like all the profit's being eaten up with loan payments."

Momma purses her lips, and the look on her face says I'm about to get a sharp verbal slap that begins with a drawled-out, *"Giiirlll..."*

But before she can speak, my father surprises me by

being the one to answer. "As we told your brother. It's not your concern."

Gerry draws in a breath to start a fresh tirade, but I reach my hand under the table, put my hand on his leg. He deflates, the air rushing out from between clenched teeth. It's rare that I'm the one advocating for calm and diplomacy, but if my father's the one putting his foot down, then the conversation definitely isn't going to go anywhere. Mom's normally the stubborn one. Dad stepping in indicates something major, something absolutely out-of-bounds. At least for now.

I decide to change the subject. "So, uh, if the surgery isn't happening tonight, do you guys think I could get the evening off? I kind of made plans."

This seems to surprise Gerry. "Plans?"

"Yeah," I say. "That's this word that means you have an intention to do something other than hanging out at your parents' restaurant for fifteen hours straight."

"It's fine," Dad says. "And thank you for taking on so much for us the last few days."

I shrug. "It's what I'm here for, right?"

Mom's lips purse again and she raises an eyebrow like she questions my motives. Which isn't very fucking cool, if you ask me, given that I broke my basketball contract and dropped my whole fucking life to come back and help. Not that I had much of a life to drop.

But before I can give her a defensive *What?,* my dad runs with the topic change like the diplomat he is.

"What have you got planned, Ani?" he asks conversationally. "Seeing old friends?"

"Something like that. It's Grace Adler's bachelorette party tonight. Turns out she's getting married this weekend."

My brother's face clouds and he squints at me skeptically. "You *hate* Grace Adler."

"Hate's a strong word, babu," I say.

"Don't fucking call me — "

"Language!" my mother snaps.

"Oh, come on. We're not teenagers anymore, Mom," Gerry says.

She points at the ceiling. "Whose roof is that, Geronimo? Mine or yours?"

He groans. "Yours. But — "

"'But' nothing," Mama says, warming up to a lecture. "My roof, my rules. I'm tired of hearing my children use foul language at my kitchen table. You'd think we never taught you any better."

It's a surrogate argument, of course. They're power-struggling over language because my parents already shut Gerry down on the topic of the restaurant.

And once again, it's my father who intervenes. Always the peacemaker.

"It's nice that you're supporting Grace," he says, as if my mother and brother aren't steaming at each other on either side of him. "And I'm sure you'll run into lots of other people you grew up with at the party. It must be a very long time since you've seen them." He smiles around a spoonful of dal. "It will be a nice reunion for you, bahini."

Gerry's still skeptical. "You'd never go to a bachelorette party voluntarily, let alone Grace Adler's. Is this about that girl? Amy?"

I give Gerry the kind of death stare older sisters reserve specifically for their younger brothers.

"Who's Amy?" asks Mom.

"Just someone I met on the plane. She's in town for Grace's wedding. Turns out they went to college together."

My mom raises her eyebrows, doesn't say anything. My dad gets interested in his breakfast. As much as they didn't like the idea of me being with Jenny, they've liked even less the parade of short-term relationships and one-night stands that have characterized my love life over the last decade. I don't blame them for thinking a girl I met on the plane and who will only be in town for a little more than a week is yet one more example of my inability to settle down with someone.

I think about defending myself, telling them whatever they're thinking is wrong and that there's something different about what's growing between Amy and me, but the truth is they're probably *not* wrong.

What I say instead is, "So you don't care if I take the night off, right?"

My father nods and smiles. "Of course. I was planning to cover the dinner shift tonight anyway. Enjoy the party."

#

After I finish breakfast and shower, I send a group text to my brothers and sister.

Sibling meeting,
my text announces.

2pm CST. Skype. It's important.

What's it about?
Dutch asks.

I'm busy at 2pm
PJ replies.

You'll find out what it's about.

PJ, clear your schedule.

This is really short notice
he answers.

Sorry. I wouldn't ask if it wasn't important.

Is this about Mom?

writes Dutch.

Goddammit you two.

**I'm not explaining over
text. That's why we're
meeting. Just show up.**

I'll see what I can do.
PJ says.

Fine
Dutch says, then inquires:
Gerry??

My phone dings immediately with Gerry's reply.

**I'll be there. And Anika's right, this
is important**
he says.
See u 2 online.

Chapter 25: Siblings. Jesus.

Back to the future: Five and a half years ago. Marcine, Ohio, at Dutch's wedding.

I've got the blonde pinned against one of the bandstand pillars, one of my hands halfway up her shirt, the other holding myself steady, braced against the railing. I've definitely met better kissers in the three years since Jenny and I broke up — this girl alternates between a full-mouthed, moaning sloppiness and this weird sort of pecking thing that I can't really say turns me on, but I'm drunk and she's drunk and her hair's almost the same color as Jenny's, and so I don't mind the fact that —

A hand grabs my elbow, yanks me away from the bandstand pillar. I spin unsteadily in the direction of the hand and am confronted with a wavering rendition of my three siblings. In my drunken haze, they look like a superhero movie poster, the three of them spread out and serious, staring at me with solemn eyes. The only thing they're missing is fucking capes.

Dutch stands point, one hip popped to the side, hands on the hips of her strapless white wedding gown. PJ is behind and to her right, looking profoundly uncomfortable; Gerry is behind and to her left. From the way he sways, from the slackened face and drooping eyelids, it's clear he's either very high or very trashed.

"Anika?" the blonde says behind me. And then she must see my siblings, because I hear an, "Oh!," and out of my peripheral vision, I see her slip away. I turn, open my mouth to call her name, but realize I can't remember it.

I spin towards my sister, almost losing my balance in the process. "What the *fuck*, Dutch?"

"Don't you 'what the fuck' me, Anika," my sister says. "This is *my* wedding."

"No, it's not. Your wedding was hours ago. This is the fucking recep..." I lose the word for a moment before I find it again. "The reception," I finish with a slur.

Arms still tight against her chest, she lifts a single finger and points at me. "We're having a family intervention," she declares.

"A family..." My face twists into an ugly sneer, and I point at Gerry. "If you want to have a family intervention, have it for the fucking junkie."

Gerry points unsteadily at himself. "Hey, not cool. This isn't junk. I've been clean for months. This is just... wedding punch and *way* too many champagne toasts."

"This isn't an intervention about drinking, anyway," PJ says. "Although you've been doing it a lot since you've been home."

I lean against the pillar the blonde girl (damned if I can remember her name) was occupying a moment earlier, mainly because Gerry's swaying is making me feel seasick and I need something that will anchor me.

"This is about you and that *girl*," Dutch says, practically spitting the word "girl."

I point in the direction of the missing blonde. "Who? Her? What's wrong with — "

"Not *her*," PJ interrupts. He's using his stop-playing-around-this-is-serious-business big man voice. "Jenny."

The name strikes like a poison dart in my chest. And as if he really did impale me in the heart, I stand there practically fucking bleeding, mouth gaping, not able to say shit.

Gerry chuckles, because apparently the way my siblings have just blindsided me amuses him.

"Jenny's married now," Dutch informs me.

"I know that," I say. "You think I don't know that?"

"And she has a son," PJ adds.

"I *know* that."

"It's been over between you two for three years, Anika, almost four," Dutch continues. Her face softens, and if I didn't know my big sister inside and out, I would almost say her tone has become sympathetic. "You have to stop acting like this is just a temporary break."

"I *know* it's over. And I'm not acting like it's a temporary break. Hell, I was fucking *acting* like it was over five minutes ago, in case you didn't notice, until you three musketeers came over here and so rudely interrupted."

Gerry laughs again. "And everyone says *I'm* the one

living in denial."

"I saw you with her, earlier today," PJ says, taking a step forward. "You had lunch together. And left the restaurant together."

"So what? You've got a problem with people who are friends with their exes? You'd better not be implying what I think you're implying," I say. "Jenny's been my best friend since high school. And we're still friends. We can still hang out."

"For her, maybe you're just friends," Dutch says. "For you, *no*. You *cannot* hang out with her anymore, because for you, it's *not* about being 'friends.'"

"The fuck? So you're *Mom* now? Telling me who I can and can't hang out with? Telling me I can't — "

Dutch cuts me off. *"She's* moved on. *You* haven't. That's the difference. And we're sick of watching you torture yourself over her."

PJ coughs gently against a closed fist, a sign he's about to say something that might actually be — God fucking forbid — confrontational. "You forget I'm staying at Mom and Dad's, too. I heard you last night after you got home from hanging out with her."

I feel a little faint, and it's not just the wedding punch. "What do you mean, you heard me?"

"I heard you crying, sis."

"The fuck you did."

Dutch squints at me. "Did you sleep with her? Since you've been back in Ohio — did you two...?"

"That's none of your fucking business."

"Oh my God. You did. Didn't you?"

I look away.

"She's married!" Dutch cries.

"You said that already," I mumble.

PJ sighs, looks down at the ground. "I could hear you crying all the way from the kitchen when you got home last night."

I grip the bandstand railing. "So I was emotional. I'd had too much to drink…"

Gerry lifts a finger, tries to shake it at me as he smirks. "Didn't anyone ever tell you? That's not an excuse."

"Shut up, Gerry," Dutch snaps. Turning back to me, she says, "How many dates have you gone on in the last three years?"

"I'm not doing this right now, assholes." I turn to walk away, but my sister grabs my arm.

"How many, Anika?" she demands.

"I *date!* I fucking… I was just… There was a girl…" I wave hopelessly towards the place in the crowd where the nameless blonde disappeared to.

"I'm not asking how many women you've *screwed* in the last three years," Dutch says with a mighty eye roll. "I'm asking how many you've *dated.* How many people you've had a relationship with that lasted longer than a couple of nights."

"Okay, so I haven't — "

"I know how many," she says.

"Oh, because you *always* know the fucking answer, right? So why d'you even ask?"

"Zero," she says, ignoring me. "And yet how often do you talk with that *girl?*"

Dutch is starting to really piss me off.

"You *never* liked Jenny," I say, my voice turning cold. "You've always treated her like she's — "

"How often do you talk with her?" Dutch repeats, so fucking shrill I have the urge to cover my ears with my hands.

"We Skype sometimes."

"And what does 'sometimes' mean?" PJ asks.

I shrug and shake my head, looking past them in the direction of the basketball courts, the ones at the far end of the park. The ones I shot hoops in not long after I found Jenny crying, sitting with Grace Adler in my apartment.

"Once or twice a week," I mumble.

"Dammit, Anika." Dutch lets out a huff, pinches the bridge of her nose. "You're right. I've *never* liked Jenny. Want to know why? Because she's always used you and manipulated you and treated you like the consolation prize she could always come back to if nothing better came along. And she's *still* doing it. And now we're finding out you're talking with her every week, and you slept with her after being home for less than a week, even though she's married? This has *got* to stop."

PJ nods in agreement, takes another step towards me, but cautiously, like I'm an unstable animal who might charge him at any moment.

"We think it's time for you to cut Jenny loose, sis," he says. "It's killing us to see you like this. We thought you'd start to move on after you left and went to Europe, but it's clear that hasn't been happening."

"How do *you* know?" I ask bitterly. "When's the last time *you* bothered to call me?"

Gerry lifts a wobbly index finger again. "But I know. 'Cause you and me, we've been talking some. Right?"

I turn my head towards my wasted baby brother. Aha. So here's the real Judas. He'd called me out of the blue after his latest stint in rehab, telling me he'd always felt closer to me than to PJ and Dutch, and that he wanted to start repairing our relationship, making amends. And I, wanting to be a supportive older sibling, had fallen for it. We'd been talking every week for almost two months. And I'd cried on his virtual fucking video chat shoulder over the unhealing wound that was Jenny more than once.

Now I was kicking myself. Never trust a fucking junkie.

"You need to stop talking to her," Dutch says.

I feel the heat of tears rising in my eyes.

"Stop calling her, stop texting her, stop *liking* her baby photos on Facebook," my sister continues. "And you *definitely* have to stop fucking her."

"It was only once," I say in my defense. "And I know it shouldn't have happened — we both know that."

"'It was only once' is an addict's line," Gerry says.

"Takes one to know one. You need Jenny rehab."

I look skyward. "It's been three years," I tell my brothers and sister with a shaky voice. I sniffle. "Three years. It's not supposed to still hurt this bad after three years, is it?"

"You're such a soft-hearted idiot," Dutch says, and this time there's no mistaking it; her voice is just as shaky as mine. Her arms finally unfold from her chest, opening wide as she steps forward. "C'mere, brat."

And because my back is pinned against the pillar of the bandstand, and because I'm drunk, and because I'm tired of hurting, and because, fuck it, I need my big sister, I let her wrap her arms around me and I drop my face into her wedding-day hairdo. Gerry crashes into us from the side, knocking us sideways as he throws his arms around Dutch and me. After a second of hesitation, PJ comes up from the other side, crushes his butterball body into our awkward group hug.

We stand there for at least a minute or two, with me sobbing into Dutch's perfect hair, and Dutch crying against my shoulder, Gerry babbling drunkenly, and PJ squeezing like he's never going to let go.

Finally, I push away from them, wipe my eyes and nose on the sleeve of the white bridesmaid suit Dutch made me wear.

"Okay," I say. I take a long, shuddering breath. "You're right. I'll stop talking to her."

"Thank *God,*" Dutch says, dabbing at her running

mascara with the tip of one well-manicured finger. "I thought I was going to have to force Gerry to steal your laptop."

PJ looks relieved but says nothing.

"That was fun," Gerry says. "We should do this shit more often."

Chapter 26: Did I already say, "Siblings. Jesus."? Once more. With feeling.

Friday, 2pm CST, Soul Mountain

"Are you guys there?" I say, leaning closer to the laptop screen.

PJ's video comes online a moment later, blurry and choppy while he adjusts the position of his phone.

"I'm here," he answers.

"I'm here, too," Dutch says, and there she is, headphones on, Sherry just visible in the background inside a playpen. "So what's this all about? The last time we had a sibling meeting, it was about — "

"I don't need the reminder," I say, flashing back to Dutch's wedding five years earlier. "This isn't about me. It's about Mom and Dad."

Gerry leans closer to me so that he can be seen in the video frame. "And it's about the restaurant."

"What about the restaurant?" Dutch asks, frowning.

"Gerry did payroll this week when Dad took a few days off to be with Mom," I say. "He found something… not good. After he did payroll, there was only, like, twenty bucks left in the checking account."

"That can't be right," Dutch says immediately. "The restaurant's been really crowded every time I've been by recently."

"It *is* right," Gerry says, leaning close again. "I checked it and double-checked it and triple-fucking-checked it. After everyone got their checks, there was twenty-three dollars and fifty-seven cents left in the bank account."

"And they've been charging groceries," I add. "At least for weeks, maybe for months. Gerry would know better than me."

"Actually... I have a copy of the credit card statement," Gerry says.

Which is news to me. I'm just hoping he didn't break the lock on Dad's filing cabinet to get to it.

He pulls out a folded-up piece of paper from his back pocket, unfolds it, and holds it in front of the laptop screen. "The card's almost maxed the fuck out."

"Gerry, will you stop dropping f-bombs? Sherry's in the room," Dutch says irritably.

"You've got headphones on, Dutch," PJ says.

"So? I still don't think it's a good habit to — "

"Can you shut up and listen, Dutch?" I say. "There are more important things right now than Ger's use of the word 'fuck.'"

"Anyway," Gerry continues. "It looks like they've only been making the minimum payment on the card for the past six months. And almost every single charge is for

groceries. There's a few other things on here, too — looks like they paid the laundry service from this card a few times recently, and there's an exterminator charge a few months ago."

"That's not like Dad," PJ says, almost like he's talking to himself, musing over this new information out-loud. "He almost always pays for everything in cash. He hates credit cards. And he's never trusted banks."

"I know," I say. "Which is why I called this meeting. You guys... I don't know exactly what's going on, but Soul Mountain's in trouble. They can't keep going like this for much longer."

"What did Mom and Dad say when you asked them about it?" asks Dutch.

"They won't talk about it," says Gerry, and from his tone, it's obvious he's still raw and irritated from his earlier fight with our parents.

"But we know that at least part of the problem is a huge loan payment they're making every month," I say. "It looks like they're having trouble staying ahead of it, and it's draining whatever profit they're bringing in. Do you guys know what the loan could be for?"

PJ and Dutch both shake their heads.

"Dad hates loans about as much as he hates credit cards," PJ says. "Remember what he used to tell us when we were growing up?"

All of us nod, remembering.

Before he and my mother married and moved to Ohio

in search of better work, Dad worked incessantly for his brother-in-law's restaurant. He bused tables, he waited tables, he went for days practically without sleeping. But lacking citizenship, and, despite his visa, constantly fearing that he would for some reason or another be deported, he never opened a bank account. Instead, living as frugally as possible, he saved almost fifteen grand in cash in a shoebox he hid behind his brother-in-law's couch. That was the money he used to move to Ohio, to marry my mother, to pay the deposit and a month's rent on their first apartment in Marcine.

Dad didn't borrow money. He didn't spend it, either. He saved it.

After a moment of silence, PJ says, "It doesn't matter what the loan's for. What matters is that we pay it off. See if you can find out how much it's for."

"I don't know how open they're going to be about that, given the reaction Gerry and I got this morning," I say.

"I'll handle it. I'm sure I can find out," Dutch states.

I snort. "And how do you propose to do that? Breaking and entering?"

"No. I'll just ask them," she says.

"They're not going to tell you," Gerry says.

"I can be very convincing. And they trust me."

I shake my head. "I don't think this is a matter of them trusting you more than they trust us, Dutch." She hadn't said that, not directly, but I know that was what she'd meant. "Gerry's right. Whatever it is, they're not going to tell you."

She quirks an eyebrow, and I realize she's interpreting my words as a challenge. "We'll see about that. Is this all you guys wanted? Because I have to go get ready to pick Nathan up from school."

I glance at the time on the clock and see that it's not quite two-fifteen. The elementary school doesn't let out for another hour and a quarter. But *of course* Dutch would need to primp for something as important as driving through the elementary school carpool line. I suppress an eye roll.

"Yeah," I say. "That's all we got. Tell Nate I say hi."

"Tell him yourself. We eat dinner at Soul Mountain every Friday night."

I shift in my seat uncomfortably. "Uh... I guess I'll have to see him some other time. I've got plans for tonight."

Dutch cocks her head to the side. "Plans?"

"She's screwing around with some chick she met on the plane on the way over here," Gerry supplies helpfully.

I punch him hard in the arm. "I am *not* 'screwing around' with Amy, you asshole."

Gerry only laughs.

"Guys, I have to go. I'm already late for a meeting," PJ says. "But I'll be home by Sunday night. Dutch, text me if you learn anything."

"Text *all* of us," Gerry says.

"I will," she says lightly, and her screen goes dark. PJ's

screen goes dark a moment later.

Gerry turns to me. "Those pricks. They're not taking this seriously."

I shrug. "You expected something different?"

"I guess I thought 'the restaurant is on the brink of fucking bankruptcy' would have had more of an effect."

"Then you have a higher opinion of them than I do. But don't worry. They'll get their shit together. And then we'll figure this out."

Chapter 27: Should auld acquaintance be forgot, / And days of auld lang syne?

Friday night

Lisa Vanderwerf's lake house is one of several dozen small cottages lining a gravel loop around a man-made lake most of the way to Youngstown. It's dark when I arrive, so I drive past Lisa's place at least twice before I finally realize that there's only one house on the road whose lawn is packed with a dozen cars. I park Mom's SUV behind Amy's blue rental car, step out into the lawn, picking up the faint sound of '80s music emanating from the little cabin.

I'm here

I text Amy.

And as if I'm a nervous kid at a high school kegger instead of a grown-ass woman showing up to a bachelorette party for other middle-aged women, I have to take a long, deep breath to steady my nerves before I weave through the cars towards the house.

A few girls sit on the cabin's front porch, their feet up on the railing in front of them, drinks in their laps. I recognize one of them vaguely as someone I think I went to high school with; the other two aren't familiar at all. They track me with their eyes as I approach, and momentarily I feel ten feet tall instead of six-three, exposed and alien and utterly out of place.

But the feeling doesn't last, because the front door opens, spilling out more '80s music and a triangle of soft light onto the porch. Amy steps out, and that beautiful smile is on her face again, and she's not looking at the girls with the tracker eyes, she's looking at only one person, and that person is me.

She's got two drinks in her hands, pushes one of them at me after I walk up the short flight of porch stairs and greet her with a peck on the cheek.

"You made it," she states. "You brought your overnight bag?"

I nod. "Even some extra nail polish and a brush so we can do each others' nails and hair later."

Amy laughs; the three girls sitting with their feet against the railing all just keep giving me a *look*.

"Do you know these lovely ladies?" Amy asks, sweeping a hand towards the girls.

I meet eyes with the one I recognize. "We went to high school together, right?"

She nods. "You're Anika Singh. You got a basketball scholarship to Rosemont."

"Yeah, that's me," I say, embarrassed that I can't come up with her name or how I know her.

But she doesn't seem bothered by it. She stands up, reaches across her friends to shake my hand. "Callie," she says. "I was in band with Grace and Jenny."

"Right, of course," I say, even though I still don't really have any fucking clue who Callie is or if we ever actually hung out in high school. There was only one band nerd I paid attention to in high school. "Nice to see you again, Callie."

After Callie, there are other, equally awkward introductions and small talk with the other girls.

When I feel like I'm small-talked out, I turn back to Amy. "Should we go in? Meet the rest of your friends? And I should say hey to Grace."

#

Inside the stuffy cabin are about a dozen more women, some of whom I recognize, some of whom I don't. Three or four play a board game at the kitchen table; Lisa Vanderwerf sits on the couch, where she and a couple others are sipping glasses of wine and exchanging tips about potty training over the high synths of what I'm pretty sure is Hall & Oates.

I let Amy take me from group to group, introducing me to everyone, including the ones I should really remember but don't. When I spot Grace Adler herself mixing a drink in the kitchen, I excuse myself from Amy to do the polite thing — go say hello and congratulate her on the upcoming marriage. Second marriage, that is.

Grace turns away from the counter just as I cross the threshold into the kitchen, and when she spots me, there's this double-take of pure shock that crosses her face that she doesn't even try to hide.

"Hey, Grace," I say. "Congrats on the — "

"Anika?" she says, not even let me get my well-mannered congratulations out. "What are *you* doing here?"

Grace closes the distance between us in two long steps, goes up on her tiptoes to give me a hug, which I am a little slow in returning. After a quick, tight squeeze from Grace, with me awkwardly kinda patting her back, she releases me and looks me up and down.

"God, you look exactly the same as the last time I saw you. Except your hair is shorter."

"Thanks... I think."

She gives a rapid shake of her head. *"Definitely* thanks. You don't look like you've aged a single day."

"I have." I think of Jenny. Of her children. Of finding Grace and Jenny in my apartment the day I found out she was pregnant. "Believe me."

"So what are you doing here? — sorry, I didn't mean like what are you doing at my bachelorette party, because, of course, I'm glad you're here, I meant more like — "

As usual, Grace Adler makes me feel as if I need to justify my presence.

"I'm here as Amy Ellis's date," I say.

Her mouth drops open — further shock — and she

closes it again quickly as her eyes dart past me to I guess wherever Amy's standing. "Amy Ellis? *My* Amy Ellis?"

You know how your stomach lurches right before you're about to throw up, and a bunch of hot fucking stomach acid starts burning your throat? When Grace says *"my* Amy Ellis," putting her stamp of ownership on the Tinkerbell Jane Lane I found in a British airport, I get that feeling for a quick second. I can't say why exactly. Maybe because I've already started thinking of Amy as *my* Amy, not Grace's Amy, not anybody else's Amy.

Maybe it's because this is the second time the catty redhead has ended up as one of the nearest-and-dearest of a girl I like.

"Yeah. *That* Amy Ellis." I hope my distaste for Grace — and the fact that I almost just threw up on her — isn't too noticeable. After all, *Amy* likes Grace, and *Jenny* likes Grace; maybe I should be trying to give her a second chance (third, fourth, fifth chance), too.

"How in the world do you know Amy?" she asks, and the way she says it offends me a little further because the implication underneath the question is something like, *What would Amy be doing with a person like* you, *Singh?*

"We met on the plane to Cleveland," I say, and briefly explain about Amy recognizing me as a basketball player, about *Snakes on a Plane,* about me distracting Amy with the story about my parents.

"Huh. Small world, I guess," is all Grace says when I finish. Then she adds, "She always was into athletes," which feels slightly demeaning again even though I'm sure she didn't intend it that way.

I'm just about to say something like, *"Well, congratulations on the wedding this weekend,"* and then excuse myself so I can get back to Amy when Grace grabs my elbow.

"Anika," she says seriously, lowering her voice, "you know Jenny's going to be here tonight, right?"

("Don't even fucking think about throwing up! I just washed these floors!" shouts the janitor who lives in my brain.)

I gently shift my arm out of Grace's grip without being rude about it. "That's fine. I've talked with Jenny a few times this week. We're cool."

And like she's a fucking shark who can smell blood at a ratio of one part-per-billion, she cocks her eyebrow in a way that's skeptical and curious at the same time.

"Honestly, Grace. Jenny and I are okay. It's not a big deal."

Annie. Ani. Yes, Jenny and I are completely cool. No drama whatso-fucking-ever.

"But you cut Jenny off," Grace says, cocking her head like a curious cat. "You two haven't spoken in five years. Now you're hanging out with her again?"

I grind my teeth. Nosy as ever. Making it her business to know everyone else's. I bet she has a fucking *logbook* she records shit like this, some leather-bound, dog-eared journal locked in a drawer somewhere. And right past the five-year-old entries about spying on her neighbors, there's probably one that reads, *Summer, wedding of Dechen ("Dutch") Singh and Matthew Raeburn: Last time Anika Singh speaks to Jennifer Pearson.* Tonight she'll add a new entry about how she found out we've been talking again.

Fucking Grace Adler.

"Well, 'hanging out' might be overstating it," I say after a moment. "I've been working at my parents' restaurant this week. Jenny stopped by a couple times; we had lunch."

There's this long pause, like she's waiting for me to elaborate, and then she says, "That's good. Because she's supposed to be here in ten or fifteen minutes. She just texted to say she'd stopped for gas on the edge of town."

"Cool." I point at the counter behind her. "Mind if I make a couple more drinks for Amy and me?"

She grins broadly. "It's a bachelorette party, silly. Drink as much as you can!"

#

I find Amy sitting on the couch with the wine sipping, potty training tips moms a minute later. She gives me a grateful smile when I settle onto the arm of the couch and hand her the martini I made in a red plastic cup, then returns her attention to the woman who's speaking.

"Left him naked," the woman says. And the statement is apparently some kind of conclusion.

"Naked?" echoes a second woman.

"As a jaybird," the first woman says. She's heavy and pink, with carefully styled shoulder-length, red-brown hair and so much makeup piled onto her face that she almost resembles a drag queen. "Something about being naked stops them from just *going* — or at least makes them slow down and think about it for a second. It worked like a charm for my daughter. My son's had a few more accidents than she has, but it's working for him, too."

Lisa Vanderwerf nods knowingly, but the second woman — a slight, pretty blonde who's younger than the rest of them and still in possession of a slim figure — looks between the other two skeptically.

"But don't you worry about... you know, number *two* getting all over the house?"

Heavy-and-Pink shakes her head. "Didn't happen even once."

Amy stands suddenly, drains the rest of the martini in three mighty swallows. Her cheeks are flushed an apple-red when she finds my eye.

"Did you see the dock behind the house?" she asks me.

"No. There's a dock?"

Lisa looks over, nods in my direction. "There is. But be careful — I don't think it's supposed to get down to freezing tonight, but it's still pretty cold out there, and the dock could be slick."

Amy gives a business-like nod. "I'm going to show Anika the dock. We'll be back in a few."

Heavy-and-Pink glances from me to Amy. Her eyes land back on me again. After talking with such gusto a moment earlier about letting her toddler run around "naked as a jaybird," she's now tight-lipped and oddly silent.

I smile at her; she looks away.

Okaaay. What was *that* look for?

Amy tugs on my hand and I stand up, drawing myself up to my full height and squaring my shoulders towards Heavy-and-Pink almost reflexively.

"Go get our jackets from the other room," Amy directs. "I put them on the green easy chair."

I do as I'm told, and the moment I walk back into the living room with our coats, the front door swings open.

Jenny.

She steps inside, wiping her feet on the mat, and her arrival immediately triggers a chorus of women calling her name with excited little sorority-girl-style squeals. She smiles and waves like a fucking movie star, kisses Lisa Vanderwerf on the cheek and gets wrapped into a hug by Grace, who'd pranced in from the kitchen as soon as she heard all the hubbub.

Alarms blare and flash inside my skull; the janitor living in my brain runs around desperately pulling levers and pressing buttons and locking doors. Out of the corner of my eye, I see Marty McFly weaving through the throng of women in an effort to get to me.

But then Amy reaches for her pea coat; I hand it to her without a word. We leave through the front door before

Jenny has a chance to close it again.

Chapter 27: Slippery when wet.

Lisa's right. The dock leading into the rippling black expanse that is the lake is covered in a combination of condensation and patches of feather-patterned frost. It's slick enough that the intrepid Amy Ellis nearly wipes out the moment she steps onto the wooden platform, but I have long arms and fast reflexes and catch her before she dumps into the frigid lake.

For a moment afterward, neither one of us moves. She stands there, off-balance, gripping my forearms, letting me hold her weight and keep her on her feet. Then she shifts at last, glances over her shoulder.

"You saved me," she says.

I let her go. "I think that's a little dramatic, Amy. They were only talking about potty-training. It's a natural fucking process, you know."

She gives a giggle at my joke, but it transforms into an irritable groan at the end.

Reaching backward, one of her hands slides down my arm until she finds my wrist. She tugs me forward, and I'm more careful than she was when I follow her down the slippery dock towards the lawn chairs sitting at the far end.

"I don't know why they have to do that," Amy complains. The lawn chairs are as damp as the rest of the dock; she brushes beads of water away from them with her palm before finally giving up and sitting down in one of them anyway.

"You don't know why who has to do what?"

"Come to a *bachelorette* party and then spend all their time talking about their children's number twos. Can't they think of anything else to talk about?"

I sit down in the lawn chair next to hers. The leather jacket I'm wearing protects my torso from the damp, but my jeans immediately get clammy. "That's what mothers do. They talk about their kids."

"Yeah, but..." She sighs and pushes dark hair behind one ear. Silver studs glint in the moonlight. "Not all mothers do *that* — show up to a party and talk potty-training. But there's this certain breed of women who can *only* talk about their children. It's like, their kids come along, and boom, they completely forget about anything else they ever were before motherhood. They start subscribing to parenting magazines, and every sentence out of their mouth begins with, 'little Johnny did the cutest thing yesterday.'"

I lean back, turn my head to the side so I can look at her. It's the first time I've seen her so worked up in our short acquaintanceship.

"Bitter much?" I ask.

"I'm not bitter," she says quickly. "I never wanted kids. Not even when I thought I was straight. I just..." She sighs again, pushes dark hair back. I'm beginning to realize the gesture is one of her tells, revealing some level of pent-up emotion. "I just hate seeing amazing women do that to themselves. Become so single-mindedly determined to erase every bit of their personality and replace it with some kind of archetypal Uber Mother. It kills me."

I chuckle, stare out at the undulating surface of the dark lake. Then something occurs to me all at once, hits me like a shotgun blast to the gut. I turn my head again before I speak, so I can watch her reaction.

"Were you with somebody who ended up having a baby?"

She shrugs, says casually, "A lot of women I've dated over the years have children now. Some with men, some with other women, some on their own."

"That's not what I mean."

She turns, looks at me. Studies my face with lake-dark eyes that undulate with something lurking beneath the surface. "Then what *did* you mean?"

I shift forward; the plastic seat of the chair crackles beneath me. "Were you with someone who — I don't know exactly — someone who left you to because they wanted kids?"

I pause, realizing this is potentially too personal and too heavy and could endanger the fun I'm hoping to have tonight with Amy. But I press it anyway, putting forth a theory that, if I'm right, will give Amy and me more in common than I ever would've thought.

"Amy. Look, I'm just guessing here, but... Did

somebody cheat on you and get herself pregnant in the process?"

She looks like she's about to say something, but doesn't. She shakes her head. "No. Not exactly." Sighs. Pushes dark hair behind an ear. "She didn't get pregnant when she cheated on me. Just thought she did. But she wound up pregnant a couple months later, anyway."

I reach across the short gap between our chairs and take her hand. "I'm sorry."

Amy won't look at me. "Don't be. It was a long time ago."

"What was her name?"

"Wendy. We met when I was in business school and she was doing an MFA."

"MFA?"

"Masters in Fine Arts. She was a painter. Did some sculpture, too, but mostly painting." She pauses, seems to think for a moment. "I never would've thought we'd end up together because she wasn't really my type — flighty and girly and filled with way more energy than me. But, I don't know, we clicked somehow. We were together most of our twenties."

Amy traces a vein on the back of my hand with her thumb. It tickles, sends a shiver through me.

"What about you?" she asks me. "Did you ever want a family?"

I think about Jenny and her kids — the solemn-looking Andrew, bouncy little Jake, the baby girl who shares my name. I think about Jenny showing me pictures of them on her phone, scrolling through with her thumb, smiling, telling stories about each of them, and I wonder if Amy would accuse Jenny of erasing her personality to become an archetypal Uber Mother.

And I think of lying in bed this morning, listening to the rhythm of my parents' interwoven voices above me, missing a family with Jenny I never had.

The memories elicit a dull throb inside my chest. Somewhere in my brain, the janitor tests a lock on a door.

"I thought I wanted kids," I say after a minute. "A lot of years ago. But at this point, I think I'm happy playing auntie to my sister's kids and godmother for Alex's two kids. Not that I get to see them that much. But that's part of what I like about it — I show up for Christmases and birthdays, give 'em a ton of presents, play with 'em, leave. All the benefit of having kids, none of the responsibility."

"Alex and Graham — they have a boy and a girl, right?"

I nod. "Danny just turned four. Aria's two and a half — and she's a total terror. I get the feeling she's going to be all Graham."

Amy laughs lightly. "So what's Graham like? Coach Woods doesn't talk about her much in the book. She only gets a few cameo appearances."

A memory surfaces from last Christmas Eve, which was the last time I saw my best friends: an exhausted Graham, asleep on the couch, face illuminated in reds and blues and yellows by the Christmas tree lights, baby Aria sleeping on her chest. Alex carefully wrapping them both up in a throw blanket, while Danny asks in a dramatic stage whisper about what's going to happen if they're still asleep like that when Santa comes in.

"What's Graham like," I muse. "She's completely fucking perfect for Alex, for starters. She's sassy, doesn't put up with Alex's shit even for a minute, stubborn as a motherfucker, and she's the glue that holds them all together. And Alex is so ridiculously in love with her that it's fucking *nauseating* to be around. I hate them both."

The thumb goes back to tracing the veins on my hand. "In other words, Graham's as amazing as Coach Woods says she is."

I sigh. "Basically. Yes."

"And when you say you hate them, what you really mean is…"

"That I love them and their kids so much I would sell my soul to the devil to help them if I needed to? Yes."

Amy laughs and leans over, kisses my cheek.

She settles back down in her seat, and we fall into a comfortable silence, the pad of her thumb still rubbing absentminded patterns on the back of my hand as we both stare out across the lake.

A couple of long, quiet minutes go by this way.

"Should we really be doing this?" Amy asks. The words are so soft that they nearly get lost in the blackness.

"Doing what? Skipping out on the male exotic dancer

portion of the evening? Because if you want my honest opinion, I was kind of looking forward to that. Nothing says 'fun' to me like a room full of drunken straight girls and a male stripper."

She doesn't laugh. "Be serious for a minute. Should we really be doing *this* — spending all this time together, acting like this is going somewhere when I'm leaving in a few days and you... you don't really even know what you're doing?"

"What's wrong with having fun for a little while? Even if it's only for a few days?" I shrug. "Why make it complicated?   Just let it be what it's going to be — something to do in Marcine for a week besides entertaining Grace Adler. You entertain Grace; I entertain you. Nothing wrong with that."

The thumb on my hand stops. "But Anika... I like you."

"Well, I should fucking hope so. After all the time I spent trying to ply you with nachos and liquor at Dillan's — "

"Stop using humor to deflect. I'm trying to say something here." She turns in her seat. "When I say I like you, I mean I really *like* you. I mean that I haven't felt so... so *right* about someone I've met in a really, really long time." Her eyes break away across the lake for a moment, then come back to mine. "But I'm getting too old for bullshit, Anika.   I don't have the patience for it anymore. So tell me the truth — do you see this going anywhere? Or is this a week-long fling and then we say our goodbyes? And I'm good either way, but I want to know. Because if this is just a week-long thing, I need to brace myself for that."

It takes me a few seconds to react, and the delay must convince Amy she's fucked everything all up, because she shakes her head like she's angry at me or herself or me or the world, sighs, pushes dark hair behind one silver-studded ear.

"Maybe I shouldn't have said... It's fine if you don't feel the same way," she starts, but I silence her by reaching over, pulling her hand away from her ear.

"Come here," I say, tugging gently at her hand. At first, she doesn't seem to understand, but I guide her out of her wilting old lawn chair, pull her towards me and onto my lap. She seems hesitant at first, uncomfortable, resting on the edge of my thigh like she's going to sprint away at any second. But I take both her hands and pull her close, wrap my arms around her until she relaxes and finally lets the side of her face settle into the space between my shoulder and my neck. I kiss her forehead.

"I don't know if this is going to go anywhere, Amy. But the way you're feeling... it's the same for me. It's just... it's so easy to be around you, and you make me feel like — like *me* again, and I haven't felt like me in a really long fucking time. Does that make any sense?"

Her eyelashes tickle my throat, and I feel her grin against my neck. "Honestly? No. It doesn't make sense."

I let out a half-laugh. "It means I like you, too. A lot. Like a dumb-ass kid in high school 'a lot.' And if you want to try to… I don't know, if you want to try to see if this can go somewhere, even if you're in fucking Basel and I'm still stuck in Ohio, well, I'm up for at least trying."

There's another butterfly kiss of eyelashes against my throat, and the next thing I know, there's a Tinkerbell-sized hand tugging at the collar of my jacket, pushing it down, exposing bare skin to the cold night air. Amy shifts against me, and the exposed skin doesn't stay exposed for long; a mouth covers the goosebumps forming there, teeth graze against my collarbone, following the line to my clavicle and sucking the skin there into a kiss.

"Amy? Please don't tell me you're giving me a hickey."

Instead of answering, her lips smile against the tender skin at the base of my throat, and the hand not holding back my collar fiddles with the jacket zipper, tugging it down. A cold hand invades the warm interior of my jacket, running down the contours of my chest and pulling up on my shirttail. Cold fingers land on my abdomen, and immediately I'm sucking in a breath.

"Holy Jesus, your hands are cold," I accuse.

"Not for long," she says against my collarbone. She pushes my jacket open further, and a second hand follows the first, joining in on the task of pulling my shirttail from my jeans and turning my bare stomach into goosebump patches of ice.

I reach down, shift her so that she's straddling my lap, gently push her away from the vampire job she's doing to my neck.

She looks up, studies my face, and in the silver moonlight, I can see there's something in her eyes I haven't seen before — something soft and open, something I guess that's more like the *real* Amy than the hard-ass business woman she's always presenting to the world.

Then her eyes dart down to my neck and back up, and she smirks, the secret soft expression disappearing. She touches a fingertip to the place her mouth had been earlier.

"Maybe a *little* bit of a hickey," she says.

I grab both her hands and pull her roughly forward. "You're so paying for that," I say over her laughter, and she tries to squirm away from me, but I'm holding her tightly and of course I'm only five-fucking-thousand times stronger than my little Jane Lane-style Tinkerbell, so she can't get away from the big-ass mouth that lands like a suction cup on the side of her neck.

"Bridesmaid!" she manages to say between bouts of giggling. "Don't forget I have to be a bridesmaid in less than forty-eight hours!"

I draw a light line with the tip of my tongue up the side of her neck, suck lightly at her jaw. "That's what you sorority girls learn all those fancy makeup tricks for, isn't it?"

She puts her cold hands on either side of my face and pushes me back. "Seriously. No hickeys."

"After the wedding?"

"I have that interview with Ohio State on Tuesday."

"You don't play fair," I say, touching a finger to the spot where I think she left a mark.

Her eyes dance down to where my finger messes with my throat. The smirk comes back. "I said I liked you. I never said anything about playing fair." She moves her hands from my cheeks to the back of my neck, lacing her fingers there, watching me.

I lean down, let my mouth find hers, pull her into a deep kiss. She obliges this time, rocks forward so that we're chest-to-chest, doesn't object when my fingers fumble with the buttons of her heavy pea coat, slide beneath her cashmere sweater.

Chapter 29: Nothing says "fun" like a room full of drunken straight girls and a male stripper.

We only head back to the cabin when we get too cold to keep making out on the dock. And after the frigid air surrounding the lake, stepping into the warm glow of the living room is like walking into a sauna.

As much as I'd hoped we'd stayed outside long enough to miss it, the table with the board game on it has been pushed aside, couches have been shoved out of the way, Hall & Oates has been replaced with something bass-ier, and the first thing that greets me when I open the door is a grinning, fish-pale white guy in a Speedo, dancing on the coffee table and thrusting his sausage skyward. Heavy-and-Pink, she of the "naked as a jaybird" toddlers, is squealing with delight and shaking what her mama gave her, dollar bill pinched between her first two fingers.

Oh, Jesus H. Fucking Christ.

These are the times when you want to firebomb your retinas until permanently blinded. But it doesn't matter, because you know that even once your eyeballs are burned out of your skull, you're still going to be *seeing* that, seeing fucking Grace Adler get pushed on top of the coffee table, dancing drunk and out-of-sync and flushed red as Mr. Sausage turns his attention onto her and starts grinding mere inches away, his mostly fit but not-quite-buff skinny body snaking up and down like one of those Gumby air tube men that used car dealerships put out in the front lot to announce a BIG SALE!!!

Amy and I slip in quietly, unnoticed by the room full of drunken, middle-aged women, and I help her out of her coat.

"I'm going to need a drink to make it through this," she says to me in a low tone.

"Only one?"

She quirks a sardonic eyebrow. "Or five. You want one?"

I nod.

"Any preference?"

"Anything," I say. "Rubbing alcohol, maybe."

"I'll be right back," she says, squeezing my hand.

"I'll put our coats away."

I watch as Amy skirts around Heavy-and-Pink and a few other women, making her way towards the kitchen. A blonde head turns when she passes.

Jenny.

She looks over her shoulder, catches my eye. Her smile falters for a moment, but then she goes back to clapping and swaying and giggling with everyone else.

Giggling. There's a lot of fucking giggling, and I'm finding that I'm glad I never spent the night in a sorority house, after all. I head for the bedroom with the pile of coats on the bed.

#

I'm draping Amy's damp pea coat on top of my leather jacket when I hear the door to the bedroom closing softly, muting the thumping music emanating from the living room.

I look over my shoulder, and there's Jenny, leaning back against the door, hands pinned behind her. Her pale face is flushed red, either from too much booze of from the heat of the makeshift, living room dance floor.

"Hey," I say, surprised and a little confused by her sudden appearance.

She rakes long blonde hair away from her face. It's the first time I've seen it unbraided this week, making her look less mom-like and more like the Jenny I once knew.

"Hey," she answers weakly. Then says nothing more.

I turn away from the pea coat. "You okay?"

Her eyes fall. She shakes her head.

Mild alarm courses through me. "Are you going to be sick?" I ask, because I know all-too-well about Jenny's low tolerance for alcohol, and the disaster that strikes when she mixes her grains. "Do you need help into the bathroom?"

"I'm not drunk," she says. Then amends herself with, "Well, I'm not *that* drunk. Only a little." She holds up her thumb and forefinger, an inch or two apart, to show me just how not-drunk she is.

Which, in other words, means she's either really tipsy or full-on fucking drunk.

"Oh. So then… what's wrong?"

She lifts an index finger slowly, points it at my chest. Rotates her hand, points at her own chest. "We are," she whispers.

I play dumb, even though I worry that I know exactly what she's talking about. "What do you mean, we're wrong? I thought we had some very fucking civil, adult lunchtime conversations this week."

She crosses the room slowly, walks around the edge of the bed. She stops when she's two feet away from me, just outside the outer boundary of Personal Space Zone, and points at my neck.

"You have something on your throat," Jenny says, and I reach up automatically, run my fingers across the place where I know there must be a hickey showing in the space left by the unbuttoned collar of my shirt. Even though I know there's nothing there that's going to magically wipe away, I look down at my hand anyway, swiping my thumb against my fingertips.

Jenny breathes out a laugh. "It's still there, Ani."

"Don't call me that."

She shrugs. Neither of us speaks.

"You must like her," she says after a moment. "To let her leave a mark like that."

"It's a hickey, Jenny, not a tattoo."

254

"You could've stopped her."

"Maybe. But why should I have?"

"Because you hate hickeys," Jenny says plainly.

Now it's my turn to shrug. "Never too late to turn over a new leaf."

A frown flashes across her face. Suddenly she asks, "Why did you stop talking to me? Five years ago? I thought we were doing fine, but then you came to town for your sister's wedding, we hung out a few times, and then... nothing. Not a single word to me for five years. Not until this week."

"I thought we agreed not to talk about the past?"

"It's just one question. Is it really that hard to answer?"

I sigh. "We did a lot more than 'hang out' when I came home for my sister's wedding. You know that. It was wrong. And it hurt too much. And I couldn't do it anymore — not to me, not to you, not even to fucking Mason. My sister found out about how much time you and I were spending together — and she guessed what we'd done — and she and my brothers confronted me. Told me I needed to take a break from you. And I realized they were right."

The frown comes back; she seems to think for a few seconds. "I get that we needed to stop... *that,* but did you really have to cut me out completely? Why couldn't we have at least just stayed friends?"

"Jenny..." I say, her name a long breath through a tightening throat.

"Five years of complete silence, Ani. And you didn't even warn me. You didn't think I deserved some sort of explanation?" She turns her head sharply away from me, blinks a few time, presses her lips together. When she looks back, her eyes are brimming with tears and her chin trembles like a child's. Her next words are high-pitched and cracking. "I thought we were doing okay. We'd gone back to being friends — *best* friends, like we always had been, but then one day you were just... *gone.* Just like that."

"Don't bullshit a bullshitter. We were never good at being 'just friends.' What we were doing... you were married."

"Mason's not you. He's never been you."

My hands curl into fists. "Jesus Christ, Jenny! Then I guess you should've fucking thought of that before you let him get you fucking pregnant!"

That does it. The dam breaks and the tears spill from her eyes, roll down her cheeks, drip off her trembling chin. Her red cheeks flush redder; her brown eyes shine with moisture.

And the sight just about kills me.

"I'm sorry," I say, voice softening. "I shouldn't have yelled."

"*I* shouldn't have made you move back to Ohio," she says, and her breath hitches around a sob. "And I shouldn't have asked you to stop playing basketball for me, it was so selfish, I was just so hurt after Rhianna, so angry with you, and it was like — I thought — if we could just go back, back home, back to the place where we'd started, when things had been good between us, then maybe… maybe…"

Her crying overwhelms her words, and she can't speak anymore; her chest and throat spasm with silent tears. She closes her eyes, presses a fist against her mouth.

"Jen…"

I can't stop myself from reaching for her. I bridge the narrow gap between us, wrap my arms around her as I pull her forward. She fits against me the way she always has, burying her face against my chest, and the moisture of her tears and the heat of her breath bleed through my shirt and dampen my skin.

I rub her back soothingly and stare at the ceiling while she cries it out, blinking back my own emotion.

And then that rat, Marty McFly, appears in the corner.

"She felt awful about Mason, you know," Marty says, hands shoved into the pockets of his letterman jacket. "Just like you felt awful about Rhianna. She would've stayed with you if you'd forgiven her. Like she'd forgiven you the year before. You could've been Andrew's second mom." He jerks a thumb over his shoulder. "Doc's got the DeLorean right outside. We could go back if you want. We could change the past right now."

I ignore stupid, All-American Marty Fucking McFly. I know better than that. You can't change the past. What's done is done.

I squeeze Jenny a little closer to me, close my eyes

when she tightens the arms around my waist.

But in my mind, I'm following Marty McFly into the driveway, stooping low to fit into the goddamn DeLorean, buckling my seatbelt when he sets the clock for

***Back to the future: Eight and a half years ago.
Marcine, Ohio.***

I walk out of the bathroom still dripping water, nothing on but a towel wrapped around my waist. I hold the dental floss I'd meant to throw away in one hand, a pregnancy test in the other, its two pink lines telling me a story I don't think I want to know.

Jenny's sitting up on the bed, kindergarten progress reports spread around her, the way I'd expected to find her when I'd first walked in a while ago.

"Is this Grace's?" I ask, but already there's an accusatory tone in my voice, because Grace was the one with dry eyes.

But it has to be Grace's. How could it be Jenny's? It couldn't be hers. She's never been with anyone but me.

Jenny looks up from her spot on the bed, her eyes still red from crying earlier, and she opens her mouth to say something, to answer me, but no words come out. Her brown eyes go big and round and start to glisten with fresh tears.

"Is this Grace's?" I repeat, shaking the pregnancy test at her as if she might not know what I'm talking about.

"Jenny? Tell me this is from Grace. Tell me that's why you guys were crying earlier."

Her bottom lip begins to tremble. "It's mine," she says, words nearly inaudible.

Somehow I already knew she would say this, but I fling the stick with the two pink lines across the room anyway, as if realizing I've been holding a poisonous snake all this time that I need to get rid of. It smacks against the bedroom window, falls to the carpet.

We lock eyes. Questions swim through my head in such a thick swamp that it's impossible to distinguish one from the other. I don't realize that I've started to cry until Jenny goes blurry before me. I swallow thickly, blink her back into focus, and finally find a question distinct enough that I manage to voice it.

"Who?"

She covers her eyes with her hand.

"Who, goddammit?"

"Ani, it doesn't matter, you don't want — "

"Don't tell me I don't want to know!" I scream, because I know that's what she was going to say. We've been completing each others' sentences for a decade.

"But it doesn't — "

"It does matter! It matters to me!"

She doesn't take her hand away from her eyes. "Mason," she whispers.

"Mason?" I repeat incredulously. "Mason who got me a job, Mason? Mason who I *fucking work with every day*

Mason?"

She nods. Hand still covering her eyes.

I swivel, slam a fist into the door frame behind me. It shivers, and I fleetingly think it's a good thing that I didn't hit the wall because my fist would've gone right through it.

Now my hand fucking hurts, and it competes with my heart to see what's going to break first. I feel faint, and so I lean back against the door frame, slide down until my wet ass hits the carpet.

"Why?" I ask, choking out my next question. "I thought things were getting better."

Finally, she takes her hand away from her face, revealing wet, red cheeks. "They were — they are," she says, pushing aside progress reports to climb off the bed.

She kneels beside me, reaches for me, but I push her away.

"It was a few months ago, when we first got here. And I — " her voice breaks " — I was still so angry at you about Rhianna, and we were barely talking, and so I — we... Mason asked what I was so upset about, and..."

"Only once?" I ask hoarsely. "It only happened once?"

Her face falls. "Twice."

"Fuck," I mutter, turning my head away from her as the tears fall freely down my face. I'm back in high school again, sitting across from Jenny on New Year's Day, and she's telling me that the kiss we'd shared was meant to be a joke. Just a fucking joke to her.

She puts her hand on my chin, turns my face towards

her. "I don't want Mason, Ani. I want *you*. You're the only one I've ever wanted."

Marty McFly materializes behind Jenny, crouching over her, listening intently, his hands on his knees. "This is it. This is the moment," he tells me. "Get ready — this is where we change everything. The whole course of your life."

"We've always said we'd start a family one day," Jenny says, and I can tell she's pleading with me. "This isn't the way we thought it would happen, but I... maybe we..."

"Fucking Christ, are you asking me to fucking raise *Mason's* fucking baby?! You *cannot* be fucking serious!"

"Listen to me, Anika," Jenny says, resting her hands on the sides of my face, wiping away my tears with her thumbs. "Please just listen. We can do this. We can — "

"No. We absolutely *can't* fucking do this." I stand up, gather my towel around me, leave Jenny kneeling on the carpet in my wet spot. "*I* can't fucking do this. Not anymore. We're done. Once and for all. Done."

Behind Jenny, Marty McFly slaps a palm to his forehead, shakes his head at me. "I brought you back here to do things differently," he says. "Not repeat the same mistakes." He straightens up, calls over his shoulder, "Doc! Reset the clock on the DeLorean — we're going to have to come back and do it all over again."

Back to the present

Jenny lets go of me at last, pushes herself back and wipes tears roughly from her face.

"I wish we'd done everything differently," she says. "I wish we hadn't been so young and stupid."

"We were who we were. And we can't change the past."

"I know. But what if we could still change the future?" She tilts her head to the side, gazes up at me with a hopeful expression on her face.

I shake my head. "We don't have a future. Not anymore."

"But we still could. You're still my soulmate."

Soulmate. The word that sounded so magical, so imbued with power twenty years ago. The word that sounds like a cruel fucking irony today.

"I don't believe in soulmates anymore." I hear the bitterness in my own words, but I can't help myself.

"I do." She looks down for a moment, then back up. "Mason and I separated two months ago. At this point, I'm just waiting for the divorce to be finalized. That, and all the custody paperwork."

Bomb.

Dropped.

When I don't respond, she says in a rush, "I was going to tell you, the first time I came to Soul Mountain. That was the whole reason I went. But you — you seemed like you were still so angry, and I could barely get you to talk to me at all, let alone tell you how I... and so I chickened out.

But when I saw you tonight, I knew I had to tell you. I knew it was maybe my last chance. I should've done this five years ago. I never should've let you go back to Switzerland." She reaches up, gingerly touches the hickey on the base of my throat. "But maybe it's already too late," she whispers.

I wrap my hand around hers, pull it away from my neck. There are a lot of things I want to say to Jenny in this moment — like how it's been too late for a long fucking time, and how I stopped talking to her, stopped touching her five years ago because I'm an addict like my brother, and how after five years of abstinence from my addiction I still teeter on the brink of relapse, and how my sister thinks she's a manipulative bitch, and how I told Amy only thirty or forty minutes earlier that I'm willing to try to have something *real* with her — but I don't say any of that.

Instead, I tilt my head towards the bedroom door, look down at her, and say, "They're going to be wondering where we went. I should get back out there."

Chapter 30: Nothing says "fun" like Celine Dion and Superwoman bedspreads.

I know what you're thinking. You're thinking a big, tough basketball player like me would only listen to music as kickass as I am. You're thinking I'd be into the kind of hard stuff Gerry likes, which was mostly crazy, screaming metal bands when he was in high school, and then way-too-explicit hip hop later on. Or you'd think that at least I'd listen to good, soulful black music — the Motown-ish tunes my mom always had playing in the house when I was growing up, singers like Marvin Gaye and Diana Ross and early-era Whitney Houston.

But my deep, dark secret is that I shared a room with Dutch until high school, okay? It wasn't my fault. And what was Dutch into back then?

Mariah Carey. Alanis Morissette. Ace of Bass. That girl with the awful glasses and the guitar who sang about how she thought she'd live forever, but now she's not so sure, and her boyfriend told her that she's clever, but that won't get him anyhow, or anywhere, with her.

(Those were song lyrics, by the way. You can look them up if you don't believe me.)

And Celine Dion. Good God, Dutch went through this

Celine Dion phase that seemed to last for fucking *years*.

And I hate to admit this, but there's this part of me —
this very *small* fucking part of me, mind you — that still
kinda likes Celine Dion.

So when I walk back out of the bedroom where all the
coats are and make my way to where Amy's drinking in the
corner, watching Mr. Sausage and leaning her back against
the wall in measured, patient silence, I don't even hear the
bass-y electronic music or the squealing women. What I
hear is

There were nights when the wind was so cold
That my body froze in bed if I just listened to it
Right outside the window

(Also fucking song lyrics.)

I reach an arm around Amy's waist and accept the drink
she hands me.

"Did you get lost in there?" she asks. "I thought I was
going to have to send in a search party."

I shake my head, hesitate, opt for honesty. "Jenny
kinda cornered me," I explain, glad that the volume of the
dance music keeps my words just for Amy's ears. I lean
against the same wall she's leaning on, slide down a little
so that I don't have to bend over to speak in her ear. "A
little unexpected drama. But it's fine."

I finished crying in the instant that you left

Just then, Jenny walks out of the bedroom — she'd opted to go to the bathroom to clean her face up at the same time that I left to head back to Amy — and Amy spots her right away, leaving the same room I'd left only moments before, which makes me goddamned glad I decided to be honest about what had happened.

And I can't remember where or when or how

"Anything I should know about?" Amy asks warily.
"No. Honestly, it's fine. She just…"

And I banished every memory you and I had ever made

"… She's had too much to drink, and she always gets weepy and nostalgic when she drinks. So she followed me in there, wanted to talk about our shitty past."

Marty McFly appears on my other side, leans back against the same wall. "That's not *exactly* what happened," he says. "She also made a pass at you."

But Amy nods like she's satisfied by this, reaches a hand behind me and sticks it into the back pocket of my jeans. "Your jeans are still wet from the dock chair," she comments.

I shrug. "They're fine."

"Did you bring another pair? We could get you out of these, put you into something dry."

I raise my eyebrows. "Is it just me, or did you just suggest you want to take off my pants?"

She answers with a one-shouldered shrug. "Sounds like you're choosing to interpret it that way."

"You're such a tease."

She blushes, eyes falling away from mine. Hesitates a moment, and then says, "There's another bedroom behind the kitchen. Technically a kids' room, I guess. I'm sure we could get you out of your pants in there. Without anyone coming in." She nods towards the knot of dancing women in front of them. "They're all too busy and too drunk to notice if we disappear again for a while."

I let the hand that's on her waist drop a little lower, run it lightly over her round behind. "I think your pants might be a little wet, themselves."

She grins. "I'm wet? That's not from the dock."

"See? Total tease."

Amy pops an eyebrow up. "Really? I thought I was being pretty obvious that time."

"Then maybe you'd better show me where that kids' room is. Help me out of these wet, wet jeans."

Her smile grows, and she takes me by the hand, leads me in the direction of the kitchen.

I must feel the eyes boring into my back, or else it's some kind of psychic fucking twinge, leftover from the days when we completed each others' sentences, because I look over my shoulder almost on instinct, and

But when you touch me like this
And you hold me like that

find Jenny watching us, brown eyes filled with sorrow and loss.

I just have to admit
That it's all coming back to me

#

Amy doesn't waste time. We aren't even all the way inside the room when she practically fucking jumps me, fingers moving as fast as they can to undo the buttons of my shirt, pulling me down into a hungry kiss at the same time as her foot fumbles behind her, kicking distractedly at the door until it clicks shut.

She manages to get the final button undone, but instead of pulling the shirt off, she runs her hands up and down my bare skin, scratching at me lightly, stopping with both hands cupping my boobs.

"God," she says. "I've wanted to rip your clothes off since the moment you touched me on that airplane."

I try to remember touching her on the airplane and come up with the moment I chose comfort over politeness and gave her shoulder a reassuring pat.

Guess I didn't know my own strength.

I answer with a kiss, pull back with a laugh when she

bites my bottom lip a little too hard. "Tell me this isn't a case of you just being some sort of weirdly obsessed basketball groupie."

"I *am* a basketball groupie," she says. "I'm not ashamed to admit it. I've been following you for *years*. But I didn't get obsessed until you started telling me stories on that plane."

"Seriously? Hearing about my parents' getting together is what — "

She pushes her fingers beneath the bottom seam of my sports bra. "Too much talking. Not enough ripping clothes off."

I help her with my bra, then lift the fancy, cashmere sweater over her head. Under the sweater is only a black tank top, accentuating her curves. I go to take the tank off, too, but she grabs my hands, pulls them away.

"Not yet," she breathes. "Please? I'm too self-conscious."

I run my fingers under the bottom edge of the tank, but don't try to take it off again. "I have a hard time imagining you being self-conscious about much of anything," I say, but at the same time, my exploring fingertips hit something that feels like it might be scar tissue, and I wonder if I've found the source of Amy's self-consciousness.

She grabs my wrists, pulls my hands to her backside, starts working at the button of my jeans while landing soft, open-mouthed kisses against my bare chest.

"I thought we said we needed to get you out of these

jeans," she says between kisses.

"Yeah, I think you might've mentioned — " But I stop with a gasp when her hand slides into my underwear, squeezes, which of course sends all the blood in my body rushing out of my brain and into my nether regions, leaving me feeling lightheaded and weak-kneed.

Fingers tease through the wetness accumulating there, and Amy pushes me back until my legs hit the end of a bed. With her free hand, she shoves me lightly backward, and I oblige, lying back onto a Super Woman bedspread.

She climbs on top of me, straddles my stomach, gazes down at me for a moment before folding down onto my chest. She sucks on the same spot at the base of my throat where she already left a hickey. Her mouth moves up my neck, her slacks scratching my ribs as she wriggles up my long-ass body. She reaches the side of my face, takes an earlobe into her mouth for a long, agonizingly slow moment before breathing into my ear, "Tell me what you want."

And because there's still no blood in my brain, it takes a while to formulate coherent words.

"I think," I start to say, but stop when lips curl around my earlobe again. I close my eyes. "I think you're doing just fine without my help," I manage at last, which is answered by a light rumble of laughter tickling my ear.

Her nails trail up my arms, down my sides.

"Is there anything I need to know about? You'd tell me if I was going to run the risk of catching anything from you, right? Because I'm about to mix a lot of bodily fluids together."

I nod, and even though it's somewhat embarrassing to admit, I tell her the truth: "It's been more than a year for me. The rumors about all the nookie professional athletes are supposed to get turned out to be completely false. At least in my case."

Her mouth moves from my ear to my neck, my neck to my jawline, my jawline to my mouth. When her kiss finishes, she runs her tongue slowly across her upper lip. "Good. Then I can have you all to myself."

"The last time was with one of my teammates in Switzerland," I tell her. She leans down, takes a nipple into her mouth. Sucks. "Cici — Rademaker," I manage to gasp out. "Did you ever see her play? We dated on and off for a couple of years, but when she got an offer in Australia — "

Amy lifts her head. "Anika. Seriously. Please stop talking."

And with that, she's traveling down my body again, pausing long enough to tease each nipple between her teeth, then trailing little kisses down the plane of my stomach, using her hands to tug the jeans off my narrow hips, down across long thighs and calves, off two enormous feet.

I'm expecting her to take my underwear when she takes my jeans, since that's all I've got left now, but she doesn't. Instead, that tongue of hers draws a light line from my ankle to my knee, my knee up the inside of my thigh, and when she reaches my hot, damp fucking Hanes Her Way

271

black bikini briefs, she drags her bottom lip up the crotch, starts kissing me right through the goddamned cotton, and I swear I almost lose it right fucking there.

"God fucking *dammit,* Amy."

My hips squirm up all on their own, and I tilt my head back, gripping the Super Woman bed spread in both fists and biting the inside of my cheek to keep from screaming. Amy laughs against me, tonguing the cotton between us, and I manage to force a ragged breath into air-starved lungs.

Her face still between my legs, she hooks both index fingers around the top of my underwear and starts to pull. Her tongue's on my bare clit a moment later.

There were moments of gold and there were flashes of light
   There were things I'd never do again
   But then they'd always seemed right
   There were nights of endless pleasure
   It was more than any laws allow

Baby, baby...

And for the first time in almost nine years, I surprise myself by being with someone and not thinking of Jenny even once.

Chapter 31: Departures and reunions.

Saturday morning

"I wish I could stay," I say between two little kisses, car keys dangling from my fingers. "But with Mom and Dad both still out... I don't want Gerry to have to be at the restaurant all day on his own."

Amy wraps Tinkerbell-sized arms around my waist, pulls me close once more, lands another kiss on the underneath side of my jaw. Then she lets go. "Okay. You're a better big sister than I've ever been."

"I seriously doubt that."

She closes my hand around the car keys. "Go. Before I change my mind and kidnap you, take you home to the B&B for the rest of the day."

"You're needed elsewhere anyway," I remind her. "Isn't the rehearsal and the dinner tonight?"

She rolls her eyes. "Yes. Unfortunately. Which — you'll come with me to the wedding on Sunday, won't you?"

I think for a second. We hadn't discussed me coming to the wedding until now, but if I'm being honest, I have to admit that I want all the time I can get with her between now and her departure from Ohio on Wednesday morning.

"What time is the wedding, again?" I ask. "The after-church crowd gets busy, but we close early Sunday nights."

"Six o'clock. At the Lutheran Church."

"St. Peter's? I know that one. How about I let you know tomorrow morning? PJ's arriving home today, so if he can cover me…"

"Can I drop by the restaurant tonight?" she asks. "After the rehearsal dinner? I could help you guys close."

"Don't be silly, you don't need to help us."

"I know I don't 'need' to, but it will give me an excuse to visit," she says with a shrug.

I kiss the top of her head. "You never need an excuse. I'd love for you to visit."

The smile she gives me in return is shy. She walks backward a few steps. "I'll see you tonight, then."

#

My phone buzzes before I make it even a mile from the lakeside cabin, a video chat request flashing at me from where the phone sits in its air vent holder. I know I should probably wait until I'm stationary and not try to video chat and drive at the same time, but when I see who's calling, I can't help myself. I accept the call with a grin.

"How's Ohio?" the voice on the other end says.

I give the screen a quick glance, see that Alex is in her living room, probably sitting on the couch with her laptop on the coffee table. A head of messy blonde hair passes by in the background behind her.

"Shitty as ever," I say cheerfully. "How's the Deep South? Warming up yet?"

"Who are you talking to?" I hear Graham ask off-screen. The blonde hair reappears in the frame, and a face hovers over Alex's shoulder. "Hey — Anika!" Then her brow crinkles and she says, "You shouldn't be video chatting while driving, you know."

"I know. But since we're practically in the same time zone for now, I didn't want to miss the chance."

"Same time zone?" Graham asks, the crease in her brow deepening.

"Alex didn't tell you? I'm in Ohio."

Graham smacks Alex playfully on the back of the head. *"Nooo.* You know she never tells me anything."

"Did she tell you my mom's sick?"

Graham nods sympathetically. "Now *that* I did hear about. How's your family?"

"Driving me fucking crazy. Gerry's clean, though. And he seems to be doing really good."

"How long are you going to be home for?" Alex asks.

I admit to her that I don't really know, reminding her of how I broke my contract to be here and that my basketball career is most likely over. Graham meanders out of the frame when we start talking basketball, while Alex and I go over the highlights of the NCAA tournament season this year. Rosemont got knocked out early, during the Sweet Sixteen, a sensitive topic that Alex is still grouchy about.

After basketball, the conversation roams to Danny and Aria, and how Aria's walking now and talking up a storm, and Danny's latest obsession is birdwatching.

"Birdwatching?" I ask, surprised.

"I think it has more to do with the binoculars than the birds," Alex says. "Graham says he'll either grow up to be a zoologist, a super spy, or a peeping tom."

We share a laugh.

"Speaking of kids…" I trail off, clear my throat. "So, uh, Jenny came by the restaurant a couple times this week. She's up to three kids now. I got to meet the two little ones."

"Jenny?" Alex says, eyebrows dipping. "As in Pearson? I thought you weren't talking to her?"

I shrug. "I wasn't. But she wanted to… mend fences or some shit."

"I think she wanted to mend a hell of a lot more than that," says Marty McFly, who has appeared in the passenger's seat next to me.

There's a moment of silence. "And?" Alex says.

"And what?"

"And did you mend your fences?"

"Go on. Tell her," McFly says.

"I don't know. Maybe," I say to Alex. "She said some shit last night… maybe it was just the alcohol speaking, but… She and Mason are splitting up, and then kind of implied that she wants us to try again."

Alex studies me thoughtfully. "It's a pretty bold move

on her part, after everything you two have gone through. But — wait. You're not actually considering that, right?"

I'm at a stop light, so I look down at the phone, meet Alex's eyes for a second. "No," I say firmly, then backpedal with, "I mean, I don't think so. Maybe if things were different for me right now... Or if..."

From the passenger's seat, McFly hums a bar of Celine Dion. I shoot the evil-ass figment of my imagination a glare before turning back to Alex.

"What I'm trying to say is — I met someone recently. On the plane from Toronto to Cleveland. And... it's too early to say anything for sure, but I really like her."

I tell Alex a little about Amy, confess that we've been seeing a lot of each other lately, and then say that even though it's only been a week, I think there might be something there. Something real. Something worth seeing through.

She chuckles when I finish. "You are *so* U-Hauling right now."

"I am not!" I say. But my face burns.

"You so are."

"Fuck you, Woods."

Alex cocks her head to the side. "Does Amy know about Jenny?"

"Yeah. They met by accident at the restaurant. And I told Amy how long Jenny and I were together and everything. So that's out in the open."

"But did you tell her what Jenny said to you last night?

About divorcing Mason and wanting another try with you?"

I shake my head. "Amy and I... spent the second half of our night a little too busy to talk."

This earns a brief arched eyebrow from Alex. It's a look so arrogantly fucking regal and knowing that I remember why we nicknamed her Commander.

"You slept with her already?" she says. "That's fast. Even for you."

I roll my eyes. "Fucking don't even. Look who's talking."

She holds up both hands defensively. "Hey. I don't know what you're talking about. I'm a happily married woman." Then she brings it back to the point. "Did you tell this Amy girl what Jenny said or not?"

"Of course I didn't," I scoff. "What was I going to do? Wait for her to go down on me and then be like, 'Oh, by the way, shorty, my ex is divorcing her husband, and named her daughter after me, and is kind of acting like she wants me back.' Talk about ruining the fucking mood."

"Hold up. Did you just say Jenny named her *daughter* after you?"

"So she says. She named her Annie."

The eyebrow arches again. Alex knows that Jenny's the only one outside my family who I ever let call me Ani. There's a long silence on the other end, so long that I check the phone a few times to make sure the call didn't drop.

"You *are* considering getting back together with Jenny," Alex says at last. "Aren't you?"

"No!" I say immediately, as indignant as I was a moment earlier when she accused me of being a fucking U-Haul lesbian. But McFly starts humming Celine Dion again, and I sigh. "I mean… Maybe somewhere way in the back of my mind, subconsciously…"

"So that's what you're calling me now?" McFly asks. "Your subconscious?"

"I don't know," I say to Alex after a moment of silence. "I can't say I didn't feel anything when I held her last night."

"Held her? Now you were *holding* her?" Alex asks, voice going up an octave.

"I told you. She was drunk — or tipsy, I don't know, but she started crying about the past, about how much she hated the way everything had gotten so fucked-up between us, and so… yeah. I gave her a hug. And it… lasted a while. I let her cry it out."

Graham reappears at the side of the frame. "Who's crying it out?" she asks me. "Your mom?"

"No," Alex says, turning her head. "Jenny."

"Jenny?" Graham repeats. She looks from me to Alex. "Anika's Jenny?"

"Yeah, that Jenny," Alex confirms. "She told Anika she named her daughter after her, and she's divorcing her husband, and she wants to get back together. And so Anika held a crying Jenny one minute, then went and fucked some new girl she just met the next."

Graham kicks Alex lightly. "Watch your language, hot

stuff. Your son is sitting at the table in the other room." Then she swivels towards the screen, bends down a bit to look at me, puts both her hands on her hips. "But *please* tell me you didn't do what Alex just said you did."

"It wasn't like that," I say, defending myself. "There was nothing... sexual about holding Jenny." Marty McFly cackles loudly from the passenger's seat. "I just wanted her to, I don't know, calm the fuck down. And feel better."

"Am I remembering incorrectly, or did you tell us that you hooked up with her a couple of times five years ago when you went back home for your sister's wedding?" Graham challenges. I don't respond right away, and of course Graham, being Graham, sees that as a reason to keep pushing. "So if Jenny were here right now, and I asked what that moment meant to *her*, would *she* say it was totally innocent?"

I heave a frustrated sigh but don't reply. Graham shakes her head disdainfully.

"Careful, buddy," Alex says. "You are about one inch away from stepping into a hot pile of steaming shit."

Graham kicks Alex again, hard enough to make her wince this time. "Language!"

"I know, I know," I admit miserably. "But it's just... it's not that easy to have a clear head when she's standing right in front of me, crying her eyes out, and I'm holding her, and she's all but saying she's available and wants to get back together."

Graham plops down on the sofa next to Alex, leans into

her. "You left Jenny for a reason. And you stopped talking to her for a reason, too," she says. "Plus, if you have someone else in your life now, your actions are going to impact more than just the two of you."

"I wouldn't say I 'have someone' in my life. That would be overstating it."

"But you slept with her?" Graham asks.

"...Yeah."

"And was there a mutual understanding that it was just a one-time thing?"

"No." *Kinda the fucking opposite,* I think, but I keep that to myself.

Graham crosses her arms against her chest. "Then you have someone else in your life."

Alex lifts her chin, which is the Alex Woods way of indicating her silent agreement.

I groan. "Jesus Christ. I think I'm having a mid-life crisis."

Graham glances at Alex, then back to me. "I think you need to figure out what you want, Anika," she says gently. "Before someone gets hurt."

"Yeah. I know," I say with a sigh. "Listen, I'm almost back at the restaurant. I should let you go."

"How's the restaurant?" Alex asks.

"Fuck, speaking of hot piles of shit, that's a whole *other* thing I have to deal with. But too much to get into right now," I add when her eyebrows quirk into an unspoken question. I reach for the phone, about to end the call. "I'll talk to you guys later."

"Bye," Alex says. "Try to be good."

"Anika, wait a second," Graham says.

"What?"

"Sort out your shit."

Alex smiles crookedly, pokes Graham's cheek. "Language," she scolds.

"Oh, hush."

"I've gotta go, guys," I tell them.

"Alright," Graham says. She and Alex wave goodbye simultaneously. They've been moving like fucking synchronized swimmers for a long-ass time, and it stings to watch, so I terminate the call quickly, right as I pull into the Soul Mountain parking lot.

A shiny silver Merc sits in the spot closest to the entrance — Dutch's car. A clean, new, but less pretentious Camry sits next to it. Pennsylvania plates. When I get out, I hear its engine still cooling.

So. PJ's arrived. The family reunion is finally complete.

Chapter 32: "Why, oh why, oh why, oh — / Why did I ever leave Ohio?"

It's a few minutes after eleven when I walk into the restaurant, right as we open. The dining room is empty except for my siblings; Dutch bounces a fussy Sherry on her knee, Gerry's messing with his baseball cap and laughing about something, PJ leans back in his chair, soda in hand, and I notice that he's put on a few pounds since the last time I saw him.

Admittedly, the last time I saw him was when he was vacationing in Europe three years ago. I'd gotten mad with him about something that I honestly can't even remember anymore, and have only barely spoken to him since then.

He gets up when he sees me walk in, smiles warmly but with a hint of caution. Whatever we fought about last time we were together, I'm still the rabid animal who might bite him at any time, I guess.

"Ani," he says, pulling me into an embrace and clapping me on the back. "It's really nice to see you. It's been way too long."

We exchange pleasantries for a while; he catches us all up on his life. Business is good, he says, and he's been seeing someone he can't wait for us to meet, an attorney he met through a dating site who completely understands why his time is so limited, because she's as devoted to her career as he is to his, and so her own time is limited, too. Isn't that great?

Yeah. Trying to date someone when both of you are too goddamned busy to actually spend time together. Sounds wonderful, PJ. You just keep going with that.

But of course I don't say anything; I keep my mouth shut and smile and make faces at Sherry, who stops fussing as soon as I begin entertaining her. A few minutes later, I've taken over Gerry's seat while he goes to answer Becker's question in the kitchen, and somehow Sherry ends up in my lap, playing with my hair and giggling while PJ and Dutch compare notes on their new cars.

"The Germans are still the best engineers in the world," Dutch declares. "I'll take a German car over a Japanese car or an American car any day of the week."

PJ chuckles. "You know your C-Class out there was probably built in Alabama, right? A lot of foreign brands are manufactured in the U.S. these days. They're all about the same."

Dutch wrinkles her nose like something smells bad. "Not true. Built here or not, the Germans still design a better product."

I chew on Sherry's fingers, making monster noises as I pretend to eat her hand, which makes her squeal with delight. And I figure it's better that my mouth's full, because if it wasn't, I'd probably be obliged to point out that the only reason Dutch owns a Mercedes Benz is for the hood ornament.

PJ, who in general is a better fucking person than I am, just shrugs and lets it drop.

Gerry returns from the kitchen, pulls up a new chair and sits backward on it, turns his baseball cap around, too. He looks at Dutch.

"So did you talk to Mom and Dad? About the loan?"

Dutch nods. "A little. I managed to get Dad alone for a few minutes. He told me the original loan was from a long time ago, and they got locked in at an interest rate that was higher than what they wanted, and so when a sales guy gave them a chance to refinance the house, they jumped at it. Said he thought it would give them a chance to pay off the original loan — and it did — but they didn't do a good job reading the fine print on the mortgage refi; sounds like the sales guy was a real sleaze. So the rate on their mortgage jumped up way, way high a couple of years ago, and they've been struggling to make ends meet ever since."

All of us fall into thoughtful silence except for Sherry, who babbles happily while she grabs fistfuls of my hair.

Gerry speaks first. Frowning, he asks, "He told you all that?"

"I told you they'd talk to me," Dutch says. Her smile is smug.

"How?" Gerry says. It's obvious he's both offended and surprised that Dad would say all this to Dutch but not to him and me.

I'm not surprised, of course, but that's why I make it a point not to live in Ohio.

"Like I said. I got Dad away from Mom. Once I had him by himself, it took a little work, but he opened up."

PJ gets a funny look on his face. "Did he say what the original loan was for?"

"No. I asked. He wouldn't say."

PJ's funny look persists. He puts his soda down, chews on his tongue, stares into space.

"PJ? What's up?" I ask. When this doesn't get a response, I try again. "Junior? Got something you wanna share with the rest of the class?"

The childhood nickname he's always hated gets his attention, and he comes back to planet Earth. "I just realized something. I think this might all be my fault."

Dutch furrows her brow. "What are you talking about?"

PJ lets out a long breath, scrubs his round face with both hands. "It probably *is* my fault," he mumbles, mostly to himself.

"What's your fault, bro?" Gerry asks.

"Five years ago, when we were all back here for Dutch and Matt's wedding," he says. "I don't know if you guys remember, but I'd just bought another restaurant. But once I got into it, I realized I'd bitten off more than I could chew. It'd been struggling before I bought it — that's why the owner unloaded it in the first place — and I thought I could turn things around quickly, but it turned out to be harder than I thought. I'd sunk a lot of money into it, and I was about to lose my shirt. Which was going to endanger the other three restaurants. So... I wasn't proud to do it, but I asked Mom and Dad for help. They gave me more than I asked for — fifty grand — and I — "

"Fifty *grand?*" Gerry echoes. *"Jesus,* dude!"

"Like I said, it was more than what I asked for. I tried to pay them back in installments, but Mom wouldn't hear it. She refused my money. Voided my checks and sent them back to me."

Dutch drums manicured nails on the glass table covering, rests her chin in her other hand. "This loan they gave you... it was at the same time as my wedding?" she asks.

PJ nods.

She sighs. "They paid for most of the wedding, too. Right after they'd loaned Matt and me some money."

"Wait," I say, untangling Sherry's hand from my hair. "When did they loan *you* guys some money?"

"A few months before the wedding. Matt got laid off the year before, remember? And he was working again, and we were doing okay, but we'd missed a few house payments. Things started to get dicey. Mom and Dad helped us out for a few months, until we could catch back up."

"How much did they give you?" I ask.

"None of your business," Dutch snaps.

"PJ told us," Gerry points out.

Dutch looks away. "It doesn't matter. We paid most of it back." She glances at PJ, looking a little troubled. "They didn't send us *our* checks back."

I study her skeptically. "How much is most?"

She crosses her arms against her chest. "We still owe them about four or five thousand dollars."

Gerry shakes his head, lets out a low whistle. "Fifty thousand to him. A wedding plus another few thousand to you... No wonder the restaurant's about to go under."

Dutch huffs and jabs a finger at him. "If I remember correctly, they sent *you* to rehab — *again* — not long after I got married. Did you ever ask them how much they spent trying to get you clean? And have you even *offered* to pay them back?"

Gerry drops his gaze, takes off his baseball cap and runs a hand through his hair.

PJ and Dutch both look at me.

"What?" I ask, already reading the silent accusation in their faces. "I hope you're not waiting for some big admission about the money they gave me. Because I haven't taken a dime of their money since high school. Unlike the rest of you, apparently, *I've* been paying my own way for a long time."

"Well, congratulations," Dutch drawls, voice dripping with sarcasm. "I guess you've proven you're the best one, once and for all."

I narrow my eyes. "What's *that* supposed to mean?"

"Nothing," she says, shaking her head.

"What? We're in a competition I didn't know about? What are you fuhh..." But I have Sherry in my lap still, and I cut out the f-bomb just in time. "What are you insinuating?"

"It's not about insinuation. It's the *truth,* Anika," Dutch says.

"The truth about what?"

"About how you've always gone to great lengths to prove how much *better* you are than the rest of us."

I snort and glance at my brothers, thinking one of them might intervene on my behalf against Queen Bee over here. But PJ's still chewing his tongue, staring into space; Gerry's still gazing down at the baseball cap he's rotating in his fidgety hands. I'm on my own.

"Me?" I say to Dutch. *"I'm* the one who goes to great lengths to prove how much better I am? This coming from the woman who was telling us all a couple of minutes ago about how much better her Mercedes is than a Camry? You're fuh... You're full of it."

Sherry glances between her mother and me, and her little face puckers like a raisin, tears brewing in her big brown eyes.

Dutch purses her lips, arches both manicured eyebrows. "You've done everything you can to avoid taking responsibility in this family, all the while making sure the rest of us know that you think you're better off without us. And when things get hard here at home, you stay as far away as you possibly can."

"Stay away? I'm sitting right here!"

"Yeah?" she shoots back. "Where were you the last time Dad had to leave to go find Gerry?"

"I'm in the room, guys," Gerry says.

This pulls PJ back from outer space. He looks from Gerry, to Dutch, to me, worry creasing his brow.

Dutch ignores both of them, continues on her tirade. "Why didn't you even *know* Gerry got clean *a year ago?* Or that he's been living at home for the past seven *months?* And how come you've seen Graham and Alex's kids more times in the last five years than you've seen your own niece and nephew?"

"Maybe because every time I come home, you start throwing crap like this in my face!"

She shakes her head. "No. Wrong. You've always been content to let everyone else do the dirty work while *you* stay as far away as possible. Hell, I'm surprised you even bothered to come home when you found out Mom was sick."

"Goddammit, Dutch, I broke my *contract* to be here!" I shout. In my lap, Sherry starts to wail, reaches for her mother. "How dare you say I can't be bothered!"

Dutch leans across the table, plucks her daughter from my arms, pats her back soothingly but turns her venomous fucking eyes on me. "You came home because your career's over and you don't know what else to do." When I don't say anything right away, she nods definitively. "Look me in the eye and tell me I'm wrong."

"This is such bullshit," I say between clenched teeth. "I'm here because Mom's sick. Because coming home was the right thing. Because the rest of you are too busy or too fucked-up to run this place if Mom and Dad can't!"

Gerry turns his head sharply, eyes turning into slits.

Whoops. I probably shouldn't have said anyone was too "fucked-up" to run the restaurant, because there's only one person in the room those words could possibly be directed at. I think I just crossed a line.

He confirms it after a pregnant moment of silence. "Funny. I'm pretty sure I was managing to run this place just fine while you were back in Switzerland, playing ball and chasing tails. But maybe I'm just so 'fucked-up' that I didn't even realize I needed your help." He stands briskly. "I need a cigarette."

"Gerry…" I say, apology in my voice.

But he doesn't wait around to hear me say I'm sorry. He spins on his heel and walks out the front door.

PJ holds up both hands, looks between Dutch and me. "Girls, come on. This isn't productive," he says. "We're here to help Mom and Dad. Not make things worse."

"And what's your plan for doing that, huh, PJ?" I ask irritably. "You got fifty grand in a shoebox somewhere that we don't know about? You gonna make everything right?"

He opens and closes his mouth a few times like a fish out of water, and then his eyes slide away from mine and onto the table. And because I know my brother, I know he's in falling into the middle of a shit storm of guilt right about now. But at the moment, I can't bring myself to care.

I turn on Dutch. "What about you, sissy? You got that four grand to give back? You planning to sell the Benz out there so you can pay them back for the cost of your wedding? Because I sure don't remember — "

"Anika, so help me God, don't finish that sentence."

"Why not? How's the sentence going to end?"

"It's going to end with 'I don't remember them paying for *my* wedding.'"

I roll my palms skyward, shrug. "What's wrong with finishing my sentence that way? You talked about telling the truth earlier, right? Well, *that's* the truth. They didn't contribute a *dime* to our wedding. They didn't even *offer.* Jenny and I paid for everything out of our own pockets."

"Grow up, Anika."

"Seriously, guys," PJ says in a warning voice, "this really isn't help — "

But I'm not done.

"I grew up a long time ago, Dutch. Unlike some people, *I* didn't have a choice in the matter."

Sherry cries harder. Dutch bounces her up and down, but keeps her eyes locked on mine.

"I am so sick and tired óf you using your sexual orientation as a whiny excuse for all the things that didn't work out in your life exactly the way you wanted them to."

My head jerks back. "Since when have I used the fact that I'm gay as an excuse?"

"Since you were in high school!" Dutch spits. "But you

know what? Have you ever considered that maybe the fact that Mom and Dad are closer to the rest of us has less to do with the fact that you're a lesbian and more to do with the fact that you're a selfish *bitch?"*

I slap my hands on the table, push myself up to my full height. I usually avoid towering over my siblings, but for once, I don't care that they have to crane their necks to look up at me.

"I don't need this," I say. "And I don't know where you think *you* get off, when it's the rest of you who're responsible for this restaurant going under. But I guess I shouldn't be surprised. You'd always rather point fingers than step up and do the work."

I turn to leave.

"That's right, Anika, just walk away. Talk your big game about showing up for us and doing the work, and then walk out. Because that's what you do best." She flaps her hand at me condescendingly, like she's shooing away a pesky fly. "Run on home to Switzerland. Let everyone else pick up the pieces you leave behind. Just like you did to Jenny."

I spin around. *"What* did you just say?"

"You heard me. Whine about us not supporting your relationship all you want, but everyone knows how hard Jenny tried to get you to stay. You think we don't know about how she *begged* you not to leave? The same way you begged *her* after Rhianna?"

I feel like I've been slapped. "How do you even know

about Rhianna?"

"How do you think? We live in Marcine."

I throw my hands in the air. "Oh my God. This is *exactly* why I fucking *hate* Ohio."

I let the door bang shut behind me, hoping it's not too late to apologize to my baby brother.

Chapter 33: Gerry makes a speech.

I find Gerry around back, smoking next to the dumpster. His eyes are cloudy and red, but I suspect it's not from cigarette smoke. He takes a last, deep drag when he sees me coming, then shakes his head, crushes out his cigarette on the brick wall and flicks the butt away.

"I'm sorry," I say when I get close enough. "Dutch pissed me off, and I said something I didn't mean."

He grunts. "Dutch pisses everyone off, eventually."

It's his way of saying he accepts my apology.

"Yeah. But I still shouldn't have said it. And it's wrong, anyway. You're not fucked-up."

He shrugs. "May as well call a spade a spade. I'm the family fuck-up. Everybody knows it. Always have been. Always will be."

"You're not. You're the family success story."

He scoffs. "Says the professional fucking athlete."

"You *are*. It took guts, getting clean, coming back here." I fall silent for a moment. We stare out together at the grey horizon. "You know how this town is," I continue, glad he wasn't inside to hear Dutch's comment about Rhianna Fucking Jerkins. "Everyone always running their mouths. Everyone up in everyone else's business." I nudge him with my elbow. "Everyone knowing your story.

But you came back anyway. That's not what a fuck-up does."

He shakes his head. "That's exactly what a fuck-up does. Comes home with his tail between his legs, begging his Mom and Dad to take him in because he has nowhere else to go and they're the only people left on Earth he can even ask."

"You could've asked me," I say softly. "I would've taken you in."

"You live in Europe. I have a record. They probably wouldn't even let me into the friggin' country."

He's right, but I don't say so out loud.

We go back to staring at the horizon. Soul Mountain's on the outer edge of town, so behind the restaurant, there's more-or-less nothing. A vacant lot. A boarded-up convenience store. A patchwork asphalt road that stretches into a no-man's-land of empty fields until it hits the highway.

"You know why I started using?" he asks, pulling another cigarette from a crumpled cardboard box.

"Because your friends were doing it?" I guess.

"Naw. I mean, they were, but that's not why I got into it the way I did. I started using because I was like, 'What's the fucking point?' I was looking around at everybody, and it was like, what were they doing, really? Why were they working so hard?" He lights his cigarette up, takes a drag, exhales the smoke through his nostrils. "Take Dad, for example. He runs away from Nepal, gets treated like a fucking slave at his brother-in-law's restaurant, scrimps and saves, gets to Ohio, slaves away some more, only to get laid off from his job a few months after he gets here. And he and Mom, they go from job to job, plant to plant, layoff to layoff, and they work and pinch pennies and they scrimp some more and finally they open the restaurant, and they *bleed* for that fucking thing, and meanwhile their kids are all fighting with each other, and fighting with everybody else, and *nobody's* all that fucking happy, and it's just like... why? For what? People struggle and struggle and struggle, and then — then they just... die. And that's it. A bunch of struggling with a fucking *death* at the end. And I figured, if I had to go through all that too, at least I was going to have some fun along the way. At least I'd find a way to get high."

I turn my head, study my brother's profile. "That's pretty fucking bleak, Ger."

"Yeah, well. That was how I saw things for a long time."

I note the past tense in his words. "And now? You still see it that way?"

"No. I don't. Which is why I came back. I mean, besides the fact that I needed Mom and Dad's help to get on my feet again."

He smokes in silence for a minute or two, and I just wait, because I know this side of Gerry. He's always had a dark, philosophical streak to him that none of the rest of us really have, a deep vein of nihilism that I've never really understood. And he doesn't show this side of himself to many people, so when it comes out, I just give him space, let him say what he needs to say.

"You know how they say addicts have to hit rock bottom before they're ready to get clean? I kept falling and falling, and I thought I just didn't have a fucking bottom, but I finally hit mine," he says after another drag. "Right before I decided to get clean once and for all. I was in Texas. San Antonio. Don't ask me how I got there, I don't even fucking know. I was with some guys, and some skanky meth-head girl, holed up in some shooting gallery or another outside of town. You know what a shooting gallery is, right?"

I nod, remembering the term from one of the "family days" I went to during Gerry's first couple rounds of rehab. It's a place where junkies go to shoot up, the kind of place that used to be called a "crack house," until crack went out of style and heroin came back in.

"Anyway. We'd been pushing too hard for too long, me in particular, and I overdosed." He crushes the cigarette out, flicks it away. "I died, Ani. Literally fucking died."

He turns, searches my face a moment, maybe checking to make sure I'm taking him seriously, then looks away. "I saw the tunnel, the white light, all that shit. And I was floating away, looking down on my body, looking down on all the other nodding fucking junkies, and I felt better than I had in my whole sorry-ass life. Higher than any high I'd ever known. Because that white light? It was like... just love, man, pure fucking love. Connected to everyone. To everything. So there I am, floating up into the light, right? *Merging* with all this love. *Disappearing* into it. And I'm looking down on my body and on everyone else in the shooting gallery, and then I have this thought: 'What a waste.' That's what I think. 'What a waste, there's so much love to give, so much love to have and to share, and these guys? They're never going to know that. They're just going to go from shit hole to shit hole, thinking that's all life is. Just like I did.'" Gerry sniffs hard, meets my eyes. "And as soon as I have that thought? Boom." He snaps his fingers. "I'm back in my body. Sitting up. Gasping for air. And you can call bullshit if you want, but I know I got sent back here for a reason. I'm supposed to share that love with people. To make things better. To help people get a little taste of what I got." He turns away from me, shakes his head a few times. "I probably sound like I'm fucking crazy," he mutters.

"It's not crazy, Ger." I feel the tears spill onto my cheeks, let them stay there a few seconds before I wipe them away. "That's why you came back home? Because of... the love?"

He attempts a smile. "Yeah. I have a lot of love I want to give back. Figured I should start with my family." There's a pause, and he sighs. "I get that I owe everyone. But sometimes? With all the drama? It's hard to remember that's what I'm here for."

His words trigger another round of tears for some

ANDREWS / ANIKA TAKES THE LONG WAY

reason, and with the lump that's clamping around my vocal cords, I just nod instead of trying to speak. Finally, I clear my throat a couple times and say quietly, "Yeah. Yeah, I hear ya on that one, baby brother."

We stand in silence next to the dumpster for a few more minutes. Gerry starts to pull another cigarette from his pack, thinks better of it, puts the pack back in his pocket.

"Hey, can I ask a favor?" I say.

He shrugs.

"Could you give me a couple hours between lunch and dinner? Just maybe from three o'clock to five o'clock? And then I promise I'll be back before the dinner rush."

"Sure."

"Why don't you take off for now?" I suggest. "I can handle lunch by myself. Maybe you could come back at three, when I leave."

He adjusts his baseball cap. "It's okay. It's not like I have anywhere else to be."

"Oh yeah? How are those applications for school coming along?"

"They're not. I haven't really worked on them in a couple weeks. Not since we found out Momma's sick."

"Then go home," I say. "Work on your applications for a while. Just be back by three."

#

Dutch and PJ are gone by the time I get back inside,

which is probably for the best. Lunch is a little busier than usual, since it's a Saturday, but nothing we can't handle. Gerry returns a little before three, giving me a chance to run home, change clothes, air up the dusty playground ball at the bottom of my closet and still make it to the park by Jenny's old house before three-thirty. Since it's Saturday, I'm expecting to have to fight for court space, but it's cold and the grey sky has turned into the lightest of drizzles, so there's only two little kids there when I arrive, and I take the side of the court they're not using.

It's nice to have a ball in my hands again; I've spent nearly a week away from courts and balls and sneakers, and the first shot I take brings pure relief. It's that *Ahhh...* feeling that Dutch gets from shopping and PJ gets from eating and Gerry used to get from sticking a needle in his arm.

We all have our addictions, I suppose. Maybe the four of us are more alike than we like to admit.

I chase the ball, shoot, rebound, shoot, chase the ball again. I fall into a comfortable rhythm, find myself wishing Alex were here so I could kick her ass. Wishing Alex were here so I could talk through all the things going through my head right now. Because there's a lot on my fucking mind — Soul Mountain, money, Mom's cancer, Dad, Dutch, Amy, Jenny, divorces, drug addictions. And the speech Gerry gave out by the dumpster in between pulls on his cigarette.

It's mainly the speech that I keep coming back to,

rebounding it in my head over and over again, like it's a ball that just fucking refuses to fall through the hoop.

Love.

Family.

Connection.

The past.

The future.

Paying it back.

Paying it forward.

Getting my life together.

"You came home because your career's over and you don't know what else to do. Look me in the eye and tell me I'm wrong." That keeps coming back to me, too. And as much as I hate to confirm Dutch's high opinion of herself and low opinion of me, I have to admit that she usually has a way of being right about these sorts of things.

By the time the alarm I set on my phone goes off at four-fifteen, I think I have a plan. It's a crazy fucking plan — scary as shit, too, that's for damned sure. But it's a plan.

Chapter 34: The beginnings of a backbone.

A text from Dutch appears on my phone screen when I'm almost back to Soul Mountain.

Sorry. I was out of line
it reads.

"Goddamned straight you were," I mutter, but I don't slide the message to reply because, you know, texting and driving and all that shit. Besides, I'd rather make her stew on it a while.

In all, it's very typical Dutch behavior. When she gets freaked out about something, especially if said "something" might be just a teensy-weensy bit her fault, she tends to revert to blaming other people. I'm not angry about it, not really. It's just Dutch. Just like running off to the basketball court until I calm back down is just me.

The good thing about Dutch is that, while most of the time she's high-strung and loud-mouthed and bossy like our mother, she has just enough of our father in her that she can eventually be made to see reason. Which is why I'll be able to get her to hear out my plan.

I get another text right as I'm walking into the restaurant, this one from Amy.

Dammit. I cracked my coffee grinder.

It's pretty much useless now.

#1stworldproblems

I grin like a giddy schoolgirl, because it's the first time Amy's texted me something like this. And by "something like this," I mean the kind of silly, mundane little details of daily life that friends and significant others send to each other. They are the details that, in and of themselves, don't carry any weight, but when taken as a whole, form the glue that binds two people's lives together.

I know it sounds like a minor fucking thing, but the text about the cracked coffee grinder lights me up from the inside out, like it's the best news I've heard all day. And given how my day has played out so far, it's kind of true.

> **You traveled all the way from Europe**
> **with your own coffee grinder?**
> I text back.

Doesn't everyone?
Amy asks.

> **Umm... no.**

> **Why are you making coffee now? It's almost 5. You won't sleep 2nite.**

I'm hoping I won't. ;-)

The grin on my face gets a little bigger as I shoulder open the door into the foyer. Just to mess with her, I write:

> **Cuz you have big plans to help Grace decorate the church until the wee hours of the morning?**

No. Try again.

> **Cuz you have a work conference call that starts at 5am GMT?**

Work? You blaspheme.

I laugh to myself. Katie, the teenage hostess, is standing behind the podium when I walk in, a spray bottle in one hand and a damp, white-grey rag in the other. I lift a hand in greeting.

"What do you think?" I ask her. "We gonna have another busy night tonight?"

She blows out a breath between pursed lips. "I hope not. You missed it last night. We literally had forty-minute wait times at one point."

I raise an eyebrow. "What was the problem?"

She shrugs. "Nothing. We were just really, really busy. People kept coming and coming. Gerry had to call your dad in to come help. And even with your Dad and Becker both on hot prep, it was still slammed until almost closing time."

I wince inwardly, guilt flashing briefly through my chest. I'd come back to Ohio to help, but I'd spent the busiest night of the restaurant week getting my rocks off at Grace Adler's bachelorette party.

My phone dings, and I glance down at it.

I should probably hang onto that guilt, but it gets slippery when I see Amy's text, which reads:

Should I come by around 10 ish?

Sounds good.

Course, I might be tired at 10.

I insert a sleepy-face emoji, followed by a wink.

I'm sure I can find a way to wake you up.

By which I mean I'll grab a coffee for you on my way. :-)

Like I said before. You're a tease.

She replies with a winking emoji.

Gotta run. Seeya in a few hours.

**Oh hey — are you any good with
business plans?**

Business plans?

You sure know the way to a girl's heart.

**It's a long story. Maybe we can talk
about it when you get here?**

'K

I hesitate a moment, and reply with a heart and kissy face emoji. Amy replies with a heart of her own, and I chuckle at the two of us, because we're both acting like a couple of sappy fucking teenage girls.

I head to the office. After I tie my apron on, I fire off a string of text messages to various people.

(1) To Dutch: **Yes. You were out of line. But I know I haven't exactly been the best sister in a while, either. I'm trying to change that. I swear that's why I'm here.**

(2) To my property manager in Phoenix: **Pls call me on Monday when you get a chance. Something important to discuss.**

ANDREWS / ANIKA TAKES THE LONG WAY

(3) To Jenny: **Can we meet on Monday? There's something I need to talk to you about.**

I'm finger-combing damp hair into a fresh pony tail when my phone dings with the first reply. I'm expecting Dutch but get Jenny, instead.

What if I just come by tonight?
she says.

Maybe around the time you guys close.
The kids will be asleep by then. I can slip
out for a few.

I shake my head, despite the fact that she can't see me do it, and pick up my phone from the desk, thumbs hovering above the keys. Even if it weren't for the fact that Amy's supposed to be by tonight at closing, I still wouldn't want Jenny coming by. She probably thinks it has something to do with what she said to me at the cabin the night before, and that's not the impression I want to give her.

Not tonight. Monday works.

Will you be at Grace's wedding
tomorrow? We could talk then.

Shit. I hadn't really thought about the fact that she'll be

at the wedding tomorrow.

Yes, but I don't want to talk there.

Monday.

Okay then. Monday.

See you at the wedding. :-)

I don't reply.

The janitor who lives inside my brain strolls down an interior corridor, pushing a cart overflowing with cleaning supplies and whistling Celine Dion under her breath.

"That's a lot of spray bottles and mop heads and paper towels," I remark. "What's it all for?"

"Oh, this?" she asks, waving a hand at her cart of supplies. "It's for the inevitable mess you're going to make at that wedding tomorrow."

"Mess? Why do you think the wedding's going to lead to a mess?"

She shrugs instead of replying, goes back to whistling and pushing her cart.

#

After exchanging a few texts towards the end of our busy Saturday night, Amy arrives at Soul Mountain at ten-thirty on the dot. I give her a light squeeze and drop a kiss onto her cheek when she walks through the door.

Her lips twitch up into a shy smile, the one that always surprises me and makes my heart skip a beat when it appears. Usually, Amy's so carefully badass — all shrewd intelligence and calculation mixed with just the right amount of aloof sarcasm. I haven't told her so yet, but as much as I like Badass Amy, I think I like Shy Amy even better. There's something about Shy Amy that's endearing, and when she shows up, I get this feeling like I've stumbled through a gate and into a secret garden, saturated with bright flowers and babbling water.

She looks me up and down, shy smile fading fast. "You look exhausted."

The words trigger an automatic reliving of my day, from the goodbye kiss I gave her this morning at the lakeside cabin, to my frank talk with Alex and Graham about my love life, to fighting with Dutch, hearing Gerry's speech, playing basketball for an hour, working through the dinner rush.

I shrug. "It's been a long day."

"Tell me about it over a drink?"

"Absolutely. But I need to help Gerry finish closing first."

Amy refuses my suggestion that she sit down and relax while we finish up odds and ends in the kitchen. She jumps in the way she did before, first helping Katie and Kiersten to clean the dining room, then tying on a full-length apron and snapping on yellow rubber gloves to help with the dishes. She speaks to Emir in easy, fluent Spanish as they scrub pots together; she trades good-natured barbs with Becker over her shoulder. All in all, it's hard for me to focus on what I'm supposed to be doing because I'm having so much fun watching her.

"I like this one," Becker tells me with a grin when I'm pulling out the trash bag on the hot prep side of the kitchen. "She's got more backbone than the other one."

He doesn't need to explain who he means by "the other one," nor do I need to ask.

"You might be right," I say.

"Oh, I *know* I'm right." He winks at me.

Chapter 35: Brotherly love.

Two rounds of drinks, one plate of nachos. Amy and I get the same booth in the shadowy back of Dillan's that we had a few nights ago, get the same twenty-something waitress as we did before. It's a lot louder tonight, though, because it's a Saturday, and so we're practically fucking shouting over the din of laughter and conversation to be able to hear each other.

We eat faster, drink faster, and when the second drink is drained, Amy turns to me and asks, "Do you want to get out of here?"

"And go where?"

I didn't know it was possible for a woman's eyes to go both smokey and shy simultaneously, but Amy pulls it off. "Back to my B&B…?"

I stand up. "I'll pay our tab."

#

I'll be honest with you. Alex was right when she said that sleeping with Amy on the third date, less than a week after we'd met, was fast, even for me. But after drinks at Dillan's and the invitation to go back to her B&B, I completely fucking admit that I'm hoping I'll get to sleep with her on the fourth date, too.

It doesn't end up going down like that. Instead, I ride

with her in the rental car back to the B&B, chatting about the weather and Grace's wedding. Somehow we end up talking about the restaurant's debt problem, which leads to telling her about my blow-up with Dutch, which leads to Gerry's speech.

"...and so I spent the afternoon at the basketball court, thinking about my life and my past and the mistakes I've made and what I want to do going forward." I look out the window, watch the houses rolling past us. "It's crazy how one little choice can set up a fucking chain reaction that changes your whole life, you know?"

"Like what?" Amy asks.

"Well, like Dutch had to bring up Rhianna Fucking Jerkins — this girl who — "

"Rhianna Jerkins? Star center for UConn, ended up in the WNBA in Indiana before she blew her knee out?"

I grin, because I'd momentarily forgotten what a women's sports junkie Amy is. "Yeah. *That* Rhianna Fucking Jerkins."

"So — why was your sister bringing up Rhianna Jerkins?"

"Because... I slept with her. When I was still married to Jenny."

It's dark in the car, but it doesn't escape me that Amy stares straight ahead, hands tightening on the steering wheel. "I thought you said Jenny was the one who cheated on you?"

"She did. About a year and a half after Rhianna...

happened. That's what I mean about how one thing can lead to a chain reaction of other things. I've always wondered if Jenny would've cheated on me if I hadn't done it to her first. And then maybe... I don't know, everything might've worked out differently. We might've stayed in Phoenix. Worked through our issues. Had kids together." I glance at her. "But then I probably never would've gone to Switzerland. And met you."

I reach across, squeeze her thigh and smile at her. She doesn't return the smile. She still isn't looking at me.

"When we were talking about sororities and college, didn't you say you'd always been loyal to Jenny?" she says.

"I was. The thing with Rhianna... it was a messed-up, one-time thing that happened when my team played hers. Jenny was in Phoenix, I was in Indiana."

Marty McFly snickers in the backseat. "You know you're just digging yourself in deeper, right?"

Amy says nothing.

"It was... we'd been having problems," I say, ignoring McFly. "I was on the road all the time for basketball. And even when I was at home, I wasn't at home. We tried to fix things. But it was like, everything we did, we got *further* apart instead of closer together."

Amy says nothing.

"Relationships," I say with a heavy sigh. "They're fucking hard. Right?"

"Yeah," she says softly. "They are." She looks over at

me, gives me half a smile. "And we all make stupid mistakes in our relationships sometimes."

I feel like she's given me a reprieve for a moment, so I grab onto the first change of subject that pops into my head. "So this guy Grace is marrying — Kyle? What's he like? He's not a tool or anything, is he?"

Amy's shoulders soften a bit. "He's not bad. For a straight white man. He's completely, insanely in love with Grace." She smiles as if she's remembering something from the distant past, lets out a laugh. "He'll treat her well. He already does — dotes on her." She shifts back in the car seat, lets go of the death grip she had on the steering wheel. Drops one hand into her lap. "It's endearing, to tell the truth. To watch someone be so utterly attentive and loving towards someone else. And — look, I love Grace, she's one of my best friends, and she's been there for me at times when no one else has, but she can be…"

I glance over, watch Amy search for the right words.

"Overbearing?" I suggest. "High and mighty? Oblivious to the feelings of others?"

Amy laughs, and the last of the dark cloud that had passed over her face when Rhianna came up disappears. "I wouldn't have chosen those exact phrases, but… yes. So I'm glad she's found someone who accepts her as she is. Warts and all."

I reach over, take the hand resting in Amy's lap. I lace our fingers together, bring the back of her hand to my lips, give it a light kiss before resting our hands together on the center console.

"We should all be so lucky," I say. "Given that we all have a few fucking warts."

"Yeah. Yeah, I guess you're right about that."

A few minutes later, we're lying on top of her neatly made bed at the B&B, each of us on our sides, facing each other, trading stories about childhood and college years and old crushes. One of my hands rests on the rise of her hip (which makes it sounds like we're all close and cuddly, but you have to keep in mind I have the wingspan of a fucking albatross, so actually we're a few feet apart), and one of her hands runs lightly up and down my arm as she talks.

I can't remember whose eyes start to dip closed first, or which one of us is the first one to say, "Should we get under the covers?" All I know is that when I open my eyes again, it's because sunlight is streaming in through the balcony window, filtering in through the gauzy white curtains that Amy's pulled only halfway shut. Sunlight dots my bare arm, softens Amy's sleeping face with a soft orange-yellow glow. Her back nestles into my chest, one of my arms is draped over her, the rest of my body curls around hers from above and below. Like Amy's a lowercase c and I'm an uppercase C.

My other arm is trapped beneath her heavy head, and even though it's uncomfortable with pins and needles and the feeling of cut-off circulation, I don't move it. I don't want to wake her. Or turn away.

Usually, when I wake up in a woman's bed, it's still

dark outside, and I dress quietly and slip out before she can wake. If she does wake, I mumble something apologetic and completely fucking made up about an early morning basketball practice and then leave anyway.

So it's been a long time since I've actually simply lain in bed and *held* someone. And it feels so fucking good that I kinda wouldn't mind if it lasted forever. The thought makes me wriggle closer, as if there is space between us that still needs closing. There's not, really. You couldn't slide a piece of fucking paper between us, but it doesn't stop me. The arm draped around Amy contracts a little, and in her sleep, she breathes out a contented sigh.

I let my eyes slip shut again, even though I know I probably won't sleep. There's still a lot on my mind. Sleep's probably going to be scarce for the next few days.

Or years.

Or decades.

#

PJ's in the kitchen when I get to Soul Mountain, shirt sleeves rolled up and a light sheen of sweat plastering his tight black curls to his temples.

"Hey, little bro number one," I call as I walk to the office.

"Hey, big sis number two," he answers.

He's bending over our industrial-sized rice cooker when I walk back out in my serving apron, finger-combing my thick hair into a ponytail.

"So hey, Peej?" I say, handing him an oven mitt. "You planning on being here all day? 'Cause I was hoping to leave around four-thirty or five to go to Grace Adler's wedding."

He closes the lid to the rice cooker, wipes sweat from his brow with one of his thick forearms as he turns. He catches his breath for a second, hands on his hips, and I suddenly realize PJ has gone corporate. He's not used to standing on the hot prep side of the kitchen anymore. When you're the restaurant owner instead of the sous chef, maybe you don't end up in the kitchen that often. Naw. You probably walk around the dining room, glad-handing and sucking up to your wealthier customers and people you suspect to be food reviewers.

"Grace Adler's getting married again?"

"Yeah. At St. Pete's today."

He uses the collar of his fancy shirt to wipe the bead of sweat off his bare upper lip. "I thought you didn't like her."

"I don't."

"So why are you going to her wedding? — which, yeah, I was planning to be here anyway, so no worries about leaving early."

"Well, because I…" But an unexpected wave of shyness about Amy overtakes me. It's one thing for Gerry to see me chumming around with her, to know I basically picked up the girl on an airplane — or she picked me up, whatever. But it's different with PJ. Where Gerry and I have always been a little rough around the edges, Dutch and PJ are both smooth, refined, sophisticated. Like a grade of wine we would never sell at Soul Mountain.

And — I'll be damned — I actually want him to approve of Amy.

"Wait," he says, eyes narrowing. "Are you going because you're hoping to run into Jenny?"

"What? No — no. Jenny's — she's — no, I'm not going because she's going to be there."

He takes the oven mitt off his hand. "So why are you going to the wedding?" PJ presses. "If you're not going to see Jenny and you don't like Grace Adler...?"

Gerry reappears, carrying a dishwasher rack of clean silverware. "I bet it's her new girlfriend."

"Girlfriend?" PJ asks.

"She's not my girlfriend," I say.

"Hmm... this kind of reminds me of high school. Or the Bible," Marty McFly says, suddenly materializing next to PJ. "Your siblings ask you about Jenny, you deny it. They ask again, you deny again."

"Hush," I tell McFly. To PJ, I say, "Her name is Amy. But we only met about a week ago. She's college friends with Grace. We've been... hanging out."

Gerry snorts. "Is that what they're calling it these days?"

I glare at him, but he and his silverware are already on their way out of the kitchen.

PJ turns back to the stove, stirs a big pot that smells like cumin and bay leaves with a giant ladle. "What's the story with Amy?"

A desire to start gushing about Amy hits me out of nowhere.

I want to tell him about our second kiss when she launched herself at me hard just to give the middle finger to the rednecks coming out of Dillan's.

I want to tell him about the way she weaseled her way into Pi Phi in college and nabbed Ohio State's star soccer player.

I want to tell him about how she cut to the chase the other night, told me she's getting too old for bullshit, and had me screaming into a superwoman pillow a half hour later.

I want to say all that, and I feel like, out of all three of my siblings, PJ would be the one who would actually listen. He would lean against the metal table behind him, and he would cross his arms against his barrel-sized chest, and smile slightly, and listen.

But I don't gush. I just shrug. "She's... I haven't met anyone like her in a while."

Even though I don't gush, he nods, still wearing that empathetic PJ smile. Then the smile morphs into a thoughtful frown. "But wait. You said she's in town for Grace's wedding? So this is only a short-term type of thing?"

"I... maybe. We've talked about that. I think we're

both at a place in our lives where we're open to, well, trying something. Even after she leaves Ohio and I... go wherever."

"And what *are* you going to do next?" PJ asks. His voice softens. "Is it true what Dutch said — about your career being over?"

I think about the crazy plan I hatched shooting hoops the day before. The call I have in to my property manager in Phoenix, the meeting I'm planning with Jenny on Monday.

"I kind of wanted to talk to you about that," I say. "But not right now. Maybe Monday?"

"Mom's surgery is Monday, right?"

"Yeah, true. Tuesday?"

He nods. "Tuesday it is. Whatever you need."

I take a step forward, give him a light, affectionate punch in the shoulder. Because I'm not exactly a hugger. "Thanks, Peej."

"Sure thing, Ani."

And thanks to PJ, I get out of Soul Mountain a little before five, which gives me more than enough time to get home, take a shower, borrow a tie and a dressy shirt out of Gerry's closet, and make it to St. Peter's a few minutes after six o'clock.

Chapter 36: The last wedding I enjoyed was my own.

I push open the heavy wooden doors of St. Peter's and step inside, scanning the crowd for the now-familiar head of Jane Lane dark hair. But then I remember she's a bridesmaid. Which means she's probably off doing bridesmaid-y things. Which means I'll have to find someone else to sit with.

Damn. Why did I agree to this, again?

Some dude bumps into me from behind, mumbles a quick "Excuse me," heads off to my left. My eyes follow him, fall on a long table draped with an elegant white tablecloth, punch bowls and clear plastic glasses stacked on top.

I head for the punch table, adjust the black blazer I'm wearing as I walk. It's tight around my shoulders, and I'm tugging down on sleeves that are a few inches too short for my long arms. It's what I get for crossing the Atlantic Ocean with only a gym bag; I had to raid Gerry's closet for a dress shirt, dress pants, tie, and blazer. Fortunately, the kid's only a couple inches shorter than I am, and we share similar tastes in clothes. I ended up going with an all-black ensemble, accented with a red tie.

It's probably more suited for a funeral than a wedding — in fact, the whole get-up probably makes me look like a six-foot-three Blasian Grim Reaper.

A bunch of dudes stand around the punch bowls, sipping red punch. They're laughing, and from the snippets of conversations I catch, the humor apparently has to do with wives and shopping and where does all their hard-earned money go?

One of them glances at me when I reach for a plastic punch cup, scoots to the side out of my way with silence and a wary look.

I ignore him, ladle myself some punch. Slices of lime float around on its surface. I hope to God there's alcohol in it.

A cluster of women stand a few feet beyond the men, all of them coated in layers of too much makeup, wearing too much jewelry, and enough perfume that I can smell them from all the way over here. One of them says something that looks like it might be conspiratorial, lifting a well-manicured hand and placing it on the shoulder of a girlfriend like it's a punctuation mark at the end of whatever story she's telling, and the girlfriend immediately gasps and covers her mouth. Little kids weave around the knees of the women, carrying on their own conversations three feet below, and one little girl looks over at me, big blue eyes climbing up my Grim Reaper frame until they meet mine.

Annie. Ani.

I give the little girl a friendly smile, which leads to her immediately hugging the calves of the woman in front of her and burying her tiny face in the back of the woman's knees.

There are no daughters in my future, I remember. No sons, either.

I take a sip of the punch, glad to taste the familiar bite of rum.

"Remind you of anything?" asks a voice on my left.

I glance over to find Marty McFly standing at my elbow. He's in his usual uniform of jeans and that ridiculous puffy red-orange vest, but tonight he's also wearing a polka-dotted bow tie. Dressed up for the wedding, I guess.

"The last wedding I was at in Marcine was Dutch and Matt's," I say. "That was five years ago. But this doesn't remind me of that wedding. Theirs was outside. In the summer."

McFly nods thoughtfully, reaches behind me for a clear plastic punch glass. "I was thinking of another Marcine wedding. A church wedding a couple weeks before Christmas." He fills his punch glass and uses it to gesture at the crowd swelling in the church pews. "It was a lot smaller ceremony than this one, though. A more select crowd, you might say."

I know what he's talking about, but I don't say anything.

"It was still a nice wedding, though," he continues.

"Remember? Simple but elegant. Intimate. You enjoyed it."

"I was so happy that day," I say.

"Would you go so far as to say it was the happiest day of your life?"

I think about his question for a moment, spin it around like a basketball in my mind.

"Maybe. I don't know."

"I can help you remember. We can go back there if you like. Then you can know for sure."

I shake my head. "Not now. This is about being here for Amy. *With* Amy. The last thing I need is to start thinking about my fucking wedding day."

He reaches up, puts his hand on my shoulder. "That's the funny thing about memories. They come on strong sometimes, whether you want them there or not."

\#

Back to the future: Sixteen years ago. My wedding day.

I choose a light grey tux for my wedding, a traditional thing with a slightly darker vest underneath, black tie tucking into it. Jenny had argued the choice with me, complaining that my color choices were too light for a winter-time wedding, and that the black tie wasn't cheery enough, but the grey and black is a nod to Rosemont

Raiders colors, and with Alex as my "best man," I wanted colors that we already knew looked good on both of us.

Jenny had intended to get married in the church she grew up in, a Lutheran place called St. Peter's, but the conservative old minister straight-up refused to marry us, so here we are in a Unitarian-Universalist church a few towns over, not quite all the way to Columbus. It's a disappointment to Jenny; a church whose sanctuary decor includes posters with liberal political slogans on them doesn't match her idea of a "traditional wedding," and I misstep by reminding her that we're not exactly a traditional Ohio couple. The statement earns me a lot of tears and at least one night of yelling in the weeks leading up to our wedding, but eventually she accepts the UU, glad to find any church that will marry us and fulfill her little girl dreams of an old-fashioned white wedding.

There are only a few minutes to go, and I'm standing in front of the altar to the minister's left, hands cupped before me, bouncing up and down on my toes.

Alex catches my eye from the back of the room, where she waits near the sanctuary entrance. She gives me a silent admonishment by raising a single eyebrow.

Relax, the look says. *Stop fidgeting.*

I force my feet to be as still as my hands, turn my head fully towards the sanctuary entrance, the place where Jenny will walk in. Despite the fact that I've forced myself into stillness and set my jaw as if I'm facing Rhianna Fucking Jerkins at a tip off, butterflies flit around inside my stomach, trying to escape up into my chest or throat.

I catch a glimpse of my mother and father when I turn towards the entrance, and the sight does nothing to calm my nerves.

My mother's never gotten to the point where she totally accepts my relationship with Jenny; at best, she accepts that she's not going to change me, but that doesn't mean she approves. I'm pretty certain that I have my father to thank for what little reluctant acceptance I have from her. I imagine he probably pointed out that between having a gay second daughter and having no second daughter at all, a gay daughter is at least slightly better.

As it is, her lips are pressed together into a tight line, and unseeing eyes stare straight ahead. While I watch, my father reaches into her lap, wraps a hand around one of hers, and his knuckles literally go white with the force of his squeeze.

She's not crying, though. At least there's that. On the other side of the aisle, Jenny's mother — who I still think of and address as "Mrs. Pearson," even after all these years — is crying up a storm. And trust me, these aren't the kind of happy tears you usually see at weddings. These are, "Oh my fucking God, my baby is marrying a fucking *woman*. No, scratch that — she's marrying a beast-sized *black* woman."

At least she came. Jenny's father didn't even show up. One of our old friends from high school, Mason, is the one giving Jenny away.

I purse my lips for a second until I realize I'm mirroring my mother's expression.

Instinctively, as if I'm back on the court and waiting for my point guard to call out the play, my eyes shift back to Alex's. She gives me the tiniest of smirks, a slight curl at the corner of her mouth. And the smirk has the same effect as the eyebrow did a moment earlier. I relax a little further into my wide-legged stance.

Something behind Alex draws her attention, and she disappears from the doorway. Moments later, the first few chords of "Somewhere Over the Rainbow" waft out of the cellos sitting in the corner. The song had been my compromise with Jenny; she'd wanted the traditional "Here Comes the Bride" song, but the thought turned my stomach, and I'd argued for something more modern. We'd settled on "Somewhere Over the Rainbow," even though I told her it had always sounded like a mournful song to me. She agreed enough that we went with the Hawaiian version of the song, which is slightly more upbeat, but then she hired these two cello players to make it fancier, and now it sounds like a fucking funeral dirge. And it's instrumental, but I can't help but think of the lyrics, and the lyrics are actually kinda fucking dark, right?

Oh, somewhere over the rainbow way up high
And the dream that you dare to, why oh, why can't I?

But Jenny walks in, arm-in-arm with Mason, and of

course she takes my breath away. I forget about my mother scowling next to my father, the crying Mrs. Pearson and the absent Mr. Pearson; I forget about the fact that St. Peter's wouldn't marry us and we had to come all the way out here to this hippie UU church; I forget that I hate Hawaiian, ukulele *a la* cello version of "Somewhere Over the Rainbow." All I see is her. And I can't help it — I'm an emotional fucking person — I start to cry.

White and radiant and glimmering and beautiful — she's perfect. So perfect. Wearing a smile so wide it takes up her whole face, blonde hair pinned up and decorated with baby's breath, her simple, strapless white gown following the contours of her tiny Tinkerbell's body, sweeping the floor behind her. Her eyes meet mine. The moment she sees the tears rolling down my cheeks, her brown eyes go glassy and wet.

All these years of waiting, our tears say to each other. *Everything we've had to go through to get to this moment. All the time apart. All the late nights, crying to each other over the phone, not sure if we could sustain a long-distance relationship even one more day... After all that, we're here. We're here, and we're going to do this; we're going to be together for the rest of our lives, and anyone who says otherwise can go to hell.*

After Jenny comes her cousin Rebecca, her hand looped around PJ's elbow. I'd wanted Gerry to be a groomsman, too, but my junkie baby brother has been too messed up to be reliable lately, so it's Ophelia who walks in behind PJ.

She's being a good sport about the whole thing and is wearing one of our grey tuxes, and dutifully holding Grace Adler's dainty hand on her elbow, but Grace herself looks very uncomfortable and irritated to have been matched up with a female groomsman.

(Female groomsman. Is that like jumbo shrimp?)

Alex and Jenny's sister bring up the tail end of the procession, and, thankfully, Jenny's sister seems a lot more at ease paired with Alex than Grace does with Ophelia.

But once Jenny's in front of me, I don't notice or care what the hell any of the rest of them are doing. I take her hands in mine, and even though I try to listen to the minister, the rest of the world fades away, and she and I are the only two people left on Earth.

#

Back to the present

Movement and the *clink-clink-clink* of plastic punch glasses bouncing into the trashcan pull me out of my memories. The men and women around me disperse, finding their places in the pews. I trail a few feet behind them, uncertain about where to go. Since Amy's in the wedding itself, I don't really have anyone to sit with.

I walk slowly down the aisle, scanning for faces I know. There's Heavy-and-Pink sitting on the end of a row, a couple orange-headed preschoolers next to her. I sweep my eyes away before she sees me, find Lisa Vanderwerf on the other side. I give her a polite nod, but keep walking.

As if some sort of weird radar system has been activated by my presence, a head of long blonde hair turns, and the brown eyes I'd been remembering only a few seconds earlier meet mine. They're glassy, and I find myself wondering if Jenny had been replaying the same memory as me. Given the abrupt end to our conversation on Friday night, I expect her to look away again, but she doesn't. She slides down the pew a few feet, makes room for me.

I hesitate. Then take a seat next to my ex-wife.

"Hey," I say.

"Hey," she says. The word is a sigh.

The processional music begins, and the whole church rises as one body.

Chapter 37: I just have to admit that it's all coming back to me.

Back to the future: Sixteen years ago. My wedding night.

We have a flight leaving for Phoenix the next morning; our honeymoon will consist of her doing some house shopping while I start practicing with my new team. Until we buy a house, we'll be living in the finished basement of a new teammate, so this night, holed up together with all our luggage in a hotel less than a mile from the John Glenn Columbus International Airport, might be the only space and time we will have to ourselves for the next several weeks.

I'm tipsy, but I manage to get the door open anyway and sweep a giggling, slightly tipsier Jenny off her feet as I cross into the hotel room.

"Ani!" she squeaks when I pick her up. "What are you doing?"

"I thought this was what you were supposed to do — carry your bride across the threshold."

"You carry your bride across the threshold of your first *home,*" she informs me. "Not across the threshold of a *hotel* room."

I laugh. "Well, sorry, little miss wedding expert. I guess I've got some more carrying of you to do later."

She doesn't even let me make it to the queen-sized bed dominating the middle of the small room. Still in my arms, she's climbing me like I'm a human jungle gym, gripping my shoulders, pulling herself up until she can reach my mouth, pushing a hot, insistent, alcohol-tinted kiss into me. And even though we've done this a thousand times before, even though we've been doing this since high school, my knees go watery and my heart races as a wave of heat cascades down my body.

I stumble forward on now clumsy, uncooperative legs, barely managing to land Jenny gently on her back before I'm leaning over her, landing nipping little kisses up her throat, across the line of her jaw, over to her ear.

Jenny reaches up, digs greedy fingers into my thick hair, pulls me down closer to her. Her lips, then her teeth, find my earlobe. I shiver involuntarily.

"Ani," she whispers into my ear, hot breath tickling and sending another wave of heat coursing through my body, "we did it. We're married. You're my wife. After everything…"

When she trails off, I push myself up a few inches, study her face. Her brown eyes are wide, shining with tears again, just like during the ceremony.

"Yes, baby," I say, stroking her cheek, pushing stray hairs from her face. "We're married. Wife and wife."

The tears spill over, sliding down her temples, leaving little rivers of mascara. "I wasn't sure if we'd ever get to this night."

I kiss her. I try to put all my tenderness, all my love, all my years of patience into my lips, my mouth, my tongue, so that she can feel my answer, know that I'm telling her not to worry, that she never needed to worry, that she'll never need to worry again.

"Of course we got here," I say when I break the kiss. "I always told you we would. We're soulmates, right?"

She pulls me back down into another kiss, but there's nothing tender about it. She ends it by tugging on my bottom lip with her teeth. "Get me out of this dress," she says, voice husky.

It takes both of us working together, along with a series of giggles, to get her out of the form-fitting wedding dress. Along the way, we throw the blazer, vest, and tie from my tux unceremoniously onto the floor, and she rips at buttons without any regard for my expensive dress shirt.

When we're both bare, I straddle her hips on my knees, careful to keep the weight of my big body off of her. Jenny's skin is milk-white and marble-smooth, its only mar a birthmark above her left breast, the place where her mother used to tell her she was kissed by an angel. She's perfectly proportioned, if a little too skinny, like a blonde-haired, brown-eyed china doll. I run the pad of my thumb over the birthmark, observing the contrast between my copper-colored skin and her pale skin.

My thumb trails down, circles her bare, pink nipple until it puckers upright. Her eyes flutter closed, and her cheeks flush with heat as she lets out a long, ragged breath from her open mouth.

"You're beautiful, Jenny."

She opens her eyes, wraps a hand around my wrist, tugs me towards her. *"You're* beautiful."

I resist her tug, shake my head. "I'm not. Dutch got all the beautiful genes. I got the King Kong genes."

She tugs harder on my wrist. "You're wrong. Dutch got the snotty genes. You got the beautiful, brave, strong, funny, talented, wonderful, kind, and loyal genes."

I follow her tug this time, kiss her on one eyebrow, then the other, then her mouth. And even as I lower myself into the kiss, tongue brushing against hers and hands sliding down across her bare chest, ribs, hips, core… I marvel at the way we fit together, at the way our disparate sizes are somehow completely perfect, completely complementary.

She gasps when my long middle finger slides through her wetness. I tease her throbbing clit with the tip of my thumb, then cup her with my whole hand as I swallow her gasp with another kiss.

"Ani," she says, the name vibrating as a moan against my lips. Fingernails scrape lightly up my back. "Please, baby… *Please,* I need to feel you insi — oh!"

She loses the ability to make words when my first two fingers slide inside her, and, God, I love her so much that I'm crying again, even as desire clouds over everything else. I push harder into her as her hips jerk and thrust against me. We breathe into each other, kissing all but forgotten except for the occasional graze of my teeth against her chin, her bottom lip. I can feel the coarse tips of hard nipples rubbing against my chest, and the sheen of sweat growing across both our bodies sticks us together momentarily as she pushes against me again.

The little noises I know so well, the breathy pants and moans and half-whispered curse words — because sex is almost the only time Jenny ever allows herself to curse freely — begin to emanate from her throat. It is the music of Jenny's arrival; it is my favorite song, the track I want to play on repeat for the rest of my life. And it turns me on so much that I drop my head to her neck, close my eyes, lick up her neck as I add a third finger below. She lets out a high-pitched, wordless cry, and less than a minute later, soft wet walls clench and close around my three fingers. I thrust one last time, earning a louder cry of pleasure, and I go still as I feel Jenny's fingernails decorating my back with eight purple half-moons. The dig of her nails hurts a little, but it's the kind of hurt that feels so good that I hope I'll wear the shape of her fingernails against my spine forever.

I pull out of her gently a few seconds later, but keep my hand between her thighs, holding her there, keeping her warm, the way she likes. Her legs clamp onto my hand, trapping it, and she wiggles close to me as I drop onto the bed beside her, catching my breath. She pushes her face into my side, drapes an arm across my torso.

The tickle of lips against my ribs breaks my skin out in gooseflesh. "I love you," she says into my side. "Hold me."

"Always," I answer obediently, pulling my hand out from between her thighs and wrapping it around her back, squeezing her close to my side. "Til death do us part."

"Til death do us part," she answers, trailing a hand down my stomach and weaving the tips of her fingers through the thick, black hair below.

I turn my face, curl forward until I can kiss the top of her head, then relax back onto the pillow. And as I lay there in the darkening room, the sound of airplanes reminding me of our trip to Phoenix tomorrow, I find myself wondering, and not for the first time — how could someone so small end up taking up my whole world?

#

Back to the present

"...And do you, Grace, take Kyle to be your lawfully wedded husband, to live together after God's ordinance in the holy state of matrimony?"

"I do," says Grace Adler. Tears glisten like jewels on her cheeks, and even I have to admit she looks very pretty in her elegant gown, with her red hair quaffed and pinned atop her head.

"Will you love him," the minister says, "comfort him, honor and keep him so long as you live?"

"I will."

My eyes and attention wander from Grace to Amy, who, in her springtime green bridesmaid dress, which comes down about mid-calf, and with her nearly black hair pinned up behind her, looks at least twice as beautiful to me as the bride does. She must feel my eyes on her, because her gaze flits down the aisle, and when she sees me, she gives a soft smile. The shy Amy smile. The gentle, open one. The Amy not being a hard-ass business woman smile. I smile back, repress a childish need to wave.

She looks away.

A thought occurs to me, and I lean down, whisper in Jenny's ear. "Hey. How come you're not up there? How come you're not a bridesmaid?"

An older woman on Jenny's other side turns her head to glare at me, and I straighten back up.

Jenny puts her hand on my leg, squeezes. "I'll tell you later," she whispers back.

She doesn't remove her hand from my thigh. I don't shift away from it, which... You know how they say "hindsight is twenty-twenty"?

Yeah. Well. Forgive me for having a moment of nostalgia.

Chapter 38: Never fuck with a Tinkerbell.

You would think, with Grace Adler being Grace Fucking Adler, that we could've had a better place than Dillan's Bar & Grill for the reception. But whatever. Dillan's is walking distance from St. Peter's, it has a dance floor, they never skimp on alcohol, and it's exactly the kind of rednecky, small-town northern Ohio joint that seems to fit Grace.

And if it fits Grace, it fits her second husband Kyle even better. It doesn't take much time after the champagne toasts and the cake cutting for his boys to start to get rowdy and loud. Blazers come off, ties get draped on the backs of chairs, and the dance floor swims with white guys who don't have any rhythm when they're sober, let alone drunk.

I roll my own sleeves up as the temperature inside Dillan's starts to heat up. We've already eaten (I'm still hungry), and Amy's hitting the open bar to get us another round. I glance around, people-watching while I wait.

Amy reappears before me a minute later, sets two drinks on the table. "Sorry that took so long. The barkeep kept trying to flirt with me."

I give her a lopsided grin. "Yeah? And what did you tell him?"

"That my girlfriend wouldn't be very pleased if I let

him give me his number."

Girlfriend. It's the first time Amy's used the word. She glides over it as if it's no big deal, while my brain snags on it. The janitor inside my head flips through her massive key ring, unlocks a door.

"What did he say to that?" I ask.

"That he bet I hadn't met the right guy yet if I was seeing a girl." She smiles wickedly. "I pointed to you in the corner and said, 'See the professional basketball player sitting in the back there? The one with at least six inches and probably twenty pounds on you? I know when I've found the right girl.' And he looked at you and I *swear* he went ghost-white."

"He did?"

"Mm-hmm. And he literally said, 'Your girlfriend's Anika Singh? Aw, shit. Never mind.'"

"Really?" I ask, mildly surprised. I lean around Amy, try to get a glimpse of the barkeep to see if I would recognize him as fast as he recognized me. Maybe we went to high school together. Sure, people in this town knew me when I carried our girls' basketball team to two state championships in a row, but that was twenty years ago.

Her eyes twinkle. "Seems I'm dating a local celebrity."

Girlfriend. Dating. A warm feeling grows in my stomach, a pleasant buzz that has nothing to do with alcohol.

"Dance with me?" I say.

"Let's finish our drinks first."

But one more drink becomes two more drinks; two more drinks becomes three, because now a tipsy Amy decides she wants to see if she can antagonize the barkeep a little more. I swear I don't condone the action, but somehow I find myself dragged to the bar anyway, ordered to look tall and intimidating as I glare and cross my arms tightly against my chest and tower over the barkeep, who's probably a perfectly respectable five-nine or five-ten, while Amy orders another drink. It seems like a mean thing to do, but it amuses Amy, so I go along with it.

Even I'm starting to feel the buzz by the time Amy drags me onto the dance floor.

I might be King Kong-huge, but I still have rhythm, and I know how to use what my Momma gave me. But still, when you're as big as I am, when you stick out the way I do, there's something that always feels inherently awkward about being on a dance floor, especially if you're this giant black dyke on the floor surrounded by a bunch of scrawny, mostly redneck middle aged white people. So I start out hesitant. But it turns out that Amy's years as an Ohio State going to Pi Phi mixers paid off, because the girl can dance.

She's definitely drunk at this point, but she guides me through slow songs and fast ones, guides my big paws to where she wants them — which ends up being her waist, her hips, her sides, her shoulders. Everywhere, more-or-less. And I should feel self-conscious about some of the looks we're starting to draw, and fucking defensive about the way some of the men are ogling her, but I'm both too

buzzed and too enamored with my Tinkerbell-sized Jane
Lane to care. We bump and we grind and then we take it
easy with a few slow songs, but eventually I get to the point
where the need to pee overcomes my need to run my hands
down that sweat-damp green bridesmaid dress before me.

At the end of another slow song, I lean down and kiss
Amy on the cheek. "I'm going to go to the bathroom."

Her eyes widen and she grins. "Oh. Okay. Let's go."

I chuckle. "Amy. Get your mind out of the gutter. I
mean I'm actually going to go, like *go,* go."

Her face falls. "You weren't just saying that to get me
some place more private?"

I land another kiss on her cheek. "I'm sure I'll get you
some place more private later, but let's make it at your
B&B and not Dillan's. Alright?"

It's hard to tell if her cheeks flush from blushing or
from drinking or from the heat of a half-hour of dancing.
At any rate, her eyes cut away from me as she reddens, and
she glances towards our cowed barkeep. "I'll get us more
drinks while you're gone."

I shake my head. "I've had enough. And I don't want
you passing out on me." I waggle my eyebrows
suggestively. "Not when I have plans for you for later."

This time, it's definitely not the dancing or the drinking
that makes her go crimson to the tips of her adorable little
Tinkerbell ears. She reaches up, wraps a hand around my
loosened necktie, pulls me down to her level. Kisses me
hard.

"Don't be gone too long," she whispers in my ear once she breaks the kiss.

I lick the taste of her off my numb lips. "Believe me. I won't."

I head to the women's room, completely fucking missing the fact that a blonde head turns as I pass by, and also completely fucking oblivious to the fact that a blonde, wispy, different Tinkerbell of a woman follows me through the crowd.

#

I'm finishing in the bathroom, washing my hands at the bathroom sink, when a stall door squeaks opens and Jenny walks out. She takes the sink next to mine, turns the hot water on, reaches across me to pump soap into her palm. Meets my eyes in the mirror.

"Hi," she says.

"Hey. Having a good time?"

In the mirror, her eyes shift from mine to her own. "Not really."

I turn my water off. "Why not? A night off from the kids. Your best friend from high school marrying a guy who seems halfway decent. Free food. An open bar. What's not to like?"

She looks down, scrubs at hands that are quickly turning a scalded red. Back of the right hand. Back of the left hand. Palms. Fingers lacing together. It's the same hand-washing ritual she's had since high school.

Hot water still sending up little clouds of steam from the sink, she reaches around me for a paper towel, not seeming to notice the way the motion brushes her left arm across my right. She turns the water off with the paper towel.

"I'm not overly fond of weddings," she says. "If it weren't for the fact that it's Grace, I wouldn't have come."

I cock my head in both suspicion and surprise. "You always loved weddings. Said they were romantic. And that a woman is always at her most beautiful on her wedding day."

"Did I?"

"You did. And you cried at every wedding we ever went to. Remember when Graham and Alex got married? And we — "

She grabs my forearm. "Please don't talk to me about Graham and Alex's wedding."

I look down at the porcelain-white hand wrapped around my tan forearm. "Why not? We had a really nice time."

"Because I can't think of *their* wedding without thinking of *our* wedding. And ever since you sat down next to me in the church, I haven't been able to get our wedding out of my mind."

Alex and Graham got married two years after Jenny and I did — a chance for Alex and me to repurpose our grey tuxes, a chance for Jenny to plan yet another romantic church wedding, since Graham wasn't much into the planning side of things herself. And like us, they married right before Christmas. Also like us, basketball season ensured that their honeymoon was approximately non-fucking-existent. Probably nothing more than a hot night or two in a hotel room. A lot like...

I pull Jenny's hand off me gently. "Maybe thinking about our wedding isn't a good idea right now. For either of us."

Her eyes meet mine. Neither one of us says anything for what seems an extremely long fucking time.

"You, too, huh?" she asks. Her voice is small.

I nod. Swallow. "You were... We were... It was a beautiful ceremony, you know. Even if it wasn't at St. Peter's like you wanted. And you..."

("Don't you fucking dare," says the janitor in my brain. She shakes a mop at me. "I *just* finished cleaning up in here.")

"...You were so beautiful that day. More beautiful than Grace Adler will ever be."

"Ani." The two syllables escape her lips like a soft prayer. Like a plea. A wish. Jenny's eyes flit from my eyes to my mouth.

I feel it coming before it happens, but I don't do anything to stop it. It tingles up my arms, my neck, into my face, my lips, the back of my throat. Blame it on alcohol. Blame it on nostalgia. Blame it on the fact that I've never had any willpower around Jenny.

Then the dam breaks and her hands are reaching up, curling into the fabric of Gerry's black dress shirt on either side of the collar, pulling me down at the same time that I step forward and wrap my hands around her waist. Our lips don't so much meet as they collide, two mouths each intent upon devouring the other, desperate and hungry and needy.

I *should* catch the movement of the bathroom door out of the corner of my eye, but my eyes have fallen shut. I *should* hear the door squeak on its hinges, but all I hear is the tiny moan Jenny breathes into my mouth — a moan I haven't heard in more than five years, a sound that used to be the opening bars to my favorite song in the world.

No, I don't realize that someone else has walked in until I hear my name.

"Anika?" Amy calls as she rounds the corner into the bathroom foyer. "Did you fall — Oh, God."

Jenny and I are already splitting apart, pushing away from each other like repelling magnets, but it's too late. Amy stands wide-eyed in the center of the bathroom, both hands flying to her face, covering her nose and mouth, eyes immediately glassing over with tears.

Mother*fucker.*

Chapter 39: #TBT: A selfie of Amy hyperventilating.

Back to the future: Amy and Wendy, ten years earlier.

To fully understand what happens next, you have to rewind Amy's life, get into a #throwbackthursday from ten years earlier. You have to scroll past old photos of Katarina, a brooding Swiss-German, who broke up with Amy six or seven months before I met her on that Toronto to Cleveland flight; past Vera, a short-lived relationship with an American ex-pat in northern France who still wanted to live *la vie boheme*; and past Terri, a professor Amy dumped after two years when it became apparent that Terri was never going to be capable of settling down and offering any kind of actual commitment. The end of Terri had been the beginning of Switzerland; Amy agreed to the transfer because it got her away from southern New Jersey, away from an Ivy League lover who was ultimately more interested in organic farmer's markets and attending conferences on social justice than she was in Amy.

But before all of them — before serious Katarina and Peter Pan Vera and Pretentious Princeton Terri — there was Wendy.

Wonderful, wacky Wendy. The girl who would rush into a restaurant with paint streaking her hair and putty beneath her nails, dropping a breathless kiss on Amy's cheek before sitting across from her.

"Sorry I'm late, honey," Wendy says. "You know I've been blocked around that commissioned piece for the last week or two. But I *finally* figured out what I wanted to do with it today..." She waves her hands while she talks, describing colors and light, textures and brushstrokes, barely noticing in time that she's about to knock over her glass of water.

And Amy? Amy listens. She moves the innocent glass of water out of the way before Wendy knocks it over, and she listens. Not so much because she cares about light and color and brushstrokes, but because there's no one she cares about more than Wendy. There's no one who makes her feel freer than Wendy, no one else who sands down the sharp edges of her strict military upbringing in quite the same way. Because Amy is composed of timetables and deadlines, spreadsheets and mathematical models. And listening to Wendy describe her work this way... it's like Wendy's voice itself unwinds the uncomfortably tense knots deep inside Amy's heart.

Wendy doesn't bother to look at the menu before her. She's too intent on describing her latest revelation. But it's okay; Amy knows what Wendy likes. She ordered for her girlfriend ten minutes ago. It's only when the food comes that Wendy realizes that Amy ordered on her behalf. She stops talking long enough to look from the hot plate before her to Amy.

"You ordered for me?"

Amy nods.

Wendy smiles. She plants paint-stained palms on the table, leans across her hot plate to plant her mouth on her girlfriend's, not caring that they're in the middle of a restaurant in a suburb of Columbus, Ohio, not caring that people stare. Amy has always loved that about Wendy — the easy obliviousness to what other people see and think. Amy has always cared what others think far too much; Wendy is changing her without even meaning to.

#

It's a month after that bold restaurant kiss that Amy comes home to find the door to their apartment unlocked. It's not terribly surprising — it's Wendy, after all, and no matter how many times Amy reminds her to lock the door, the woman's flighty, dreamy brain just can't seem to hold the instruction.

"Wendy?" Amy calls as she steps inside, closing the door with her butt and dropping her keys into the hand-blown glass bowl on the coffee table. "Wen?" She thinks she hears noise coming from the bedroom, so she heads in that direction. She expects to find Wendy on the bed with her sketchpad in her lap, music playing softly on her laptop as she stares out the window in pensive silence.

Wendy's on the bed, alright. And there's something in her lap. But it isn't a sketchpad. It's a face. And the sounds Amy heard? The sounds are coming from Wendy. They're sounds Amy knows and loves, but they are private sounds, and she never thought she'd be hearing them like this.

Wendy's eyes are closed, her head is thrown back, her mouth is open. And the face between her legs — the face that, judging from the rest of the bare body attached to it, must belong to a male — is obscured by Wendy's thighs. Even though Amy's never seen the naked legs and back and hairy ass before her, she recognizes the back of the head. It's something about the bald spot, the way the wispy hair is combed over it but only poorly conceals it. It's the bald spot that belongs one of Wendy's MFA professors. Amy can't quite remember his name. Not now. Not in this moment.

The bundle of textbooks and binders cradled in Amy's arms tumbles to the ground with what might be a loud clatter, but Amy can't hear it. She can't hear anything anymore — she can't hear the traffic outside the apartment, she can't hear Wendy's whimpers of pleasure, she can't hear the sound of licking. The only thing she can hear is the sound of her heart, which sounds like a military marching cadence sped up to an unnatural rate. Blood rushes into her ears. Her legs water as if they are melting away from her. Without willing them to, her hands fly to her face, covering her nose and mouth.

My God, the rational part of her brain thinks, *I'm having a heart attack.*

When the books hit the wooden floor, the man's head jerks up from between Wendy's legs, and Wendy's eyes open.

Amy can see Wendy's mouth moving, can see words forming, but Amy can't hear them, either.

Amy? is what the mouth looks like it's saying.

Amy should know; she's seen that mouth say her name hundreds of times before. Under all circumstances. For many years.

But never a circumstance like this.

Amy? the mouth seems to ask again.

There's movement now; Wendy's trying to get up, the MFA professor with the bald spot rolls away from her, looks in Amy's direction with an expression on his face like a guilty child caught eating sweets. Except it's not chocolate that smears the black-and-grey hairs of his thin goatee.

If it really was a heart attack, I'd probably be dead by now, Amy reasons.

It's the last thought she has for a couple minutes, because she turns her back on the nightmare scene before her, intending to walk out of the room. But she doesn't get far. She takes only one step, and somehow the world goes black.

She regains consciousness on her own bedroom floor three minutes later,　flat on her back, *Theories of*

Management and Leadership textbook digging into her spine. Wendy's concerned face hovers inches above her own, damp palms on Amy's cheeks. Damp palms coated in the unfamiliar scent of a stranger.

"Baby? Amy?" Wendy says. And Amy observes that she can apparently hear again, which she takes to be a good sign. "Oh — thank God. Thank God, you're awake. When you fell, I thought — I really thought that maybe you — "

"Get your hands off of me," Amy says. She can hear, but she can't see clearly anymore, because tears blur her vision. Amy blinks away the tears, pushes her girlfriend back, manages to stand on two unsteady feet. She grabs her keys from the hand-blown glass bowl, slams the apartment door on her way out.

It's the first panic attack she's ever had. The second one comes when she's driving away from the apartment complex five minutes later, and she doesn't even see the silver pickup truck until the moment before it slams into the driver's side. The world goes black yet again, and this time it's Grace Adler's face that hovers above her own when she wakes — not in an apartment this time, but in a hospital bed.

"Ames? Are you actually awake?" Grace asks. "You had me worried out of my mind."

The panic attacks become a regular feature of Amy's life after that. They come on unexpectedly and predictably at the same time. Every time a meeting at work gets a little too stressful. Every time her step-mother calls her to give her more bad news about her father's health. Even when it seems like there's no reason to panic, a panic attack comes on. It comes on, and she tries to laugh at herself, *Why are you doing* this, *now? This is stupid. Stop it,* but telling her body to knock it off never works.

She tries medication. She gets counseling. But although they get fewer and further between, the attacks never leave. Neither do the scars that crisscross her abdomen, the left-over battle wounds from the car accident on the worst day of her life.

#

Back to the present

Like the rest of me, like my mother, like my sister, I have a big motherfucking mouth. And I've never been shy about using it. But with Amy standing there? Her feet rooted to the floor, her hands over her nose and mouth? Staring at me with these huge brown eyes full of a pain so sharp I can practically feel it slicing through my fucking soul?

I lose the ability to speak.

Not that I don't try. I open my big mouth. I try to will a sound to come out — even a single syllable, a squeak. But nothing comes. The moment stretches out like Silly Putty, going on and on and fucking on without breaking,

Amy and me and Jenny all standing in middle of Dillan's women's restroom in a collective, dumbfounded silence.

Amy's the one who moves first, swaying a little as she spins on her heel and heads away from us.

"Amy? Wait," I call as she walks away.

But of course my words are already too late.

I don't think anything about her unsteady gate. At the time, it doesn't even register. We've both been drinking, after all, and she's smaller than I am, and the fact that she's stumbling a little as she pushes out of the women's bathroom doesn't seem surprising, given everything.

But that's because I don't know about Wendy and the MFA professor and the panic attack and the car accident. I don't know about Katarina or Vera or Terri. I don't have any #throwbackthursday photos of Amy. Not yet.

Someone at this party does know about Amy's panic attacks, though. Which is why a few seconds later, when Amy collapses, pitching forward against a table to the dramatic accompaniment of splashing drinks and shattering glass, Grace Adler is the one who reaches her first, just as she collapses to the floor.

"She's having a panic attack!" Grace yells on the way to Amy. "Give her some space. Did she hit her head? Did anyone see if she hit her head? She's bleeding. Oh, God, there's blood everywhere! Somebody call an ambulance!"

Chapter 40: Don't look at me like that. I'm serious. What? You think I can't do it?

Monday morning

You know what I hate worse than airports? Hospital waiting rooms. There's not a single thing about a waiting room I like. I don't like the elevator music. I don't like the mind-numbing women's magazines. I don't like the chairs — which, okay, is not entirely the fault of the hospital. When you're just fucking big, it's hard to find a chair that's actually comfortable to sit in for longer than five minutes at a time.

Maybe this was the hospital they took Amy to last night. But now I'll only remember it forever as the hospital where my mom had surgery for her osteosarcoma.

"Anika. Will you *please* stop pacing?" Dutch says.

I stop my trek across the waiting room, turn around. Lots of people multitask, but Dutch? Dutch multi-micromanages.

"Sorry," I mutter. I head back to a chair across the coffee table in front of my siblings, drop into it. Bounce a knee up and down.

Across from me, next to Dutch, Gerry. He's slouching slightly down, elbows on the chair arms, hands laced across his chest. His eyes are closed, but I know he's not asleep. He kind of looks like he's meditating. A half-black Buddha with a baseball cap.

Next to him, PJ straightens, studies me for a moment. "So how was Grace's wedding?"

"Shitty."

Dutch glances over. "Don't cuss in front of the baby."

I shrug.

But her curiosity's stronger than her annoyance. "What made it so bad?"

"Jenny." I shift in my chair.

Gerry's eyes open. Fix on me.

I hate it when they all stare at me like this.

"Are you going to elaborate?" Dutch asks.

"No."

My gaze flits to the old-fashioned clock above her head, watching the red second hand circle smoothly around the face. I think about my dad, standing in the surgery viewing room, watching the whole procedure anxiously. He's not supposed to be there. Viewing rooms are supposed to be for visiting doctors only, but they must've picked up on the fact that my dad was going to have a fucking nervous break down if he didn't get to be as close to her as possible, so I guess they made an exception for him.

"It's already been three hours," I say. "I thought they said it should only take two hours?"

"Two to three," says PJ. "They said two to three hours."

I pull my phone out from my pocket. My property manager in Phoenix hasn't gotten in touch yet. But I suppose that's not surprising; it's only about eight-thirty in the morning there.

"Should we call Becker?" I ask Gerry. "Tell him he might need to open up without us?"

"I'll go," Gerry says without moving from his meditative posture. "If we don't hear anything in a half hour, I can leave and help him open."

I shake my head. "Don't. I'll go. I'm supposed to meet Jenny there at eleven fifteen anyway."

My statement earns a row of three sets of surprised, raised eyebrows and a gurgle from baby Sherry.

Dutch clicks her tongue against the roof of her mouth. "I thought you said the wedding was bad because of her? But you're not even waiting for the carcass to cool, are you?"

"What?"

"Jenny's divorce. From what Jodie told me, it's not even finalized yet. You're swooping in a little fast, don't you think?"

I give Dutch a look that I hope is completely fucking incredulous. This woman.

"It's not about her divorce. I need her to sign some paperwork. I'm selling the house in Phoenix."

"Really? Why?" PJ asks.

Jenny and I never sold the house when we moved back to Marcine. And when we split up, we kept it in both our names, even though I was the one who'd bought it and the one who was still paying the mortgage. My property manager had reliably kept a tenant in it ever since, bringing in a nice, tidy little sum of money every month. A good supplement to my income, considering that female professional athletes don't get paid *nearly* what our male counterparts get.

But since the house was still in both of our names, I still needed Jenny's cooperation to sell it.

"Well," I say carefully, "I kept it as an investment property, and it's appreciated in value even more than I expected it to. I'm ready to cash it in."

Dutch narrows her eyes, immediately suspicious. "Cash it in for what?"

I hesitate under three stares. For a second, I think I'll deflect. Change the subject. But I need to talk to them anyway, and now might be the last time for a while that we'll all be in the same place at the same time, with nothing else to focus on but each other.

"I'm going to talk to Mom and Dad once all this stuff with the surgery is over," I say. "I, uh, I'm going to ask them to sell me Soul Mountain."

I get three shocked reactions simultaneously:

(1) Dutch lets go of the toy she's holding for baby Sherry as her head spins towards me. "What?!"

(2) Gerry's hands come unlaced from his chest and his

eyes open wide. He leans forward as if he's going to spring out of his chair.

(3) PJ's mouth literally drops open at the same moment that his eyebrows fly upward.

"You want to buy the restaurant?" PJ asks. "Do you even know what kind of work it takes to own a restaurant?"

Now, *that* is just fucking offensive.

"Let me think about that a second, Peej," I say, pretending to think.   I snap my fingers like I've had a brilliant idea. "Yeah. As a matter of fact, I'm pretty sure I know exactly the kind of fucking work it takes, since I've been working there on and off since I was — wait for it — *thirteen.*"

Dutch shakes her head.   "You haven't been working there.   Okay — maybe in high school for a while, weekends and summers.   But then you ran off to Rosemont — "

"I didn't 'run off.' I had a basketball scholarship to one of the best schools in the country.   And worked *every* school break that I was home.   As if I didn't have anything fucking better to do."

"It's not the same," Dutch insists. "PJ worked there all through high school. *I* worked there through high school *and* college. Every weekend. Sometimes during the week, too.   And even Gerry..."   She glances sideways, thinks better of completing her statement, shakes a thought away. "It's not the same," she says again. "You've never had the patience for it, you — "

"You always said you hated the restaurant," PJ says. And he sounds hurt when he says it, as if it's his girlfriend we're talking about instead of Soul Mountain.

"I do — or, did, I mean," I say. "But I've been doing a lot of thinking since I got back. About a lot of things." My mind flashes back to the day I asked Gerry to cover the restaurant while I hit the basketball court.

Love.

Family.

Connection.

Getting my life together.

I turn towards Dutch. "As fucking rude as you were the other day — "

She throws her hands in the air. "Stop cussing in front of the baby!"

"Sorry. As *rude* as you were the other day, you were right about a couple things. My basketball career is basically over." I look from her to my two brothers. "And I haven't been here for you guys. Or for Mom and Dad. Not the way I should've. I've been running from Ohio for as long as I can remember, and... well, I think it's time I man up. For lack of a better fuh... for lack of a better word."

There's this frozen moment where all three of them continue to stare at me in utter silence, and I would swear that when Dutch opens her mouth again, she's going to tell me I've completely fucking lost it, but instead, she says,

"Oh my God, Anika. I think that's the first adult thing

I've ever heard you say in your entire life."

For the second time in the past ten minutes, I give her a look that I hope is incredulous.

"You're serious, aren't you?" Gerry asks.

I nod.

"Are you *sure?*" PJ asks. "Are you *absolutely sure* you want to take this on? Restaurants aren't easy."

"I'm sure," I say, trying and somewhat succeeding at pretending that PJ isn't being more fucking patronizing than usual. "I made my mind up a few days ago. This is what I want to do."

"It means staying in Ohio," says Gerry.

I meet his eyes, and an unspoken conversation passes between us. Gerry, the black sheep. Anika, the dark grey one. Gerry, the reformed junkie who had the courage to come back home, to face his demons, to pay off the invisible debts that dragged him down for so long. We have a lot in common. We both know it. We both understand why I'm doing this.

After a few seconds pass in silence, I shrug. "Ohio's home," I say. "Right?"

He hesitates. Nods. "Yeah. For better or worse. It is."

I lean back, slouching low in my chair, lacing my hands behind my head. "I'll need to go back to Switzerland, once things settle down here. I have things to clean up there. Move out of my apartment. Officially get fired from my basketball team. But then... Yeah. If Mom and Dad agree to sell me Soul Mountain, I'm coming back. Maybe buy a house." I glance at Gerry. "I'll need a roommate."

He grins. Nods again, but it's relaxed this time.

I sit back up, watch the red second hand make another trip around the clock face. I surprise myself by managing to sit still for almost an entire fucking minute before I push up to my feet.

"Speaking of Soul Mountain, I'm gonna go ahead and get there. I'm sure Becker and Emir don't want to be by themselves for the whole lunch shift."

"And Kiersten," Gerry puts in. "Don't forget she's doing a double for us today. She's supposed to be there by about ten-thirty."

I manage not to roll my eyes. Fucking Kiersten. If my parents agree to me buying the restaurant, Kiersten will be one of the first things to go. That, and the bad, stained canvas paintings that are supposed to be the Himalaya Mountains. Both of them are nothing more than poor imitations of something far more fucking original. The paintings try and fail to capture the majesty of the Himalayas; Kiersten tries and fails to capture the real glory and attitude of a Strong Black Woman. She has nothing on my mother. And for that, she can kiss my Blasian ass.

I say goodbye to my siblings, make Dutch promise that she'll call me as soon as Mom gets out of surgery. On my way out the front door, I text Amy.

Can we talk? Please?

She hasn't answered the other two texts I've sent. I don't have high hopes she'll answer this one.

Chapter 41: How to stop warping the time-space continuum.

Back to the future: Eight and a half years ago. Marcine, Ohio.

"Can we talk? *Please,* Ani," Jenny says. Her face is puffy, her eyes are bloodshot from days of crying. "We can still work this out."

"We can't."

"We can," she insists. "I know we can. We're meant to be together."

I shake my head, swallow past my own tears. "Just because we've been together since we were kids doesn't mean we were meant to be together forever."

"That's not why," she says. Her eyes are welling with tears again. She's cried so much in the past forty-eight hours that I'm surprised she still has any water left in her body to cry. "Or at least — it's not the only reason why. You... you're my everything."

"I'm your everything?" I echo, shaking my head again.

This is fucking sad and it fucking sucks and I want to let myself fall apart and scoop her up into my arms and tell her everything's going to be okay, but I know better. And I know better because we've been like this for too long. For years.

"When was the last time you were happy, Jen? Tell me the truth." She doesn't answer, so I try to help her out. "You were miserable in Phoenix."

Her gaze falls to the floor.

"You spent the last four years angry with me. You spent the four years before that crying almost every time we Skyped. You've tried to break up with me three different times. We're a mess, Jenny. We've been a mess. For way too fucking long."

"But at least we're a mess *together*," she whispers, still staring at the floor.

I take my hand off the door knob, reach under her chin, tilt her head up and wait for her to look at me. I don't speak again until she does.

"We were unhappy with each other all the way through college. We thought it would be better after college. It wasn't. Then we thought it would be better after we got married. It wasn't. We thought it would be better during the off-season. It *still* wasn't. We thought we could patch things up by coming back to Ohio. Instead, you fucking…" I let go of her chin, and without meaning to do it, my eyes flit to her stomach. To the place where she has a child growing inside her. *Mason's* child. "Coming to Ohio didn't make it better, either. We have to stop. We have to stop hurting each other."

She brushes tear-damp blonde hair out of her face.

"We've just been... we have growing pains. We've been growing up. Changing."

"We're not growing up. We're growing *apart*. It's been happening slowly, ever since high school." My voice cracks when I say it, and I don't fight the sting of tears that come with the words *high school*. "What have we been hanging onto all these years, Jen? Tell me what you're hanging onto, because I sure as fuck don't know what I'm hanging onto anymore. Not *you*. *You've* been out of reach for almost as long as I can remember."

"I can't lose you," she says. Fresh tears spill from her eyes, down her cheeks. "I don't even know who I *am* without you."

"Yeah? Well, that's *exactly* why I have to leave. You said it yourself in Phoenix. You can't build your whole life around me. You have to build your life around *you.*" I sniff, wipe tears from my face. "You know what I think we've been holding onto all this time? An idea. Just an idea of who we're supposed to be. An idea we came up with at seventeen. But we're not seventeen anymore. It's time we both let go."

She shakes her head; the tears come harder, faster.

It's almost impossible to get the next words out. They hitch and tangle around my half-swallowed sob. "I'm not going to be one of those people who spends the rest of my life fucking *trudging* through something I don't want to be in anymore. And I don't want you to do that, either. I don't want us to stay together just because we said we would a long time ago. Not when both of us are unhappy. I don't know who I am without you, either, but I've got the rest of my life to figure it out. And you've got to do that, too."

She cries so hard she can't speak, cries so hard that she probably can't even fucking see me through her tears. And I may not be *in* love with Jennifer Pearson anymore, but I still *love* her, and I still hate seeing her in agony. I reach out a hand, stroke blonde hair one last time without a word, and then, because there's nothing else to do, nothing else to say, I walk out the door.

Marty McFly waits for me inside the DeLorean in the parking lot outside our apartment. I open a batwing door, throw my duffle into the backseat, and climb inside. I glance in the rearview mirror, skeptically eyeing the trailer attached to the back of the car.

He watches me a second before starting the car. "Hey, I've got a joke for you."

"I'm not in the mood for jokes, McFly."

"You'll like this one."

"I said I'm not in the moo — "

"What does a lesbian bring to the second date?"

"A U-Haul," I say irritably. "You need some new material. That's like, thirty fucking years old."

"No, no, that's not the end of the joke," he says with a grin. He leans forward, sets the digital clock on the dashboard for eight and a half years into the future. "What does a lesbian bring to an apartment complex thirteen years *after* the second date?"

I give him a you-can't-be-fucking-serious look.

"Another U-Haul!" He cackles with delight, waiting for me to laugh with him. When I don't so much as crack a grin, his laughter dies off awkwardly. He points at the seat belt. "You should buckle up. Sometimes time travel gets crazy."

I wipe drying tears from my cheeks. "Tell me about it." I fasten the buckle. When he puts the DeLorean in reverse, I reach across, put my hand on his shoulder. "McFly."

"Hmm?"

"I'm tired of time traveling, okay? I don't want to come back anymore. There's nothing I can do here that's going to make a difference."

He looks disappointed. "You only say that because you've never tried to change anything."

"The *fuck,* McFly? They call the past 'past' because you *can't* fucking change anything. It is what it is — or was what it was, or whatever — and there's not a goddamn thing you can do except live with it. Mistakes and all."

"Not true!" he says. He pats the flux capacitor on the dash. "I used this baby to go all the way back to 1955. I saved my parents' marriage." .

"That was a movie."

"The hell it was! It was my *life!*"

"It was your life in a *movie,"* I correct. "A classic fucking movie. But still a movie. In real life, there's no going back. Except in your head. And after a while, all that going back makes your head crazy. So I'm serious, okay? Don't show up with your goddamned DeLorean again. I'm not going back anymore. Only forward."

Marty McFly heaves out a mighty sigh, but he nods his acceptance. "Well, I guess it's a good thing we've got all your stuff with us in the U-Haul, then." His face brightens. "Hey, speaking of which. I've got another joke for you."

"I don't want to hear it."

"When the zombie apocalypse comes — "

"I *told* you. I'm not in the mood for jokes."

"No, listen. This is a good one. When the zombie apocalypse comes, how come the gay guys are going to be the first ones to get out of town?"

I give him a stare of death.

"Because their shit's already packed!" He cackles again.

I groan. "That was... *really* politically fucking incorrect."

"I know! But it's funny, right?!"

"No. It's tasteless and borderline homophobic. And you're a *straight* figment of my imagination. So... not fucking cool, okay?"

"Oh, lighten up, Anika. It was only a joke."

I scowl at him. "I've got a restaurant to open, McFly. Let's go."

#

Back to the present

I make it from the hospital one town over to Soul Mountain just after ten-fifteen AM. Becker and Emir are there already, preparing for the day, and when I push the door open into the main body of the restaurant, the first thing that hits me is the smell of rice and dal.

Rice and dal are... how do I even explain it?

Rice and dal aren't just rice and dal. It's not just food to me. Encoded within those smells is every memory I have of home and family. Dal is standing on a step stool next to my father at eight while he explains to me in accented English how and when to add the tamarind, onion, garlic. Rice is high school on the weekends, fighting in Soul Mountain's kitchen with Dutch as I lay out all the reasons why I should get the car instead of her.

Rice and dal are my past. Rice and dal are my present. And if my parents agree to my plan, rice and dal are my future.

I greet Becker and Emir in the kitchen. I roll silverware. I power up our aging computer system, making a mental note to update it as soon as I can afford to. I scoop ice into plastic pitchers, fill them with water, leave them at the wait station.

Kiersten comes in at ten forty-five, grumpy-assed as ever, and at eleven, I unlock the main door and switch on the neon OPEN sign in the front window.

Jenny arrives right on time at eleven fifteen, a white to-go cup of coffee in her hand.

She smiles weakly. "Hey."

"Hey," I say. I point to a table near the back, as far away from prying ears as we can get. "Let's sit down."

ANDREWS / ANIKA TAKES THE LONG WAY

Chapter 42: Grown-up questions with grown-up answers. Like a fucking boss.

We sit across from one another a few seconds later, with my hands laced together on the glass table top, Jenny gripping her to-go cup.

"How was the rest of the reception last night?" I ask. "After Amy and I, uh…"

I was going to say "after Amy and I left," but of course that sounds as if we left together. Just another happy fucking couple at another happy fucking wedding, happily leaving arm-in-happy-arm after they'd had their fill of the happy-ass reception.

But of course that's not what happened. We were a happy couple until Amy came into the bathroom to find Jenny and me sucking face. Which triggered Amy's panic attack. Which triggered Amy's fainting.

And when Amy came-to a minute later, far from wanting to see me, the sight of my face floating over hers nearly triggered a second panic attack.

No shit.

I followed the ambulance to the hospital, but when I went into the emergency room, Grace Fucking Adler, still in her wedding dress, shooed me away. And in the twelve hours since? Amy won't see me, won't text me back, won't take my calls. Probably deletes every voicemail without listening.

"The rest of the reception was about the same," Jenny says with a shrug. She taps an irregular rhythm on the black plastic lid of her to-go cup. "Are you and Amy still...?"

"Talking? Starting a relationship?" I ask. I shake my head. "Doesn't look like it."

"I'm sorry about... if I..."

"Don't be. It shouldn't have happened, but it did. It's not like I didn't participate."

She tries to smile. "Seems like this always happens, when we get close enough. Like at your sister's wedding."

I try to smile back. I don't need a fucking mirror to know that my smile doesn't reach my eyes anymore than hers does. "Maybe it's a wedding thing."

"Maybe." She takes a sip of her coffee. Looks down. Looks back up. "Or maybe it's an 'us' thing. A sign that we still have something, that we always will. Something neither of us can deny."

"Jenny..." I let out a long breath. "All we have together anymore are memories."

"Memories are what knit people together."

I slowly shake my head. "And memories push people apart. Don't you remember why we broke up?"

She takes a breath. "I got pregnant."

"No. It was more than you getting pregnant. It was you pulling away from me. It was me cheating on you. It was the two of us constantly arguing. For years."

"There were good times, too."

"Yeah, but the good times got fewer and further between. By the end, there *weren't* any good times."

"That was then. Maybe it would be different if we tried again. We're older now, more mature. I don't think we'd hurt each other in the same ways that we did back then." She pauses, studies my face. "Will you try? Will you try again with me?"

"I didn't ask to meet so we could talk about us."

"That's not an answer to my question."

I rest my elbows on the table, press the heels of my hands into my eyes. Rub. Lace my hands on the table again. "Jenny. I have a question of my own. You have to answer it honestly."

"Anything," she says softly. "Ask me anything."

"What do you want from your life?"

Her brow creases. Obviously not the question she was expecting. "What do you mean?"

"I mean what I said. What do you want from your life? What do you want your life to be about?"

"Why are you asking me this?"

"Because I've been asking myself that question for the past two years. As soon as I realized my career wasn't going to last much longer. For a long fucking time, I made my life about basketball — basketball, and you. And once

I realized you and I weren't going to last forever, it was just basketball. But now you know what I've figured out?" I wait for her to answer, but she says nothing, so I keep going. "It sounds like a fucking no-brainer, but I realized basketball's not going to last forever, either. And basing my life around a person, or around a game... that's not enough. Not for me. Not anymore."

"Why are you telling me this?"

"Because you're fucking *lost,* Jen. I see it all over your face every time we run into each other. You're lost, and you think I'm the one who's gonna make you found again. Like I'm your fucking 'Amazing Grace.'"

She shakes her head. "I'm not los — "

"You are. I know you are, because I know you, and because I've been lost for a long-ass time, too. Takes one to know one and all that shit. You're holding onto me — onto the idea of us — because us being together was the last time you knew what your life was about. And I get it, because I did the same thing for a really long time. But I can't be the center of your life. You have to find your own center."

Her eyes water and she looks down at her coffee cup. She pulls in a deep breath, lets it out slowly. Sniffs. When she speaks again, her voice is small. "What about you? What do you want from your life? What's your center?"

I reach across the table, pry her hands from her coffee cup, hold them in my own. They still fit together, our hands. Even after all these years. Her hands are cool; my hands are warm. I run my thumbs across her knuckles.

"I'm working on that. And for starters, I have to stop running," I say. "From my family, from Ohio. From my own fucking memories. I need to stay in one place for once. Give back. Take care of my mom and dad. Take care of the restaurant. This place is my center. I've fought against it for a long fucking time, but I think a part of me has always known it."

Her breath hitches in her throat. "But I'm centered here, too. Why can't we be centered here together?"

There's a part of me that's exasperated. There's another part of me that's infinitely patient, because this is Jenny, after all. The sun that the planet of my life rotated around for a very long time. I can't give her my heart anymore, but at least I can give her my patience.

"Because we can't," I say softly. "Because we stopped working a long, long time ago, when we started outgrowing each other but refused to admit it. And if we got back together, we'd be going backward. Back in time instead of forwards. Back to when we were fucking clinging to each other because we didn't know what else to do. I have to stop trying to bring the past back to life. I didn't know that for sure until yesterday, at the reception, but I know now." I swallow, meet her eyes. "I can't be with you again."

She cries in silence, won't look me in the eyes.

Another way of explaining it occurs to me, and I squeeze her hands again. "Jenny. Do you know what we are to each other?"

"Exes who wish they'd never messed things up so badly?"

I shake my head. "We're dal bhat. We're fried chicken and cornbread. We're collard greens seasoned with curry."

She lets out a wet laugh. "We're your parents' cooking?"

"No, we're comfort food. We're familiar to each other, but that doesn't mean we're good for each other. Not anymore." I sigh. "Comfort food... Too much of it just leads to a fucked-up heart. My heart's been fucked-up a long time, Jen. Yours has, too. We make each other sick, not better. You know I'm right."

She shakes her head. "You're not."

"I am. You know I am. You have to let go — we both do."

She retracts her hands, uses her index fingers to swipe at the tears pooling in her eyes. When that doesn't make the tears disappear, she tries gazing up at the ceiling for a few seconds. She blinks a few times. I wait in silence. In patience.

After a last mighty sniff, she pulls her eyes off the ceiling, puts them back on me. "So why did you want to meet me today? If you didn't want to talk about us?"

I take a breath. "I need you to do something. I'm selling the house in Phoenix, but it's still in both of our names. I need you to sign some paperwork."

She freezes in place, suddenly a statue. A dead, unbreathing, wax museum version of herself. Mouth poised halfway open. Hands completely still.

And I'm thinking, *Oh, shit. We're going to have a problem here, aren't we?*

I paid for the house when we moved out to Phoenix, because back then, I was making money and she wasn't. But we'd put it in both of our names, the idea being that if anything ever happened to me, my family couldn't pull any crazy-ass homophobic drama and try to kick Jenny out of our home. When we split up, I somehow never bothered to take her name off the deed. Maybe there was a part of both of us that didn't want to. The house was the last thing we could call "ours" instead of "mine" / "hers."

Which means that technically, she's still half-owner. Technically, she could stop me from selling it if she really wanted to.

After a couple more seconds of wax museum stillness, Jenny comes back to life. Nods. "Okay. I'll sign whatever you need me to. But why are you selling the house? I thought you were keeping it as an investment property."

I repeat the same explanation I'd given to my siblings earlier.

Her eyes widen. "You've always hated the restaurant."

I shrug. "It's like I told you. My basketball career is coming to an end. I need to do *something,* and I don't want to coach or teach. My sociology degree is about worth the paper it's printed on. If that. Being back here... My sister still drives me nuts, and I can't handle living with my parents for any length of time, but the restaurant? It hasn't been that bad. And I think... Well, I've been talking with Gerry a lot. Thinking things over. And this is what I want to do next."

She seems like she's taking all my words in, letting them steep somewhere in the back of her brain. "Do you think... if you're living here... we could end up being friends again? Just friends — that's all I'm asking."

"Depends." I laugh. "You're not going to keep throwing yourself at me in spare bedrooms and public bathrooms, are you?"

"Not if you don't want me to." She takes a deep breath. "No, I won't. I promise I'll stop."

I return her smile. "So... are you okay to fill out some paperwork now?"

"Yeah."

I stand up. "Okay. I'll get it from the office."

I get a text from Gerry on my way into the back:

Mom's out of surgery. Doctor says there's a problem.

Chapter 43: God save the queen. Long live the queen.

I meet my anxious siblings at the hospital thirty minutes later, leaving Soul Mountain under the watch of Becker and an irritated Kiersten. Kiersten, of course, is always fucking irritated about something, so… sorry, Kiersten, but all my fucks have been officially already given. I have no more fucks to give you for your irritation.

When I walk into the waiting room, I find Dutch sitting with baby Sherry, PJ texting, Gerry pacing. Dutch's eyes flash up to meet mine when I walk into the room; she looks away just as quickly. PJ doesn't stop texting, but Gerry stops his pacing, turns, crushes me in a hug.

"What's going on?" I ask. My heart pounds in my chest, and I'm unsure if I'm ready to hear what my brothers and sister might tell me.

Gerry sniffs, wipes tears from his eyes. He keeps one hand on my bicep, though whether it's to comfort me or steady him, I don't know. "They almost lost her. Almost. And they couldn't get it all."

I glance from Gerry to Dutch, Dutch to PJ. "Almost lost her? And what do you mean — they couldn't get it all?"

"They nicked an artery," Dutch says. "She almost bled out on the table."

"And they think it's metastasized," PJ says, looking up from his phone at last. "That's why they couldn't get it all."

I shake my head. "No, it hadn't metastasized. They did scans. It was only in the pelvis."

Whether or not the cancer in Mom's pelvis had metastasized and spread to other parts of the body or not was a majorly big fucking deal. If osteosarcoma is caught early, if it hasn't spread to other regions of the body, then Mom's five-year survival rate stood at forty to sixty percent. I could live with those odds. If it had metastasized, however...

"No," I repeat stubbornly. "They did scans. It hasn't spread."

Dutch's eyes water; she covers her mouth with her hand. Gerry lets go of me, resumes his pacing.

"What now?" I ask, and I direct my question to PJ because he seems like he's the least freaked out of the three of them.

"Aggressive radiation," PJ answers with a heavy sigh. "Five days per week, three or four weeks. Followed by more chemotherapy. The radiation will likely make her sick; the chemo sicker."

"But she's already been on chemo," I argue. "I thought we were done with chemo — that was the point of the surgery. To remove what was left."

PJ shrugs. "I'm not a doctor, Ani."

My fists curl; I need something to hit. This surgery was

supposed to be easy. The ten weeks of chemo leading up to the surgery — the throwing up in the middle of the night, the weight loss, the hair loss — that was supposed to be done. The surgery was supposed to be the finishing touch, and then Momma could start the recovery process. Now, though… Now, everything has changed.

I'm glad Jenny signed that paperwork this morning. My parents are going to need money sooner rather than later.

#

We wait.

Gerry paces. PJ texts. Sherry bounces on Dutch's knee.

I stand leaning against a wall, one knee up, shoe planted on the wall behind me, arms crossed tight against my chest. Hands curled into fists.

They did scans. They fucking did scans. It hasn't metastasized.

Another half-hour passes. Gerry paces. PJ texts. Sherry bounces on Dutch's knee.

Finally, a man in a white coat emerges through a side door, my father beside him. Dad's cheeks are wet with tears; when he exhales, his whole body trembles as if the nuts and bolts holding him together are about to all come out at once. The man in the white coat, who is taller than my father but shorter than me, places his hand on Dad's shoulder, squeezes it, and turns away.

Alone, my father stands in the center of the waiting room. And something miraculous occurs to me: I can't remember the last time I've seen my father standing alone. More than almost any couple I've ever known, my mother and father have always been a single unit, moving through life in unison. Even Alex and Graham, as fucking sickening as their unending romance may be, aren't like my mother and father. Graham goes to school each morning, teaches little kids how to finger paint; Alex yells at college basketball players during layup drills. My mother and father, on the other hand, have barely parted in the twenty-five years since Soul Mountain opened. They go to work each morning together; they work side-by-side all day together; they come home together. All the time together would drive any normal couple fucking crazy. But for them, it works. For them, they are two limbs of one body.

So seeing my father standing by himself, still and isolated like a fucking park statue, is unnerving. Like seeing a bloody, disembodied arm lying by itself in the middle of the floor.

"She's not completely awake yet," he says in accented English. His accent has always been a barometer of his mood; the more upset he is, the heavier it gets. And since he's rarely upset, I rarely hear it this thick. "But they're about to move her out of the recovery room. When they're finished, we can all go in."

"*Should* we all go in?" PJ asks. "Will it be too much

for her — having all of us in there at once?"

Dad shakes his head. "No. She will want all her children around her. At least right now." He takes a few steps forward, collapses into a chair. The movement makes him look small and old. A sudden urge arises to cradle him like a child, to pull him close to my chest and wrap my albatross wingspan around him.

We wait.

Gerry paces. PJ texts. Sherry bounces on Dutch's knee.

I stand against the wall, a foot planted behind me, arms crossed tight against my chest. Hands curled into fists.

A nurse appears a little while later. She glances between our faces, a practiced softness in her expression. "They've moved her into a regular room," she says. "And she's starting to feel a little more alert. You can see her now if you want."

We follow the woman's directions, traveling out of the wing of the hospital we're in and into another. Dutch leads the way; the rest of us trail behind like lost ducklings. My father walks beside her and little behind; PJ flanks him. Baby Sherry gets transferred to Gerry somewhere along the way. He hugs the baby to his shoulder and walks behind their triangle.

I bring up the rear, a yard or two after Gerry.

My mother sits halfway up in bed, a sleepy, drugged, contented smile growing on her face when our party of six crowds into the small hospital room.

"Hello, my darlings," she says.

Baby Sherry lifts her sleepy head off Gerry's shoulder at the sound of her grandmother's voice. Little hands push against her uncle's chest as she twists to see what's happening.

"Mammaw," she says, reaching a hand towards my mother.

My mother reaches out for her granddaughter automatically, stretching out ashy arms decorated with hospital bands and plastic IV tubes. "There's my girl," she says.

We all watch and smile as Gerry hands the toddler over, but I wonder if anyone else is wondering the same thing I am — will baby Sherry get a chance to know her namesake? Will Momma be around for Sherry's kindergarten graduation ceremony? Will she still be there when Sherry enters high school? When Sherry goes to prom?

Maybe the rest of my family has the same thoughts, because everyone seems to hold their breath when Mom cuddles Sherry into her chest, when both grandma and baby gurgle at each other happily.

Mom looks up. "I'm still here, babies," she declares.

Her words break the spell. Everyone shifts and breathes at once.

"We knew you would be," Gerry says. "You're too tough not to be."

"Mmm-hmm," my mother agrees, squeezing Sherry a

little closer and tickling her cheek. "Tumor-free now. How you like that?"

PJ casts a glance at my father; Gerry adjusts the Buckeyes cap on his head and shifts his eyes out the window.

My father steps forward, runs his hand tenderly along my mother's hairline before leaning down to kiss her forehead. "Tumor-free," he says, even though it's a lie. "You did well, *rani*."

"Rani" means "queen" in Nepalese, by the way. It is my father's favorite name for my mother.

But somehow, the use of the nickname twists my stomach, so much so that my hand automatically comes up to my middle. I want to double over and retch. I stop myself from doing so.

Dutch moves to the head of my mother's bed, strokes her baby's curls absentmindedly. Dutch smiles, starts chattering to Momma about something distracting and inconsequential. Anything other than the truth of the situation.

I wonder how long they can keep their conspiracy up. How long it will be before someone tells my mother the truth. They're probably hoping the doctor will do it.

But I don't think it should come from a doctor. My mother is as strong and stubborn as a fucking mule; I can't stand watching everyone tread around her so lightly, like she's made of crystal.

My momma ain't no crystal. She's obsidian. Black and

hard and beautiful. A scalpel-sharp tongue and mind. The product of the fire that rumbles beneath the Earth.

"Momma," I say, interrupting Dutch. The room turns to me as one body, and Dutch's eyes are already flashing with anger, because she knows what I'm about to do. "They didn't get the whole tumor. You're going to have to come back for more treatment. Radiation, probably. And more chemo."

Everyone deflates at once, collective breath hissing out of them like a dying balloon. My father glances over his shoulder, meets my eyes for a moment. His expression is both a show of disappointment in me and a signal of relief.

"Anika!" Dutch says.

My mother turns towards Dutch, gives her that *look,* the one I haven't seen much of since we were kids, then she locks eyes with my father. He nods slowly.

"Okay. Can't say as I'm surprised." She sighs. "I could feel the little booger growing. Even when I was on the chemo."

"I'm sorry," I say, though I don't really know who the apology is directed at.

"Girl, don't be sorry," Momma says immediately. "Just because they didn't get it all doesn't mean y'all need to start worryin' and fussin' over me." She gives my father a pointed look. "Treatin' me like I can't handle some bad news. Treatin' me like I'ma stop fighting just because it didn't work the first go-round. That's how these things go, you know. They don't always take on the first go-round.

ANDREWS / ANIKA TAKES THE LONG WAY

That doesn't mean we're done."

My dad takes a step closer to her bed, reaches for the hand that isn't around Sherry. He says nothing, just squeezes her hand in both of his, and I don't need to see his face to know that his cheeks are wet with tears again.

Despite Momma's brave words, there's a realignment happening in this moment, and I'm sure everyone feels it. Fire is rumbling beneath the surface again, but maybe the volcano that is my mother is going dormant. Maybe it's time for someone else to be the family's active volcano.

PJ moves to stand beside Dutch; he and my sister and my mother begin a conversation I don't tune into.

Maybe it's time for the *rani,* the long-time matriarch of Soul Mountain, the ruling queen of downtown Marcine, the town's other gravitational center outside Jodie's hair salon, to pass her crown to someone else.

After a few more minutes of conversations I can't listen to, I pull out my phone, glance at the time. "I should get back to the restaurant," I say to everyone. "I don't trust Kiersten enough to leave her there all day on her own."

My mother looks over to me from where she's been deep in dialog with Dutch and PJ. There's a long pause. Then her face shifts into something that she's directed at me only rarely over the years — approval.

She nods once. Snorts. "You won't get an argument from me over *that,"* she says. "That girl's about as trustworthy as a mobster in a casino."

I chuckle, nod. Lift my hand in a silent goodbye wave

to my mother and turn to leave the room without another word.

"Anika?" my mother calls.

I turn back. "Yeah?"

"Emir still tends to burn the dal on the bottom, and he lets the chicken dry out. You have to stay on him. He's still new."

"I will, Momma."

She stares at me for a moment. She nods again. "Good. I believe you will."

I give her a nod of my own, and then — I can't help it — I grin. This is probably one of the first times in my life I've been on the same page as my mother.

Whether the rest of them understand what just happened or whether it was a silent transaction that passed only between me and Momma doesn't matter. She knows. I know. And that's what counts.

The queen's crown just got passed.

Chapter 44: Best possible outcomes.

Four days later — Friday

I bring fresh flowers with me — pink tulips from my mother's own garden — when I arrive at the hospital a few days later. She's there with my father for her radiation appointment, and although I wasn't going to join them, I decided at the last minute to go. Gerry's holding down Soul Mountain and it's late afternoon, anyway — that interminable lull between the end of the lunch rush and the beginning of the dinner rush.

My father rises when I walk in, surprise etched on his face, and takes the flowers from me when I extend them in his direction.

"Look, *rani,*" he says, showing them to my mother. "Your tulips are blooming."

She gives a pained nod, says nothing. Dad hands them to her gingerly and rubs her back.

As always, his love for my mother is as plain as the fucking sun in the spring sky, which is a bittersweet thing to see. It's heartening and hopeful that two people can be together for so long and still love each other so much, but it underscores my feeling of being a complete fucking failure in the relationship department.

It underscores my loneliness.

Jenny and I haven't talked since she signed the paperwork that puts the Phoenix house solely in my possession. And that's probably good. It's probably what needed to happen, but now that she's stopped pursuing me and has given me the space I asked for, I find I miss her even more than I did before.

Amy and I, meanwhile, haven't talked since the disastrous wedding reception. I don't think she's even still in town anymore. I could swing by the B&B to see if her rental car's still there, but why? If it's there, it'll just hurt, because it will mean she still hasn't forgiven me. If it's not there, it'll still hurt, because it will mean the first girl I had actual fucking feelings for in a long time is long gone.

My mother gazes at the tulips. "They're from my garden?"

I come back to the present, nod.

She rotates them, inspecting, brushes a bit of dirt from a soft pink petal with an index finger. "Why didn't I notice they were in bloom already?" she says, mostly to herself.

It's hard seeing her like this, pale and grey from the chemo, hollow and wasting away from the radiation. The strongest woman I've ever known has finally stepped into the ring with an opponent she might not be able to beat.

She looks up, and my mother and I stare at each other in silence for a moment.

"How're you feeling?" I ask. It's a stupid question, but what the hell else am I supposed to say?

She shrugs noncommittally. "I've felt better." She nods towards the flowers. "Did I ever tell you how your father courted me with flowers when we first met? Used to bring me fresh ones every single day."

The mention of the story I've heard a million times before makes my eyes sting with tears. "Yeah. You might've mentioned it once or twice."

She smiles at this. "That's right. We've told you kids that story, haven't we?"

"Yes, ma'am."

My dad gets up. "Maybe I can find something to put the flowers in?"

Momma hands him the flowers. "Cut the stems down while you're at it," she says, pointing to the place she wants them cut.

He heads for the nursing station.

I sit down. Clear my throat. "Momma? There's something I want to talk to you about."

"Hmm?"

"I put my house in Phoenix on the market. The one Jenny and I lived in? Only listed it on Wednesday, but we've already had a few bites. I think I should make a nice profit on it."

My mom knows me way too well. She frowns and cocks her head. "Why you sellin' the house? You need money? I thought you had it rented, and you were making a profit from the rent?"

"I was making money from it, yeah. But listen, I've

thinking... With your... hip, and with Dad spending so much time taking care of you... and..." I bite down hard on my tongue right before I say *with the debt the restaurant's in* because she already made it clear once *that* topic isn't up for discussion. "And with you guys getting close to retirement age anyway... and given that this was probably my last season playing basketball..."

Her frown gets skeptical as I trail off.

I've never been good at asking things of my parents. I love them. I know they love me. But it's like Gerry told me when I came back to town — I'm not exactly the black sheep, but I'm pretty dark fucking grey. Positive communication, especially with my mother, hasn't always been my strong suit over the years.

"Spit it out, girl," is what she says. She's giving me a real stink-eye now. "What you need to sell that house for?"

"I want to — I want to use the money to buy Soul Mountain," I say in a rush, my stomach exploding with unexpected butterflies. No one but my mother has the power to turn me into a stammering, nervous idiot. "If you guys would be open to it..."

My dad picks that moment to walk back into the waiting room, tulips cut down to size and drooping out of a plastic cup he's filled with water. Picking up on the tension immediately, he glances from me to Mom.

"Open to what?" he asks.

Momma heaves a big sigh, reaches for the tulips. She takes them and sticks them right under her nose, inhaling their fresh scent deeply before placing them on a stack of health and women's magazines on the end table beside her. She pats the seat next to her.

"Sit down," she orders.

I take a step forward, prepared to fit my big awkward body into yet another hospital waiting room chair, but she waves me off.

"Not *you*. Your father."

Chastened, I retreat a few steps, make room for Dad. Clearly he's wondering what's up, because he sits down in the chair slowly and carefully like there's a frigging bomb beneath it that he might set off if he moves too quickly.

My mother turns to him. "Our second daughter just offered to buy Soul Mountain."

Dad looks up in surprise, from me back to her. "Buy the restaurant?"

"Yeah," I say. "You guys deserve a real retirement, and I know you don't want to talk about it, but with the shape the restaurant's in now, you're not going to be able to afford to retire until you're both, like, fucking ninety or something."

"Watch your language," Momma says, lips puckering into a sour frown.

"Sorry," I mutter.

"I am surprised you would ask, Anika," my father says. "You've never particularly liked Soul Mountain."

I anticipated this question, so I already have an answer ready. "I'm surprised, too. But over the last week... I've realized a few things. I've missed being part of a family. Seeing the progress that Gerry's made... seeing how big Sherry's gotten..." I pause. "Seeing you guys. Seeing how much you love each other — and your kids, and this town, and..." My mind flashes to Jenny, to the daughter named after me, to the things I opted out on that now I have second thoughts about. "I haven't been a part of this family — or had a real home, actually — in a really long time. And life's short. So... I think I should do something about that. While I still have a chance."

My last sentences fall into an abyss of pained silence, a silence that contains within it my mother's unknown future. A future that might be shorter than any of us wanted it to be.

She's the first one to speak. "And what if you change your mind? What if you start running the restaurant, only to realize it's not what you want to do after all, hmm? Owning a restaurant... that's not the same as a normal job, Ani. You do something like this because just you feel obligated, you're settin' yourself up to be unhappy later. And then Soul Mountain suffers."

"I know it's not like a normal job. But basketball's going to be over for me soon." I shrug. "I have to do *something*. But it's not — I mean, I don't want to make it sound like I want to own Soul Mountain just because I don't have any better options. Being back here this week, it made me realize... there's something special about Soul Mountain. It's a part of this community, of Marcine. It *gives* something to people. And it should stay in the family. Gerry's going back to school, Dutch is busy raising her kids, and PJ... PJ could do it, but he'd have to manage it from afar. So that leaves me. And... I've thought about it. A lot. It's what I want to do. Really."

Instead of responding to me, my parents meet eyes, stare at each other for a long few seconds in silence. After a lifetime of watching them do this, I know they're having an entire, complicated conversation in those few moments of subtle eye flickers and twitched lips. But I've never been a part of their psychic inner circle, so all I can do is stand there and wait for an answer.

Momma turns back to me. "We'll think about it."

"Okay," I say, knowing that *We'll think about it* was the best possible outcome I could've hoped for, and much better than the outright *No* I halfway expected.

It ends up taking them two weeks and five more radiation treatments before they give me a definitive answer. By then, Mom's losing weight rapidly. She has no appetite, and what Dad's able to force into her she often throws back up, anyway. Life in my basement room is punctuated by the sound of my father's words drifting down from the kitchen —

"But you have to eat, *rani.*"

When they get home from the hospital after the fifth treatment in six days, they call me at the restaurant.

"Anika?" my father says. "Your mother and I have thought about your offer on Soul Mountain. We agree. We will sell it to you."

Chapter 45: Did I mention that I fucking hate airports?

Seven weeks later

As if God or Buddha or the fucking Universe or whatever was waiting for my parents to finally make a decision, everything starts happening really fast once they say they'll sell me the restaurant. My house in Phoenix sells in less than two weeks; Gerry ends up getting into community college; PJ announces he's getting married; Dutch turns up preggo with Baby Number Three.

Another month goes by. Kiersten quits before I have to fire her, which is fucking awesome, and I hire two new servers I really like, one a new friend of Gerry's from the community college, one a friend of Katie-the-high-school-hostess. Without the weight of debt dragging the restaurant down, it starts doing pretty well. I buy a condo; Gerry moves in as my roommate.

Jodie and Ben come in every Tuesday to play Scrabble, and Jodie updates me on all the gossip in town. Every week she asks after my mother, and every week I tell her the same thing: *"The doctors say it's too soon to guess yet."*

I settle into a comfortable routine. Gerry takes classes at the college during the day — all prerequisites so he can get into an actual four-year degree program at Ohio State. He relieves me at the restaurant around five every evening, and I let him handle the dinner rush but make it back in time to help him close.

The kid's in school, after all. I don't want him staying up too late.

After a drunk driver almost takes Gerry out when he's walking home from the restaurant one night, Dutch takes it upon herself to buy us a car. It's a compact that neither one of us even really fit in, but we start driving it home every night, and I let Gerry take it to school each morning.

It's not an exciting life. But it's a good life, a quiet life.

Jenny comes to the restaurant about once per week. A lot of times, she comes with kids in tow; once in a while, she comes by herself. I sit and talk with her on the days that I have time. Things are... as normal as they will ever get between us, I suppose.

She comes in by herself one day, and I bring her a menu, but she says, "Two menus, actually, Ani."

I give her a curious look but she won't meet my eye. Five minutes later, I find out why. A woman walks in the front door, gazing around like she's looking for someone. She's on the tall side (shorter than me, obviously), with a lean, athletic build and short-cropped dark hair. I don't have to look at her twice to know she's gay as hell.

When she sees Jenny, her whole face lights up, breaks into this huge smile, and she strides across the restaurant without so much as noticing that I'm standing there. Jenny is her sun; this girl is a planet that's fallen inside her gravitational pull.

I glance at Jenny. She's smiling just as broadly as the short-haired girl, and when the short-haired girl reaches her, Jenny stands, and the girl gives her a peck on the cheek.

I smile. I'm happy for Jenny. I really am.

But the peck on the cheek is a glaring neon sign pointing to the one thing still missing in my life: I'm as alone as I was the day I left her.

Maybe I should just get used to it. Maybe it's going to be like this from now on. Or maybe I should try some online dating or some shit.

Yeah, right. I want to try online dating about as much as I want to try a root canal without novocaine.

#

"You're sure you're okay with this?" I ask Gerry one last time. "You aren't going to get stressed running things on your own? Don't skip any classes — leave Soul Mountain with Becker if you have to."

He laughs. "Sis, it's going to be fine."

"So you say."

He smirks at me. "You're a better businesswoman than you give yourself credit for. Which means that Soul Mountain is going to be *fine* without you. Okay? So get going."

I hesitate; he raises an eyebrow. "Alright, alright," I huff, picking up my duffle. I follow him into our ridiculous compact car outside. "I *really* don't want to go back to Switzerland, Ger," I say once he gets in and starts the engine.

The little fucker just laughs some more.

"You're going to sit there and fucking laugh at me?"

"I can't help it. It's funny. I'm just thinking that the Anika who came home a couple months ago. She never would've said something like that." We roll to a stop at the end of the street, and he gives me a sideways glance before he speaks again. "Amazing how quickly life changes sometimes, right?"

I slouch down in the seat. "Don't try out your future social worker techniques on me, asshole."

Gerry chuckles. A few minutes later, we're on the highway, heading for the Cleveland airport.

#

I have a long fucking flight path. The first leg is a little puddle-jumper from Cleveland to Chicago O'Hare. Then it's Chicago to London — an overnight flight in which I'll be guaranteed to get absolutely no fucking sleep and be surrounded by babies screaming in British accents — and from London, it's an hour and a half to Basel.

Once I get to Basel, I'll have a lot of cleaning up to do, starting with my basketball contract. I know the whole organization's already pissed at me, but whatever. If I didn't take myself out of the game this season, they would've done it for me next season. Or the season after that. Or I would end up injuring myself and wind up needing surgery and being gimpy the rest of my life. The way things worked out might just be for the best, in the end.

I contemplate all this over my eight-fucking-dollar salad in the Chicago airport, feeling ripped off because it was labeled "gourmet" and yet the lettuce leaves are tinged with brown and the dressing tastes like somebody mixed in some ranch powder and corn syrup with water and squeezed it into a plastic ramekin.

God. Owning a restaurant is starting to making me a fucking food snob.

A few minutes after I finish my salad, I'm walking onto the plane to London, navigating my duffle bag in front of me, stooping occasionally to avoid whacking my head on overhead bins and protruding suitcase wheels.

I settle into my aisle seat at last, splaying my knees wide around the seat back in front of me, wondering, not for the first time, why airlines seem to think all passengers are the size of fucking African pygmy people. At least I got an aisle seat. And so far, the window seat next to me is empty. Maybe it'll stay that way and I can turn sideways or some shit and manage to almost sleep for an hour or two.

I pull out the magazine from the seat pocket and start flipping through it. Glossy pages tell me about places that I absolutely *must* visit before I die, foods I should try, bike paths I should ride. I pause for a second at an article about an NFL guy who loves traveling to Asia, skimming through the interviewer's questions and wondering idly if I could ever afford to take my family on a trip to Nepal.

The daydream is interrupted when a voice next to me says, "Hey. Anika."

I glance in the direction of the voice. The window seat that had been empty a moment before is now filled. With Marty McFly.

I groan. "What are you doing here, McFly? I thought I told you I didn't want to go on any more head-trips to the past?"

He shakes his head, keeps his voice low. "That's not why I'm here."

He points up the aisle, and my eyes follow his gesture. Four rows ahead of me, sitting in the center row in the aisle seat, there's a dark head of hair, cut Jane Lane-style. A row of silver earrings glints in the light.

"Guess who else is flying to Heathrow today?" McFly says.

"No *fucking* way," I say, and although I usually speak to McFly only in my head, I accidentally make the statement out-loud this time. A British woman my mother's age (but about half of her size) catches my cursed mutter, purses her lips in my direction.

"You should go talk to her," my imaginary seat mate says.

"No," I say quickly, and this time I manage to keep my conversation with him silent. "She's made it *plenty* clear that she doesn't want to talk to me."

Now McFly is the one pursing his lips at me. "What kind of attitude is that? You're an *Olympian,* for chrissakes, Anika, not a quitter." He makes a curt gesture up the aisle. "Get up. Go over there. *Talk* to her."

"Not only does she not want to talk to me," I say, "but also, after what happened at Grace's reception, I think it's pretty fair to say she doesn't ever want to lay *eyes* on me again."

"Okay, so you have some explaining to do. Some begging for forgiveness, maybe."

"I begged on at least five separate voicemails. I texted her an apology every day for a week. She didn't answer any of them. She wants me to leave her alone."

Marty McFly considers this for a few seconds. Then he says, "Maybe she does. Maybe she just wants you to try harder. To demonstrate that you're not ready to give up on your relationship with her."

I roll my eyes. *"What* relationship, McFly? We met on a plane a couple of months ago. We had all of a fucking *week* of hanging out together before I screwed up and kissed Jenny right in front of her."

McFly shrugs. "Yeah, it was only a week. But it was a *good* week. A *special* week. You both thought so."

"Yeah, and we also both thought I was over my past," I mumble. I stare at the dark hair a couple yards in front of me and heave a heavy sigh. "Besides, if she's on the plane for London, it probably means she's going back to Basel. What are we supposed to do, enter into a long-distance relationship when we haven't even really dated yet? Fat fucking chance of *that* working out. And ever since Jenny, I've pretty much had it on long-distance relationships."

McFly stares at me a long moment. "Anika. Just go talk to her."

I shake my head. "Nuh-uh. No way."

"Go. Talk. To her."

"No."

"You're being a baby."

I hesitate. Unbuckle my seat belt. Glance over at McFly. "If this ends up totally sucking, I'm sending you back to fucking 1955. Permanently."

"Go," is all he says.

Against my own better fucking judgment, I stand up.

One of the few good things about my height is that I'm like a fucking watchtower. I can scope things out from my vantage point without making myself known, getting a bird's eye view on everything below me. That's what I do now, checking out what's happening in Amy's aisle a few feet ahead of me.

On the far side of her row of seats is what looks like a mother and daughter pair. The girl's about eleven, twelve, with crazy carrot-top red-orange frizzy hair. She giggles over something her mother's showing her, and I catch a hint of a British accent. Next to the mother, there's a balding man reading a newspaper. At first, I assume he's the father of the carrot-top girl, and I think, well, fuck, I guess that's it — there's no way I can switch seats with one-third of a family of three. But as I watch him read the newspaper, his body language — and the fact that he's completely fucking ignoring both the women sitting on either side of him — makes me realize that he's not with the mother and the middle-school girl.

Which makes him a prime target for seat switching. After all, who in their right mind would turn down an aisle seat in a row of two, with a possible *empty fucking seat* next to it, to stay in an row of four, in the middle of the plane, stuck between a mother and a daughter on one side and a stranger on the other?

No one. That's who.

Rather than striding right up the aisle and making myself known to Amy, I turn around, head towards the back of the plane as if I'm going to the bathroom behind me. But instead of going to the bathroom, I cross over to the other aisle, and work my way up towards Amy's row, apologizing for every bag and body and baby I have to squeeze by as I work against traffic. When I get to Amy's row after a minute of this, I reach one of my long, albatross arms out and tap the man with the newspaper on the shoulder. The mom and carrot-top daughter look a little annoyed at me for reaching over their heads, but I'm sure they'll get over it.

"Excuse me, sir?" I start, and at the sound of my voice,

Amy's head whips around. I see her eyes go wide with surprise, then narrow with anger a nanosecond later. "I was wondering if you would like to switch seats with me so I can sit to my friend?"

Amy shakes her head vigorously, but the man's facing me and doesn't see her frantic hell-no signals. Mom and carrot-top do, though. They look from the man, to Amy's violently shaking head, to me with open curiosity.

The man seems like he doesn't know what to say, so I help him out.

"It's an aisle seat," I say. "About four rows back from where you are now." I gaze over the heads of the passengers seated in the middle rows. "And the window seat is still empty, so far."

"Anika…" Amy says, a warning tone in her voice.

"I'd be really grateful," I say to the man.

The man folds up his newspaper, spares Amy a quick glance over his shoulder, looks back at me. "Of course," he says.

From his spot next to my previous seat, Marty McFly gives me a double thumbs-up.

It takes newspaper guy a minute to gather all his things and scoot past Mom and carrot-top, but he finally untangles himself from the row of seats and steps into the aisle. Once he's clear, I squeeze past the mother and daughter with several apologies for my enormous girth, and at last drop down into the seat beside Amy.

She won't look at me. Her arms are crossed tight

against her chest; her mouth is pressed into a thin, white line. The Mom on my right gives us a quick look, but then turns back to her daughter. She can tell that something's up, but doesn't say anything about it.

Which is actually one of the best qualities of the British: They absolutely hate it when people cause scenes, and they're generally really good at minding their own fucking business.

I adjust my knees for a second, trying to get as comfortable as I can while squashed between Amy on my left and the Mom (mum, really) on my right.

"Hi," I say to Amy.

She gives no indication that she's heard me.

"So, uh, are you flying back to Basel, too? Crazy that we ended up on the same plane again. Right?"

"Anika," she says in a low voice between clenched teeth. "I am trying really, *really* hard not to have a panic attack right now. So if you want to help with that, you can stop speaking *right now* and leave me alone."

Chapter 46: Snakes on a plane. Again.

The mom on my other side catches Amy's comment and suddenly becomes even more absorbed in whatever she's looking at with her daughter.

"Okay," I tell Amy. "If you need me to be quiet for a while, I can be quiet."

A beat passes. Amy doesn't turn to look at me. I get the message, reach in front of me and go back to reading the article in the airline magazine about the football player who likes traveling to Asia.

Soon enough, we're taxiing down the runway, and the little monitor above my tray starts playing a safety video populated by little British cartoon people showing me things like how to buckle my seatbelt, how to use the floatation cushion beneath my seat, which exit to use if we have to evacuate.

I let my eyes slide to the left to see if Amy's watching the video or doing something else. She makes a good show of watching it; her eyes are glued to the small screen, but her posture is stiff, almost rigid, with her arms still folded tightly against her chest and her lips still pressed into their thin line.

But I can see her pulse vibrating in an artery up her neck, and it seems to me it's much faster than it should be.

Her breath hitches at the sound of the engines revving; the pulse in her neck looks like it's getting even faster. She squeezes her eyes shut.

"Amy," I say softly, turning so that only she can hear me. "Aren't you supposed to try to relax when a panic attack comes on? It doesn't help to get stiffer with an attack... does it?"

"Of course I'm trying to relax," Amy snaps. "What did you *think* I was trying to do? Panic more?"

I want to say, *"Well, you have a weird fucking way of trying to relax,"* but that doesn't seem like it's going to help the situation.

The engines rev again; we're starting down the runway now.

"Oh, God," Amy says, and she moves her hands onto each armrest, white knuckling against plastic and metal as the plane gathers speed.

"Breathe, Amy," I say when it looks like she isn't. Then I say something I heard in a movie one time: "Just focus on your breathing, okay? Big, deep breaths, into your belly."

But instead of breathing, Amy literally fucking stops breathing the moment I feel the plane leave the earth. I pry the hand closest to me from its place on the armrest and put it inside my own big paw. I close my fingers around Amy's hand.

"If you can't focus on your breathing, focus on my voice, okay?" I say. I'm still speaking softly, but with the background noise of the plane, I could probably yell and the woman on my other side still wouldn't hear me. "Listen, Amy. This is a big, bad monster of an airplane. The fucking height of human engineering. It wants to fly. More than anything, that's what this plane wants to do. It wants to stay in the air and ride the currents. It's fine; we're safe." Amy closes her eyes, seems to relax by about one millimeter. The plane banks; she squeezes my hand harder. "Focus on my voice, Amy, not the plane. Just focus on me. I've got you. We're okay."

It goes on like this for about five more minutes — Amy squeezing my hand every time the plane turns or its engines change, me rubbing my thumb on the back of her hand and telling her that everything's going to be fine.

At the end of five minutes, the plane starts to level out, shifts and changes get less dramatic. Amy extracts her hand from mine, lets out a breath.

"Thank you," she says without looking at me.

"You're welcome," I say. "Are you... Does this mean we can talk?"

"No. Not at all."

This might end up being a long fucking flight.

#

Two hours pass like.

Damn Marty McFly. Why do I ever listen to anything he says? *"Talk to her,"* he'd said. *"She wants you to try harder,"* he'd said.

Amy refuses to look at me; she puts in earbuds and begins watching a bad chick flick comedy I've never heard of before. When it becomes obvious she really doesn't plan to acknowledge my presence again, I give up trying to read the airline magazine and turn the entertainment system on myself. I end up picking a cooking show, hoping I can find something I can tweak as a special for Soul Mountain. At one point I think I see Amy glance at my screen in surprise, but if she's going to ignore me, then I'm more than fucking capable of ignoring her.

At the end of two hours, though, I can't ignore the urge that I've been fighting against any longer. I take my earbuds out, tap Amy on the shoulder.

She ignores me.

I sigh in frustration, tap her on the shoulder again. "I have to pee," I say, pointing at the aisle at the same time in case she truly can't hear me with the earbuds in.

She nods curtly, gets out of her seat long enough for me to squeeze past her place and into the aisle.

You think the economy section is bad when you're almost six-four? Let me tell you what's even worse: fucking airplane toilets.

Anyway, I wait in line for the bathroom for a while, use the facilities, make my way back up the aisle. I pass the guy I'd swapped seats with on my way back, and sure enough, the window seat never got filled, so he has the whole damned row to himself.

Fucking Marty McFly.

When I get back to my row, Amy gets up again to let me back in. I settle into my seat, doing my best to get my legs comfortable in the cramped space, reaching for my earbuds.

But before I can put them back into my ears, Amy touches my forearm and asks, "How's your mom? Did the surgery go alright?"

I shake my head. "It didn't go so well. Turns out her cancer had metastasized, which means it spread to other parts of her body and needs radiation therapy and more chemo."

Her face scrunches in sympathy. "I'm really sorry to hear that. Truly."

I shrug. "It's..." I mean to say *"It's alright,"* but obviously it's fucking *not* alright. Instead, I say, "It's like Momma always told us. 'Getting old definitely ain't for sissies.' But she's definitely not a sissy, so I'm sure she'll make it out of this."

"I'm sure she probably will," Amy says sympathetically.

I hesitate, not sure if I should push my luck, but also not wanting to miss the opportunity to open up a conversation. "So... how was the rest of your trip?"

"It was alright," she says, looking away from me.

"Did you get to see your dad and your step-mom?"

"Yeah. My dad's a little like your mom — struggling with health stuff. It's hard to watch him starting to decline like this."

"But your dad sounds like he's as tough as my mom." I pause, and then add — against my better fucking judgment, "You've got to get your stubbornness from somewhere, right?"

"Mmm," she says noncommittally.   She puts the earbuds back in, turns to face her screen.

Oops.

I guess our conversation's over.

The rest of the flight goes basically in the same way — long periods of silence with occasional strained small-talk. By the time we're beginning our descent into Heathrow, I've only managed to draw about a paragraph's worth of conversation from her. I tell myself that part of the reason we didn't talk is that it was an overnight flight, and Amy spent a good third of it either sleeping or pretending to sleep.

I tell myself that. I don't really believe it, though.

When we land and the fasten seatbelt light goes off for the last time and everyone starts deplaning, I grab her carry-on out of the overhead bin and hand it to her.

"Are you flying to Basel today?" I ask her.

"Yeah."

"Maybe we'll be on the same flight again. Funny how that works with us, right?   Wacky fucking coincidence." She doesn't respond.   "Hey — do you want to grab some breakfast? I'm buying."

"No."

"Are you sure? You know, the English breakfasts they have are pretty — "

"I said *no,* Anika."

"Alright," I say, and I'm planning to say more, but the line moves, and Amy turns her back to me, heading towards the front of the plane.

Chapter 47: It's not exactly *Breakfast at Tiffany's*, but it still counts for something.

We do end up on the same flight, of course. London Heathrow might be one of the most important airports in the world, but there are only so many flights from there to Basel on any given weekday morning.

Which means I see Amy sitting in the DMV-style airport waiting area not far from one of the breakfast places. I grab stuff for both of us, including a coffee each (and I still fucking hate drinking coffee in Britain, that hasn't changed any), and head over to where she sits, flopping down into the seat next to her without dropping all the breakfast goodies I'm cradling in my arms.

"I got you some food," I say. I unbend an arm carefully, dropping a container of scrambled eggs and sautéed tomato into my lap, and try to hand her one of the coffees. "And a coffee. Even though I can't vouch for the quality."

The way Amy looks at me…

Okay — are you familiar with cats at all? Cats are the single snootiest domesticated animal you'd ever care to meet. When they aren't in the mood to be playful or bratty, they look at you like you're lower than the dirt attached to

ANDREWS / ANIKA TAKES THE LONG WAY

the bottom of a sandal.

That look, that superior Cat Master of the Fucking Universe Look, is the look that Amy gives me.

But my hands are full and my lap is full and she has to *take the fucking coffee* if I'm going to be able to grab the plastic silverware and start to eat, and somehow she realizes that, so she sighs and relieves me of one of the two coffees.

"I told you I didn't want any food. Or coffee, for that matter," she says, but she pops the plastic lid off at the same time and sticks her nose close, inhaling its earthy smell.

I set the remaining coffee down between my feet and start to sort through my lapful of breakfast goodies.

"I've got some sausage here, plus two containers of scrambled eggs, some tomatoes — you know they love their tomatoes here — and some toast."

"I don't need anything to eat. They fed us on the plane."

"You called that food?" I snort. "That cheesy, doughy, stale imitation of pizza and the two green apple slices? I don't know what that was, but I would *not* call it breakfast."

I open one of the containers of scrambled eggs, and when the steamy smell hits my nostrils, my mouth waters immediately.

"You ate the 'stale imitation of pizza,'" Amy says.

I gesture at myself. "Do you see this, Amy? It's six

feet, three-and-a-half inches of mostly muscle. I haven't hit the court much since I've been back in Ohio, but I'm willing to bet that I still have a body fat percentage of less than eighteen percent. All that means it takes a lot of fucking calories to keep this machine moving. So yes, I ate the goddamned imitation pizza."

Is that a smile? Just like on the plane, she won't look at me, but nevertheless, I can see her mouth twitch around the corners. It doesn't quite transform into a real smile, but it's a good start.

"See?" McFly says on my other side, because of *course* he would choose now to re-materialize. "What did I tell you about her just wanting you to try a little harder?"

She sips her coffee.

"Have some eggs," I say, sticking a plastic fork in the open container and setting it on her lap. "You say they fed us on the plane, but you seem to be forgetting that I sat right next to you. You took two bites of that nasty fake pizza and gave up on it. Don't tell me you didn't."

She sighs, balances the coffee between her knees so that she can start eating eggs. Satisfied for now, I pop open the other container and start eating my own.

We go on like this, eating in silence, watching businessmen and families with little kids walk by, rolling their suitcases behind them, when, without any fucking warning whatsoever, Amy sets her fork down, wipes her mouth, and asks me,

"How could you *do* that to me, Anika?"

It takes me about two point thirty-seven seconds to understand what she's talking about. For two full seconds, I think she's referring to the coffee and it's actually worse than I could've anticipated. For point three seconds, I think she might mean the sausage that I'm in the middle of chewing, the sausage I didn't offer to share with her. But during the final seven-hundredths of a second, my sleep-deprived, jet-lagged brain realizes she's talking about what happened at Grace Adler's wedding reception.

I swallow my sausage quickly, turn in my seat to face her. "I'm sorry. I'm so, *so* sorry. I regret it more than…"

— and the image that pops up in my head is Rhianna Fucking Jerkins, naked and looming over me. Could I possibly regret *kissing* Jenny more than *sleeping* with Rhianna? It didn't really compute — I'd been with Jenny for years when I cheated on her; I'd barely even call what Amy and I had "dating."

But it's true — I regretted that kiss even more than Rhianna.

Because I'd looked at Amy and I'd seen the possibility of a new life, of an entire future, and then, somehow, my past waltzed into the bathroom and ruined everything.

"I regret it more than I've ever regretted anything in my entire life," I tell Amy. "And that's the honest fucking truth."

"Do you know how it felt, Anika? To walk into that bathroom to find you — to find you with her…" She closes her eyes, shakes her head, lets out a breath. "I should've known better," she says, almost like she's talking to herself. "I should've known. The first time I saw you two together, I *knew* there was something there. Even if you couldn't see it, I could. It was clear as day — *is* clear as day."

"No. You were right the first time. *Was* clear as day. Jenny and I talked. We both know that kiss never should've happened. Things with her are done. Once and for all, done."

She opens her eyes, turns to look at me. "How am I supposed to believe you? You told me she was in the rearview mirror. Those were your exact words — 'Jenny's been in the rearview mirror for a long fucking time.' So either you lied to *me,* or you lied to *yourself.* I don't even know which one is worse, but either way, I can't trust you."

"Give me a chance to earn your trust back. What happened with Jenny — that's not who I am."

"It's not? But you told me yourself about the time you cheated on her."

"Amy. I've been alive almost four fucking decades. I cheated *one* time. One time! And I felt horrible about myself afterward."

Amy meets my eyes. "Twice."

"What?"

"Twice. You say you cheated once; you cheated twice. You cheated on *me.* "

"But that — it was only — we weren't even — "

"Whatever you're trying to say, Anika, don't. *Don't* say

it doesn't count because it was just a kiss. And *don't* say we weren't anything official. You were at that reception with *me,* as my date. If that's not official, I don't know what the fuck is."

I open my mouth to argue, but then I see tears pooling around the rims of Amy's dark eyes.

"You're right," I say. "I'm sorry. I'm so totally fucking sorry."

Amy sniffs, blinks the tears away. "I don't know how you can affect me like this," she says. "You're just some… some stranger I met on a plane. Some basketball player I never thought I'd see in person. You're not even real."

"I'm not?" I say, completely confused.

I look down at my scrambled eggs, and it sucks because they're going to get cold, but I put them down next to my coffee. Then I get out of my plastic chair and drop down onto one knee in front of Amy.

"Amy Ellis," I start, but she interrupts me before I can go any further.

"Oh, God, Anika, what are you doing? Don't tell me you're about to fucking propose or something."

"No — I — well, not this time, anyway." I place my hands on her knees, which are still holding a coffee cup between them, and I start again. "Amy Ellis, I am so, so sorry. When I look at you, I see my future. And I don't know exactly what that means, because who the fuck knows what the future holds, but there's one thing I know for sure about my future — I want you in it. I *need* you in it. So, please, *please* will you give me another chance? One get-out-of-jail-free card, that's all I'm asking."

Her gaze falls to my face, and she seems to study me for a moment. Then she smiles. It's a smirk, really, one of those devious Amy Ellis smirks. That smirk. I didn't even realize how much I'd missed that smirk until it hits my heart with a sharp pang.

"I tell you what," she says. *"One* date. One chance to impress me. Show me something in Basel that you truly love, something that doesn't have anything to do with basketball. And if it impresses me, then... I'll consider forgiving you. But I'm not making any promises."

I nod. "I'll take those odds."

I don't try to sit next to Amy on our flight to Basel. I figure it's better to give her space. At baggage claim, I tell her I'll get in touch about the date, which she agrees to.

Two days later, a little after ten in the morning, I'm standing on the stoop outside her building, two cups of coffee *(good* coffee) in hand. I press the buzzer on her door.

Chapter 48: Oh, the places you'll go!

"So. A morning date?" Amy says when she steps outside and accepts her cup of coffee. "Bold."

I grin. "You're going to like this."

She raises an eyebrow. "Maybe I will. Maybe I won't."

"You will."

I open the door to the dark grey Mercedes parked at the curb for her; she glances between it and me in surprise.

"Have you always owned a Mercedes? Women's basketball salaries must be higher than I thought."

"They're not," I say. "Trust me. But I already sold my car; I just rented this one for the day." I shrug. "A Mercedes is really more Dutch's thing than mine, but... You told me to impress you."

She smiles a little. "So I did."

I climb in behind the wheel, put the car into gear.

"Why did you sell your car?" she asks curiously.

"Oh — I didn't tell you? I'm moving back to Ohio."

Her shock is evident on her face. "Really? Why? I thought you said you'd rather move to Antartica than Ohio?"

"Yeah, it's true. I did say that. But... you know, with my mom being sick... Plus all my family's there. I mean,

PJ's in Philadelphia, but that's close enough. I figured it was time to get back to my roots. Or grow some roots. I realized when I was home that I've been running from Ohio for way too long."

She thinks about this a moment. "So what are you going to do in Ohio? It's not exactly known for its booming economy, you know."

"Well... I kinda bought my parents' restaurant."

Now she's looking *really* fucking shocked.

"When I really sat down and asked myself, 'What do I care about, other than basketball?' the answer was — and look, I know this sounds like a fucking Hallmark card, but seriously — I decided that what matters most is my family. I love Alex and Graham and their kids, and they're like family to me, but they're far from everyone else I love. And... I haven't really done a good job at being a good daughter or a good sister or a good auntie over the years. So I wanted to make up for that."

"I can understand that," Amy says, "but I'm still a little surprised you decided to buy the restaurant."

"I know. I'm still a little surprised, too. But you know what? When I stopped thinking about it as just 'restaurant' and started thinking about it in other ways, I realized that it really isn't all bad."

"So what does that mean, exactly? How are you thinking about it now?"

"As a piece of my family, for one. It's almost like Soul Mountain has been my parents' fifth child. And it was in rough shape, financially, due to — eh, well, it's a long story, but it was a fifth child that was on life support. And it was going to break my parents' heart if they ended up having to take it off life support and close it. So that's one part of it."

"Is there another part?"

I glance over at Amy while I wait for the light to change. "There is. You know what I figured out from working there during the last couple months? Soul Mountain doesn't just belong to my family; it belongs to the whole goddamned town. It's an institution there. If it disappeared... it would be like the statue of Custer disappearing."

Amy shakes her head, lets out a small laugh.

"What?" I ask. "Is that too sappy?"

"It *is* sappy," she agrees. "But it's also... I don't know, it's sweet. That you would care about your family enough and Marcine enough to sink your future into a restaurant."

"Hey," I admonish. "Let's not use the words 'sink' and 'restaurant' in the same sentence, okay?" I see an open parking space, pull into it before it has a chance to disappear. "We're here, by the way."

"Where's here?"

"You told me to show you one thing here that I truly love. Well, I love this place. As a matter of fact, I think it's fair to say that it's my favorite place in all of Basel."

She glances around, looking for something remarkable. But we're parked on a side street, next to a nondescript hotel.

"It's actually behind us," I say. "We're going to have to walk a block."

"It's not the Spalentor, is it?" she asks, referring to the old, castle-like city gate.

"Nah. Too touristy."

"Then what is it?"

I chuckle. "Follow me."

#

Switzerland is a mountainous nation, cloudy, rainy, snowy for large chunks of the year. Summer is pleasant in Basel, but the daytime high doesn't usually climb much above seventy. We've had eighty-degree days, for sure, but for the most part, I'd call the weather on the cool side of "temperate."

That's why, for the past several years that I've lived here, I've made the botanical gardens at the University of Basel my second home. Inside the big glass greenhouse, I can pretend I'm in a tropical climate. I can lose myself amongst the rows of orchids and water lilies and Seussian-like flowers, drinking coffee and thinking about life.

I brought Cici here once, the girl I dated for a couple years. She was bored and antsy here, had a "So?" attitude that led to us leaving almost as soon as we arrived. I never brought anyone to the botanical gardens after that. It's become like my own private retreat space, the place no one knows about but me.

I mean, of course it's not actually fucking true that no one else knows about this place; people are in here all the time. But somehow, whenever I'm there, I feel like I'm in an insulated world all my own, and for a while, I can forget about my fucked-up problems.

I tell all this to Amy as she follows me into the main, domed greenhouse, where we are met by humid air. I let her get a few steps ahead, take in the green while I linger behind.

She stops in front of the pond that sits beneath the dome's center, gazing out at otherworldly lily pads.

"How did you find this place?" she asks.

"By accident. Just wandering around the city one day."

"And you come here a lot?"

"Probably at least once per week. Twice if it's a shitty week."

She turns around, and there's a smile on her face. A genuine smile, an Amy smile. The kind I grew to love in the days leading up to Grace Adler's wedding. "Anika Singh, you never cease to surprise me. You know that?"

"Is that a good thing? Or a bad thing?"

"In this case, it's a good thing."

We end up spending the rest of the day together, eating lunch outside at a cafe because it's shaping up into a warm, near-summer's day, then taking a leisurely walk back to where I parked the Mercedes.

"Well," I say to Amy, leaning against the passenger's

side of the car. "Did I do okay? Am I still relegated to the doghouse, or is there a chance I can be forgiven?"

Amy reaches up, puts her hands lightly on my shoulders. Her touch sends an unexpected jolt of energy into me as if I'd gotten a miniature electrocution. She runs her hands down my arms, over my wrists, squeezes my fingers.

"Do you understand how badly you hurt me?" she asks, voice soft.

"I do. And I'm sorry."

She shakes her head. "No. I don't think you do understand. Ever since I met you..." She trails off, staring at a far away place beyond me. She tries again. When she speaks again, she sounds more like she's talking to herself than to me. "You can't understand how it felt because I don't completely understand it myself. You're not supposed to be anyone to me, Anika. Just a stranger. Just a few days of fun in Ohio while I waited for Grace's wedding. But somehow, I fell for you so fast, so hard, that I..." Her eyes regain focus, and she looks up at my face. "You're not the only one who looked at us and saw the future. I saw it, too. I saw it from the time you told me the story of how your parents met. But I assumed... I'm not a rash person, Anika. I don't just fall for people like that. But with you... and then at that reception... I think you might've broken my heart. And I'm long past the age where I thought anyone would break my heart ever again."

I lean forward, plant a gentle kiss on her forehead

experimentally. When she doesn't flinch, doesn't pull away from me, I lean in a little further, open her mouth with mine. She doesn't fight me; she sinks into it, kisses me back.

I don't push my luck and try to stretch the kiss out; I figure Amy and I are back into baby steps mode. I run my thumb along her cheek.

"I can try to put your heart back together again," I say. "If you let me."

She smiles; there's a hint of sadness in it this time. "Maybe," she says. "Take me home?"

"Alright," I say. I turn to unlock and open her door for her.

"Will you have dinner with me tonight? At my place. I'll cook."

I try not to show how completely fucking awesome that invitation makes me feel, try not to do the happy dance right there on the sidewalk like a flamboyant NFL player in the end zone.

All I do is grin and say, "Okay. What time?"

Chapter 49: A romantic second date.

I bring flowers. I'm not usually a bring-flowers-to-a-date kind of girl, but it seems like the right move. I'm still barely out of the doghouse, after all.

Amy opens the door, sees me, sees the flowers, smiles. She takes them out of my hand once we're inside her apartment, and she rewards me with a peck on the cheek.

"I'll put these in some water," she says, and for some reason, I can't help but think of my parents, of my father refusing to take "no" for an answer when he first asked my mother out.

Hell, maybe Marty McFly was right. Maybe I'd simply needed to try harder, and God or the Universe or fucking British Airways decided to give my sorry ass one more chance by putting Amy and me on a plane together again.

"Told you so," McFly says at my elbow while Amy's in her small kitchen, digging for a vase.

"Go away, McFly," I mutter. I don't turn to look at him; I think if I do, it'll only encourage him.

Dinner goes smoothly. Afterward, Amy puts on some music and we both retire to her sofa, each of us working on a second glass of red wine. Amy opens up to me a little, tells me the story about her and Wendy and the professor who came between them. She tells me about the panic attacks. She tells me about the car accident — and shyly, self-consciously, she unbuttons the bottom of her blouse and pulls it to one side to show me the scars. I don't need her to tell me that she's insecure about the scars; it's written all over her face.

I reach out to touch them but stop myself a few inches from the surface of her skin. I feel the energy crackling there between my fingertips and her ribs, the miniature electrocution waiting to happen all over again.

My eyes flit up to hers. She's breathing hard, but she also looks more open, more vulnerable than I've ever seen her.

"May I?" I ask. "Is it okay to…?"

"Yes," she says quietly, almost inaudibly.

The electrocution I expected comes the moment the pads of my fingertips meet her scars. Goosebumps and heat run like a rash up both my arms and down my center, melting lower into a pool of something warm and wet.

Amy must feel something similar, because she gasps and lets her eyes flutter closed.

"Anika," she whispers. "Put my heart back together. And promise me you'll never break it again."

I take the glass of red wine out of her hand, place it on the coffee table. Put mine next to it. I trace the scars with the pad of my thumb, bring my other hand to her face. I stroke her cheek with the back of my fingers.

"I promise."

I lean Amy back onto the couch slowly and gently,

kissing my way up her throat, nipping gently at her jaw.

"I promise," I say again, and kiss her while I undo the rest of the buttons of her blouse. My hand skirts up her stomach, across a bra-covered breast, thumb stopping long enough to tease her nipple into hardness.

"Baby," she breathes.

I sit her up far enough to take off her shirt, her bra. I suck against her clavicle. And you know what the good thing about long fucking albatross arms is? I can suck on Amy's clavicle and unbutton her pants at the same time.

"Are you... Are you giving me a hickey?" she asks.

I push myself up. "Why? You don't have to be a bridesmaid anytime soon, do you?"

"Anika," she says, my name a blend between want and chastisement.

I only smirk, drop my mouth back down to the base of her throat while I push her pants down past her hips. She lets out a soft moan, which tells me I'm on the right track.

I kiss her hard, sliding my hand beneath the band of her silky underwear. She's wet, so fucking wet, that it makes me answer her moan with one of my own, totally losing track of my kiss. I dip the tip of my index finger inside her — just the tip — reveling in the way her hips buck up to meet my hand.

"Anika," she says into my mouth. "I want you. I've always wanted you."

I push two fingers in this time, moving inside further, stroking against her front wall.

Amy's hands come up, fingers digging into my shoulder blades, squeezing me towards her.

I rock my hips forward, thrusting deeper, finding Amy's rhythm until we're moving together, our breaths coming out in short, matching pants. I drop my face into the side of her neck, licking up with the tip of my tongue until I find her ear, taking it between my lips as she drives down against my fingers.

She mutters something in German, then French, then her hips jerk up against me so hard that I nearly lose my balance. But I don't. I put one foot on the floor to steady myself and push harder. For a split second, my mind rushes back to the night I lost my virginity with Jenny on a park bench outside Columbus, one foot digging into the earth, the other on the bench. And instead of the memory hurting, it tastes sweet, like red wine on the back of my tongue, like I've completed a circle that had been broken for too long. Then the memory goes, and my mouth finds Amy's.

A couple minutes later, I feel the earthquake of her orgasm shudder down her body, squeeze itself around my fingers, dissipate out through her hips. Her body goes limp beneath me.

"Mother*fucker,*" she says once she catches her breath.

I smile against her neck, begin to pull myself out of her.

"No," she says quickly, catching my wrist. "Not yet — *oh.*"

An aftershock tremors through her.

She tugs on my wrist. "It's okay now. Just — just don't go anywhere yet, okay?"

I laugh. "I'm not going anywhere. Do you really think I'd just, 'wham, bam, thank you, ma'am'?"

"No, I just — I don't know." She wriggles to the edge of the sofa. "Just lie here with me a minute. Will you?"

I'm much too fucking big for Amy's modern little European sofa, but I comply anyway, wedging my right side into the narrow gap she's created for me, threading my arm under her neck and around her shoulders. I drape my other arm across her chest, nestling her into me.

She sighs contentedly. "You're tall," she remarks.

"So I've heard," I say drily.

She tugs at the arm draped across her chest, wraps a hand around two of my fingers, puts them into her mouth. Her lips close around my second knuckles, her tongue slides into the gap between my fingers as she pulls them from her mouth, slowly.

My breath catches.

"And you're *long,*" she whispers. "All over."

She drops my hand back onto her chest, smiles, and closes her eyes.

We lie there for a while in comfortable silence. I listen to the slowing sound of her breathing, smell the rich scent of red wine coming off her breath in little puffs.

"Amy?"

Heavy eyelids flicker open. "Hmmmm?"

"What's going to happen with us? You're here in Basel.

434

I'm going back to fucking Ohio… Is this it? Is tonight all there is for us? I've done long distance relationships before. I don't want another one."

Instead of looking concerned like I think she should, she just smiles and lets her eyelids drift closed again. "We can talk about it in the morning," she says. "For now, you're going to be here five more nights, right?"

"Yeah, but I — "

"Shhh. Then let's just focus on five more wonderful nights, okay?"

She smiles again, turns so that she's lying on her side, too, nuzzling her face into my chest.

Amy sleeps. I lie awake, thinking that I've resolved my past but still don't have a future.

*"There is a tipping point in midlife, a midpoint in your
journey, a day when you feel that middleness
of having equal parts past and future, of the life that you've
lived and the life that you will live,
of what is done and what is still possible."*

— Michael Lipsey

*"The only time you really live fully is from thirty to sixty.
The young are slaves to dreams;
the old servants of regrets. Only the middle-aged have all
their five senses in the keeping of their wits."*

— Theodore Roosevelt

Chapter 50: Home is where the heart is.

One week later

I have my first full day back at work on a Tuesday, which means that, right on time, Jodie and Ben show up at noon for their weekly game of Scrabble and dal bhat tarkari. I fill their water glasses when they sit down, ask if they need a menu.

"No," Ben says. "Just the usual today, thanks."

"How was Switzerland?" Jodie asks, studying my face like it might reveal some mysterious new secret she can share with her salon clients.

I smile, but it's wan. "It was fine."

And truthfully, it *was* fine — more than fine. It was nearly a full week of Amy, nearly a full week of lovemaking, interrupted only by the pesky tasks of daily life like "work" and "moving." But since I arrived home two days ago, I haven't heard from her at all. I've texted. I've emailed. I tried Skyping once or twice.

Nada. Amy's gone dark. Again. And I alternate between worried as hell that Swiss cat burglars broke into her home and raped and murdered her, and angry as hell that, after everything we've been through, she's decided I'm not worth the trouble.

Wham, bam, thank you, ma'am.

"Only fine?" Jodie probes, picking up immediately on my sullen mood like the seasoned gossip she is.

"Yeah, you know," I say with a shrug. "Moving isn't ever fun. It was a lot of packing, a lot of shipping stuff to Ohio, a lot of closing accounts and ending basketball contracts and breaking my apartment lease."

"Mmm," Jodie says. Then her face brightens. "Oh — did you hear about Dillan McElroy? You know, of Dillan's Bar & Grill?"

"No," I say. "What about him?"

"Had a heart-attack last week," she says. She adds sagely, "It's not surprising, really. He eats his own food too much. And you know they're practically a greasy spoon…"

I let her go on for a while, glad she's stopped probing me, even if I'm not that interested in Dillan McElroy's heart attack. I nod at the appropriate moments, raise my eyebrows and say, "Oh really?" at other appropriate moments, just as I watched my mother do with Jodie for years upon years.

The bell above the door rattles with a customer coming in, so I tell Jodie and Ben, "Excuse me for a minute," and turn to wait on my new patron, my welcoming restaurant owner's smile already plastered on my face.

My smile falters when I see who it is.

"Amy?"

She lifts a hand in greeting, gives me one of her

trademark smirks.

"What are you doing here?"

"Is that how you greet all your customers — 'what are you doing here'?" She raises an eyebrow. "No wonder the restaurant's been struggling."

I glance over my shoulder, and of *course* Jodie has already turned her attention from Scrabble to Amy and me. I'm sure we're looking way more interesting to her than a TRIPLE LETTER SCORE square. I cross the distance between Jodie's table and Amy in a few long-legged strides. When I reach her, I take her shoulders and turn her physically towards the door.

"Outside," I say. "We're not talking in here."

"Okay, okay, I'm going," Amy says, still light as a feather, as if she hasn't completely fucking ignored me for the past two days.

I grab Amy's arm, half-guiding, half-pulling her to the alleyway on the far end of Soul Mountain. Becker's back there, dropping trash in the dumpster.

"I'm going to be out here for a second," I tell him. "Keep an eye on the front of the house?"

He smiles, nods, and wisely slips back inside the kitchen door.

"What are you doing here?" I ask Amy. "And why have you completely ignored me for the past two days? I've been worried."

"I'm sorry," Amy says, and it sounds like it's a genuine apology. "For most of the past forty-eight hours, I've been traveling. And I didn't tell you because, well, I thought it would be fun to surprise you."

I throw my hands in the air. "Consider me fucking surprised."

She grimaces. "I'm sorry. Seriously. I didn't mean to worry you or upset you." She takes a step closer, reaches up and tucks a wily strand of hair behind my ear. "Can you forgive me?"

"Depends. On whether or not you're going to answer my question. You still haven't told me why you're in Ohio. And *please* don't tell me it was just because you missed the cornbread."

Amy laughs, lets go of my face. "You do have the best cornbread I've ever tasted. But no, that's not why I'm here." She chews on her bottom lip for a moment, pensive. "I'm here because... I took the job at Ohio State. I just moved to Columbus yesterday."

"You — *what?!*" This new news is almost as shocking as seeing her walk through the front door.

"I did another phone interview with them when I was in Florida visiting my parents," she explains. "And a couple days after that, right before I left for Basel, they offered me the position. I was trying to decide whether or not I should take it when you just... showed up on the plane. And then told me you were moving to Ohio to put down roots. It seemed like... does it sound ridiculous to say it seemed like a sign?"

I shake my head and take her hands in mine. And don't

make fun of me — I'm an emotional fucking person, okay? — but my eyes start to mist over with tears.

"No," I say. "It's not ridiculous. It sounds like as clear a sign as the universe ever bothers to offer."

She gets teary, too. "That's what I thought. And then you got down on your knees in the middle of Heathrow to beg my forgiveness..." She gives a wet chuckle. "No one's ever made an apology like that to me before. No one's ever bothered to try. And then the botanical gardens... and the dinner at my place... and everything else..." She looks up at me, totally crying at this point. "I had to say yes," she whispers. "To Ohio State, I mean. I had to see if you and I could..."

I'm crying, too, and my voice cracks when I say, "You said yes... for me? You moved to motherfucking *Ohio* for *me?"*

She shrugs. "Home is where the heart is, right?"

I nod, and just like that, I feel something click into place. It's like putting in the last piece of a jigsaw puzzle and going, *"Yesssss!"* because now you're finally done with that fucking puzzle. No — it's better than that; it's more like the fist-pumping feeling you get when you sink a clutch shot in a tournament game with the clock running down its final few seconds. Or like the janitor in your brain unlocking all the doors that have been sealed shut for way, way too long.

I gather up my Tinkerbell-sized Jane Lane in my arms and kiss her.

Amy's here, and I'm here, and I'm home at last.

* * *

Thanks for reading.

Support independent authors — leave a review at Amazon.com.

Amazon did for writers what the MP3 and YouTube did for music. It used to be that in order to publish a book (and actually get people to read it), you had to work through a publisher. Authors didn't work for their readers; authors worked for their publishers. Being able to publish independently, without a big publishing house, is absolutely revolutionary and extraordinary.

Will you support this publishing revolution by taking two or three minutes to leave a review? If you loved Anika's story and think others should read it, let them know by leaving a review.

Unlike big publishing houses, with massive marketing budgets and the ability to advertise books in national magazines and subway stations, all we indies really have is our reputation. So please review this book if you liked it. It really does make an enormous difference.

Would you like a free short story?

Guess what: A friend of mine unearthed something I

thought I'd lost a long time ago — a semi-autobiographical short story that got published in an anthology of lesbian erotica that has long since gone out of print.

I wrote it when I was twenty-three, almost twenty-four, and when my friend took photos of the pages (the anthology doesn't exist as an ebook — it's *that* old!) and texted them to me, I laughed and laughed and laughed. I honestly hadn't even remembered I'd written it, but thinking back, I realize it was the first time I'd ever gotten paid for something I'd written. It made me feel like a "real" writer.

Anyway, would you like it for free? If so, sign up for my Reader's Club here: AuthorElizaAndrews.com/ReadersClub

Also, getting older's a bitch. (My customary rant at the end of my novels.)

In my last book, I wrote a bit of a longish "About the Author" that morphed into a rant about lesbian representation in mainstream media. I felt a little embarrassed that I wrote it at the time, but in the reviews for my book, a lot of people mentioned that they appreciated it, so I figured, hey, why not. There's a fantasy writer who used to include what was basically a personal essay at the end of each of his novels. I thought, "Maybe I could be like that. Share a little something personal with my readers when they reach the end of each book."

So, at the risk of boring you, annoying you, and possibly coming across as self-absorbed (if you already think it's any of the three, then I would suggest you stop reading now), I thought I'd tell you a bit about how this book came about.

A lot of you probably already know the basic story of where this book came from. It's a sequel / spin-off of my other lesfic novel, *To Have Loved & Lost,* in which Anika was a side character. I liked Anika so much that I wanted to give her a novel of her own.

But also, in case you didn't notice, this book you just read is less about Anika and more about going through a mid-life crisis.

When I started writing this book, I was *not* having a mid-life crisis. I had just published *To Have Loved & Lost,* life was good except for the 2016 presidential election, and I was pleasantly surprised to watch my latest book climb the charts on Amazon into the number one spot. But somewhere about halfway through writing the first draft of *this* novel, my mid-life crisis hit, BAM, full force.

Look, I'll spare you the gory details. They are personal and dramatic at a "truth is stranger than fiction" sort of level. You can use your imagination to guess my situation, but I promise you that you won't guess right. I doubt you'll even come close. Let me put it this way: If I fictionalized my mid-life crisis into a novel, people would complain that it "just wasn't realistic."

Ha! It's not realistic… until it's your life.

But what I do want to share with you is what I've learned from my experience. With any luck, it will help you in some way, provide you with some comfort. So here it goes, broken into six stages:

(1)

When we are in our twenties, and to a large extent our thirties, I think we have a tendency to do whatever the "next thing" is that appears before us. We might choose a college major based upon what our parents think is good for us, for example, or we might move in with the person we're dating because it seems simpler at the time than supporting two households. We end up "going with the flow" without even realizing there's a flow or that we're going. Weighty decisions don't seem weighty at the time; they don't seem like they steer our lives into the paths of invisible tractor beams (sorry, that's a nerdy *Star Trek* reference), but they are and they do. Unfortunately, these early big decisions don't always correspond with who we are at our core, but we don't realize that yet because we're still young and living with a black-and-white idealism that we'll never replicate again in our lives.

So we take jobs that we're going to eventually grow bored with, we fall in love with people who aren't right for us, and we move to places we don't necessarily want to live because it all seems magical and wonderful and obvious at the time. But we haven't acquired any long-term vision yet. We don't realize that these decisions are dominoes that are going to continue to knock things over when we are well into our thirties, forties, fifties, sixties... And we don't realize how hard dominos are to stop once they start falling.

(2)

Then there comes this moment, as Michael Lipsey mentions in the quote I used in the final chapter, where we feel the "middleness" of our lives, when we recognize that somehow, our lives are already halfway over, and — here's the big, scary question — are we actually living the life that we want to be living? Or have we been dragged along by a tractor beam all this time, and now we realize we don't want to be there anymore?

But now it might be too late.

(3)

This is the moment when the mid-life crisis actually begins to hit us full-force.

It's like being in the middle of a thunderstorm.

For an hour or two before the storm, you watch the sky slowly darken, the air becomes still, the clouds grow in size. Then the air takes on that electric smell, the sky changes into a deep blue-grey, and then — the first raindrops. In life, this is the phase where we look around and go, "Wait a second. Is this who I actually *am?* Is this

what I actually want to be *doing* for the rest of my life?
Where *am* I? Why am I doing this?"

(4)

To carry on with the thunderstorm analogy:

It's like a storm that starts to rage outside, and you're
just coming out of the grocery store, your reusable,
environmentally friendly bags in hand. You watch the rain
pelt the parking lot, and in the distance, you see your car,
alone and soaked and hoping you will come rescue it.

But what do you do? Do you brave the storm? Do you
step out into the rain and embrace the thorough drenching?
Or do you simply wait, and hope it will pass?

That's what a mid-life crisis is like. You stand on the
brink, you see your options laid out in front of you. You
know what your choices are:

A) You can change. You can be bold, and take the risk,
and upend your life. You brace yourself and step into the
rain with your grocery bags, hoping that the rain won't ruin
what's inside by the time you get to your car.

B) Or you can wait. You say to yourself, "This, too,
shall pass," and you really, *really* hope that it does. You put
down your grocery bags and you just stand there, watching
it rain, hoping you won't feel this trapped by your
circumstances for the rest of your life.

(5)

Here's the thing. I'm a run into the rain kind of girl. In

the end, I figure, it's only water. You might argue, "But that's where your analogy breaks down, Eliza. Because when it comes to your life, it's *not* just water. There are consequences. The storms of career change and divorce, sickness and loss — these things don't just dry out. They're real and they suck and they're serious business. You can't just step out into the rain with groceries. You're not a teenager anymore."

But consider this, my friend. You are a speck of dust on a speck of dust on a speck of dust. You are this tiny, self-aware bit of biology held by the magical, invisible force of gravity to a water-logged *rock* hurtling through space at speeds that boggle the mind. And the rock we lovingly call Earth is just one rock among gazillions of other rocks, all of which are hurtling through space in anonymous galaxies populated by anonymous stars, anonymous rocks, and, who knows, maybe other anonymous little bits of biology.

Another way to think of it:

Go to a beach. Pick up a single grain of sand. Hold it on the tip of your finger. Look at it. Say to yourself, "This is me."

Then look up the beach, towards the pier. Look down the beach, towards the line of hotels and kites and scampering children. Look at all the other grains of sand. And think, "These grains of sand are all the other living beings in this world. All the jet-setting billionaires; all the hipsters; all the poor kids in Sub-Saharan Africa my mother always told me would be grateful to have my vegetables;

all the shelter dogs; all the shelter cats; all the frogs and toads and salamanders and crickets; all the sea cucumbers and jellyfish and whale sharks and dolphins and *Finding Nemo* clown fish."

Maybe it feels nihilistic to think of yourself as so small. But you know what thinking in this way can do for you?

It can liberate you. Absolutely, enormously liberate you. It teaches you that you're just *not* that important. Your problems aren't that important. They never have been. Hell, even your mid-life crisis isn't really all that important.

And by thinking this way, you can let go.

You can let go of thinking you have to hold onto the dysfunctional constellation your life has become, and you can reorganize everything, even the parts of your life you thought could never be questioned. You can step into the rain. You can be daring enough to let your grocery bags get wet, and give the world your best Barbaric Yawp. Then you laugh like a madman and enjoy getting soaked.

(6)

Or… you can live the rest of your life standing at the edge of those automatically opening grocery store doors, the cold breeze of air-conditioning at your back, the soothing music of Elton John wafting out towards you.

"It's not the life I wanted," you'll say to yourself. "It's not the life I'd planned for, but here I am. It's familiar. It's safe. It's dry. I know my place in it, and I have people who love me, so…"

And you will waste away there, staring at your own version of the Mirror of Erised for the rest of your life. Just because you're afraid of a little water. Just because you've imbued far more import to your problems than they've really earned.

That's not for me, friend. I'm stepping into the rain. Join me and let's Yawp together.